P9-CDP-802

ATLANTIC NARRATIVES

First Series

ATLANTIC CLASSICS

ATLANTIC NARRATIVES

Modern Short Stories

EDITED WITH AN INTRODUCTION BY

CHARLES SWAIN THOMAS, A. M.

Lecturer in the Harvard Summer School

The Atlantic Monthly Press
BOSTON

Copyright, 1918, by

THE ATLANTIC MONTHLY PRESS

THIRD PRINTING

PRINTED IN THE UNITED STATES OF AMERICA

CONTENTS

INTRODUCTION

THE SHORT STORY

THERE is a story current among companionable golfers of a countryman who reluctantly accepted an invitation from a group of friendly associates to try his unpracticed hand at golf. When they all arrived at the links, his friends carefully placed the little carbonadoed sphere upon the tee, and told their aged neophyte that he must try to send this little painted ball to the first hole — plainly marked by the distant waving red flag toward which they pointed. The stalwart old man swung his club valiantly, hit the golf-ball a square, ringing blow, and watched it eagerly as it made its long, swift flight toward the far-off putting-green. His three friends, all loudly congratulating him upon his stroke, went with him in his silent search for the ball. Finally they found it lying just three or four inches from the edge of the first hole. A look of exultant astonishment was upon their faces; a look of keen disappointment upon the face of the old man. "Gee, I missed it," he muttered in disgust. His stroke had been the traditional stroke of the ignorant lucky beginner; he had unwittingly accomplished a feat beyond the dream of the trained expert.

Something similar to this triumphant accomplishment of the golf links has occasionally happened in the realm of story-telling. An untrained narrator, with a good tale to tell and with a natural instinct to select the dramatic incidents and arrange them luckily in effective sequence, has held his hearers in continuously rapt attention, and won from them, at the close of his story, round upon round of spontaneous applause. But as the literary world has grown older and more mature in its æsthetic judgments, it has naturally grown more exacting. As narrator after narrator has told his stories, the critical public and the academic critics have come to impose certain definite technical demands — demands not so definite or so exacting, however, that the splendor of success in certain ways has not pardoned even rather glaring neglects and defects along certain other concurrent ways.

Now it has been my pleasant task during the recent months to read or to reread scores upon scores of short stories that have been published in the *Atlantic Monthly*. My object has been to select from the Atlantic files some of the best and most representative of these narratives for publication in book form, and thus make these significant stories more readily available for the college, school, and the reading public. Out of this study, as it has combined and recombined with all my impressions of past readings, have come certain convictions that have grown more persistent as the reading and the selecting have progressed.

The net result of this thinking, I may at the beginning assert, has been to expand and liberalize my convictions concerning the art and technique of short-story writing. The choice of theme is multitudinous, the methods of allowable treatment generously variable, the emphasis upon character, plot, and setting easily shiftable, and the ultimate effects as diversified as our human moods and interests. Contrary to a currently repeated assertion, there is, I am convinced, no strict Atlantic type of story — at least none so rigorously conceived as not to allow unquestioned commendation of the narrative art of such varied personalities as Bret Harte, Thomas Bailey Aldrich, Sarah Orne Jewett, John Galsworthy, Mrs. Comer, Mrs.

Gerould, E. Nesbit, Jack London, or indeed that whole luminous galaxy of skilled story writers — many of them without fame — who for the past sixty years have been contributing the best of their literary selves to the *Atlantic*. Yet a study of these contributions of such varied types convinces one of certain large demands which each successive editor has, with somewhat latitudinarian rigor, pretty positively held in mind while he was determining the worth of the given product. What, we may be interested in asking, are these larger and more persistent demands?

The unified impression

Perhaps the most obvious requirement is that one upon which Edgar Allan Poe, in his brilliant critical essays on the art of the short story, laid the strongest stress — the demand that the narrator produce an unquestioned unified effect or impression. An examination of the narrative method of the old Metrical Romances and of many of the Arabian Nights Tales will by contrast illustrate Poe's comment. In those writings there was often no apparent plan. The hero started out and had an adventure. This the story-teller narrated as Episode No. 1. The hero continued and had another adventure, similar or dissimilar to the first. This we recognize as Episode No. 2. And thus the story continued until the narrator's powers of invention or endurance were exhausted. We close the reading with no sense of satisfied unity — no oneness of impression. At the beginning of the story, the writer of these Romances and Tales apparently had no definitely preconceived plan, he allowed no foreshadowing of catastrophe, he was careless alike of both beginning and end, he made no conscious use of suspense, setting, character-contrast, reverting narrative, climax, or any of the numerous devices that make up the technique of modern short-story writing. More particularly did he ignore the principle of unified impression.

Unified impression secured by character domination

While unity of impression is the sovereign demand in the modern short story, the ways in which this impression may be secured possess interesting variety. One of the most important of these ways is evident in the pervading or directing influence of some strongly dominant character. Events move in accordance with the will of some one person — or, it may be some group of persons with closely related powers and aims.

An interesting example of single character domination is seen in Miss Sherwood's story, *The Clearest Voice*. Alice, the wife, has been dead five years, yet it is her personality that still pervades and governs the home. Her spirit of kindly interest, her instinct for the æsthetic, her household control — all these have persisted through the long months that have intervened since her death. But it is when the husband is faced by the temptation to accept an inheritance which legally, though not justly, belongs to him — it is then that the influence of the wife's assertive character silently and determinedly dictates the correct decision. The husband's pressing financial difficulties, the urgings of the relatives, the unquestioned legality of the bequest — these are all finally swept aside by the subtle workings of a quietly persisting ethical force.

Sometimes an author reveals the strength and wisdom of one of his characters by allowing this character to yield to the wisdom and domination of another. I am thinking of Mrs. Comer's story, *The Wealth of Timmy Zimmerman*.[1] As we read the first part of this narrative, we are

[1] *The Atlantic Monthly*, vol. 113, p. 733.

interested only in Timmy Zimmerman and the personal
character problems which the huge profits of the tobacco
trust suddenly thrust upon this uncultured but good-
souled parvenu. We watch him in his early struggles so
full of energy and bold emprise; we rejoice with him in
his significant financial triumphs, and later we watch him
as he tries, by an expensive building enterprise, by tours
through Europe, by the rapid and careless driving of his
ten-thousand dollar red automobile, to win back the nervous contentment that was the happy companion of those
early years of adventurous poverty. He dominates each
separate situation, but he does not solve his problem. It
is only when he meets Molly Betterton and sees himself
as analyzed by her candid native acumen, that he learns
his own weakness and the true potentialities of his wealth.
Her character is strong enough to win dominion over him;
it is not strong enough to dominate the story and lure the
reader away from the controlling interest in the personality whose career the reader has so intently watched.
The unity of impression is firmly and continuously cen-
tered in the portrayal of Timmy Zimmerman's character,
and it is that which tautly holds the reader's attention
in leash.

A more recent story that secures its chief interest from
character portrayal is Mr. Arthur Russell Taylor's *Mr.
Squem*. Mr. Squem is a traveling man who sells Mercury rubber tires. He wears clothes that arrest attention
— broad striped affairs that seemed stripes before they
were clothes; his talk is profusely interlarded with vulgar
but picturesque slang; he is far removed from the academy.
Brought into direct contrast with the Reverend Allan Dare
and Professor William Emory Browne, his crudity is the
more grossly apparent. It is later enhanced by the glimpse
we get of his room — 'extremely dennish, smitingly red as

to walls, oppressive with plush upholstery. A huge deer-head, jutting from over the mantel, divided honors with a highly-colored September Morn, affrontingly framed. On a shelf stood a small bottle. It contained a finger of Mr. Squem, amputated years before, in alcohol.'

But in the midst of a railroad wreck, we lose all thought of these banalities and crudities; we take Mr. Squem for what he really is — a genuine, large-hearted, efficient minister unto his fellow men. The impression he creates dominates the entire situation.

Of the classic stories which admirably illustrate this method of securing a unity of impression through concentrated character interest, we like to revert to Bret Harte's *Tennessee's Partner*. It is of small moment that we do not know this man's name — of small moment indeed that he seems, throughout his mining career at Sandy Bar, to have been content to have his personality dimmed by the somewhat more luminous aura of Tennessee. But when Tennessee's repeated offences bring him to trial before Judge Lynch, and finally to his doom on the ominous tree at the top of Morley's Hill, Tennessee's partner comes suddenly upon the scene and overpoweringly dominates the situation. We close our reading of the story completely impressed by the devoted loyalty of Tennessee's partner — the loyalty that creates the unified impression.

And this same unity of impression thus secured in *The Clearest Voice*, *The Wealth of Timmy Zimmerman*, *Mr. Squem*, and *Tennessee's Partner* by concentrated interest in character, is easily discernible, in scores of other stories. The method is artistically employed by Hawthorne in *The Great Stone Face*, in Maxim Gorky's *Tchelkache*, Turgenef's *A Lear of the Steppes*, J. M. Barrie's *Cree Queery* and *Myra Drolby*, Thomas Nelson Page's *Marse Chan*,

Henry James's *The Real Thing*, Joseph Conrad's *The Informer*, and such well-known Atlantic stories as Anna Fuller's *The Boy*, Esther Tiffany's *Anna Mareea*, Florence Gilmore's *Little Brother*, Ellen Mackubin's *Rosita*, Charles Dobie's *The Failure*, Clarkson Crane's *Snipe*, and Christina Krysto's *Babanchik*. Indeed the list is well-nigh inexhaustible, and is constantly being increased by the many gifted writers who, enriching our current literature, see in personal character the germ of story-interest.

Unified impression secured by plot

Just as in looking at a finished piece of artistic tapestry we get a sense of harmonious design, so in contemplating the events of a well-told story, our sense of artistic completeness is satisfied by the skill displayed in the weaving and interweaving of incident — such weaving and interweaving as bring the significant events into the immediate foreground, and group the items of lesser moment in such an unobtrusive manner as to merge them into harmony with the main design.

Preceding the beginning of any story, we assume the existence of a state of repose. Either there is nothing happening, or, if events are happening, they are simply happening in the atmosphere of dull and inconsequential routine, and are accordingly without the pale of narratable notice. Then, suddenly, or gradually, something happens to disturb this repose; and to this initial exciting force are traceable the succeeding events, with such varied culminations as prosperity, or poverty, or dejection, tragedy or joy, or restored calm, or any one of the multitudinous finalities that life brings with her in her equipage.

The whole principle of plot, as here briefly analyzed, is simply and artistically revealed in Mr. Ernest Starr's *The Clearer Sight* — an admirable example of a story whose unity is secured largely by the effective handling of situation and incident. To Noakes, the young scientist who is the central character in the story, the master chemist, Henry Maxineff, has given certain general suggestions for a formula which will give an explosive of great value and of high potential power. The young man, following these general lines, discovers that, by slight additions and alterations, he can successfully work out the formula and immediately sell his secret to a foreign government. The sum he would thus secure would amply justify him in proposing marriage to Becky Hallam, the girl of his choice. We watch him in his brisk experiments and in his conclusive yielding to the temptation. We see him betraying his employer and at the same time failing to meet the standard of confidence which is demanded by the girl he loves. Right in the midst of these scientific successes and these ethical failures comes the terrible explosion in the laboratory where Noakes was working in secret. He is blinded by the accident — permanently, he thinks. Harassed by his sufferings — more particularly by his spiritual sufferings — he makes his confessions to Mr. Maxineff and Miss Hallam, and looks despairingly toward the empty future. The story closes with the physician's hope that the loss of his sight is after all but temporary. As we end our reading and view the events in retrospect, we are conscious of having seen the various threads of interest woven into a complete and unified design.

Again, the principles of plot structure are clearly seen quietly creating their unified impression in *A Sea Change*, one of Alice Brown's homely stories.[1] Cynthia Miller, a New England housewife, had lived for years her life of dull routine in an isolated mountain farm eight miles from the nearest village. Her husband, Timothy, 'was a son of the

[1] *The Atlantic Monthly*, vol. 86, p. 180.

soil, made out of the earth, and not many generations removed from that maternity.' Cynthia gradually comes to despise her life and her husband's crude carelessness — exemplified by his habitual animal aura and his newly-greased boots by the open oven door. With little ado, but with grim determination, she leaves him and goes to the sea-side home of her sister Frances. Cynthia is taken ill, but is at length cured by the kindly village doctor and the silent ministrations of the neighboring sea. Timothy, changed by the sudden departure of his wife and the opportunity for introspection that his lonely life now brings him, shakes off a bit of his earthiness and goes, after several weeks, to find his wife. We listen to the brief reconciliation and see Timothy begin to breathe in new life of aroused love and appreciation. The author's skillful manipulation of the action makes us live in the glow of a clearly perceived oneness of impression.

There are, of course, thousands of stories which secure this singleness of effect by a similar skill in the handling of situations and incidents. Among these many we need mention only a few whose unity is largely secured by plot-interest — Thomas Bailey Aldrich's *Marjorie Daw*, Maupassant's *The Necklace*, Poe's *Murders in the Rue Morgue*, Stockton's *A Tale of Negative Gravity* and *The Lady or the Tiger*, Kipling's *Without Benefit of Clergy*, Pushkin's *The Shot*, A. Conan Doyle's *The Adventures of Sherlock Holmes*, and Jack London's *A Day's Lodging*.

Unified impression secured by setting

Perhaps the most significant critical comment on setting — the third important element in the story-weaving process that secures oneness of impression — is that frequently quoted conversation of Stevenson with Graham Balfour: 'You may,' said Stevenson, 'take a certain atmosphere and

get action and persons to express it.   I'll give you an example — *The Merry Men*.   There I began with the feeling
of one of those islands on the west coast of Scotland, and I
gradually developed the story to express the sentiment
with which the coast affected me.'

There is no sensitive reader who will not sympathize
with this feeling and immediately understand how the
atmosphere of a particular place will act upon inventive
genius and become the exciting force for the production of
a story.   The squalid surroundings in the city slums, the
gay glamour of a garishly-lighted casino, the unending
stretch of desert waste, the dim twilight or the shrouded
darkness of the pine forest, the bleakness of the beaches in
midwinter, the sounding cataracts, haunting one like a
passion — how rich in storied suggestiveness may be each
of these to him who already has within him the instinct of
story or romance.

How the mood of place may effect its influence is well
expressed in the opening passages of John Galsworthy's
Buttercup-Night, which sensitively analyzes the feelings
for an unnamed bit of land in the 'West country' as the
author experienced them one Sunday night of a by-gone
early June.

'Why is it that in some places there is such a feeling
of life being all one; not merely a long picture-show
for human eyes, but a single breathing, glowing, growing thing, of which we are no more important a part
than the swallows and magpies, the foals and sheep
in the meadows, the sycamores and ash trees and
flowers in the fields, the rocks and little bright streams,
or even the long fleecy clouds and their soft-shouting
drivers, the winds?

'True, we register these parts of being, and they —

so far as we know — do not register us; yet it is impossible to feel, in such places as I speak of, the busy, dry, complacent sense of being all that matters, which in general we humans have so strongly.

'In these rare spots, that are always in the remote country, untouched by the advantages of civilization, one is conscious of an enwrapping web or mist of spirit, the glamorous and wistful wraith of all the vanished shapes that once dwelt there in such close comradeship.'

We can readily see, as we read *Buttercup-Night*, that it is the atmosphere of the place that subtly dictates the telling of the story, and at the end leaves the reader breathing this delicious June air and living within the charmed romance of this accumulated mass of magical yellow. What happens is interesting, but it is interesting largely because the incidents are fused and integrated with the hovering spirit of place and time — here as dominating in their charm as is the weird, mysterious Usher homestead in its gloom.

While such stories as Stevenson's *Merry Men* and Galsworthy's *Buttercup-Night* and Poe's *The Fall of the House of Usher* illustrate in a particularly striking way the dominant influence of setting, we recall scores upon scores of stories that have an added power because their authors have shown skill in the creation of a permeating and directing environment. Among the more famous of these stories are Sarah Orne Jewett's *The Queen's Twin*,[1] Israel Zangwill's *They that Walk in Darkness*, Prosper Mérimée's *Mateo Falcone*, Hardy's *Wessex Tales*, Lafcadio Hearn's *Youma*,[1] Jack London's *Children of the Frost*, John Fox's *Christmas Eve on Lonesome*, Edith Wyatt's *In November*,[1] and Mrs. Gerould's *The Moth of Peace*.[1]

[1] Atlantic stories.

Unified impression secured by theme

Another element of the story which we find interesting to discover and analyze is the author's dominant theme — what in the older days we might have unapologetically called the moral of the story. But along with the development of the technique of the short story, there came a school of critics and writers that shied terribly at this mention of the word moral; and such writers as Stevenson often seemed over-conscious of its lurking danger. In such consciousness, Stevenson wrote wonderful stories of adventure and mystery, such as *Treasure Island* and *The Sire de Maletroit's Door.* Yet the native instinct toward emphasis upon theme allowed him to write such powerful ethical stories as *Markheim* and *Dr. Jekyll and Mr. Hyde.* But in these, as in most of the modern thematic stories, the ethical truth pervades rather than intrudes. It is so firmly woven into incident and character and surroundings and natural dramaturgy that its identity is not exposed to naked bareness, but combines with other elements to produce a perfect unity through harmony of tone and effect.

Among the recent Atlantic story-writers this harmonious linking is seen happily existent in the deft workmanship of Mrs. C. A. P. Comer and Anne Douglas Sedgwick. In each number of three notable trilogies which these gifted writers have contributed, there is an artistic treatment of three notable themes. In Mrs. Comer's *Preliminaries, The Kinzer Portraits*, and *The Long Inheritance* we find the author's implied comments on Engagement, Marriage, and Divorce. In Anne Douglas Sedgwick's unconnected floral trilogy — *Hepaticas, Carnations*, and *Pansies* — there is in turn reflected Miss Sedgwick's attitude toward three themes which are less concrete and which demand a longer phrasing. In the first there is the world-old story of a noble spirited woman's love and sacrifice and ardent wishings for her self-victimized son. In *Carnations* we have the story of a husband, Rupert Wilson, released from the bondage of an unfortunate infatuation and restored to the sanity of love. In *Pansies* we have a generous tribute to quiet sentiment, developed by a study in character contrasts — the simple-hearted woman, loving a simple garden, contrasted with the kindly disposed but worldly-environed Mrs. Lennard, fond of display and Dorothy Perkins effects, and laying a disproportioned stress upon the expensive and the modern.

In none of these six stories is there the slightest suggestion that the narrative has been conceived in the spirit of propaganda. It would be impossible to say even that it was the underlying theme which gave the initial conception to the narrative and directed its progress. Any one of these six stories I can fancy beginning in plot, or in character, or in setting. Plot, character, setting, and theme — all are here, but all are so happily combined that I feel no disproportionate emphasis, and hence no forcing of a technical element. I only know that, personally, when I think over these stories, I find the theme of each leaving its strong and lingering impression.

What is true regarding this effective combination of elements in these stories of Mrs. Comer's and Miss Sedgwick's is of course true of many of the Atlantic stories which I have been reading. Perhaps in the majority of the best there is such a thorough merging of all the elements that the final impression falls upon neither character nor plot nor setting nor theme. The author has had something worth while to relate, and he has related it in a simple and natural way, — all unconscious of, or happily triumphant over, any studied technique in the art of narration. It has indeed been a conviction in the minds of some of the Atlantic editors that most persons, even though untrained in manipulating the story-maker's gear, have at least one experience — real or imagined — that is abundantly worth telling and worth writing. Unconsciously of course this artless narrator might throw into bold relief theme, character, setting, or plot. Or he might unconsciously merge these separate interests.

The woman writers

Aside from the mere contemplation of story-element technique, there are many other interesting observations which naturally come to one who reads critically the currently published fiction. He who examines the recent Atlantic files will be immediately impressed by the dominant place held by women writers of the short story — Mrs. Wharton, Mrs. Comer, Mrs. Gerould, Sarah Orne Jewett, Alice Brown, Mary Antin, Zephine Humphrey, Edith Ronald Merrielees, Margaret Prescott Montague, Kathleen Norris, E. Nesbit, Laura Spencer Portor, Anna Fuller, Edith Wyatt, Margaret Lynn, Elizabeth Ashe, Anne Douglas Sedgwick, Elsie Singmaster, Margaret Sherwood. Among the Atlantic contributors we should find it difficult indeed to match this list with an equal number of men equally gifted in story-telling power. But even if we should succeed in such a fatuous pairing of talent, we should still be impressed with the high place attained by the women writers — high in contrast with the place which they have attained in painting, sculpture, architecture, drama, and music.

And why this high attainment in the realm of the short story? Perhaps it is partially due to a lighter-winged fancy native in the feminine mind — a fancy that roves with more natural ease and grace among the animals and flowers of earth, among the clouds and stars and spirits of the sky, among the demon-haunted grottoes of the underworld. From all these easily-directed journeys perhaps it turns more naturally to the penetrable secrets of human motive — penetrable, however, only to those hearts which yield quickly, spontaneously — even wantonly — to the springs of love, hate, beauty, justice, jealousy, fear, vengeance, and the silent routine of daily duty. Doing all this of its natural self, the heart can more readily guide the mind in the deft record of vicarious action. Leastwise, to make a simple record of a real or an imagined experience is a task which can be more easily done by girls than by boys.

As boys and girls grow into maturity and the desire for contact with life increases, the masculine mind finds its natural outlet in business, in wrestlings with the soil, in contests of law and — at the present moment, alas! — in the chaos of relentless war. Woman's sphere, though continually enlarging, is still relatively narrowed, and she seeks her freedom in the realm of imagination, thus identifying herself oftentimes in the work-a-day contests of men. This mental exercise within the wide gamut of imagined emotions naturally helps her to enter sympathetically into varied contests. And it is perhaps because of her broadened understanding that she is fuller and truer in her written record.

The feminine mind, moreover, is more observant of detail and more ready to perceive a lack of harmony in arrangement; and while mere fullness of observation might in isolated cases lead to incontinent garrulousness, the generous flow is usually held in sufficient check by that nicer feminine perception of an æsthetic effect that dictates shearing and compression.

Perhaps the widening of the educational field, the world's

fuller acknowledgment of woman's varied ability, her easier mastery of delicate technique, a more habitual access to a writing-pad — perhaps all these combine with other facts and circumstances to encourage her in this prolific output of marketable fiction. At any rate, the fact is easily apparent.

The stamp of authenticity

A further interesting fact revealed in an examination of Atlantic narratives is the encouragement of that type of story which carries with it the stamp of an authentic atmosphere. More than a generation ago this magazine was printing the stories of Bret Harte — stories that revealed with great accuracy and skill and sympathy the spirit of the California mining camp. Bret Harte had lived and breathed the grim and romantic spirit of this environment. Fusing this experience with an imagination that emotionalized a native instinct for story-telling, Bret Harte was able to lend to his writing a verisimilitude that easily won the reader's interest in the charm and novelty of that strenuous and elemental western life.

While the work of Bret Harte perhaps most strikingly illustrates this power of authentic portrayal of experience and place, there are scores of Atlantic stories that employ the same general method. Sarah Orne Jewett, in such stories as *The Queen's Twin*, *The Life of Nancy*, and *A Dummet Shepherd*, has admirably re-created the simple life of rural New England. Lafcadio Hearn has realistically brought to us the spirit of Japan, Jacob Riis has portrayed for us many pictures of New York tenement life, Joseph Husband has brought us into the atmosphere of industrialism, H. G. Dwight and Charles Johnson have allowed us to breathe the spirit of Orientalism. And scores of other writers, such as Dallas Lore Sharp,

E. Morlae, Margaret Prescott Montague, Abraham Rih-
bany, Mary Antin, Mildred Aldrich, Simeon Strunsky,
after they have lived their separate experiences, have
shared with us the intimate memories which those personal experiences have bequeathed.

Sordidness rejected

The Atlantic traditions, for the most part, have rejected the harrowing and the sordid and the meretricious.
Contrasted with the tone of tragic realism so often dominant in Gorky, Dostoevsky, Turgenef, Maupassant, and
Zola, we usually find in the pages of the *Atlantic* an emphasis upon themes which suggest a gentler and more
humane spirit. The winds of heaven do, of course, sometimes blow over places that are bleak, barren, and desolate.
They shriek and moan through winter wilds, and sometimes the human mood that corresponds to this despair
has found its reflection in stories which the *Atlantic* has
printed. But the mission of the magazine has in general
been in the sunlit fields or near the hearthfire's glow. If
it sometimes has witnessed tragedy, it has never found
delight in the disclosure of grimness for grimness' sake.
It has been more watchful of scenes within the common-
places of human action; here the writers have found
themes of quiet pathos, of homely humor, and of rich romance. Small wonder, indeed, if since August, 1914,
grimmer scenes than usual should not sometimes shadow
the pages! But even so; the writers have not yet lost
their sanity, their hopefulness, or their quiet sense of
humor.

Possibilities within the future

After these comments on the more dominant charac-
teristics of the short story it is natural to inquire into the

possible future of the art.   It is apparent that writers are paying careful attention to technique, and there is real danger to the art if technique is to be too narrowly interpreted and too slavishly followed.   A credulous acceptance of a guide has always worked havoc in the field of creative literature.   Aristotle, and Horace, and Longinus — to revert to a literary period now far distant — showed admirable critical acumen, but it may be sincerely questioned whether they enhanced the worth of Grecian and Roman literature.   We may be quite sure that the critical writings of neither Boileau nor Pope deepened or improved French or English poetry.   Will our short stories be any better here in America because Brander Matthews, Bliss Perry, Clayton Hamilton, Henry S. Canby, W. B. Pitkin, Miss Albright, Miss Ashmun, and a score of others have written so entertainingly about them?   As I have read these criticisms and as I have seen new writers apparently influenced by these criticisms and by the methods obvious in Poe, Bret Harte, Kipling, and O. Henry, I have been reluctantly made to feel that we were perhaps on the verge of yielding to the technique of the telling rather than to the substance of the experience.

Where art becomes too self-conscious and too critical, it sacrifices spontaneity and elemental power, and smothers itself in the wrappings of its self-woven web.   Reliance upon technique and long practice in its use will help crudeness to rise to mediocrity, but the process will never lift the mediocre writer to the plane of the supremely excellent or the austerely great.

Perhaps the present danger lies partly in the attitude of the magazine editor whose sceptre is his check-book. Let us not deceive ourselves.   Literature is now a business — or if not wholly commercialized, it is acutely sensitive to the laws of the trade.   The purely commercial editors, with their eyes riveted to the main chance, have come to recognize the power of technique, and to it they have been paying bountiful tribute. The public has in turn learned to expect the sudden start, the swift pace, the placarded climax, the clever paradox, the crisp repartee, the pinchbeck style, the bared realism, the concluding click. It is all very perfect and very regular, and the editor in accepting the manuscript that adheres to each conventional requirement encloses his check for two hundred dollars in a letter that contains an order for a half dozen more of the identical type. One of the deplorable adjuncts of this procedure is that the editor often realizes the emptiness of this technically correct story, and his own best literary judgment spurns it. But trying to objectify what his clientele would applaud, he pays the price and orders more.

Conversely, a story with genuine substance and sincere feeling comes to his desk. He reads it and approves. Then he asks that fateful question — What will my reading public say? He concludes that they will note the utter lack of climax, of cleverness, of ingenuity, of realistic contact with unadorned everydayness. He closes the incident by a return of the manuscript with a printed rejection slip enclosed.

But this procedure is sometimes happily reversed: an editor has had the fortitude to ignore the fancied judgment of his readers and has relied upon his own impressions of what constitutes literary worth. He is conscious that the story he has accepted is written in utter ignorance or in total disregard of traditional propriety and the laws of modern technique; yet it carries a message, it reveals character, it shows real thinking powers. Accepted and published, as was Arthur Russell Taylor's *Mr. Squem*, it has been enthusiastically received by its readers.

There is one final conviction that emerges from the varied and the multitudinous impressions that come from the reading of all these stories. Every individual has an experience worth narrating; and most individuals have scores upon scores of experiences — real or imagined — that are worth narrating. To succeed in the attempt one does not necessarily need to be a conscious master of technique. He must, of course, have a reasonably firm command of his vernacular — indeed, to succeed in any large degree, he must attain unquestioned mastery and fittingly fashion his style to the theme immediately at hand. He should have a sense of organization that deftly orders the proper sequence of events and skillfully adjusts both minor and major incidents to secure a unified impression. There is, I am convinced, no single minor rule that critics may formulate which will stand a rigid acid test. Genius abrogates every law; talent may abrogate most laws. A great experience, a great situation, a great theme, a great character, a great scene, a great emotion — any one of these may direct even an ordinary writer to successful narration. The skilled story-teller will win success from even scanty material — but the scanty material will be enriched by a sense of humor, an ingenious fancy, a felicitous style, a controlling imagination, a deft craftsmanship, or a keen perception of the value and regulation of detail.

ATLANTIC NARRATIVES

THE PRELIMINARIES

BY CORNELIA A. P. COMER

I

Young Oliver Pickersgill was in love with Peter Lannithorne's daughter. Peter Lannithorne was serving a six-year term in the penitentiary for embezzlement.

It seemed to Ollie that there was only one right-minded way of looking at these basal facts of his situation. But this simple view of the matter was destined to receive several shocks in the course of his negotiations for Ruth Lannithorne's hand. I say negotiations advisedly. Most young men in love have only to secure the consent of the girl and find enough money to go to housekeeping. It is quite otherwise when you wish to marry into a royal family, or to ally yourself with a criminal's daughter. The preliminaries are more complicated.

Ollie thought a man ought to marry the girl he loves, and prejudices be hanged! In the deeps of his soul, he probably knew this to be the magnanimous, manly attitude, but certainly there was no condescension in his outward bearing when he asked Ruth Lannithorne to be his wife. Yet she turned on him fiercely, bristling with pride and tense with over-wrought nerves.

'I will never marry any one,' she declared, 'who does n't respect my father as I do!'

If Oliver's jaw fell, it is hardly surprising. He had expected her to say she would never marry into a family where she was not welcome. He had planned to get around the natural objections of his parents somehow — the details of this were vague in his mind — and then he meant to reassure her warmly, and tell her that personal merit was the only thing that counted with him or his. He may have visualized himself as wiping away her tears and gently raising her to share the safe social pedestal whereon the Pickersgills were firmly planted. The young do have these visions not infrequently. But to be asked to respect Peter Lannithorne, about whom he knew practically nothing save his present address!

'I don't remember that I ever saw your father, Ruth,' he faltered.

'He was the best man,' said the girl excitedly, 'the kindest, the most indulgent — That's another thing, Ollie. I will never marry an indulgent man, nor one who will let his wife manage him. If it had n't been for mother —' She broke off abruptly.

Ollie tried to look sympathetic and not too intelligent. He had heard that Mrs. Lannithorne was considered difficult.

'I ought n't to say it, but can't explain father unless I do. Mother nagged; she wanted more money than there was; she made him feel her illnesses, and our failings, and the overdone beefsteak, and the under-done bread, — everything that went wrong, always, was his fault. His fault — because he did n't make more money. We were on the edge of things, and she wanted to be in the middle, as she was used to being. Of course, she really has n't been well, but I think it's mostly nerves,' said Ruth, with the terrible hardness of the young. 'Anyhow, she might just as well have stuck knives into him as to say the things she did. It hurt him — like knives, I could see him wince — and try harder — and get discouraged — and then, at last —' The girl burst into a passion of tears.

Oliver tried to soothe her. Secretly he was appalled at these squalid revelations of discordant family life. The domestic affairs of the Pickersgills ran smoothly, in affluence and peace. Oliver had never listened to a nagging woman in his life. He had an idea that such phenomena were confined to the lower classes.

'Don't you care for me at all, Ruth?'

The girl crumpled her wet handkerchief. 'Ollie, you're the most beautiful thing that ever happened — except my father. He was beautiful, too; indeed, indeed, he was. I'll never think differently. I can't. He tried so hard.'

All the latent manliness in the boy came to the surface and showed itself.

'Ruth, darling, I do n't want you to think differently. It's right for you to be loyal and feel as you do. You see, you know, and the world does n't. I'll take what you say and do as you wish. You must n't think I'm on the other side. I'm not. I'm on your side, wherever that is. When the time comes I'll show you. You may trust me, Ruth.'

He was eager, pleading, earnest. He looked at the moment so good, so loving and sincere, that the girl, out of her darker experience of life, wondered wistfully if it were really true that Providence ever let people just live their lives out like that — being good, and prosperous, and generous, advancing from happiness to happiness, instead of stubbing along painfully as she felt she had done, from one bitter experience to another, learning to live by failures.

It must be beautiful to learn from successes instead, as it seemed to her Oliver had done. How could any one refuse to share such a radiant life when it was offered? As for loving Oliver, that was a foregone conclusion. Still, she hesitated.

'You're awfully dear and good to me, Ollie,' she said.

'But I want you to see father. I want you to go and talk to him about this, and know him for yourself. I know I'm asking a hard thing of you, but, truly, I believe it's best. If *he* says it's all right for me to marry you, I will — if your family want me, of course,' she added as an afterthought.

'Ought n't I to speak to your mother?' hesitated Oliver.

'Oh, — mother? Yes, I suppose she'd like it,' said Ruth, absent-mindedly. 'Mother has views about getting married, Ollie. I dare say she'll want to tell you what they are. You must n't think they're my views, though.'

'I'd rather hear yours, Ruth.'

She flashed a look at him that opened for him the heavenly deeps that lie before the young and the loving, and he had a sudden vision of their life as a long sunlit road, winding uphill, winding down, but sunlit always — because looks like that illumine any dusk.

'I'll tell you my views — some day,' Ruth said softly. 'But first —'

'First I must talk to my father, your mother, your father.' Oliver checked them off on his fingers. 'Three of them. Seems to me that's a lot of folks to consult about a thing that does n't really concern anybody but you and me!'

II

After the fashion of self-absorbed youth, Oliver had never noticed Mrs. Lannithorne especially. She had been to him simply a sallow little figure in the background of Ruth's vivid young life; some one to be spoken to very politely, but otherwise of no particular moment.

If his marital negotiations did nothing else for him, they were at least opening his eyes to the significance of the personalities of older people.

The things Ruth said about her mother had prepared

him to find that lady querulous and difficult, but essentially negligible. Face to face with Mrs. Lannithorne, he had a very different impression. She received him in the upstairs sitting-room to which her semi-invalid habits usually confined her. Wrapped in a white wool shawl and lying in a long Canton lounging-chair by a sunshiny window, she put out a chilly hand in greeting, and asked the young man to be seated.

Oliver, scanning her countenance, received an unexpected impression of dignity. She was thin and nervous, with big dark eyes peering out of a pale, narrow face; she might be a woman with a grievance, but he apprehended something beyond mere fretfulness in the discontent of her expression. There was suffering and thought in her face, and even when the former is exaggerated and the latter erroneous, these are impressive things.

'Mrs. Lannithorne, have you any objection to letting Ruth marry me?'

'Mr. Pickersgill, what are your qualifications for the care of a wife and family?'

Oliver hesitated. 'Why, about what anybody's are, I think,' he said, and was immediately conscious of the feebleness of this response. 'I mean,' he added, flushing to the roots of his blond hair, 'that my prospects in life are fair. I am in my father's office, you know. I am to have a small share in the business next year. I need n't tell you that the firm is a good one. If you want to know about my qualifications as a lawyer — why, I can refer you to people who can tell you if they think I am promising.'

'Do your family approve of this marriage?'

'I have n't talked to them about it yet.'

'Have you ever saved any money of your own earning, or have you any property in your own name?'

Oliver thought guiltily of his bank account, which had a

surprising way of proving, when balanced, to be less than
he expected.

'Well, — not exactly.'

'In other words, then, Mr. Pickersgill, you are a young
and absolutely untried man; you are in your father's employ and practically at his mercy; you propose a great
change in your life of which you do not know that he approves; you have no resources of your own, and you are not
even sure of your earning capacity if your father's backing
were withdrawn. In these circumstances you plan to
double your expenses and assume the whole responsibility
of another person's life, comfort, and happiness. Do you
think that you have shown me that your qualifications are
adequate?'

All this was more than a little disconcerting. Oliver was
used to being accepted as old Pickersgill's only son —
which meant a cheerfully accorded background of emi-
nence, ability, and comfortable wealth. It had not occurred to him to detach himself from that background and
see how he looked when separated from it. He felt a little
angry, and also a little ashamed of the fact that he did not
bulk larger as a personage, apart from his environment.
Nevertheless, he answered her question honestly.

'No, Mrs. Lannithorne, I don't think that I have.'

She did not appear to rejoice in his discomfiture. She
even seemed a little sorry for it, but she went on quietly: —

'Don't think I am trying to prove that you are the most
ineligible young man in the city. But it is absolutely necessary that a man should stand on his own feet, and firmly,
before he undertakes to look after other lives than his own.
Otherwise there is nothing but misery for the woman and
children who depend upon him. It is a serious business,
getting married.'

'I begin to think it is,' muttered Oliver blankly.

'I don't *want* my daughters to marry,' said Mrs. Lanni-thorne. 'The life is a thousand times harder than that of the self-supporting woman — harder work, fewer rewards, less enjoyment, less security. That is true even of an ordinarily happy marriage. And if they are not happy — Oh, the bitterness of them!'

She was speaking rapidly now, with energy, almost with anguish. Oliver, red in the face, subdued, but eager to refute her out of the depths and heights of his inexperience, held himself rigidly still and listened.

'Did you ever hear that epigram of Disraeli — that all men should marry, but no women? That is what I believe! At least, if women must marry, let others do it, not my children, not my little girls! — It is curious, but that is how we always think of them. When they are grown they are often uncongenial. My daughter Ruth does not love me deeply, nor am I greatly drawn to her now, as an individual, a personality, — but Ruth was such a dear baby! I can't bear to have her suffer.'

Oliver started to protest, hesitated, bit his lip, and subsided. After all, did he dare say that his wife would never suffer? The woman opposite looked at him with hostile, accusing eyes, as if he incarnated in his youthful person all the futile masculinity in the world.

'Do you think a woman who has suffered willingly gives her children over to the same fate?' she demanded passionately. 'I wish I could make you see it for five minutes as I see it, you, young, careless, foolish! Why, you know nothing — nothing! Listen to me. The woman who marries gives up everything, or at least jeopardizes everything: her youth, her health, her life perhaps, certainly her individuality. She acquires the permanent possibility of self-sacrifice. She does it gladly, but she does not know what she is doing. In return, is it too much to ask that she be assured a roof over her head, food to her mouth, clothes to her body? How many men marry without being sure that they have even so much to offer? You yourself, of what are you sure? Is your arm strong? Is your heart loyal? Can you shelter her soul as well as her body? I know your father has money. Perhaps you can care for her creature needs, but that is n't all. For some women life is one long affront, one slow humiliation. How do I know you are not like that?'

'Because I'm not, that's all!' said Oliver Pickersgill abruptly, getting to his feet.

He felt badgered, baited, indignant, yet he could not tell this frail, excited woman what he thought. There were things one did n't say, although Mrs. Lannithorne seemed to ignore the fact. She went on ignoring it.

'I know what you are thinking,' she said, 'that I would regard these matters differently if I had married another man. That is not wholly true. It is because Peter Lannithorne was a good man at heart, and tried to play the man's part as well as he knew how, and because it was partly my own fault that he failed so miserably, that I have thought of it all so much. And the end of all my thinking is that I don't want my daughters to marry.'

Oliver was white now, and a little unsteady. He was also confused. There was the note of truth in what she said, but he felt that she said it with too much excitement, with too great facility. He had the justified masculine distrust of feminine fluency as hysterical. Nothing so presented could carry full conviction. And he felt physically bruised and battered, as if he had been beaten with actual rods instead of stinging words; but he was not yet defeated.

'Mrs. Lannithorne, what do you wish me to understand from all this. Do you forbid Ruth and me to marry — is that it?'

She looked at him dubiously. She felt so fiercely the things she had been saying that she could not feel them continuously. She, too, was exhausted.

Oliver Pickersgill had a fine head, candid eyes, a firm chin, strong capable hands. He was young, and the young know nothing, but it might be that there was the making of a man in him. If Ruth must marry, perhaps him as well as another. But she did not trust her own judgment, even of such hands, such eyes, and such a chin. Oh, if the girl would only believe her, if they would only be content to trust the wisdom she had distilled from the bitterness of life! But the young know nothing, and believe only the lying voices in their own hearts!

'I wish you would see Ruth's father,' she said suddenly. 'I am prejudiced. I ought not to have to deal with these questions. I tell you, I pray Heaven none of them may marry — ever; but, just the same, they will! Go ask Peter Lannithorne if he thinks his daughter Ruth has a fighting chance for happiness as your wife. Let him settle it. I have told you what I think. I am done.'

'I shall be very glad to talk with Ruth's father about the matter,' said Oliver with a certain emphasis on *father*. 'Perhaps he and I shall be able to understand each other better. Good-morning, Mrs. Lannithorne!'

III

Oliver Pickersgill Senior turned his swivel-chair about, bit hard on the end of his cigar, and stared at his only son.

'What's that?' he said abruptly. 'Say that again.'

Oliver Junior winced, not so much at the words as at his father's face.

'I want to marry Ruth Lannithorne,' he repeated steadily.

There was a silence. The elder Pickersgill looked at his son long and hard from under lowered brows. Oliver had never seen his father look at him like that before: as if he were a rank outsider, some detached person whose doings were to be scrutinized coldly and critically, and judged on their merits. It is a hard hour for a beloved child when he first sees that look in heretofore indulgent parental eyes. Young Oliver felt a weight at his heart, but he sat the straighter, and did not flinch before the appraising glance.

'So you want to marry Peter Lannithorne's daughter, do you? Well, now what is there in the idea of marrying a jail-bird's child that you find especially attractive?'

'Of course I might say that I've seen something of business men in this town, Ross, say, and Worcester, and Jim Stone, and that if it came to a choice between their methods and Lannithorne's, his were the squarer, for he settled up, and is paying the price besides. But I don't know that there's any use saying that. I don't want to marry any of their daughters — and you wouldn't want me to. You know what Ruth Lannithorne is as well as I do. If there's a girl in town that's finer-grained, or smarter, or prettier, I'd like to have you point her out! And she has a sense of honor like a man's. I don't know another girl like her in that. She knows what's fair,' said the young man.

Mr. Pickersgill's face relaxed a little. Oliver was making a good argument with no mushiness about it, and he had a long-settled habit of appreciating Ollie's arguments.

'She knows what's fair, does she? Then what does she say about marrying you?'

'She says she won't marry anybody who doesn't respect her father as she does!'

At this the parent grinned a little, grimly it is true, but appreciatively. He looked past Oliver's handsome, boyish head, out of the window, and was silent for a time. When he spoke, it was gravely, not angrily.

'Oliver, you're young. The things I'm as sure of as two and two, you don't yet believe at all. Probably you won't believe 'em if I put them to you, but it's up to me to do it. Understand, I'm not getting angry and doing the heavy father over this. I'm just telling you how some things are in this world, — facts, like gravitation and atmospheric pressure. Ruth Lannithorne is a good girl, I don't doubt. This world is chuck full of good girls. It makes *some* difference which one of 'em you marry, but not nearly so much difference as you think it does. What matters, from forty on, for the rest of your life, is the kind of inheritance you've given your children. You don't know it yet, but the thing that's laid on men and women to do is to give their children as good an inheritance as they can. Take it from me that this is Gospel truth, can't you? Your mother and I have done the best we can for you and your sisters. You come from good stock, and by that I mean honest blood. You've got to pass it on untainted. Now — hold on!' he held up a warning hand as Oliver was about to interrupt hotly. 'Wait till I'm through — and then think it over. I'm not saying that Peter Lannithorne's blood is n't as good as much that passes for untainted, or that Ruth is n't a fine girl. I'm only telling you this: when first you look into your son's face, every failing of your own will rise up to haunt you because you will wish for nothing on God's earth so much as that that boy shall have a fair show in life and be a better man than you. You will thank Heaven for every good thing you know of in your blood and in your wife's, and you will regret every meanness, every weakness, that he may inherit, more than you knew it was in you to regret anything. Do you suppose when that hour

comes to you that you'll want to remember his grandfather
was a convict? How will you face that down?'

Young Oliver's face was pale. He had never thought of
things like this. He made no response for a while. At last
he asked, —

'What kind of a man is Peter Lannithorne?'

'Eh? What kind of —? Oh, well, as men go, there have
been worse ones. You know how he came to get sent up.
He speculated, and he borrowed some of another man's
money without asking, for twenty-four hours, to protect
his speculation. He did n't lose it, either! There's a point
where his case differs from most. He pulled the thing off
and made enough to keep his family going in decent comfort, and he paid the other money back; but they concluded to make an example of him, so they sent him up. It
was just, yes, and he said so himself. At the same time
there are a great many more dishonest men out of prison
than Peter Lannithorne, though he is in it. I meet 'em
every day, and I ought to know. But that's not the point.
As you said yourself, you don't want to marry their daughters. Heaven forbid that you should! You want to marry
his daughter. And he was weak. He was tempted and fell
— and got found out. He is a convict, and the taint sticks.
The Lord knows why the stain of unsuccessful dishonesty
should stick longer than the stain of successful dishonesty.
I don't. But we know it does. That is the way things are.
Why not marry where there is no taint?'

'Father —?'

'Yes, Ollie.'

'Father, see here. He was weak and gave way — *once!*
Are there any men in the world who have n't given way
at least *once* about something or other? — are there,
father?'

There was a note of anguish in the boy's voice. Perhaps

he was being pushed too far. Oliver Pickersgill Senior cleared his throat, paused, and at last answered sombrely,—

'God knows, Ollie. I do n't. I won't say there are.'

'Well, then —'

'See here!' his father interrupted sharply. 'Of course I see your argument. I won't meet it. I shan't try. It does n't change my mind even if it is a good argument. We'll never get anywhere, arguing along those lines. I'll propose something else. Suppose you go ask Peter Lannithorne whether you shall marry his daughter or not. Yes, ask him. He knows what's what as well as the next man. Ask Peter Lannithorne what a man wants in the family of the woman he marries.'

There was a note of finality in the older man's voice. Ollie recognized it drearily. All roads led to Lannithorne, it seemed. He rose, oppressed with the sense that henceforward life was going to be full of unforeseen problems; that things which, from afar, looked simple, and easy, and happy, were going to prove quite otherwise. Mrs. Lannithorne had angered rather than frightened him, and he had held his own with her; but this was his very own father who was piling the load on his shoulders and filling his heart with terror of the future. What was it, after all, this adventure of the married life whereof these seasoned travelers spoke so dubiously? Could it really be that it was not the divine thing it seemed when he and Ruth looked into each other's eyes?

He crossed the floor dejectedly, with the step of an older man, but at the door he shook himself and looked back.

'Say, dad!'

'Yes, Ollie.'

'Everybody is so terribly depressing about this thing, it almost scares me. Are n't there really any happy times for married people, ever? You and Mrs. Lannithorne make me feel there are n't; but somehow I have a hunch that Ruth and I know best! Own up now! Are you and mother miserable? You never looked it!'

His father surveyed him with an expression too wistful to be complacent. Ah, those broad young shoulders that must be fitted to the yoke! Yet for what other end was their strength given them? Each man must take his turn.

'It's not a soft snap. I don't know anything worth while that is. But there are compensations. You'll see what some of them are when your boys begin to grow up.'

IV

Across Oliver's young joy fell the shadow of fear. If, as his heart told him, there was nothing to be afraid of, why were his elders thus cautious and terrified? He felt himself affected by their alarms all the more potently because his understanding of them was vague. He groped his way in fog. How much ought he to be influenced by Mrs. Lannithorne's passionate protests and his father's stern warnings? He realized all at once that the admonitory attitude of age to youth is rooted deep in immortal necessity. Like most lads, he had never thought of it before save as an unpleasant parental habit. But fear changes the point of view, and Oliver had begun to be afraid.

Then again, before him loomed the prospect of his interview with Peter Lannithorne. This was a very concrete unpleasantness. Hang it all! Ruth was worth any amount of trouble, but still it was a tough thing to have to go down to the state capital and seek one's future father-in-law in his present boarding-place! One ought n't to have to plough through that particular kind of difficulty on such an errand. Dimly he felt that the path to the Most Beautiful should be rose-lined and soft to the feet of the approaching bridegroom. But, apparently, that was n't the way such paths were laid out. He resented this bitterly, but he set his jaws and proceeded to make his arrangements.

It was not difficult to compass the necessary interview. He knew a man who knew the warden intimately. It was quickly arranged that he was to see Peter Lannithorne in the prison library, quite by himself.

Oliver dragged himself to that conference by the sheer strength of his developing will. Every fibre of his being seemed to protest and hold back. Consequently he was not in the happiest imaginable temper for important conversation.

The prison library was a long, narrow room, with bookcases to the ceiling on one side and windows to the ceiling on the other. There were red geraniums on brackets up the sides of the windows, and a canary's cage on a hook gave the place a false air of domesticity, contradicted by the barred sash. Beneath, there was a window-seat, and here Oliver Pickersgill awaited Lannithorne's coming.

Ollie did not know what he expected the man to be like, but his irritated nerves were prepared to resent and dislike him, whatever he might prove. He held himself rigidly as he waited, and he could feel the muscles of his face setting themselves into hard lines.

When the door opened and some one approached him, he rose stiffly and held out his hand like an automaton.

'How do you do, Mr. Lannithorne? I am Oliver Pickersgill, and I have come — I have come —'

His voice trailed off into silence, for he had raised his eyes perfunctorily to Peter Lannithorne's face, and the things printed there made him forget himself and the speech he had prepared.

He saw a massive head topping an insignificant figure.

A fair man was Peter Lannithorne, with heavy reddish hair, a bulging forehead, and deep-set gray eyes with a light behind them. His features were irregular and unnoticeable, but the sum-total of them gave the impression of force. It was a strong face, yet you could see that it had once been a weak one. It was a tremendously human face, a face like a battle-ground, scarred and seamed and lined with the stress of invisible conflicts. There was so much of struggle and thought set forth in it that one involuntarily averted one's gaze. It did not seem decent to inspect so much of the soul of a man as was shown in Peter Lannithorne's countenance. Not a triumphant face at all, and yet there was peace in it. Somehow, the man had achieved something, arrived somewhere, and the record of the journey was piteous and terrible. Yet it drew the eyes in awe as much as in wonder, and in pity not at all!

These things were startlingly clear to Oliver. He saw them with a vividness not to be overestimated. This was a prison. This might be a convict, but he was a man. He was a man who knew things and would share his knowledge. His wisdom was as patent as his suffering, and both stirred young Oliver's heart to its depths. His pride, his irritation, his rigidity vanished in a flash. His fears were in abeyance. Only his wonder and his will to learn were left.

Lannithorne did not take the offered hand, yet did not seem to ignore it. He came forward quietly and sat down on the window-seat, half turning so that he and Oliver faced each other.

'Oliver Pickersgill?' he said. 'Then you are Oliver Pickersgill's son.'

'Yes, Mr. Lannithorne. My father sent me here — my father, and Mrs. Lannithorne, and Ruth.'

At his daughter's name a light leaped into Peter Lannithorne's eyes that made him look even more acutely and painfully alive than before.

'And what have you to do with Ruth, or her mother?' the man asked.

Here it was! The great moment was facing him. Oliver caught his breath, then went straight to the point.

'I want to marry your daughter, Mr. Lannithorne. We love each other very much. But — I have n't quite persuaded her, and I have n't persuaded Mrs. Lannithorne and my father at all. They do n't see it. They say things — all sorts of dreadful things,' said the boy. 'You would think they had never been young and — cared for anybody. They seem to have forgotten what it means. They try to make us afraid — just plain afraid. How am I to suppose that they know best about Ruth and me?'

Lannithorne looked across at the young man long and fixedly. Then a great kindliness came into his beaten face, and a great comprehension.

Oliver, meeting his eyes, had a sudden sense of shelter, and felt his haunting fears allayed. It was absurd and incredible, but this man made him feel comfortable, yes, and eager to talk things over.

'They all said you would know. They sent me to you.'

Peter Lannithorne smiled faintly to himself. He had not left his sense of humor behind him in the outside world.

'They sent you to me, did they, boy? And what did they tell you to ask me? They had different motives, I take it.'

'Rather! Ruth said you were the best man she had ever known, and if you said it was right for her to marry me, she would. Mrs. Lannithorne said I should ask you if you thought Ruth had a fighting chance for happiness with me. She does n't want Ruth to marry anybody, you see. My father — my father' — Oliver's voice shook with his consciousness of the cruelty of what was to follow, but he forced himself to steadiness and got the words out — 'said I was to ask you what a man wants in the family of the woman he marries. He said you knew what was what, and I should ask you what to do.'

Lannithorne's face was very grave, and his troubled gaze sought the floor. Oliver, convicted of brutality and conscience-smitten, hurried on, 'And now that I've seen you, I want to ask you a few things for myself, Mr. Lannithorne. I — I believe you know.'

The man looked up and held up an arresting hand. 'Let me clear the way for you a little,' he said. 'It was a hard thing for you to come and seek me out in this place. I like your coming. Most young men would have refused, or come in a different spirit. I want you to understand that if in Ruth's eyes, and my wife's, and your father's, my counsel has value, it is because they think I see things as they are. And that means, first of all, that I know myself for a man who committed a crime, and is paying the penalty. I am satisfied to be paying it. As I see justice, it is just. So, if I seem to wince at your necessary allusions to it, that is part of the price. I don't want you to feel that you are blundering or hurting me more than is necessary. You have got to lay the thing before me as it is.'

Something in the words, in the dry, patient manner, in the endurance of the man's face, touched Oliver to the quick and made him feel all manner of new things: such as a sense of the moral poise of the universe, acquiescence in its retributions, and a curious pride, akin to Ruth's own, in a man who could meet him after this fashion, in this place.

'Thank you, Mr. Lannithorne,' he said. 'You see, it's this way, sir. Mrs. Lannithorne says —'

And he went on eagerly to set forth his new problems as they had been stated to him.

'Well, there you have it,' he concluded at last. 'For myself, the things they said opened chasms and abysses. Mrs. Lannithorne seemed to think I would hurt Ruth. My father seemed to think Ruth would hurt me. *Is* married life something to be afraid of? When I look at Ruth, I am sure everything is all right. It may be miserable for other people, but how could it be miserable for Ruth and me?'

Peter Lannithorne looked at the young man long and thoughtfully again before he answered. Oliver felt himself measured and estimated, but not found wanting. When the man spoke, it was slowly and with difficulty, as if the habit of intimate, convincing speech had been so long disused that the effort was painful. The sentences seemed wrung out of him, one by one.

'They have n't the point of view,' he said. 'It is life that is the great adventure. Not love, not marriage, not business. They are just chapters in the book. The main thing is to take the road fearlessly, — to have courage to live one's life.'

'Courage?'

Lannithorne nodded.

'That is the great word. Don't you see what ails your father's point of view, and my wife's? One wants absolute security in one way for Ruth; the other wants absolute security in another way for you. And security — why, it's just the one thing a human being can't have, the thing that's the damnation of him if he gets it! The reason it is so hard for a rich man to enter the kingdom of Heaven is that he has that false sense of security. To demand it just disintegrates a man. I don't know why. It does.'

Oliver shook his head uncertainly.

'I don't quite follow you, sir. Ought n't one to try to be safe?'

'One ought to try, yes. That is common prudence. But the point is that, whatever you do or get, you are n't after all secure. There is no such condition, and the harder you demand it, the more risk you run. So it is up to a man to take all reasonable precautions about his money, or his happiness, or his life, and trust the rest. What every man in the world is looking for is the sense of having the mastery over life. But I tell you, boy, there is only one thing that really gives it!'

'And that is —?'

Lannithorne hesitated perceptibly. For the thing he was about to tell this undisciplined lad was his most precious possession; it was the piece of wisdom for which he had paid with the years of his life. No man parts lightly with such knowledge.

'It comes,' he said, with an effort, 'with the knowledge of our power to endure. That's it. *You are safe only when you can stand everything that can happen to you.* Then and then only! Endurance is the measure of a man.'

Oliver's heart swelled within him as he listened, and his face shone, for these words found his young soul where it lived. The chasms and abysses in his path suddenly vanished, and the road lay clear again, winding uphill, winding down, but always lit for Ruth and him by the light in each other's eyes. For surely neither Ruth nor he could ever fail in courage!

'Sometimes I think it is harder to endure what we deserve, like me,' said Lannithorne, 'than what we don't. I was afraid, you see, afraid for my wife and all of them. Anyhow, take my word for it. Courage is security. There is no other kind.'

'Then — Ruth and I —'

'Ruth is the core of my heart!' said Lannithorne thickly. 'I would rather die than have her suffer more than she must. But she must take her chances like the rest. It is the law of things. If you know yourself fit for her, and feel reasonably sure you can take care of her, you have a right to trust the future. Myself, I believe there is Some One to trust it to. As for the next generation, God and the mothers look after that! You may tell your father so from me. And you may tell my wife I think there is the stuff of a man in you. And Ruth — tell Ruth —'

He could not finish. Oliver reached out and found his hand and wrung it hard.

'I'll tell her, sir, that I feel about her father as she does! And that he approves of our venture. And I'll tell myself, always, what you've just told me. Why, it *must* be true! You needn't be afraid I'll forget — when the time comes for remembering.'

Finding his way out of the prison yard a few minutes later, Oliver looked, unseeing, at the high walls that soared against the blue spring sky. He could not realize them, there was such a sense of light, air, space, in his spirit.

Apparently, he was just where he had been an hour before, with all his battles still to fight, but really he knew they were already won, for his weapon had been forged and put in his hand. He left his boyhood behind him as he passed that stern threshold, for the last hour had made a man of him, and a prisoner had given him the master-key that opens every door.

BUTTERCUP-NIGHT

BY JOHN GALSWORTHY

WHY is it that in some places there is such a feeling of life being all one; not merely a long picture-show for human eyes, but a single breathing, glowing, growing thing, of which we are no more important a part than the swallows and magpies, the foals and sheep in the meadows, the sycamores and ash trees and flowers in the fields, the rocks and little bright streams, or even the long fleecy clouds and their soft-shouting drivers, the winds?

True, we register these parts of being, and they — so far as we know — do not register us; yet it is impossible to feel, in such places as I speak of, the busy, dry, complacent sense of being all that matters, which in general we humans have so strongly.

In these rare spots, that are always in the remote country, untouched by the advantages of civilization, one is conscious of an enwrapping web or mist of spirit, the glamorous and wistful wraith of all the vanished shapes which once dwelt there in such close comradeship.

It was Sunday of an early June when I first came on one such, far down in the West country. I had walked with my knapsack twenty miles; and, there being no room at the tiny inn of the very little village, they directed me to a wicket gate, through which by a path leading down a field I would come to a farmhouse where I might find lodging. The moment I got into that field I felt within me a peculiar contentment, and sat down on a rock to let the feeling grow. In an old holly tree rooted to the bank about fifty yards away, two magpies evidently had a nest, for they were coming and going, avoiding my view as much as possible, yet with a certain stealthy confidence which made one feel that they had long prescriptive right to that dwelling-place.

Around, as far as one could see, there was hardly a yard of level ground; all was hill and hollow, that long ago had been reclaimed from the moor; and against the distant folds of the hills the farmhouse and its thatched barns were just visible, embowered amongst beeches and some dark trees, with a soft bright crown of sunlight over the whole. A gentle wind brought a faint rustling up from those beeches, and from a large lime tree that stood by itself; on this wind some little snowy clouds, very high and fugitive in that blue heaven, were always moving over. But what struck me most were the buttercups. Never was field so lighted up by those tiny lamps, those little bright pieces of flower china out of the Great Pottery. They covered the whole ground, as if the sunlight had fallen bodily from the sky, in tens of millions of gold patines; and the fields below as well, down to what was evidently a stream, were just as thick with the extraordinary warmth and glory of them.

Leaving the rock at last, I went toward the house. It was long and low and rather sad, standing in a garden all mossy grass and buttercups, with a few rhododendrons and flowery shrubs, below a row of fine old Irish yews. On the stone verandah a gray sheep-dog and a very small golden-haired child were sitting close together, absorbed in each other. A pleasant woman came in answer to my knock, and told me, in a soft, slurring voice, that I might stay the night; and dropping my knapsack, I went out again.

Through an old gate under a stone arch I came on the farmyard, quite deserted save for a couple of ducks moving slowly down a gutter in the sunlight; and noticing the upper half of a stable-door open, I went across, in search of

something living. There, in a rough loose-box, on thick
straw, lay a long-tailed black mare with the skin and head
of a thoroughbred. She was swathed in blankets, and her
face, all cut about the cheeks and over the eyes, rested on an
ordinary human's pillow, held by a bearded man in shirt-
sleeves; while, leaning against the whitewashed walls, sat
fully a dozen other men, perfectly silent, very gravely and
intently gazing. The mare's eyes were half closed, and
what could be seen of them dull and blueish, as though she
had been through a long time of pain. Save for her rapid
breathing, she lay quite still, but her neck and ears were
streaked with sweat, and every now and then her hind-legs
quivered spasmodically. Seeing me at the door, she raised
her head, uttering a queer half-human noise, but the
bearded man at once put his hand on her forehead, and
with a 'Woa, my dear—woa, my pretty!' pressed it down
again, while with the other hand he plumped up the pillow
for her cheek. And, as the mare obediently let fall her head,
one of the men said in a low voice, 'I never see anything so
like a Christian!' and the others echoed, in chorus, 'Like a
Christian—like a Christian!'

It went to one's heart to watch her, and I moved off down
the farm lane into an old orchard, where the apple trees
were still in bloom, with bees — very small ones — busy on
the blossoms, whose petals were dropping on the dock leaves
and buttercups in the long grass. Climbing over the bank
at the far end, I found myself in a meadow the like of which
— so wild and yet so lush — I think I have never seen.
Along one hedge of its meandering length was a mass of
pink mayflower; and between two little running streams
grew quantities of yellow water-iris — 'daggers,' as they
call them; the 'print-frock' orchid, too, was everywhere in
the grass, and always the buttercups. Great stones coated
with yellowish moss were strewn among the ash trees and

dark hollies; and through a grove of beeches on the far side, such as Corot might have painted, a girl was running, with a youth after her, who jumped down over the bank and vanished. Thrushes, blackbirds, yaffles, cuckoos, and one other very monotonous little bird were in full song; and this, with the sound of the streams and the wind, and the shapes of the rocks and trees, the colors of the flowers, and the warmth of the sun, gave one a feeling of being lost in a very wilderness of nature. Some ponies came slowly from the far end, — tangled, gypsy-headed little creatures, — stared, and went off again at speed. It was just one of those places where any day the Spirit of all Nature might start up in one of those white gaps that separate the trees and rocks. But though I sat a long time waiting — hoping — She did not come.

They were all gone from the stable when I went back up to the farm, except the bearded nurse and one tall fellow, who might have been the 'Dying Gaul' as he crouched there in the straw; and the mare was sleeping — her head between her nurse's knees.

That night I woke at two o'clock to find it almost as bright as day, with moonlight coming in through the flimsy curtains. And, smitten with the feeling that comes to us creatures of routine so rarely, — of what beauty and strangeness we let slip by without ever stretching out hand to grasp it, — I got up, dressed, stole downstairs, and out.

Never was such a night of frozen beauty, never such dream-tranquillity. The wind had dropped, and the silence was such that one hardly liked to tread even on the grass. From the lawn and fields there seemed to be a mist rising — in truth, the moonlight caught on the dewy buttercups; and across this ghostly radiance the shadows of the yew trees fell in dense black bars.

Suddenly I bethought me of the mare. How was she

faring, this marvelous night? Very softly opening the door
into the yard, I tiptoed across. A light was burning in
her box. And I could hear her making the same half-human noise she had made in the afternoon, as if wondering
at her feelings; and instantly the voice of the bearded
man talking to her as one might talk to a child: 'Oover,
my darlin'; yu've a-been long enough o' that side. Wa-ay,
my swate — yu let old Jack turn yu, then!' Then came
a scuffling in the straw, a thud, that half-human sigh, and
his voice again: 'Putt your 'ead to piller, that's my dandy
gel. Old Jack would n' 'urt yu; no more 'n if yu was the
Queen!' Then only her quick breathing could be heard,
and his cough and mutter, as he settled down once more
to his long vigil.

I crept very softly up to the window, but she heard me at
once; and at the movement of her head the old fellow sat
up, blinking his eyes out of the bush of his grizzled hair and
beard. Opening the door, I said, —

'May I come in?'

'Oo ay! Come in, zurr, if yu'm a mind tu.'

I sat down beside him on a sack. And for some time we
did not speak, taking each other in. One of his legs was
lame, so that he had to keep it stretched out all the time;
and awfully tired he looked, gray-tired.

'You're a great nurse!' I said at last. 'It must be tiring
work, watching out here all night.'

His eyes twinkled; they were of that bright gray kind
through which the soul looks out.

'Aw, no!' he said. 'Ah, don't grudge it vur a dumb
animal. Poor things they can't 'elp theirzelves. Many's
the naight ah've zat up with 'orses and beasts tu. 'T es
en me — can't bear to zee dumb creatures zuffer.' And
laying his hand on the mare's ears, 'They zay 'orses 'ave
n't no souls. 'T es my belief they've souls zame as us.

Many's the Christian ah've seen ain't got the soul of an
'orse. Same with the beasts — an' the ship; 't es only
they'm can't spake their minds.'

'And where,' I said, 'do you think they go to when they
die?'

He looked at me a little queerly, fancying perhaps that
I was leading him into some trap; making sure, too, that I
was a real stranger, without power over his body or soul —
for humble folk must be careful in the country; then, reassured, and nodding in his beard, he answered know-
ingly,—

'Ah don't think they goes so very far!'

'Why? Do you ever see their spirits?'

'Naw, naw; I never zeen none; but, for all they zay, ah
don't think none of us goes such a brave way off. There's
room for all, dead or alive. An' there's Christians ah've
zeen—well, ef they'm not dead for gude, then neither are
n't dumb animals, for sure.'

'And rabbits, squirrels, birds, even insects? How about
them?'

He was silent, as if I had carried him a little beyond the
confines of his philosophy; then shook his head.

''T es all a bit dimsy. But you watch dumb animals,
even the laste littlest one, an' yu'll zee they knows a lot
more'n what we du; an' they du's things tu that putts
shame on a man 's often as not. They've a got that in
them as passes show.' Not noticing my stare at that unconscious plagiarism, he went on, 'Ah'd zooner zet up of a
naight with an 'orse than with an 'uman — they've more
zense, and patience.' And stroking the mare's forehead,
he added, 'Now, my dear, time for yu t' 'ave yure bottle.'

I waited to see her take her draft, and lay her head down
once more on the pillow. Then, hoping he would get a
sleep, I rose to go.

'Aw, 't es nothin' much,' he said, 'this time o' year; not like in winter. 'T will come day before yu know, these buttercup-nights.'

And twinkling up at me out of his kindly bearded face, he settled himself again into the straw.

I stole a look back at his rough figure propped against the sack, with the mare's head down beside his knee, at her swathed black body, and the gold of the straw, the white walls, and dusky nooks and shadows of that old stable illumined by the dimsy light of the old lantern. And with the sense of having seen something holy, I crept away up into the field where I had lingered the day before, and sat down on the same halfway rock.

Close on dawn it was, the moon still sailing wide over the moor, and the flowers of this 'buttercup-night' fast closed, not taken in at all by her cold glory! Most silent hour of all the twenty-four — when the soul slips half out of sheath, and hovers in the cool; when the spirit is most in tune with what, soon or late, happens to all spirits; hour when a man cares least whether or no he be alive, as we understand the word.

'None of us goes such a brave way off — there's room for all, dead or alive.' Though it was almost unbearably colorless, and quiet, there was warmth in thinking of those words of his; in the thought, too, of the millions of living things snugly asleep all round; warmth in realizing that unanimity of sleep. Insects and flowers, birds, men, beasts, the very leaves on the trees — away in slumberland.

Waiting for the first bird to chirrup, one had perhaps even a stronger feeling than in daytime of the unity and communion of all life, of the subtle brotherhood of living things that fall all together into oblivion, and, all together, wake. When dawn comes, while moonlight is still powdering the world's face, quite a long time passes before one realizes how the quality of the light has changed; so it was day before I knew it. Then the sun came up above the hills; dew began to sparkle, and color to stain the sky. That first praise of the sun from every bird and leaf and blade of grass, the tremulous flush and chime of dawn! One has strayed so far from the heart of things, that it comes as something strange and wonderful! Indeed, I noticed that the beasts and birds gazed at me as if I simply could not be there, at this hour that so belonged to them. And to me, too, they seemed strange and new — with that in them 'that passed show,' and as of a world where man did not exist, or existed only as just another form of life, another sort of beast. It was one of those revealing moments when we see our proper place in the scheme; go past our truly irreligious thought: 'Man, hub of the Universe!' which has founded most religions. One of those moments when our supreme importance will not wash either in the bath of purest spiritual ecstasy, or in the clear fluid of scientific knowledge; and one sees clear, with the eyes of true religion, man playing his little, not unworthy, part in the great game of Perfection.

But just then began the crowning glory of that dawn — the opening and lighting of the buttercups.   Not one did I actually see unclose, yet, all of a sudden, they were awake, the fields once more a blaze of gold.

HEPATICAS

BY ANNE DOUGLAS SEDGWICK

I

OTHER people's sons were coming home for the three or four days' leave. The first gigantic struggle — furious onslaught and grim resistance — was over. Paris, pale, and slightly shuddering still, stood safe. Calais was not taken, and, dug into their trenches, it was evident that the opposing armies would lie face to face, with no decisive encounter possible until the spring.

There was, with all their beauty and terror, an element of the facetious in these unexpected holidays, of the matter-of-factness, the freedom from strain or sentiment that was the English oddity and the English strength. Men who had known the horrors of the retreat from Mons or the carnage of Ypres, who had not taken off their clothes for ten days at a stretch or slept for four nights, came home from trenches knee-deep in mud, from battlefields heaped with unburied dead, and appeared immaculate and cheerful at breakfast; a little sober and preoccupied, perhaps; touched, perhaps, with strangeness; but ready for the valorous family jest, and alluding to the war as if, while something too solemn for adequate comment, it were yet something that lent itself to laughter. One did such funny things, and saw them; of the other things one did not speak; and there was the huge standing joke of an enemy who actually hated one. These grave and cheerful young men hated nobody; but they were very eager to go back again; and they were all ready, not only to die but to die good-humoredly. From the demeanor of mothers and

wives and sisters it was evident that nothing would be said
or done to make this readiness difficult; but Mrs. Bradley,
who showed serenity to the world and did not, even when
alone, allow herself to cry, suspected that the others, beneath their smiles, carried hearts as heavy with dread as
her own.

It had been heavy, with hope now as well as with dread,
for the past week. It was a week since she had last heard
from Jack. Mrs. Crawley, over the hill, had had her wire,
and her husband was now with her; and Lady Wrexham
expected her boy to-morrow. There was no certainty at
all as regarded herself; yet at any moment she might have
a wire; and feeling to-day the stress of waiting too great to
be borne in passivity, she left her books and letters, and
put on her gardening shoes and gloves, and went out to
her borders.

For weeks now the incessant rain had made the relief and
solace of gardening almost an impossibility; but to-day was
mild and clear. There was no radiance in the air; curtains
of pearly mist shut out the sky; yet here and there a soft
opening in the white showed a pale, far blue, gentle and
remote as the gaze of a wandering goddess, and the hills
seemed to smile quietly up at the unseen sun. Mrs. Bradley, as she went along the river-path, could look across at
the hills; the river-path and the hills were the great feature
of Dorrington — the placid, comely red brick house to
which she and Jack had come fifteen years ago, after the
death of her husband in India. Enclosed by woods, and
almost catching sight of the road, — from its upper windows and over its old brick wall, — the house could have
seemed to her too commonplace and almost suburban, in
spite of the indubitably old oak-paneling of the drawing-
room, had it not been for the river and the hills. Stepping
out on to the lawn from the windows of the drawing-room,

she and Jack, on that April day, had found themselves con-
fronting both — the limpid, rapid little stream, spanned
near the house by its mossy bridge, and the hills, beyond
the meadows, streaked with purple woodlands and rising,
above the woods, to slopes russet, fawn, and azure. Jack,
holding her by the hand, had pointed at once with an eager
'Is n't it pretty, mummy!' — even at eight he had cared
almost as much as she, and extraordinarily in the same
way, for the sights of the country; and if the hills had not
settled the question, it was settled, quite finally, ten minutes later, by the white hepaticas.

They had come upon them suddenly, after their tour of
the walled kitchen garden and their survey of the lawn
with its ugly shrubberies, — now long forgotten, — penetrating a thicket of hazels and finding themselves in an opening under trees where neighboring woods looked at them
over an old stone wall, and where, from an old stone bench,
one could see the river. The ground was soft with the
fallen leaves of many an autumn; a narrow path ran, half
obliterated, down to the river; and among the faded brown,
everywhere, rose the thick clusters, the dark leaves, and the
snowy flowers — poignant, amazing in their beauty.

She and Jack had stopped short to gaze. She had never
seen such white hepaticas, or so many, or so placed. And
Jack, presently, lifting his dear nut-brown head and nut-
brown eyes, had said, gazing up at her as he had gazed at
the flowers, 'They are just like you, mummy.'

She had felt at once that they were like her; more like
than the little boy's instinct could grasp. He had thought
of the darkness and whiteness; her widow's weeds and pale
face had suggested that; but he could not know the sorrow,
the longing, the earthly sense of irreparable loss, the heavenly sense of a possession unalterably hers, that the dark,
melancholy leaves and celestial whiteness of the flowers ex-

pressed to her. Tears had risen to her eyes and she had stooped and kissed her child, — how like her husband's that little face! — and had said, after a moment, 'We must never leave them, Jack.'

They had never left them. Dorrington had been their home for fifteen years, and the hepaticas the heart of it, it had always seemed to them both; the loveliest ritual of the year that early spring one when, in the hazel copse, they would find the white hepaticas again in flower. And of all the autumnal labors none were sweeter than those which cherished and divided and protected the beloved flowers.

Mrs. Bradley, to-day, worked in her long border, weeding, troweling, placing belated labels. She was dressed in black, her straw hat bound beneath her chin by a ribbon and her soft gardening gloves rolling back from her firm, white wrists. Her gestures expressed a calm energy, an accurate grace. She was tall, and when she raised herself to look over the meadows at the hills, she showed small, decisive features, all marked, in the pallor of her face, as if with the delicate, neutral emphasis of an etching: the gray, scrutinizing eyes, the charming yet ugly nose, the tranquil mouth which had, at the corners, a little drop, half sweet, half bitter, as if with tears repressed or a summoned smile. Squared at brow and chin, it would, but for the mildness of the gaze, have been an imperious face; and her head, its whitened hair drawn back and looped in wide braids behind, had an air at once majestic and unworldly.

She had worked for over an hour and the last label was set beside a precious clump of iris. The hazel copse lay near by; and gathering up her tools, drawing off her wet gloves, she followed the path under the leafless branches and among the hepaticas to the stone bench, where, sinking down, she knew that she was very tired. She could see, below the bank, the dark, quick stream; a pale, diffused light in the sky showed where the sun was dropping toward the hills.

Where was Jack at this moment, this quiet moment of a monotonous English winter day? — so like the days of all the other years that it was impossible to think of what was happening a few hours' journey away across the Channel. Impossible to think of it; yet the thick throb of her heart spoke to the full of its significance. She had told herself from the beginning, — passionate, rebellious creature as, at bottom, she knew herself to be, always in need of discipline and only in these later years schooled to a control and submission that, in her youth, she would have believed impossible to her, — she had told herself, when he had gone from her, that, as a soldier's widow, she must see her soldier son go to death. She must give him to that; be ready for it; and if he came back to her it would be as if he were born again — a gift, a grace, unexpected and unclaimed. She must feel, for herself as well as for her country, that these days of dread were also days of a splendor and beauty unmatched by any in England's history, and that a soldier's widow must ask for no more glorious fate for her son than death in such a cause. She had told herself all this many times; yet, as she sat there, her hands folded on her lap, her eyes on the stream below, she felt that she was now merely motherhood, tense, huddled, throbbing and longing, longing for its child.

Then, suddenly, she heard Jack's footsteps. They came, quick and light, along the garden path; they entered the wood; they were near, but softened by the fallen leaves. And, half rising, afraid of her own joy, she hardly knew that she saw him before she was in his arms; and it was better to meet thus, in the blindness and darkness of their embrace, her cheek pressed against his hair, his head buried close between her neck and shoulder.

'Jack! — Jack!' she heard herself say.

He said nothing, holding her tightly to him, with quick breaths; and even after she had opened her eyes and could look down at him, — her own, her dear, beautiful Jack, — could see the nut-brown head, the smooth brown cheek, the firm brown hand which grasped her, he did not for a long time raise his head and look at her. When, at last, he did look up, she could not tell, through her tears, whether, like herself, he was trying to smile.

They sat down together on the bench. She did not ask him why he had not wired. That question pressed too sharply on her heart; to ask might seem to reproach.

'Darling, you are so thin, — so much older, — but you look — strong and well.'

'We're all of us extraordinarily fit, mummy. It's wholesome, living in mud.'

'And wholesome living among bursting shells? I had your last letter telling of that miraculous escape.'

'There have been a lot more since then. Every day seems a miracle — that one's alive at the end of it.'

'But you get used to it?'

'All except the noise. That always seems to daze me still. Some of our fellows are deaf from it. — You heard of Toppie, mother?' Jack asked.

Toppie was Alan Thorpe, Jack's nearest friend. He had been killed ten days ago.

'I heard it, Jack. Were you with him?'

'Yes. It was in a bayonet charge. He did n't suffer. A bullet went right through him. He just gave a little cry and fell.' Jack's voice had the mildness of a sorrow which has passed beyond the capacity for emotion. 'We found him afterwards. He is buried out there.'

'You must tell Frances about it, Jack. I went to her at

once.'   Frances was Toppie's sister.   'She is bearing it so bravely.'

'I must write to her.   She would be sure to be plucky.'

He answered all her questions, sitting closely against her, his arm around her; looking down, while he spoke, and twisting, as had always been his boyish way, a button on her coat.   He was at that enchanting moment of young manhood when the child is still apparent in the man.   His glance was shy, yet candid; his small, firm lips had a child's gravity.   With his splendid shoulders, long legs, and noble little head, he was yet as endearing as he was impressive. His mother's heart ached with love and pride and fear as she gazed at him.

And a question came, near the sharp one, yet hoping to evade it: —

'Jack, dearest, how long will you be with me?   How long is the leave?'

He raised his eyes then and looked at her; a curious look. Something in it blurred her mind with a sense of some other sort of fear.

'Only till to-night,' he said.

It seemed confusion rather than pain that she felt. 'Only till to-night, Jack?   But Richard Crawley has been back for three days already.   I thought they gave you longer?'

'I know, mummy.'   His eyes were dropped again and his hand at the button — did it tremble? — twisted and untwisted.   'I've been back for three days already. — I've been in London.'

'In London?'   Her breath failed her.   The sense of alien fear became a fog, horrible, suffocating.   'But — Jack — why?'

'I did n't wire, mummy, because I knew I'd have to be there for most of my time.   I felt that I could n't wire and tell you. I felt that I had to see you when I told you. Mother — I'm married. — I came back to get married. — I was married this morning. — O mother, can you ever forgive me?'

His shaking hands held her and his eyes could not meet hers.

She felt the blood rush, as if her heart had been divided with a sword, to her throat, to her eyes, choking her, burning her; and as if from far away she heard her own voice saying, after a little time had passed, 'There's nothing I could n't forgive you, Jack. Tell me. Don't be afraid of hurting me.'

He held her tightly, still looking down as he said, 'She is a dancer, mother, a little dancer. It was in London, last summer. A lot of us came up from Aldershot together. She was in the chorus of one of those musical comedies. Mother, you can never understand. But it was n't just low and vulgar. She was so lovely, — so very young, — with the most wonderful golden hair and the sweetest eyes. — I don't know. — I simply went off my head when I saw her. We all had supper together afterwards. Toppie knew one of the other girls, and Dollie was there. That's her name — Dollie Vaughan — her stage name. Her real name was Byles. Her people, I think, were little trades-people, and she'd lost her father and mother, and an aunt had been very unkind. She told me all about it that night. Mother, please believe just this: it was n't only the obvious thing. — I know I can't explain. But you remember, when we read *War and Peace*,' — his broken voice groped for the analogy, — 'you remember Natacha, when she falls in love with Anatole, and nothing that was real before seems real, and she is ready for anything. It was like that. It was all fairyland, like that. No one thought it wrong. It did n't seem wrong. Everything went together.'

She had gathered his hand closely in hers and she sat there, quiet, looking at her hopes lying slain before her. Her Jack. The wife who was, perhaps, to have been his. The children that she, perhaps, should have seen. All dead. The future blotted out. Only this wraith-like present; only this moment of decision; Jack and his desperate need the only real things left.

And after a moment, for his laboring breath had failed, she said, 'Yes, dear?' and smiled at him.

He covered his face with his hands. 'Mother, I've ruined your life.'

He had, of course, in ruining his own; yet even at that moment of wreckage she was able to remember, if not to feel, that life could mend from terrible wounds, could marvelously grow from compromises and defeats. 'No, dearest, no,' she said. 'While I have you, nothing is ruined. We shall see what can be done. Go on. Tell me the rest.'

He put out his hand to hers again and sat now a little turned away from her, speaking on in his deadened, bitter voice.

'There was n't any glamour after that first time. I only saw her once or twice again. I was awfully sorry and ashamed over the whole thing. Her company left London, on tour, and then the war came, and I simply forgot all about her. And the other day, over there, I had a letter from her. She was in terrible trouble. She was ill and had no money, and no work. And she was going to have a child — my child; and she begged me to send her a little money to help her through, or she did n't know what would become of her.'

The fog, the horrible confusion, even the despair, had passed now. The sense of ruin, of wreckage almost irreparable, was there; yet with it, too, was the strangest sense of gladness. He was her own Jack, completely hers, for she saw now why he had done it; she could be glad that he had done it; she could be glad that he had done it. 'Go on, dear,' she said. 'I understand; I understand perfectly.'

'O mother, bless you!' He put her hand to his lips, bowing his head upon it for a moment. 'I was afraid you could n't. I was afraid you could n't forgive me. But I had to do it. I thought it all over — out there. Everything had become so different after what one had been through. One saw everything differently. Some things did n't matter at all, and other things mattered tremendously. This was one of them. I knew I could n't just send her money. I knew I could n't bear to have the poor child born without a name and with only that foolish little mother to take care of it. And when I found I could get this leave, I knew I must marry her. That was why I did n't wire. I thought I might not have time to come to you at all.'

'Where is she, Jack?' Her voice, her eyes, her smile at him, showed him that, indeed, she understood perfectly.

'In lodgings that I found for her; nice and quiet, with a kind landlady. She was in such an awful place in Ealing. She is so changed, poor little thing. I should hardly have known her. Mother, darling, I wonder, could you just go and see her once or twice? She's frightfully lonely; and so very young. — If you could — if you would just help things along a little till the baby comes, I should be so grateful. And, then, if I don't come back, will you, for my sake, see that they are safe?'

'But, Jack,' she said, smiling at him, 'she is coming here, of course. I shall go and get her to-morrow.'

He stared at her and his color rose. 'Get her? Bring her here, to stay?'

'Of course, darling. And if you don't come back, I will take care of them, always.'

'But, mother,' said Jack, and there were tears in his eyes, 'you don't know, you don't realize. I mean — she's a dear little thing — but you couldn't be happy with her. She'd get most frightfully on your nerves. She's just — just a silly little dancer who has got into trouble.'

Jack was clear-sighted. Every vestige of fairyland had vanished. And she was deeply thankful that they should see alike, while she answered, 'It's not exactly a time for considering one's nerves, is it, Jack? I hope I won't get on hers. I must just try and make her as happy as I can.'

She made it all seem natural and almost sweet. The tears were in his eyes, yet he had to smile back at her when she said, 'You know that I am good at managing people. I'll manage her. And perhaps when you come back, my darling, she won't be a silly little dancer.'

They sat now for a little while in silence. While they had talked, a golden sunset, slowly, had illuminated the western sky. The river below them was golden, and the wintry woodlands bathed in light. Jack held her hands and gazed at her. Love could say no more than his eyes, in their trust and sorrow, said to her; she could never more completely possess her son. Sitting there with him, hand in hand, while the light slowly ebbed and twilight fell about them, she felt it to be, in its accepted sorrow, the culminating and transfiguring moment of her maternity.

When they at last rose to go it was the hour for Jack's departure, and it had become almost dark. Far away, through the trees, they could see the lighted windows of the house which waited for them, but to which she must return alone.

With his arms around her shoulders, Jack paused a moment, looking about him. 'Do you remember that day — when we first came here, mummy?' he asked.

She felt in him suddenly a sadness deeper than any he

had yet shown her. The burden of the past she had lifted
from him; but he must bear now the burden of what he had
done to her, to their life, to all the future. And, protesting
against his pain, her mother's heart strove still to shelter
him while she answered, as if she did not feel his sadness,
'Yes, dear, and do you remember the hepaticas on that
day?'

'Like you,' said Jack in a gentle voice. 'I can hardly
see the plants. Are they all right?'

'They are doing beautifully.'

'I wish the flowers were out,' said Jack. 'I wish it were
the time for the flowers to be out, so that I could have seen
you and them together, like that first day.' And then, putting his head down on her shoulder, he murmured, 'It will
never be the same again. I've spoiled everything for you.'

But he was not to go from her uncomforted. She found
the firmest voice in which to answer him, stroking his hair
and pressing him to her with the full reassurance of her
resolution. 'Nothing is spoiled, Jack, nothing. You have
never been so near me — so how can anything be spoiled?
And when you come back, darling, you'll find your son,
perhaps, and the hepaticas may be in flower, waiting for
you.'

II

Mrs. Bradley and her daughter-in-law sat together in the
drawing-room. They sat opposite each other on the two
chintz chesterfields placed at right angles to the pleasantly
blazing fire, the chintz curtains drawn against a rainy evening. It was a long, low room, with paneled walls; and, like
Mrs. Bradley's head, it had an air at once majestic, deco-
rated, and old-fashioned. It was a rather crowded room,
with many deep chairs and large couches, many tables with
lamps and books and photographs upon them, many

porcelains, prints, and pots of growing flowers. Mrs. Bradley, her tea-table before her, was in her evening black silk; lace ruffles rose about her throat; she wore her accustomed necklace of old enamel, blue, black, and white, set with small diamonds, and the enamel locket which had within it Jack's face on one side and his father's on the other; her white hands, moving gently among the teacups, showed an ancient cluster of diamonds above the slender wedding-ring.

From time to time she lifted her eyes and smiled quietly over at her daughter-in-law. It was the first time that she had really seen Dollie, that is, in any sense that meant contemplative observation. Dollie had spent her first week at Dorrington in bed, sodden with fatigue rather than ill. 'What you need,' Mrs. Bradley had said, 'is to go to sleep for a fortnight'; and Dollie had almost literally carried out the prescription.

Stealing carefully into the darkened room, with its flowers and opened windows and steadily glowing fire, Mrs. Bradley had stood and looked for long moments at all that she could see of her daughter-in-law, — a flushed, almost babyish face lying on the pillow between thick golden braids, sleeping so deeply, so unconsciously, — her sleep making her mother-in-law think of a little boat gliding slowly yet steadily on and on, between new shores; so that, when she was to awake and look about her, it would be as if, with no bewilderment or readjustment, she found herself transformed, a denizen of an altered world. That was what Mrs. Bradley wanted, that Dollie should become an inmate of Dorrington with as little effort or consciousness for any of them as possible; and the drowsy days and nights of infantine slumbers seemed indeed to have brought her very near.

She and Pickering, the admirable woman who filled so

skillfully the combined positions of lady's maid and parlor-maid in her little establishment, had braided Dollie's thick tresses, one on either side — Mrs. Bradley laughing a little and both older women touched, almost happy in their sense of something so young and helpless to take care of. Pickering understood, nearly as well as Jack's mother, that Master Jack, as he had remained to her, had married very much beneath him; but at this time of tragic issues and primitive values, she, nearly as much as Jack's mother, felt only the claim, the pathos of youth and helplessness. It was as if they had a singularly appealing case of a refugee to take care of: social and even moral appraisals were inapplicable to such a case, and Mrs. Bradley felt that she had never so admired Pickering as when seeing that for her, too, they were in abeyance. It was a comfort to feel so fond of Pickering at a time when one was in need of any comfort one could get; and to feel that, creature of codes and discriminations as she was, to a degree that had made her mistress sometimes think of her as a sort of Samurai of service, a function rather than a person, she was even more fundamentally a kind and Christian woman. Between them, cook intelligently sustaining them from below and the housemaids helpful in their degree, they fed and tended and nursed Dollie, and by that eighth day she was more than ready to get up and go down and investigate her new surroundings.

She sat there now, in the pretty tea-gown her mother-in-law had bought for her, leaning back against her cushions, one arm lying along the back of the couch and one foot in its patent-leather shoe, with its sparkling buckle and alarming heel, thrusting forward a carefully arched instep. The attitude made one realize, however completely tenderer preoccupations held the foreground of one's consciousness, how often and successfully she must have sat to theatrical photographers. Her way of smiling, too, very softly, yet with the effect of a calculated and dazzling display of pearly teeth, was impersonal, and directed, as it were, to the public *via* the camera rather than to any individual interlocutor. Mrs. Bradley even imagined, unversed as she was in the methods of Dollie's world, that of allurement in its conscious and determined sense, she was almost innocent. She placed herself, she adjusted her arm and her foot, and she smiled gently; intention hardly went further than that wish to look her best.

Pink and white and gold as she was, and draped there on the chesterfield in a profusion of youth and a frivolity that was yet all passivity, she made her mother-in-law think, and with a certain sinking of the heart, of a Dorothy Perkins rose, a flower she had never cared for; and Dollie carried on the analogy in the sense she gave that there were such myriads more just like her. On almost every page of every illustrated weekly paper, one saw the ingenuous, limpid eyes, the display of eyelash, the lips, their outline emphasized by just that touch of rouge, those copious waves of hair. Like the Dorothy Perkins roses on their pergolas, so these pretty faces seemed — looped, draped, festooned — to climb over all the available spaces of the modern press.

But this, Mrs. Bradley told herself, was to see Dollie with a dry, hard eye, was to see her superficially, from the social rather than from the human point of view. Under the photographic creature must lie the young, young girl — so young, so harmless that it would be very possible to mould her, with all discretion, all tenderness, into some suitability as Jack's wife. Dollie, from the moment that she had found her, a sodden, battered rose indeed, in the London lodging-house, had shown herself grateful, even humble, and endlessly acquiescent. She had not shown herself at all abashed or apologetic, and that had been a relief; had counted for her, indeed, in her mother-in-law's eyes, as a sort of innocence, a sort of dignity. But if Dollie were contented with her new mother, and very grateful to her, she was also contented with herself; Mrs. Bradley had been aware of this at once; and she knew now that, if she were being carefully and commendingly watched while she poured out the tea, this concentration did not imply unqualified approval. Dollie was the type of young woman to whom she herself stood as the type of the 'perfect lady'; but with the appreciation went the proviso of the sharp little London mind, — versed in the whole ritual of smartness as it displayed itself at theatre or restaurant, — that she was a rather dowdy one. She was a lady, perfect but not smart, while, at the same time, the quality of her defect was, she imagined, a little bewildering and therefore a little impressive. Actually to awe Dollie and to make her shy, it would be necessary to be smart; but it was far more pleasant and perhaps as efficacious merely to impress her, and it was as well that Dollie should be impressed; for anything in the nature of an advantage that she could recognize would make it easier to direct, protect, and mould her.

She asked her a good many leisurely and unstressed questions on this first evening, and drew Dollie to ask others in return; and she saw herself stooping thoughtfully over a flourishing young plant which yet needed transplanting, softly moving the soil about its roots, softly finding out if there were any very deep tap-root that would have to be dealt with. But Dollie, so far as tastes and ideas went, hardly seemed to have any roots at all; so few that it was a question if any change of soil could affect a creature so shallow. She smiled, she was at ease; she showed her complete assurance that a young lady so lavishly endowed with all the most significant gifts, need not occupy herself with mental adornments.

'You're a great one for books, I see,' she commented, looking about the room. 'I suppose you do a great deal of reading down here to keep from feeling too dull'; and she added that she herself, if there was 'nothing doing,' liked a good novel, especially if she had a box of sweets to eat while she read it.

'You shall have a box of sweets to-morrow,' Mrs. Bradley told her, 'with or without the novel, as you like.'

And Dollie thanked her, watching her cut the cake, and, as the rain lashed against the windows, remarking on the bad weather and cheerfully hoping that 'poor old Jack' was n't in these horrid trenches. 'I think war's a wicked thing, don't you, Mrs. Bradley?' she added.

When Dollie talked in this conventionally solicitous tone of Jack, her mother-in-law could but wish her upstairs again, merely young, merely the tired and battered refugee. She had not much tenderness for Jack, that was evident, nor much imaginativeness in regard to the feelings of Jack's mother. But she soon passed from the theme of Jack and his danger. Her tea was finished and she got up and went to the piano, remarking that there was one thing she *could* do. 'Poor mother used to always say I was made of music. From the time I was a mere tot I could pick out anything on the piano.' And placing herself, pressing down the patent-leather shoe on the loud pedal, she surged into a waltz as foolish and as conventionally alluring as her own eyes. Her inaccuracy was equaled only by her facility. Smiling, swaying over the keys with alternate speed and languor, she addressed her audience with altogether the easy mastery of a music-hall *artiste:* 'It's a lovely thing — one of my favorites. I'll often play, Mrs. Bradley, and cheer us up. There is nothing like music for that, is there? it speaks so to the heart.' And, whole-heartedly indeed, she accompanied the melody by a passionate humming.

The piano was Jack's and it was poor Jack who was made of music. How was he to bear it, his mother asked herself, as she sat listening. Dollie, after that initiation, spent many hours at the piano every day — so many and such noisy hours, that her mother-in-law, unnoticed, could shut herself in the little morning-room that overlooked the brick wall at the front of the house and had the morning sun.

It was difficult to devise other occupations for Dollie. She earnestly disclaimed any wish to have proper music lessons; and when her mother-in-law, patiently persistent, arranged for a skillful mistress to come down twice a week from London, Dollie showed such apathy and dullness that any hope of developing such musical ability as she possessed had to be abandoned. She did not like walking, and the sober pageant of the winter days was a blank book to her. Sewing, she said, had always given her frightful fidgets; and it was with the strangest sense of a privilege, a joy unhoped-for and now thrust upon her, that Mrs. Bradley sat alone working at the little garments which meant all her future and all Jack's. The baby seemed already more hers than Dollie's.

Sometimes, on a warm afternoon, Dollie, wrapped in her fur cloak, would emerge for a little while and watch her mother-in-law at work in her borders. The sight amused and surprised, but hardly interested her, and she soon went tottering back to the house on the preposterous heels which Mrs. Bradley had, as yet, found no means of tactfully banishing. And sometimes, when the piano again resounded, Mrs. Bradley would leave her borders and retreat to the hazel copse, where, as she sat on the stone bench, she could hear, through the soft sound of the running water, hardly more than the distant beat and hum of Dollie's waltzes; and where, with more and more the sense of escape and safety, she could find a refuge from the sight and sound and scent of Dollie—the thick, sweet, penetrating scent which was always to be indelibly associated in her mother-in-law's mind with this winter of foreboding, of hope, and of growing hopelessness.

In her letters to Jack, she found herself, involuntarily at first, and then deliberately, altering, suppressing, even falsifying. While Dollie had been in bed, when so much hope had been possible of a creature so unrevealed, she had written very tenderly, and she continued, now, to write tenderly, and it was not false to do that; she could feel no hardness or antagonism against poor Dollie. But she continued to write hopefully, as, every day, hope grew less.

Jack, himself, did not say much of Dollie, though there was always the affectionate message and the affectionate inquiry. But what was difficult to deal with were the hints of his anxiety and fear that stole among the terse, cheerful descriptions of his precarious days. What was she doing with herself? How were she and Dollie getting on? Did Dollie care about any of the things she cared about?

She told him that they got on excellently well, that Dollie spent a good deal of time at the piano, and that when they went out to tea people were perfectly nice and understanding. She knew, indeed, that she could depend on her friends to be that. They accepted Dollie on the terms she asked for her. From friends so near as Mrs. Crawley and Lady Wrexham she had not concealed the fact that Dollie was a misfortune; but if others thought so, they were not to show it. She still hoped, by degrees, to make Dollie a figure easier to deal with at such neighborly gatherings. She had abandoned any hope that Dollie would grow: anything so feeble and so foolish could not grow; there was no other girl under the little dancer; she was simply no more and no

less than she showed herself to be; but, at this later stage of
their relationship, Mrs. Bradley essayed, now and then, a
deliberate if kindly severity — as to heels, as to scents, as
to touches of rouge.

'Oh, but I'm as careful, just as careful, Mrs. Bradley!'
Dollie protested. 'I can't walk in lower heels. They hurt
my instep. I've a very high instep and it needs support.'
She was genuinely amazed that any one could dislike her
scent and that any one could think the rouge unbecoming.
She seemed to acquiesce, but the acquiescence was followed by moods of mournfulness and even by tears. There
was no capacity in her for temper or rebellion, and she was
all unconscious of giving a warning as she sobbed, 'It's
nothing — really nothing, Mrs. Bradley. I'm sure you
mean to be kind. Only — it's rather quiet and lonely here.
I've always been used to so many people — to having
everything so bright and jolly.'

She was not rapacious; she was not dissolute; she could
be kept respectable and even contented if she were not
made too aware of the contrast between her past existence
and her present lot. With an air only of pensive pride she
would sometimes point out to Mrs. Bradley, in the pages
of those same illustrated weeklies with which her mother-
in-law associated her, the face of some former companion.
One of these young ladies had recently married the son of a
peer. 'She *is* in luck, Floss,' said Dollie. 'We always
thought it would come to that. He's been gone on her for
ages, but his people were horrid.'

Mrs. Bradley felt that, at all events, Dollie had no ground
for thinking her 'horrid'; yet she imagined that there lay
drowsing at the back of her mind a plaintive little sense of
being caught and imprisoned. Floss had stepped, triumphant, from the footlights to the registrar's office, and apparently had succeeded in uniting the radiance of her past and

present status. No, Dollie could be kept respectable and contented only if the pressure were of the lightest. She could not change, she could only shift; and although Mrs. Bradley felt that for herself, her life behind her, her story told, she could manage to put up with a merely shifted Dollie, she could not see how Jack was to manage it. What was Jack to do with her? was the thought that pressed with a growing weight on her mother's heart. She could never be of Jack's life; yet here she was, in it, planted there by his own generous yet inevitable act, and by hers — in its very centre, and not to be evaded or forgotten.

And the contrast between what Jack's life might have been and what it now must be was made more poignantly apparent to her when Frances Thorpe came down to stay from a Saturday to Monday: Frances in her black, tired and thin from Red-Cross work in London; bereaved in more, her old friend knew, than dear Toppie's death; yet with her leisurely, unstressed cheerfulness almost unaltered, the lightness that went with so much tenderness, the drollery that went with so much depth. Dearest, most charming of girls, — but for Jack's wretched stumble into 'fairyland' last summer, destined obviously to be his wife, — could any presence have shown more disastrously, in its contrast with poor Dollie, how Jack had done for himself?

She watched the two together that evening — Frances with her thick, crinkled hair and clearly curved brow and her merry, steady eyes, leaning, elbow on knee, to talk and listen to Dollie; and Dollie, poor Dollie, flushed, touched with an unbecoming sulkiness, aware, swiftly and unerringly, of a rival type. Frances was of the type that young men married when they did not 'do for themselves.' There was now no gulf of age or habit to veil from Dollie her disadvantage. She answered shortly, with now and then a dry, ironic little laugh; and, getting up at last, she went to the piano and loudly played.

'He couldn't have done differently. It was the only thing he could do,' Frances said that night before her bed-room fire. She did not hide her recognition of Jack's plight, but she was staunch.

'I wouldn't have had him do differently. But it will ruin his life,' said the mother. 'If he comes back, it will ruin his life.'

'No, no,' said Frances, looking at the flames. 'Why should it? A man doesn't depend on his marriage like that. He has his career.'

'Yes. He has his career. A career isn't a life.'

'Isn't it?' The girl gazed down. 'But it's what so many people have to put up with. And so many haven't even a career.' Something came into her voice and she turned from it quickly. 'He's crippled, in a sense, of course. But you are here. He will have you to come back to always.'

'I shall soon be old, dear, and she will always be here. That's inevitable. Some day I shall have to leave her to Jack to bear with alone.'

'She may become more of a companion.'

'No; no, she won't.'

The bitterness of the mother's heart expressed itself in the dry, light utterance. It was a comfort to express bitterness, for once, to somebody.

'She is a harmless little thing,' Frances offered after a moment.

'Harmless?' Mrs. Bradley turned it over dryly and lightly. 'I can't feel her that. I feel her blameless if you like. And it will be easy to keep her contented. That is really the best that one can say of poor Dollie. And then, there will be the child.   I am pinning all my hopes to the child, Frances.'

Frances understood that.

Dollie, as the winter wore on, kept remarkably well. She had felt it the proper thing to allude to Jack and his danger; and so, now, she more and more frequently felt it the proper thing to allude, humorously, if with a touch of melancholy, to 'baby.' Her main interest in baby, Mrs. Bradley felt, was an alarmed one. She was a good deal frightened, poor little soul, and in need of constant reassurances; and it was when one need only pet and pity Dollie that she was easier to deal with. Mrs. Bradley tried to interest her in plans for the baby; what it should be named, and how its hair should be done if it were a little girl — for only on this assumption could Dollie's interest be at all vividly roused; and Mrs. Bradley hoped more than ever for a boy when she found Dollie's idle yet stubborn thoughts fixed on the name of Gloria.

She was able to evade discussion of this point, and when the baby came, fortunately and robustly, into the world on a fine March morning, she could feel it as a minor but very real cause for thanksgiving that Dollie need now never know what she thought of Gloria as a name. The baby was a boy, and now that he was here, Dollie seemed as well pleased that he should be a commonplace Jack, and that there should be no question of tying his hair with cockades of ribbon over each ear. Smiling and rosy and languid, she lay in her charming room, not at all more maternal, — though she showed a bland satisfaction in her child and noted that his eyes were just like Jack's, — yet subtly more wifely. Baby, she no doubt felt, with the dim instinct that did duty for thought with her, placed and rooted her and gave her final rights. She referred now to Jack with the pensive but open affection of their shared complacency, and made her mother-in-law think, as she lay there, of a soft and sleepy and tenacious creeper, fixing tentacle after tentacle in the walls of Jack's house of life.

If only one could feel that she had furnished it with a treasure. Gravely, with a sad fondness, the grandmother studied the little face, so unfamiliar, for signs of Jack. She was a helplessly clear-sighted woman, and remembrance was poignantly vivid in her of Jack's face at a week old. Already she loved the baby since its eyes, indubitably, were his; but she could find no other trace of him. It was not a Bradley baby; and in the dreamy, foreboding flickers of individuality that pass uncannily across an infant's features, her melancholy and steady discernment could see only the Byles ancestry.

She was to do all she could for the baby: to save him, so far as might be, from his Byles ancestry, and to keep him, so far as might be, Jack's and hers. That was to be her task. But with all the moulding that could, mercifully, be applied from the very beginning, she could not bring herself to believe that this was ever to be a very significant human being.

She sent Jack his wire: 'A son. Dollie doing splendidly.' And she had his answer: 'Best thanks. Love to Dollie.' It was curious, indeed, this strange new fact they had now, always, to deal with; this light little 'Dollie' that must be passed between them. The baby might have made Jack happy, but it had not solved the problem of his future.

III

A week later the telegram was brought to her telling her that he had been killed in action.

It was a beautiful spring day, just such a day as that on which she and Jack had first seen Dorrington, and she had

been working in the garden. When she had read, she
turned and walked down the path that led to the hazel
copse. She hardly knew what had happened to her; there
was only an instinct for flight, concealment, secrecy; but,
as she walked, there rose in her, without sound, as if in a
nightmare, the terrible cry of her loneliness. The dark wet
earth that covered him seemed heaped upon her heart.

The hazel copse was tasseled thickly with golden green,
and as she entered it she saw that the hepaticas were in
flower. They seemed to shine with their own celestial
whiteness, set in their melancholy green among the fallen
leaves. She had never seen them look so beautiful.

She followed the path, looking down at them, and she
seemed to feel Jack's little hand in hers and to see, at her
side, his nut-brown head. It had been on just such a morning. She came to the stone bench; but the impulse that had
led her here was altered. She did not sink down and cover
her face, but stood looking around her at the flowers, the
telegram still open in her hand; and slowly, with stealing
calm, the sense of sanctuary fell about her.

She had lost him, and with him went all her life. He was
dead, his youth and strength and beauty. Yet what was
this strange up-welling of relief, deep, deep relief, for Jack;
this gladness, poignant and celestial, like that of the hepaticas? He was dead and the dark earth covered him; yet he
was here, with her, safe in his youth and strength and
beauty forever. He had died the glorious death, and no
future, tangled, perplexed, fretful with its foolish burden,
lay before him. There was no loss for Jack — no fading,
no waste. The burden was for her, and he was free.

Later, when pain should have dissolved thought, her
agony would come to her unalleviated; but this hour was
hers, and his. She heard the river and the soft whisperings
of spring. A bird dropped lightly, unafraid, from branch

to branch of a tree near by. From the woods came the rapid, insistent tapping of a woodpecker; and, as in so many springs, she seemed to hear Jack say, 'Hark, mummy,' and his little hand was always held in hers. And, everywhere, telling of irreparable loss, of a possession unalterable, the tragic, the celestial hepaticas.

She sat down on the stone bench now and closed her eyes for a little while, so holding them more closely — Jack and the hepaticas — together.

POSSESSING PRUDENCE

BY AMY WENTWORTH STONE

I

'A LIE's an abomination unto the Lord a hundred and twenty-four, a lie's an abomination unto the Lord a hundred and twenty-five, a lie's an abomination unto the Lord a hundred and twenty-six,' recited Prudence Jane, and paused.

'Go on,' said Aunt Annie, looking up from her sewing and fixing her eyes severely on the small blue back across the room.

Prudence Jane, with the heels of her little ankle-ties together and her hands clasped tightly behind her, was standing in the corner, saying what was known in the family as her punish-sentence. Whenever she had been unusually naughty she had to say one four hundred times up in Aunt Annie's room. It was, no doubt, a silly sort of punishment, but it was one that Prudence Jane strongly objected to — and that, after all, is the essence of a punishment. Prudence Jane had seven teasing, mimicking brothers, and whenever one of them caught her saying a punish-sentence it was days before she heard the last of it. Already in the garden below there was audible a shrill voice singing, 'A *lie* is an a*bom*-i-*na*-tion *un*-to the *Lord*,' to the tune of 'Has anybody here seen Kelly?' And out of the corner of her eye, which was supposed to be fastened on the rosebuds of Aunt Annie's wall-paper, Prudence Jane could see an impudent little person in corduroys, straddling the gravel walk and squinting up at the window.

'Is "a lie's an abomination" in the Bible?' inquired Prudence Jane.

'Yes,' said Aunt Annie, 'go on.'

'Where?' demanded Prudence Jane.

'Where?' repeated Aunt Annie a little blankly. 'Why — why — in the middle of the Bible. Don't you listen to the minister, Prudence Jane?'

'The middle of the minister's Bible?' pursued Prudence Jane.

'Yes, of course,' said Aunt Annie, 'Prudence Jane, if you don't go on at once I shall have you say it five hundred times.'

'A lie's an abomination unto the Lord a hundred and twenty-seven,' resumed Prudence Jane hastily.

Prudence Jane's sentences varied from day to day, it being Aunt Annie's idea to fit the sentence to the crime whenever possible. Thus, for being late to school it was, naturally, 'Procrastination is the thief of time.' While for telling Lena, the cook, that Uncle Arthur had said she was more of a lady than Aunt Annie, the sentence had been nothing less than, 'Truth crushed to earth will rise again.'

This particular fib had been very disastrous in its consequences. We will not dwell upon them here. They make a story in themselves. Suffice it to say that there was no possible excuse for Prudence Jane.

It was otherwise with the fib for which she was this morning serving a sentence up in Aunt Annie's room. Those who also have been named after their two grandmothers will at once forgive Prudence Jane for telling the new minister, the very first time she met him, that her name was Imogen Rose. It was, to be sure, a stupid little fib, and was therefore quite unworthy of Prudence Jane. For Prudence Jane almost never told stupid little fibs. The fibs of Prudence Jane were little masterpieces, with a

finish and distinction all their own. Her brother Will, who
adored her, and had a large mind, declared when he came
home from college that she was the greatest mistress of
imaginative fiction since George Eliot. Her Aunt Annie,
who had not had the advantages of a college course, and
who roomed with Prudence Jane, said that she was a
'simple little liar.'

Now this was unfair of Aunt Annie, for whatever else
Prudence Jane might be, she was *not* simple. Even her
looks belied her. With her big confiding eyes, as round
and blue as two forget-me-nots, and her pale yellow hair
held demurely back from her forehead by a blue ribbon
fillet, she gave an impression of gentle innocence that was
altogether misleading.

'She is so like little Bertie,' dear old Grandma Piper
would say; 'that same frail, flower-like look that he had
toward the last. I almost tremble sometimes. Have n't
you noticed a transparency about her lately, Annie?'

But Aunt Annie never had.

It may be said in passing that there was only one person
to whom Prudence Jane was really transparent, and that
was her youngest brother, Peter. Peter was a square, solid
little person, with a vacant countenance; but nothing
important that Prudence Jane did escaped him.

'Just to look into that sweet little face is enough for me,'
Grandma Goodwin would declare; 'I don't want anybody
to tell *me* that Prudence Jane is untruthful. No child
could look straight at you out of her little soul as she always
does, and tell a fib. The trouble is they don't understand
her at home. I've always said Annie Piper had a suspicious nature.'

To do Aunt Annie justice, it should be said that rooming
with Prudence Jane did not tend to cultivate in one a
nature that was trustful and confiding. And yet at heart

Prudence Jane was really not at all the incorrigible little fibber that she seemed. She told fibs, not because she wished to deceive, but because the dull facts of life were so much less interesting than the lively little romances which she could make up out of her own head. When one is a creative genius one naturally rebels at being shackled to anything so tedious as a fact. Prudence Jane, looking back over a day, could rarely separate the things which had really happened from those she had invented.

Her brother Horace, who was studying law, said that he would give a hundred dollars to see Prudence Jane on the witness stand. This was one night at supper when she was being cross-examined by Aunt Annie. For five minutes she had kept the family spellbound by a circumstantial account of how that afternoon she had seen an automobile truck, loaded with a thousand boxes of eggs, go over the embankment. With eggs at sixty-five cents a dozen this was really a very shocking tale.

'Prudence Jane,' said Aunt Annie, who had private sources of information, 'you know well enough that no truck went over the embankment. Whatever do you mean by telling such an outrageous fib?'

Prudence Jane looked across the supper table at her aunt out of two round candid eyes.

'That wasn't a fib; that was just a story,' she explained.

'Well, it wasn't true; and stories that aren't true are very wicked,' said Aunt Annie with decision.

'Are all the stories in books true?' inquired Prudence Jane, the picture of innocence behind her bowl of bread and milk.

'No,' Aunt Annie was forced to admit, 'but stories written in books are different. The writers don't mean for us to believe them.'

'Do they say so in the books?' went on Prudence Jane relentlessly.

'Of course not,' said Aunt Annie; 'we know their stories are n't true, so they don't deceive us.'

'But you always know *my* stories are n't true, too,' objected Prudence Jane; 'so I don't deceive you, either.'

'Prudence Jane,' said Aunt Annie, 'I shan't argue with you. You are a very naughty little girl. I sometimes think that you don't belong to us at all; you're so different from your brothers.'

This was true. All the other little Pipers had been simple, virtuous children, with imaginations under perfect control — 'a remarkable family' everybody had said, until the Pipers became quite complacent about themselves. This was why Prudence Jane seemed like such a judgment upon them. They had waited long and patiently, as Aunt Annie put it, for Providence to see fit to send them a dear little girl to inherit her grandmothers' names — and they received Prudence Jane. Had she appeared at an earlier date, or had there been another girl in the family, she might have escaped either the Prudence or the Jane. But for fifteen years little masculine Pipers had arrived in the household with unbroken regularity, and been named, one by one, after all the available grandfathers and uncles. For the last one, indeed, there had not been even a cousin left, and he had been christened by common consent Peter Piper. And still the grandmothers waited.

From the moment, therefore, when bluff old Doctor Jones looked in upon a parlor full of aunts, and announced that it was 'a girl at last, by Jove,' there had been no choice left for Prudence Jane. The only point discussed in the solemn family conclave was as to whether she should not be Jane Prudence.

'Oh, for mercy's sake, call the poor little kid Jurispru-

dence, and be done with it,' said a flippant uncle — and
that had settled it. Prudence Jane was duly entered at
the end of the list in the middle of the Family Bible, and
her career began.

Through eight years she was just unmitigated Prudence
Jane, — not a syllable of it could ever be omitted lest one
grandmother or the other be slighted, — and then suddenly one day she decided that it was a combination no
longer to be borne. She hated her name with all her little
soul; therefore she would discard it and take another.
This sounded simple, but there were, in fact, several com-
plications. The most important was Aunt Annie. Never
a really progressive spirit, in this matter of names Aunt
Annie showed herself to be an out-and-out stand-patter.

'You wish that you had been called Gwendolin?' she
echoed in horror, as she combed out the pale yellow hair
at bed-time. 'Why, Prudence Jane, I'm ashamed of you.
Gwendolin is a very silly name indeed, and you have two
such noble ones. I only hope that you will grow up to be
like the beautiful grandmammas who gave them to you'
— which was a truly lovely little bit of optimism on Aunt
Annie's part.

II

Prudence Jane did not consult Aunt Annie further.
That very night, however, staring up into the darkness
from her little white bed, she decided upon a new combination. And when the Reverend Mr. Sanders came up
to her the next day after Sunday School, and inquired
kindly what little girl this was, Prudence Jane was quite
prepared to tell him, with the transparent look which so
frightened dear old Grandma Piper, that it was Imogen
Rose.

She fully meant to inform her family of this interesting

change as soon as she got home from Sunday School, but
when she tiptoed into the parlor Aunt Annie, in all the
majesty of her plum-colored satin, was sitting in a straight-
backed chair reading *The Christian Word and Work*, and
looked unreceptive to new ideas. So Prudence Jane tiptoed out again, to await a more favorable moment.

Unfortunately, before that moment arrived she had a
falling-out with her brother Peter. This was a mistake,
for it was the part of prudence always to make an ally of
Peter Piper. He had discovered Prudence Jane flat on
the floor in a corner of the library, scratching her name
out of the Family Bible with an ink-eraser.

'Did the minister tell you to write Imogen in?' he inquired blandly, as he stood in the doorway with his hands
in his corduroys.

'None of your business,' retorted Prudence Jane, closing
the Bible with a bang and sitting down upon it.

The result was that Peter Piper, from whom nothing
was ever hidden, went off and told Aunt Annie all about
Imogen Rose and the minister. Whereupon Aunt Annie,
with her usual limited point of view, had pronounced it a
very monstrous fib indeed, and had sent Prudence Jane
instantly into the corner.

'A lie's an abomination unto the Lord three hundred and
ninety-eight, a lie's an abomination unto the Lord three
hundred and ninety-nine, a lie's an abomination unto the
Lord four hundred,' finished Prudence Jane at a canter,
and whisked around from her corner.

Aunt Annie beckoned with solemn finger.

'To-morrow, Prudence Jane,' she said, looking across the
sewing-table, 'I am going to take you to see the minister
and you must tell him yourself what your real name is,
and what a dreadful story you have told him. I shall ask
him what he thinks should be done with a little girl who

cannot speak the truth. I'm sure I don't know what he will say. But we can't deceive a minister. They always know when they hear a fib.'

'Do they?' asked Prudence Jane, openly interested, her round eyes fastened upon her aunt.

'Always,' replied Aunt Annie rashly.

'Then why do I have to go and tell him?' asked Prudence Jane.

'Prudence Jane,' said Aunt Annie, 'you are a very saucy little girl, and I'm sure I don't know what is going to become of you.'

Prudence Jane walked slowly out of the room. She was considering what Aunt Annie had said about ministers, and she wondered if it were true. As she went tripping down the stairs she decided to put the Reverend Mr. Sanders to a test the very next time she met him. And that was why it was so surprising, when she peeked through the hall window at the foot of the stairs, to behold him diligently wiping his feet on the door-mat.

'How do you do?' said Prudence Jane politely, as she opened the door.

'Why, good afternoon, Imogen,' said the minister, shaking hands cordially.

Prudence Jane made the little knix that she had learned at German school. It was always the finishing touch to Prudence Jane. The Reverend Mr. Sanders looked down upon it with a most friendly smile.

'Is your aunt at home?' he asked, placing his hat on the table and following Prudence Jane into the parlor.

'Yes,' she said with simple candor. A fib of that sort was quite beneath Prudence Jane.

Then she sat down on a velvet sofa, spread out her little blue skirt, folded her hands in her lap and crossed her ankle-ties. She had never in her life looked so much like little Bertie. The Reverend Mr. Sanders, regarding her from an opposite chair, waited for her to open her lips and say, 'Speak, Lord, for thy servant heareth.' Instead, this is what she said:—

'Is Eliza Anna Bomination your grandmother?'

'I beg pardon,' said the Reverend Mr. Sanders.

'Is she dead and gone to heaven, and that's why you say "unto the Lord"?' continued Prudence Jane.

'I wonder, Imogen,' he said, 'if you would mind beginning over again.'

'I say, is Eliza Anna Bomination your grandmother?' repeated Prudence Jane. 'Aunt Annie says she's written down in the middle of your Bible where all people's relations are, and she sounded like a grandmother; they always have such horrid names.'

The minister looked across at the velvet sofa with eyes that entirely contradicted the gravity of his face.

'No,' he said, 'I'm sorry, but she is n't. I wish she were. I never heard of such a jolly grandmother.'

'Is she an aunt?' pursued his small interlocutor.

'I'm afraid that she's not even related by marriage,' he replied.

'Is n't she written down in the middle of your Bible at all?' said Prudence Jane.

The minister shook his head.

'No,' he said, 'I'm afraid not.'

'Then Aunt Annie told a whopper,' announced Prudence Jane with satisfaction.

'We should not malign the absent,' said the Reverend Mr. Sanders. 'And that being the case, suppose you go up at this point, Imogen, and tell your Aunt Annie that I am here.'

Prudence Jane wondered what 'maligning the absent' was. She distrusted gentlemen who made cryptic remarks of this sort. It was a way her brother Horace had. She saw that the moment had now arrived to test Aunt Annie's theory about ministers and fibs.

'She can't come down,' she replied.

'Can't come down?' repeated the minister.

'No,' said Prudence Jane, looking at him out of the depths of her forget-me-not eyes, 'she's washed her hair.'

'Oh,' said the Reverend Mr. Sanders, in the tone of one who finds the conversation getting definitely beyond him.

At this moment an apparition with a round face and a pair of corduroy shoulders suddenly darkened the open window.

'A *lie* is an a-*bom*-i-*na*-tion *un*-to the *Lord*,' it sang; and, catching sight of the clerical back, vanished hastily.

'Interesting chorus,' observed the Reverend Mr. Sanders.

Prudence Jane paid no heed to this interruption.

'It's hanging down her back now,' she pursued, launching upon the details with her usual aplomb. 'It comes clear down to here.' And standing up, she indicated a point halfway between her ankle-ties and the bottom of her ridiculous skirt.

The minister gazed fascinated. Prudence Jane sat down again.

'She washed it with Packer's Tar Soap,' she said, her eyes fixed upon her victim.

She was quite unable to make out whether Aunt Annie was right about ministers or not. The Reverend Mr. Sanders looked like the Sphinx.

'She gave a piece to a gentleman once,' went on Prudence Jane, warming to her work. 'He was n't a very nice gentleman. He was a — a —' she hesitated a moment over a fitting climax, — 'a - - a Piskerpalyan,' she finished.

'Mercy!' said the Reverend Mr. Sanders, finding his voice at last. 'And what, may I ask, are you?'

Prudence Jane looked faintly surprised.

'I,' she said, with pride and composure, 'am an Orthy Dox Congo Gationist.'

'Yes,' said the Reverend Mr. Sanders, 'so I suspected from the first.'

And now *what* did he mean by that, thought Prudence Jane to herself. She could no longer see his face. He had turned abruptly in his chair and was watching something through the aperture in the portières.

Prudence Jane heard the thump of a pair of shoes plodding up the stairs and along the upper hall. She knew that it was Peter Piper going to find Aunt Annie. There was a stir in the room overhead, then the muffled sound of a rocking-chair suddenly abandoned, followed by the swish of skirts coming along the passage and down the stairs.

Prudence Jane sat with parted lips on the edge of the sofa.

The Reverend Mr. Sanders looked decidedly nervous, but he rose and presented a bold front to whatever might be coming to him through those portières. In another moment they were pushed hastily aside, and Aunt Annie, crowned with a quite faultless coiffure, hurried into the room.

'Why, Mr. Sanders,' she said, 'I did not know until this minute that you were here.'

Then her eye fell upon her niece. Prudence Jane was now standing in front of the sofa, tracing the pattern of the carpet with the toe of an ankle-tie.

'Why did n't you tell me that Mr. Sanders was waiting?' demanded Aunt Annie sternly.

Prudence Jane continued to gaze at the carpet.

'Mr. Sanders,' said Aunt Annie, who never postponed a

disagreeable duty, 'we have a little girl here who cannot speak the truth, and we are going to ask you to tell us what becomes of people who tell wrong stories.'

The Reverend Mr. Sanders looked ill at ease.

'Come here,' continued Aunt Annie, holding out her hand toward the velvet sofa.

Prudence Jane moved reluctantly across the room.

'And now,' went on the voice of the accuser, 'she has even deceived her minister, and she has come to make her little confession. Tell Mr. Sanders,' directed Aunt Annie, 'the truth about that wicked fib.'

'Which one?' inquired Prudence Jane meekly.

'You know very well which,' answered her exasperated aunt; 'the last one.'

Prudence Jane lifted her blue eyes from the carpet and looked straight at the unfortunate Mr. Sanders.

'She did n't give any of it to the Piskerpalyan,' she said.

Then she turned and walked discreetly through the portières. She felt that it was no moment to stay and learn what became of little girls who told whoppers.

'Did n't give who what?' she could hear Aunt Annie saying vaguely on the other side of the curtains.

But Prudence Jane decided to let her minister explain.

THE GLORY-BOX

BY ELIZABETH ASHE

I

In Southern Ohio a girl's wedding chest is her Glory-Box. If, like Mabel Bennet, you are the daughter of a successful druggist, the box is of cedarwood, delivered free of charge by the Dayton department stores; but if, like Eunice Day, you are the daughter of an unsuccessful bookkeeper who has left a life insurance inadequate even when supplemented by the salary you earn teaching primary children, then the box is just a box, covered with gay cretonne, and serving the purpose very nicely.

When Eunice Day's engagement became known, Mabel, remembering the scalloped guest-towels which Eunice had given her some months before, brought over one afternoon an offering wrapped in tissue paper.

'I hope you'll like this, Eunice,' she said. 'It's just a sack, — what they call a matinée. I've found them very useful.'

Mabel spoke with the slightly complacent air of the three months' bride.

'Why, it's ever so dear of you to go to so much trouble,' said Eunice, taking the package into her hands. She was a tall, slender girl, with dark eyes and a pretty dignity of bearing. 'I'll have to open it right now, I guess. You are n't in a hurry, are you?'

'Oh, no, not especially. Harry does n't get home until quarter past six, and I've fixed the vegetables. Just you go ahead.'

Eunice untied the white ribbon. 'Why, Mabel, it's beautiful, and such a delicate shade of pink!'

She held the sack at arm's length.

'I'm glad you like it. It's nothing wonderful, of course.'

'It couldn't be more pretty, and Stephen loves pink. I wrote him the other day that I had made a pink kimono and I hoped he would like it. He wrote back that pink was — was the color of dawn and apple-blossoms.'

Mabel laughed. 'Stephen has a funny way of saying things, hasn't he?'

'Why, I don't know,' said Eunice, flushing.

'Oh, well,' went on Mabel good-naturedly, 'I do think you look nice in pink with your dark hair. Harry always tells me to stick to blue. It's the color for blondes. Don't you want to show me your things? I won't mind if the ribbons are n't all run in yet.'

'I'd like to show them to you, of course. Come upstairs. They'll look nicer though when they are all pressed out,' said Eunice, laying the sack carefully back in its paper wrappings. She carried it on outstretched palms.

'Do you know when you're going to be married?' asked Mabel as she reached the top of the narrow stairs.

'We have n't made plans yet. Probably Stephen won't want to for another year. It depends on so many things.'

'I suppose so,' said Mabel, following Eunice into her bedroom. It was a small room but pretty. Eunice had recently put four coats of white paint on her oak set. 'Lawyers,' continued Mabel sympathetically, 'have to wait so much longer. Now Harry knew to a cent what salary he was getting when he proposed to me, and he knew what his raise would probably be for the next two years. The Wire Company is a square concern. There's your Glory-Box! It looks awfully nice. You made it, didn't you?'

'Stephen made it when he was on for his vacation last

summer. We happened to have the cretonne in the house.
Mother wanted me to buy a cedar chest but I thought this
would do.'

'Oh, one does n't really need a cedar chest,' said Mabel
cheerfully, 'and they're terribly expensive, you know.'

'Yes, I do know.' Eunice's face twinkled. 'I'll lay this
sack on the bed so it won't get mussed while I'm showing
you the things.'

She raised the lid of the Glory-Box, then glanced shyly
at the other girl. 'You're the first person I've shown
them to. I hope you'll think they're dainty. There isn't
much lace on them, but mother put in a lot of handwork
— feather-stitching.'

'Lace is a bother to do up,' Mabel said amiably. 'I've
been almost distracted doing up mine.'

'Your things were beautiful, though.' Eunice was laying piles of carefully folded garments on the edge of the
box.

'There, I've got it now,' she said, getting up from the
floor. 'This is my prettiest set. I've kept it wrapped in
dark blue paper. Mother said it would keep white longer.'

'Why, they are sweet, Eunice!' Mabel touched the soft
white stuff with appraising fingers. 'And all made by
hand. My, what a lot of work! Your mother must have
spent hours on them.'

'She did. She said she wanted to do it, though. The
other things are plainer.' Eunice took them up one by
one and showed them. 'I won't let you see the table
linen to-day. I've done a lot of initialing, but they don't
look really well until they have been washed.'

'No, they don't. Anyway I have to be going. You
certainly have nice things, Eunice. That kimono is
awfully pretty.

'I like it,' said Eunice simply.

'Well, I can't stay another minute. Don't you come down to the door now. You have to put away everything. I'll just run along. Come and see me. I've got the flat all settled.'

'I shall love to, Mabel. Just a moment! You must let me go to the door with you. The Glory-Box can wait.'

Eunice found her mother standing by the bed when she came back. She was a meagre-looking woman with a thin mouth. Her eyes had once been soft and dark like Eunice's, but the glow had gone out of them, leaving them a little hard.

'I've been looking at the sack Mabel brought you. It's a nice pattern. That sort of lace looks almost like real val. What did she say to your things?'

'She said they were sweet, mother.'

'Well, I suppose they are as nice as any one could have without spending money. You did n't show her the table-cloth I gave you?'

'No, I thought I'd wait to show the linen until it was all done up.'

Her mother fingered the lace on the sack.

'I don't believe she has a much better tablecloth than that one, Eunice. Do you suppose so?'

'No,' answered Eunice, 'probably not. It's very beauti-ful.' She laid down the garment she was folding and looked up, troubled, into her mother's face. 'Oh, it seems so selfish for me to have it all. You've always wanted nice fine linen, mother.'

'I've given up wanting, I guess. I don't care as long as you have them. You had better lay tissue paper in that sleeve, Eunice, the way I showed you. I'll start supper so that you can put these things away. They won't look like anything if you leave them about.'

When her mother was gone, Eunice took up the pink

kimono and spread it out on the bed. She could fold it more carefully that way. She touched it with caressing fingers. 'Dawn and apple-blossoms,' she repeated softly. Then she smiled, remembering Mabel's remark: 'Stephen has a funny way of saying things.'

Stephen was different somehow from Harry, from any of the men whom her friends had married. They were nice young men, of course, all of them. One was superintendent of the Sunday School, besides getting a good salary in the Cash Register Company; another had gone to college, had been in Stephen's class at the Ohio State University in fact, and was now doing well as part owner of the garage on Main Street; still another was paying-teller in the bank next to the garage; he wore very 'good-looking' suits, usually with a tiny line of white at the edge of the waistcoat. Still Stephen was different.

When he had got his B.A. degree at Ohio, he decided that he wanted to be a lawyer, and that he would go to one of the best schools in the country. He chose Columbia. He had worked his way through college, but he considered that it would not pay to work his way through Law School. He wanted the time to get something out of New York. His father was unable to advance the money, so Stephen went to a friend of his father's, a prosperous coal-dealer in the town, and asked that he lend him enough to put him through economically, but not, he plainly said, too economically. He would give the coal-dealer notes, payable with interest four years after he was admitted to the bar.

The coal-dealer, taking into consideration the fact that the young man had broken every record at the university in scholarship, and two other facts, the young man's forehead and mouth, lent him the money. He said that the interest need not begin until he was admitted.

Stephen thanked him and went to Columbia. One of

the professors there took a great fancy to him. He introduced him to his sister, a maiden lady living in Washington
Square, who, finding him very likable, introduced him to
other people living in the Square.

Stephen was very happy. He wrote to Eunice, — he had
been engaged to her since the end of his second year at the
Law School, — 'Washington Square is rather terrifying
from the outside, but once inside you feel beautifully at
home. I think it's the perfect breeding you find there.
I've met women more intellectual, greater perhaps, than
Professor Lansing's sister, but never one who gives such an
impression of completion. There are no loose ends. You
will like her, Eunice.'

In another letter he said, 'We won't have much money
to start with, of course, but if we put a little dignity into our
kitchenette apartment, it will be a home that people will
love to come to. It's partly the dignity of their living
that makes these Washington Square people so worth while
to be with.'

And last week he had written, 'You won't find New York
lonely. They will love you, dear. You belong. You
have not only charm but the dignity that belongs. I wonder if I'm foolish to care so much for that word dignity.
Perhaps it's because I associate it with you, or perhaps —
I love you because you have it.'

And Eunice too was happy and proud: happy that
Stephen was coming into his own, and proud that he should
think her equal to the occasion. It would not be an easy
task, being equal to Stephen. Stephen was a great man,
or would be a great man. She knew it and Stephen knew
it. 'We are going to be great, you and I,' he had said more
than once. And yet one day when she had answered, 'You
and I, Stephen?' his eyes, which had been alight with the
glorious vision of the future, softened, and he had come and

knelt beside her and had laid his head down. 'Oh, Eunice,'
he had whispered, 'I've got brains; I'm pretty sure to be
successful; but if I'm worth while, it will be because of you.
You are a great woman, dear.'

And Eunice had mothered him and had hoped — so fer-
vently that the hope was a prayer—that she would really
be great enough to meet his needs.

Sometimes she doubted. She had dignity; Stephen had
said so; but inside she was deprecating and shy. People
like Mabel Ashley made her shy, and most of the people
she knew were like Mabel. They thought Stephen's way
of saying and thinking things 'funny.' There was only
one woman whom she could talk with, a High-School
teacher who had come to board next door. She and the
High-School teacher took long walks together.

The High-School teacher had been to Europe twice.
She knew how people lived outside of this little Ohio town
— outside of the United States even. She was full of
shrewd comment. Eunice talked to her about the books
that she and Stephen were reading, and sometimes about
Stephen himself. Several times the High-School teacher
had said, 'He is splendid, Eunice.'

Eunice thought about her this afternoon as she put the
last things away in the Glory-Box. She hoped that, if the
Washington Square people were like this teacher, she would
get along. And there came another encouraging thought.
The people in the Square were sure of themselves of course,
but perhaps they were sure because they had things and
had always had things. She would one day have the
things in her Glory-Box, and she would have Stephen.
After she was quite used to having them and to having a
person like Stephen, she would be sure of herself too.

'Supper will be ready in five minutes, Eunice.'

'I'm coming in a moment.'

The room had grown quite dark. Eunice lighted two candles standing on her bureau. They were in common glass candlesticks which she had bought at the Ten Cent store: she had wanted to have brass; but then, Stephen and she were going to have brass candlesticks in every room of their house. They both loved candle-light.

Eunice smoothed her dark hair. Then she washed her hands very carefully. Stephen had said once that they were not wonderfully pretty hands, but that they had distinction. He had kissed them.

'I guess I'm all right now,' said Eunice, glancing into the mirror. She picked up a photograph of Stephen from the bureau and laid her face against it. Then she blew out the candles and went downstairs.

II

Stephen's letter that awaited her when she came home from school the next afternoon was a one-page scrawl. 'My head is ringing so with the quinine I've taken that I can't write to-night. By to-morrow I shall probably be rid of this beastly cold. I want to tell you about a book I've just read. It's great stuff.' He added a postscript: 'Don't ask me, dear, if I wore my rubbers day before yesterday. You know I did n't.'

In Eunice's eyes was a smile of amused tenderness as she put the letter back in its envelope. If the cold were 'beastly,' perhaps he might remember next time. She was afraid though that only married men wore rubbers.

No letter came the next day, or the next.

'If I don't hear to-morrow, I'll telegraph.'

'He's probably busy,' said her mother.

'I'm afraid he's sick.'

Eunice waited for the postman on Saturday morning,

but he brought her no letter. She put on her hat and coat.

'I'll be back in a half hour, mother.'

As she went down the steps a boy riding a bicycle stopped at the curb. He handed her a telegram. It was from Stephen's landlady. Stephen had died that morning at two o'clock — of pneumonia.

Eunice was conscious of being very collected and calm as she went back into the house; quite wonderfully calm. Her mother was in the kitchen. Eunice went to her and told her — very gently. She had the feeling that it was her mother's sorrow. Her mother's dry, hard sobs and bowed figure brought the tears to her eyes. She laid her hand on the thin convulsed shoulders. 'Mother, don't — don't, dear, it's all right, you know.' She stood by her chair until the sobs ceased.

'I'm going around to — to Stephen's, mother. I'll not be gone long.'

Mrs. Day followed her to the steps; her face was pitifully pinched, almost old. At the gate Eunice turned and saw her.

'Poor mother!' She wanted to go back and kiss her but she dared not.

Stephen's home was on the other side of the town. It was a small frame house painted light gray, with a gable back and front, and a narrow porch running across it. This morning the shades in the parlor were drawn down.

Eunice had to wait some moments before the door was opened by Stephen's young sister — a slip of a thing but a capable housekeeper. Her eyes were swollen with crying. 'She's so little,' thought Eunice, and took her in her arms.

When the girl was able to speak, she told Eunice that her father had gone to New York, and that he would bring Stephen home. Eunice stayed an hour, comforting, talking, planning. Then she left her.

'I'm so quiet. I did n't know it could be like this.'

The March wind blew the dust into her face. The grit irritated her. She wished there were snow on the ground and then wondered that she should care. That was how it was the next two days: she went on thinking and acting, with every now and then this strange awareness of being alive.

But on Monday afternoon when they came home from the cemetery, Eunice went upstairs to her room.

'I'm going to lie down a while, mother.'

Her mother made no answer as she turned into the kitchen.

Eunice lay down on the bed. A pale yellow sunset gleamed through the branches of the tree outside her window. She had seen the yellow streak in the sky as they had left the cemetery. She closed her eyes to shut it out. Her heart was no longer numb. It was waking to its misery. She lay very still with clenched hands. She had learned to bear physical pain that way. She thought perhaps she could bear this if she lay very still.

'I want to tell you about a book I've just read. It's great stuff.'

'O Stephen, Stephen, laddie!'

The tears came, and great sobs that shook and twisted her rigid body. Once she thought her mother came up the stairs and stopped outside her door. She buried her face in the pillow. Her mother must not hear. By and by, — she had been quiet for an hour, — her mother came in with a tray.

'I've made you some toast and tea, Eunice. You must keep up your strength.'

Her tone was flat and emotionless. She set the tray down by her in the darkness. Then she lighted the gas.

Eunice swallowed the tea obediently, she was so very

tired. As she put the cup down her eyes fell on the cretonne-covered box in the window.

'Mother, my Glory-Box! Don't let me see it! Oh, don't let me see my Glory-Box!'

Mrs. Day came up to the bed. 'I'll take it out to-morrow while you are at school. I meant to do that.' Her face worked as she left the room.

When the door closed, Eunice sat up and pushed her tumbled hair back from her face. She wanted to look at the Glory-Box. To-morrow her mother was going to take it away. She clasped her hands tightly about her drawn-up knees and stared at the box with hot, miserable eyes. Of course it would have to be taken away, but she wanted to look at it now because it was her Glory-Box and because it was Stephen's. Stephen had made it.

'That's a decent job for just a lawyer,' he had said, when the last nail was driven in and they were taking a critical survey of it.

Stephen had laughed when she regretted that the roses in the cretonne were yellow, because the things to go into the box very likely would be pink. He had laughed and kissed her and told her she had better get a pair of pink specs, then the roses would be pink enough.

And Stephen had taken such an interest in what she had written about the things she was embroidering for household use. When she had reported a whole dozen napkins hemmed and initialed, he had thought it would be jolly to have nice linen. They would probably be short on silver at first, but good linen made you feel respectable. He remembered his mother taking so much pride in what had been left of hers. For a moment the words of that letter were so vividly recalled that she forgot that Stephen was dead. For quite a moment she was happy. Then she remembered, but the realization brought no tears, only a swelling wave of misery.

'I can't bear it, oh, I can't!'

But even as she moaned she knew that she would bear it, that she would go on living for years and years and years. Other girls she had known or heard about — in her own town — had gone on living: little Sadie Smith whose lover had been killed three days before her wedding, and even Milly Petersen, who had been engaged for five years when the man asked to be released because he wanted to marry the girl who had recently moved to Milly's street. These girls had lived; they had grown pale and faded, or hard. People felt very sorry for them: they were spoken of as 'poor Milly,' or 'Sadie Smith, poor child'; but they had lived. Eunice saw herself moving among her little circle, brave and sad-eyed like these girls.

Suddenly — she never remembered just how it came about — suddenly her humor flashed a white light over the vision. This sad-eyed Self seemed something not to pity but to scorn. It was grotesque standing in your friend's parlor with clenched hands, as it were, and compressed lips, saying, 'Don't mind me, please. I'm bearing it.' If one were going to live one must live happily. Stephen was such a happy person. He was happy when he was working or playing or just loving. Even hurdy-gurdys made him happy.

'When I hear one grinding away in the morning,' he had written, 'I have to kick a few Law Journals about just to keep in tune with the darn thing.'

It had been a delightful surprise to her, his overflowing happiness, for Stephen's face in repose was very grave. She herself only occasionally had his joy in mere living, but she had always thought that Stephen's joyfulness would prove infectious. Suppose, now, without Stephen she should make the experiment of being happy.   It would be a wonderful experiment to see, — she spoke the words aloud, deliberately, — to see if she could kill this terrible thing, Sorrow, and keep Stephen to love and to remember.

Eunice was still staring at the Glory-Box, but it was more than her Glory-Box.   It was part of the problem that she was trying to think out clearly.   For perhaps sorrow was a problem that you could work out like other problems, if only you could see it, not as one solid, opaque mass, but as something made up of pieces that you could deal with one at a time.   The Glory-Box was a piece.   She had wanted it taken away because it was a thing so filled with pain that she could not bear to have it about.   If — Eunice got up in her excitement and walked up and down the room — if the Glory-Box could become a box again, just a box covered with cretonne, and the things in it become things, then a great piece of misery would disappear.   Love, a girl's love, was like — she groped a moment for words — like a vine that puts forth little shoots and tendrils; love even went into things.   When Death trampled on the vine, the shoots and tendrils were crushed with it.   But if you cut them off, these poor bruised pieces of the vine, the vine itself would perhaps have a chance to become strong and beautiful.

Eunice played with the idea, her cheeks flushed, her eyes very bright.   She felt as she did sometimes when talking on paper with Stephen.

She went over to the Glory-Box and raised the cover. On top lay the matinée that Mabel had brought on that day not quite a week ago.   She unfolded it and touched it.   'This is n't — Stephen,' she said aloud, quite firmly. 'It's cotton voile and val lace.   It's cotton voile.'

She took out garment after garment.   When she came to the pink kimono her eyes blinded with tears.   'It's a

lovely shade.   Pink is pretty with dark hair.'   Her quivering lips could scarcely frame the words.   'It's not Stephen.
It's — it's just a kimono.'

She put the things back and closed the box.   'I'll look
at the rest in a day or two.   I'll keep looking at them.
Probably I shall never be able to use them, but I'll keep
looking until I get accustomed to seeing them.   Mother
will get used to seeing the box here.   If she put it in the
storeroom she would always dread going in.'

Mrs. Day was getting breakfast the next morning when
Eunice came down.   She went on mechanically with her
preparation, avoiding looking at her.   At the table she
glanced up.   Eunice's face was white and haggard, but
her eyes, strangely big, were shining.   Eunice's mother
watched her furtively throughout the meal.   As they left
the table Eunice put her arms about her.

'Don't take the box out, mother.   It's better to get used
to it.   I'm trying to get used to things.   Don't you worry
about me.   You'll see.'

She kissed her and hurried to school.   In her exalted
mood the sympathetic attentions of the other teachers
seemed almost surprising.   They were dear and kind, but
why should they be so kind?   She was going to be happy.
At the end of the day, however, Eunice let herself softly
into the house, too wretched to want to meet her mother.
She carried to her room the letters of condolence that were
on the dining-room table.   She read them impassively,
even the kindly one from Miss Lansing, wondering why
they did not touch her.   'It's because I'm tired,' she
concluded, and knelt down by the Glory-Box, bowing her
head on her outstretched arms.

'Stephen, dear,' she prayed, 'I can't look at the things
to-night.   I'm too tired.'

But the next day she took them all out.   And on a Sat-

urday afternoon three weeks later she startled her mother
by coming into her room dressed in the suit and hat that
were her 'best.' Her mother laid down the skirt on which
she was putting a new braid.

'Why, where are you going, Eunice?'

'I thought I'd call on Mabel. I've never been to see her
since she started housekeeping. I promised to, long ago.'

Mrs. Day looked at her keenly, her mouth tightening.
'You're foolish to go and see all her wedding presents about
the house. You won't be able to stand it.'

'I shall, mother. That's why I'm going to stand it. I
shan't mind calling there after I've been this once. I've
thought it out.'

'You're a queer girl, Eunice. I do n't understand you.
But I suppose you know your — your own business best,'
she ended, taking up her work again.

Eunice felt quite sure that she did, and yet there were
days when the experiment seemed a failure, or at least only
just begun: days when she would read in a paper of brilliant
social events in New York, in Stephen's New York. Stephen might have been there at that dinner, his eyes, which
looked so gravely from his picture, lighted with the joyfulness of the occasion, his splendid head towering above
the other men as he joined in the toasts — Stephen had
told her they always made toasts at these dinners; she could
hear his laugh, his hearty boyish laugh. And those other
days in early spring, when a hurdy-gurdy would play
'Turkey in the Straw,' and she could see Stephen pitching
his Law Journals about, exulting in the glorious fact that
he was alive. Oh, how she longed for him, wanted him
these days — with a passionate yearning that for moments maddened her. But as the months went by the
times of overwhelming wanting came less and less frequently. 'I shall soon be happy,' Eunice told herself.

And on a morning of June loveliness, a morning of very blue sky, white clouds, and butter-cups, Eunice knew that she was happy.

'I'm glad to-day, Stephen, I'm glad, just because it's all so beautiful.'

She wondered now and again why, since she herself was so surely leaving the sorrow behind her, her mother should still droop under its weight. They seldom talked about Stephen. They had agreed at the beginning not to do that often, but there was bitterness in her mother's face and bitterness on occasion in her words. 'I've got used to seeing your box around, but don't ever ask me to look inside.' It occurred to Eunice that perhaps it was because to her mother had come only the grief. She was not having Stephen to love.

III

One afternoon late in February, Eunice was met in the hall by her mother. 'A letter came for you this morning. It's from New York.' She stood watching her as Eunice opened it with unsteady fingers.

Eunice looked up in a few moments, very white. 'It's from Professor Lansing's sister,' she faltered. 'Miss Lansing is coming on to Chicago this week. She says she would like to see me. She'll stop off in Dayton over night, Saturday probably, and will come out for lunch if it's convenient for us to have her. She can make connections by doing that. Oh, mother, it's beautiful of her to want to come.'

'I don't know that it will do you much good to see her. You'll probably get upset.'

'No, I won't be upset because I'll be so glad. Stephen said she was a wonderful woman, and — we can talk about

him. He was at her house only a few days before he —
caught cold.'

'Well, I don't know,' said her mother. 'You had better
come into the kitchen where it's warm. You look like a
ghost, Eunice. I'll give you a cup of soup to drink. It's
on the stove now.' She laid nervous compelling fingers
on Eunice's arm. 'I suppose,' Mrs. Day was pouring out
the soup as she spoke, 'I suppose that Miss Lansing has n't
any idea of the way we live. Even the front stoop looks
a sight. It's needed a coat of paint for years.'

'I know,' Eunice answered, her face clouding. 'I wish
things were different for Stephen's sake. But we can't
help it.'

'No,' said her mother harshly, 'we can't help it. But I
wish she was n't coming for a meal. The last decent
tablecloth was cut up into napkins a month ago. I was
ashamed of the one we set Mabel Bennet down to the other
night.'

Eunice walked to the window. She looked out upon the
backyard, upon the snow that was reflecting the sunset, a
sentence of one of Stephen's letters in her mind. 'It's the
dignity of their living that makes these Washington Square
people so worth while.' And then she recalled that other
letter. 'It will be jolly to have nice linen. Good linen
makes you feel respectable.'

It pained her that they must offer this friend of Stephen's what they had been ashamed to offer Mabel Bennet.
Stephen's pride would be hurt, Stephen who had loved
that word 'dignity'; and Stephen's pride was her own pride
just as much as if she were his wife, as if he were living.

Eunice stood a long time looking out upon the snow,
until the rose of the sunset had gone from it, leaving it
blue and cold. She turned from the window.

'Mother,' — she was glad that in the darkening kitchen

she could not see her mother's face distinctly, — 'mother, don't you think we had better use that very fine cloth you gave me, and the napkins, to make the table look nice? Had n't we better use them?'

'Use your things out of your Glory-Box, Eunice!'

'Yes, they are just pretty things, now, mother. All the pain is out of them. I'm going to wear the best set you made me. I think if I have on those nice clothes under my dress I won't be so shy with Miss Lansing. I want — O, mother, I want Stephen to — to feel proud of me.'

Mrs. Day bent to rake the fire, then straightened up. 'If you can stand wearing that set, I've nothing to say. You have a right to your own notions. But I do n't see how I can bear to look at the cloth.'

'After it's been done up and on the table once, you'll forget there was anything sad connected with it. I know you will,' said Eunice, with her brave, pleading eyes fixed on her mother's set face.

'I do n't know; maybe I could forget. But I do n't see how I could bring myself to use something out of your own Glory-Box. It seems almost indelicate. They're all your things.'

Eunice crossed the room and laid her face down on her mother's shoulder. 'You gave me the things, mother, and you've had so little of what you've always wanted. Can't it be our Glory-Box, for us both to use on special occasions — like this?' Her arms tightened about her mother's neck. 'Can't we use them this time for Stephen's sake?'

After a moment's silence Mrs. Day pushed her gently away.

'If they are to be washed you'll have to bring them down to-morrow. I'll want to get them on the line while this good weather lasts. Saturday is only four days off.'

Saturday evening Eunice lighted the candles on her

bureau; lighting the candles seemed like another ceremony of this perfect day. She had got up early so as to put her room and the rest of the house in order. While her mother was finishing in the kitchen she had set the table. It had been a joy to do that, to spread the cloth so that the creases would come in just the right place, and the large initial 'D' show without being too conspicuous, and to fold the napkins prettily and arrange the dishes. At the last moment she had decided that it would not be too extravagant to buy a little plant of some sort for a centre-piece. So there was just time for her to slip into the clothes that had been spread out on the bed, and do over her hair, before Miss Lansing arrived.

Stephen had said, 'You will like her, Eunice.' Like her! — she was the most wonderful woman she had ever met. She was elderly, but strangely enough you did not wonder whether she had been pretty or beautiful when she was young. She was wonderful just as she was now. You could not think of her as being different. She was tall, a little taller than Eunice herself. Her face was finely cut, the sort of face you saw in engravings of old portraits; there were not many lines in it. Her eyes were dark and young too, though she had quite gray hair and evidently did n't care to be in the fashion, for her black silk fell all around in ample lengths. Eunice had watched her hands. They were not small, but long and slender and very white; the two rings she wore seemed made for them.

And Eunice had not felt shy. At first she had thought she was going to, Miss Lansing had seemed at first so like a personage; but the thought of Stephen, and of the feather-stitched best set she was wearing made her forget that Washington Square was, as Stephen had said, rather terri-fying on the outside. It was Stephen's friend whom they were entertaining, and Stephen's friend was not a personage really, but a wonderful woman who had loved Stephen too.

After lunch they talked together in the parlor while her mother was clearing things away. Miss Lansing said that she had seen a great deal of Stephen that last year. He had seemed to enjoy coming to the house. He had come to dinner sometimes, but more often he had dropped in on Saturday or Sunday afternoons for tea. One afternoon he had not been quite himself. She had questioned him a little and he had confessed with a laugh that he was homesick for Ohio.

'That was the time he talked for two hours about you, my dear,' Miss Lansing said, smiling. 'Fortunately no one else came in, so he was uninterrupted. I liked to listen to his talk; he had charm.' But Eunice saw her eyes kindle. 'He was more than charming. He was great.'

'Yes,' Eunice answered very low. 'He would have been a great man, Miss Lansing. I always knew he would.'

At that Miss Lansing put out both hands and covered Eunice's that were clasped tightly in her lap. 'He would have been a great man,' she repeated, 'and you, my dear, would have made him a great wife.'

Eunice felt that never, unless she should hear Stephen's voice again, should she listen to such wonderful words as those. Ever since Miss Lansing had gone they had sung themselves in her heart like a sacred refrain. She was glad that it was night now so that she could fall asleep repeating them.

'Getting ready for bed, Eunice?'

'I'm beginning to.' Eunice opened the door to her mother, who stood outside winding the clock.

'Do you know,' said Mrs. Day as she set the alarm, 'I've been thinking again what a good idea it was to open that can of peas. They did make the chops looks so tasty,

and they were almost as tender as the French.   I helped
Miss Lansing twice.'

Eunice kissed her as she turned away.

'It was a nice dinner throughout, mother, and the table
looked lovely.'

'Well, I saw Miss Lansing look at the cloth.   She was
too much of a lady to say anything, of course, but I could
tell she noticed it.'

'Yes,' said Eunice, 'I think she did.'

Mrs. Day was closing her door.

'Put out the light in the hall before you go to bed,
Eunice.'

'Yes, mother,' said Eunice, softly closing her own door.

She stood still a moment in the centre of the candle-
lighted room.   Then she went over to the Glory-Box and
took out the kimono and laid it over the footboard so that
the pink folds could catch the light.   When she had undressed, she put it on.   'It will be a beautiful ending to the
day,' she said, as she stood before the mirror braiding her
hair.

Her eyes rested on Stephen's picture.

'I think you would have been proud to-day, dear, and
I think you would have liked this.'

She turned to the mirror, and looked at the girl reflected
there, at the dark eyes and hair and at the kimono draping
her soft white gown.

'Dawn and apple-blossoms,' she whispered and then
stretched out her arms.

'Stephen, my dear!   O Stephen.'

THE SPIRIT OF THE HERD*

BY DALLAS LORE SHARP

I

We were trailing the 'riders' of P Ranch across the plains
to a hollow in the hills called the 'Troughs,' where they
were to round up a lot of cattle for a branding.   On the
way we fell in behind a bunch of some fifty cows and year-
lings which one of the riders had picked up; and, while he
dashed off across the desert for a 'stray,' we tenderfeet
drove on the herd.   It was hot, and the cattle lagged, so
we urged them on.   All at once I noticed that the whole
herd was moving with a swinging, warping gait, with
switching tails, and heads thrown round from side to side
as if every steer were watching us.   We were not near
enough to see their eyes, but the rider, far across the desert,
saw the movement and came cutting through the sage,
shouting and waving his arms to stop us.   We had pushed
the driving too hard.   Mutiny was spreading among the
cattle, already manifest in a sullen ugly temper that would
have brought the herd charging us in another minute, had
not the cowboy galloped in between us just as he did — so
untamed, unafraid, and instinctively savage is the spirit
of the herd.

It is this herd-spirit that the cowboy, on his long, cross-
desert drives to the railroad, most fears.   The herd is like
a crowd, easily led, easily excited, easily stampeded, —
when it becomes a mob of frenzied beasts, past all control,
— the spirit of the city 'gang' at riot in the plains.

* Published also in Professor Sharp's book, *Where Rolls the Oregon*,
and here reprinted through the courtesy of Houghton Mifflin Company.

If one would know how thin is the coat of domestication worn by the tamest of animals, let him ride with the cattle across the rim-rock country of southeastern Oregon. No better chance to study the spirit of the herd could possibly be had. And in contrast to the cattle, how intelligent, controlled, almost human, seems the plainsman's horse!

I share all the tenderfoot's admiration for the cowboy and his 'pony.'

Both of them are necessary in bringing four thousand cattle through from P Ranch to Winnemucca; and of both is required a degree of daring and endurance, as well as a knowledge of the wild-animal mind, which lifts their hard work into the heroic, and makes of every drive a sage-brush epic — so wonderful is the working together of man and horse, a kind of centaur of the plains.

From P Ranch to Winnemucca is a seventeen-day drive through a desert of rim-rock and greasewood and sage, which, under the most favorable conditions, is beset with difficulty, but which, in the dry season, and with anything like four thousand cattle, becomes an unbroken hazard. More than all else on such a drive is feared the wild herd-spirit, the quick, black temper which, by one sign or another, ever threatens to break the spell of the riders' power and sweep the maddened or terrorized herd to destruction. The handling of the herd to keep this spirit sleeping is oft-times a thrilling experience.

II

Some time before my visit to P Ranch, in the summer of 1912, the riders had taken out a herd of four thousand steers on what proved to be one of the most difficult drives ever made to Winnemucca. For the first two days on the trail the cattle were strange to each other, having been

gathered from widely separated grazing grounds, — from
Double-O and the Home Ranch, — and were somewhat
clannish and restive under the driving. At the beginning
of the third day signs of real trouble appeared. A shortage
of water and the hot weather together began to tell on the
temper of the herd.

The third day was long and exceedingly hot. The line
started forward at dawn, and all day kept moving, with
the sun cooking the bitter smell of the sage into the air, and
with sixteen thousand hoofs kicking up a still bitterer
smother of alkali dust which inflamed eyes and nostrils
and coated the very lungs of the cattle. The fierce desert
thirst was upon the herd long before it reached the creek
where it was to bed for the night. The heat and the dust
had made slow work of the driving, and it was already late
when they reached the creek, only to find it dry.

This was bad. The men were tired, but the cattle were
thirsty, and Wade, the 'boss of the buckaroos,' pushed the
herd on toward the next rim-rock, hoping to get down to
the plain below before the end of the slow desert twilight.
Anything for the night but a dry camp.

They had hardly started on when a whole flank of the
herd, suddenly breaking away as if by prearrangement,
tore off through the brush. The horses were as tired as the
men, and, before the chase was over, the twilight was gray
in the sage, making it necessary to halt at once and camp
where they were. They would have to go without water.

The runaways were brought up and the herd closed in
till it formed a circle nearly a mile around. This was as
close as it could be drawn, for the cattle would not bed
— lie down. They wanted water more than they wanted
rest. Their eyes were red, their tongues raspy with thirst.
The situation was a difficult one.

But camp was made. Two of the riders were sent back

along the trail to bring up the 'drags,' while Wade, with his
other men, circled the uneasy cattle, closing them in, quiet-
ing them, and doing everything possible to make them bed.

They were thirsty; and instead of bedding, the herd began to 'growl' — a distant mutter of throats, low, rum-
bling, ominous, as when faint thunder rolls behind the hills.
Every plainsman fears the growl, for it too often is a
prelude to the 'milling,' as it proved to be now, when the
whole vast herd began to stir — slowly, singly at first and
without direction, till at length it moved together, round
and round a great compact circle, the multitude of clicking
hoofs, of clashing horns and chafing sides, like the sound of
rushing rain across a field of corn.

Nothing could be worse for the cattle. The cooler twilight was falling, but, mingling with it, rose and thickened
and spread a choking dust from their feet which soon covered them, and shut from sight all but the wall of the herd.
Slowly, evenly, swung the wall, round and round, without
a break. Only one who has watched a milling herd can
know its suppressed excitement. To keep that excitement
in check was the problem of Wade and his men. And the
night had not yet begun.

When the riders had brought in the drags, and the chuck-
wagon had lumbered up with supper, Wade set the first
watch.

Along with the wagon had come the fresh horses —
among them Peroxide Jim, a supple, powerful, clean-
limbed buckskin, that had, I think, as fine and intelligent
an animal-face as any creature I ever saw. And why
should he not have been saved fresh for just such a need
as this? Are there not superior horses as well as superior
men — a Peroxide Jim to complement a Wade?

The horse plainly understood the situation, Wade told
me; and though there was nothing like sentiment for horse-

flesh about the boss of the P Ranch riders, his faith in Peroxide Jim was absolute.

The other night-horses were saddled and tied to the
wheels of the wagon. It was Wade's custom to take his
turn with the second watch; but shifting his saddle to Peroxide Jim, he rode out with the four of the first watch, who,
evenly spaced, were quietly circling the herd.

The night, for this part of the high desert, was unusually
warm. It was close, still, and without a sky. The near,
thick darkness blotted out the stars. There is usually a
breeze at night over these highest rim-rock plains which,
no matter how hot the day may have been, crowds the
cattle together for warmth. To-night not a breath stirred
the sage as Wade wound in and out among the bushes, the
hot dust stinging his eyes and caking rough on his skin.

Round and round moved the weaving shifting forms,
out of the dark and into the dark, a gray spectral line like
a procession of ghosts, or some morris dance of the desert's
sheeted dead. But it was not a line, it was a sea of forms;
not a procession, but the even surging of a maelstrom of
hoofs a mile around.

Wade galloped out on the plain for a breath of air and a
look at the sky. A quick cold rain would quiet them; but
there was not a feel of rain in the darkness, no smell of it on
the air. Only the powdery taste of the bitter sage.

The desert, where the herd was camped, was one of the
highest of a series of table-lands, or benches; it lay as level
as a floor, rimmed by a sheer wall of rock from which there
was a drop to the bench of sage below. The herd had been
headed for a pass, and was now halted within a mile of the
rim-rock on the east, where there was a perpendicular fall
of about three hundred feet.

It was the last place an experienced plainsman would
have chosen for a camp; and every time Wade circled the

herd, and came in between the cattle and the rim, he felt the nearness of the precipice. The darkness helped to bring it near. The height of his horse brought it near — he seemed to look down from his saddle over it, into its dark depths. The herd in its milling was surely warping slowly in the direction of the rim. But this was all fancy, the trick of the dark and of nerves — if a plainsman has nerves.

At twelve o'clock the first guard came in and woke the second watch. Wade had been in the saddle since dawn, but this was his regular watch. More than that, his trained ear had timed the milling hoofs. The movement of the herd had quickened.

If now he could keep them going, and could prevent their taking any sudden fright! They must not stop until they stopped from utter weariness. Safety lay in their continued motion. So the fresh riders flanked them closely, paced them, and urged them quietly on. They must be kept milling and they must be kept from fright.

In the taut silence of the stirless desert night, with the tension of the herd at the snapping-point, any quick, unwonted sight or sound would stampede them; the sneezing of a horse, the flare of a match, would be enough to send the whole four thousand headlong—blind, frenzied, trampling — till spent and scattered over the plain.

And so, as he rode, Wade began to sing. The rider ahead of him took up the air and passed it on until, above the stepping stir of the hoofs, rose the faint voices of the men, and all the herd was bound about by the slow plaintive measures of some old song. It was not to soothe their savage breasts that the riders sang to the cattle, but to prevent the shock of their hearing any loud and sudden noise.

So they sang and rode and the night wore on to one

perilous path at top speed, had outrun the herd and turned it from the edge of the rim-rock, without a false step or a tremor.

Bred on the desert, broken at the round-up, trained to think steer as his rider thinks it, the horse knew as swiftly, as clearly as his rider, the work before him. But that he kept himself from fright, that none of the wild herd-madness passed into him, is a thing for wonder. He was as thirsty as any animal of the herd; he knew his own peril, I believe, as none of the herd had ever known anything; and yet, such coolness, courage, wisdom, and power!

Was it training? Was it more intimate association with the man on his back, and so, a further remove from the wild thing which domestication does not seem to touch? Or was it all suggestion, the superior intelligence above riding — not the flesh, but the spirit?

IN THE PASHA'S GARDEN

A Stamboul Night's Entertainment

BY H. G. DWIGHT

I

As the caïque glided up to the garden gate the three boatmen rose from their sheepskins and caught hold of iron clamps set into the marble of the quay. Shaban, the grizzled gatekeeper, who was standing at the top of the water-steps with his hands folded respectfully in front of him, came salaaming down to help his master out.

'Shall we wait, my Pasha?' asked the head *kaïkji*.

The Pasha turned to Shaban, as if to put a question. And as if to answer it, Shaban said, —

'The madama is up in the wood, in the kiosque. She sent down word to ask if you would go up too.'

'Then don't wait.' Returning the boatmen's salaam, the Pasha stepped into his garden. 'Is there company in the kiosque or is madama alone?' he inquired.

'I think no one is there — except Zümbül Agha,' replied Shaban, following his master up the long central path of black and white pebbles.

'Zümbül Agha!' exclaimed the Pasha. But if it had been in his mind to say anything else he stopped instead to sniff at a rosebud. And then he asked, 'Are we dining up there, do you know?'

'I don't know, my Pasha, but I will find out.'

'Tell them to send up dinner anyway, Shaban. It is such an evening! And just ask Mustafa to bring me a coffee at the fountain, will you? I will rest a little before climbing that hill.'

'On my head!' said the Albanian, turning off to the house.

The Pasha kept on to the end of the walk. Two big horse-chestnut trees, their candles just starting alight in the April air, stood there at the foot of a terrace, guarding a fountain that dripped in the ivied wall. A thread of water started mysteriously out of the top of a tall marble niche into a little marble basin, from which it overflowed by two flat bronze spouts into two smaller basins below. From them the water dripped back into a single basin still lower down, and so tinkled its broken way, past graceful arabesques and reliefs of fruit and flowers, into a crescent-shaped pool at the foot of the niche.

The Pasha sank down into one of the wicker chairs scattered hospitably beneath the horse-chestnut trees, and thought how happy a man he was to have a fountain of the period of Sultan Ahmed III, and a garden so full of April freshness, and a view of the bright Bosphorus and the opposite hills of Europe and the firing West. How definitely he thought it, I cannot say, for the Pasha was not greatly given to thought. Why should he be, as he possessed without that trouble a goodly share of what men acquire by taking thought? If he had been lapped in ease and security all his days, they numbered many more, did those days, than the Pasha would have chosen. Still, they had touched him but lightly, merely increasing the dignity of his handsome presence and taking away nothing of his power to enjoy his little walled world.

So he sat there, breathing in the air of the place and the hour, while gardeners came and went with their watering-pots, and birds twittered among the branches, and the fountain plashed beside him, until Shaban reappeared carrying a glass of water and a cup of coffee in a swinging tray.

'Eh, Shaban! It is not your business to carry coffee!' protested the Pasha, reaching for a stand that stood near him.

'What is your business is my business, my Pasha. Have I not eaten your bread and your father's for thirty years?'

'No! Is it as long as that? We are getting old, Shaban.'

'We are getting old,' assented the Albanian simply.

The Pasha thought, as he took out his silver cigarette-case, of another pasha who had complimented him that afternoon on his youthfulness. And, choosing a cigarette, he handed the case to his gatekeeper. Shaban accepted the cigarette and produced matches from his gay girdle.

'How long is it since you have been to your country, Shaban?'

The Pasha, lifting his little cup by its silver *zarf*, realized that he would not sip his coffee quite so noisily had his French wife been sitting with him under the horse-chestnuts. But with his old Shaban he could still be a Turk.

'Eighteen months, my Pasha.'

'And when are you going again?'

'It is not apparent. Perhaps in Ramazan, if God wills. Or perhaps next Ramazan. We shall see.'

'Allah Allah! How many times have I told you to bring your people here, Shaban? We have plenty of room to build you a house somewhere, and you could see your wife and children every day instead of once in two or three years.'

'Wives, wives—a man will not die if he does not see them every day! Besides, it would not be good for the children. In Constantinople they become rascals. There are too many Christians.' And he added hastily, 'It is better for a boy to grow up in the mountains.'

'But we have a mountain here, behind the house,' laughed the Pasha.

'Your mountain is not like our mountains,' objected Shaban gravely, hunting in his mind for the difference he felt but could not express.

'And that new wife of yours,' went on the Pasha. 'Is it good to leave a young woman like that? Are you not afraid?'

'No, my Pasha. I am not afraid. We all live together, you know. My brothers watch, and the other women. She is safer than yours. Besides, in my country it is not as it is here.'

'I don't know why I have never been to see this wonderful country of yours, Shaban. I have so long intended to, and I never have been. But I must climb my mountain or they will think that I have become a rascal too.' And, rising from his chair, he gave the Albanian a friendly pat.

'Shall I come too, my Pasha? Zümbül Agha sent word —'

'Zümbül Agha!' interrupted the Pasha irritably. 'No, you needn't come. I will explain to Zümbül Agha.'

With which he left Shaban to pick up the empty coffee cup.

II

From the upper terrace a bridge led across the public road to the wood. If it was not a wood it was at all events a good-sized grove, climbing the steep hillside very much as it chose. Every sort and size of tree was there, but the greater number of them were of a kind to be sparsely trimmed in April with a delicate green, and among them were so many twisted Judas trees as to tinge whole patches of the slope with their deep rose bloom. The road which the Pasha slowly climbed, swinging his amber beads behind him as he walked, zigzagged so leisurely back and forth among the trees that a carriage could have driven up it.

In that way, indeed, the Pasha had more than once
mounted to the kiosque, in the days when his mother used
to spend a good part of her summer up there, and when he
was married to his first wife. The memory of the two,
and of their old-fashioned ways, entered not too bitterly
into his general feeling of well-being, ministered to by the
budding trees and the spring air and the sunset view.
Every now and then an enormous plane tree invited him
to stop and look at it, or a semi-circle of cypresses.

So at last he came to the top of the hill, where in a grassy
clearing a small house looked down on the valley of the
Bosphorus through a row of great stone pines. The door
of the kiosque was open, but his wife was not visible. The
Pasha stopped a moment, as he had done a thousand times
before, and looked back. He was not the man to be in-
sensible to what he saw between the columnar trunks of the
pines, where European hills traced a dark curve against the
fading sky, and where the sinuous waterway far below still
reflected a last glamour of the day. The beauty of it, and
the sharp sweetness of the April air, and the infinitesimal
sounds of the wood, and the half-conscious memories involved with it all, made him sigh. He turned and mounted
the steps of the porch.

The kiosque looked very dark and unfamiliar as the
Pasha entered it. He wondered what had become of
Hélène — if by any chance he had passed her on the way.
He wanted her. She was the expression of what the evening roused in him. He heard nothing, however, but the
splash of water from a half-invisible fountain. It reminded
him for an instant, of the other fountain, below, and of
Shaban. His steps resounded hollowly on the marble pavement as he walked into the dim old saloon, shaped like a T,
with the cross longer than the leg. It was still light enough
for him to make out the glimmer of windows on three sides

and the square of the fountain in the centre, but the painted
domes above were lost in shadow.

The spaces on either side of the bay by which he entered,
completing the rectangle of the kiosque, were filled by two
little rooms opening into the cross of the T. He went into
the left-hand one, where Hélène usually sat — because
there were no lattices. The room was empty. The place
seemed so strange and still in the twilight that a sort of
apprehension began to grow in him, and he half wished he
had brought up Shaban. He turned back to the second,
the latticed room — the harem, as they called it. Curiously
enough it was Hélène who would never let him European-
ize it, in spite of the lattices. Every now and then he discovered that she liked some Turkish things better than he
did. As soon as he opened the door he saw her sitting on
the divan opposite. He knew her profile against the
checkered pallor of the lattice. But she neither moved nor
greeted him. It was Zümbül Agha who did so, startling
him by suddenly rising beside the door and saying in his
high voice, —

'Pleasant be your coming, my Pasha.'

The Pasha had forgotten about Zümbül Agha; and it
seemed strange to him that Hélène continued to sit silent
and motionless on her sofa.

'Good evening,' he said at last. 'You are sitting very
quietly here in the dark. Are there no lights in this place?'

It was again Zümbül Agha who spoke, turning one question by another: —

'Did Shaban come with you?'

'No,' replied the Pasha shortly. 'He said he had had
a message, but I told him not to come.'

'A-ah!' ejaculated the eunuch in his high drawl. 'But
it does not matter — with the two of us.'

The Pasha grew more and more puzzled, for this was not

the scene he had imagined to himself as he came up through the park in response to his wife's message. Nor did he grow less puzzled when the eunuch turned to her and said in another tone, —

'Now will you give me that key?'

The Frenchwoman took no more notice of this question than she had of the Pasha's entrance.

'What do you mean, Zümbül Agha?' demanded the Pasha sharply. 'That is not the way to speak to your mistress.'

'I mean this, my Pasha,' retorted the eunuch: 'that some one is hiding in this chest and that madama keeps the key.'

That was what the Pasha heard, in the absurd treble of the black man, in the darkening room. He looked down and made out, beside the tall figure of the eunuch, the chest on which he had been sitting. Then he looked across at Hélène, who still sat silent in front of the lattice.

'What are you talking about?' he asked at last, more stupefied than anything else. 'Who is it? A thief? Has any one — ?' He left the vague question unformulated, even in his mind.

'Ah, that I don't know. You must ask madama. Probably it is one of her Christian friends. But at least if it were a woman she would not be so unwilling to unlock her chest for us!'

The silence that followed, while the Pasha looked dumbly at the chest, and at Zümbül Agha, and at his wife, was filled for him with a stranger confusion of feelings than he had ever experienced before. Nevertheless, he was surprisingly cool, he found. His pulse quickened very little. He told himself that it wasn't true and that he really must get rid of old Zümbül after all, if he went on making such preposterous gaffes and setting them all by the ears. How could anything so baroque happen to him, the Pasha, who owed what he was to the honorable fathers and who had passed his life honorably and peaceably until this moment? Yet he had had an impression, walking into the dark old kiosque and finding nobody until he found these two sitting here in this extraordinary way, as if he had walked out of his familiar garden, which he knew like his hand, into a country he knew nothing about, where anything might be true. And he wished, he almost passionately wished, that Hélène would say something, would cry out against Zümbül Agha, would lie even, rather than sit there so still and removed and different from other women.

Then he began to be aware that if it were true — if ! — he ought to do something. He ought to make a noise. He ought to kill somebody. That was what they always did. That was what his father would have done — or certainly his grandfather. But he also told himself that it was no longer possible for him to do what his father and grandfather had done. He had been unlearning their ways too long. Besides, he was too old.

A sudden sting pierced him at the thought of how old he was, and how young Hélène. Even if he lived to be seventy or eighty, she would still have a life left when he died. Yes, it was as Shaban said. They were getting old. He had never really felt the humiliation of it before. And Shaban had said, strangely, something else — that his own wife was safer than the Pasha's. Still he felt an odd compassion for Hélène, too — because she was young, and it was Judas-tree time, and she was married to gray hairs. And although he was a pasha, descended from great pashas, and she was only a little French girl *quelconque*, he felt more afraid than ever of making a fool of himself before her — when he had promised her that she should be as free as any other European woman, that she should live her life. Besides, what had the black man to do with their private affairs?

'Zümbül Agha,' he suddenly heard himself harshly saying, 'is this your house or mine? I have told you a hundred times that you are not to trouble the madama, or follow her about, or so much as guess where she is and what she is doing. I have kept you in the house because my father brought you into it; but if I ever hear of your speaking to madama again, or spying on her, I will send you into the street. Do you hear? Now get out!'

'*Aman*, my Pasha! I beg you!' entreated the eunuch. There was something ludicrous in his voice, coming as it did from his height.

The Pasha wondered if he had been too long a person of importance in the family to realize the change in his position, or whether he really —

All of a sudden a checkering of lamplight flickered through the dark window, touched the negro's black face for a moment, traveled up the wall. Silence fell again in the little room — a silence into which the fountain dropped its silver patter. Then steps mounted the porch and echoed in the other room, which lighted in turn, and a man came in sight, peering this way and that, with a big white accordeon lantern in his hand. Behind the man two other servants appeared, carrying on their heads round wooden trays covered by figured silks, and a boy tugging a huge basket. When they discovered the three in the little room they salaamed respectfully.

'Where shall we set the table?' asked the man with the lantern.

For the Pasha the lantern seemed to make the world more like the place he had always known. He turned to his wife apologetically.

'I told them to send dinner up here. It has been such a

long time since we came.   But I forgot about the table.
I don't believe there is one here.'

'No,' uttered Hélène from her sofa, sitting with her head
on her hand.

It was the first word she had spoken.   But, little as it
was, it reassured him, like the lantern.

'There is the chest,' hazarded Zümbül Agha.

The interruption of the servants had for the moment
distracted them all.   But the Pasha now turned on him so
vehemently that the eunuch salaamed in haste and went
away.

III

'Why not?' asked Hélène, when he was gone.   'We can
sit on cushions.'

'Why not?' echoed the Pasha.   Grateful as he was for
the interruption, he found himself wishing, secretly, that
Hélène had discouraged his idea of a picnic dinner.   And
he could not help feeling a certain constraint as he gave the
necessary orders and watched the servants put down their
paraphernalia and pull the chest into the middle of the
room.   There was something unreal and stage-like about
the scene, in the uncertain light of the lantern.   Obviously
the chest was not light.   It was an old cypress-wood chest
that they had always used in the summer, to keep furs in,
polished a bright brown, with a little inlaid pattern of dark
brown and cream color running around the edge of each
surface, and a more complicated design ornamenting the
centre of the cover.   He vaguely associated his mother
with it.   He felt a distinct relief when the men spread the
cloth.   He felt as if they had covered up more things than
he could name.   And when they produced candlesticks and
candles, and set them on the improvised table and in the

niches beside the door, he seemed to come back again into the comfortable light of common sense.

'This is the way we used to do when I was a boy,' he said with a smile, when he and Hélène established themselves on sofa cushions on opposite sides of the chest. 'Only then we had little tables six inches high, instead of big ones like this.'

'It is rather a pity that we have spoiled all that,' she said. 'Are we any happier for perching on chairs around great scaffoldings and piling the scaffoldings with so many kinds of porcelain and metal? After all, they knew how to live — the people who were capable of imagining a place like this. And they had the good taste not to fill a room with things. Your grandfather, was it?'

He had had a dread that she would not say anything, that she would remain silent and impenetrable, as she had been before Zümbül Agha, as if the chest between them were a barrier that nothing could surmount. His heart lightened when he heard her speak. Was it not quite her natural voice?

'It was my great-grandfather, the Grand Vizier. They say he did know how to live — in his way. He built the kiosque for a beautiful slave of his, a Greek, whom he called Pomegranate.'

'Madame Pomegranate? What a charming name! And that is why her cipher is everywhere. See?' She pointed to the series of cupboards and niches on either side of the door, dimly painted with pomegranate blossoms, and to the plaster reliefs around the hooded fireplace, and the cluster of pomegranates that made a centre to the gilt and painted lattice-work of the ceiling. 'One could be very happy in such a little house. It has an air — of being meant for moments. And you feel as if they had something to do with the wonderful way it has faded.' She

looked as if she had meant to say something else, which she
did not. But after a moment she added, 'Will you ask
them to turn off the water in the fountain? It is a little
chilly, now that the sun has gone, and it sounds like rain —
or tears.'

The dinner went, on the whole, not so badly. There
were dishes to be passed back and forth. There were
questions to be asked or comments to be made. There
were the servants to be spoken to. Yet, more and more,
the Pasha could not help wondering. When a silence fell,
too, he could not help listening. And least of all could he
help looking at Hélène. He looked at her, trying not to
look at her, with an intense curiosity, as if he had never
seen her before, asking himself if there were anything new
in her face, and how she would look if — Would she be like
this?

She made no attempt to keep up a flow of words, as if
to distract his attention. She was not soft either; she was
not trying to seduce him: And she made no show of gratitude toward him for having sent Zümbül Agha away.
Neither did she by so much as an inflection try to in-
sinuate or excuse or explain. She was what she always
was, perfect — and evidently a little tired. She was indeed more than perfect, she was prodigious, when he
asked her once what she was thinking about and she said
Pandora, tapping the chest between them. He had never
heard the story of that Greek girl and her box, and she told
him gravely about all the calamities that came out of it,
and the one gift of hope that remained behind.

'But I cannot be a Turkish woman long!' she added in-
consequently with a smile. 'My legs are asleep. I really
must walk about a little.'

When he had helped her to her feet she led the way into
the other room. They had their coffee and cigarettes

there. Hélène walked slowly up and down the length of
the room, stopping every now and then to look into the
square pool of the fountain and to pat her hair.

The Pasha sat down on the long low divan that ran under
the windows. He could watch her more easily now. And
the detachment with which he had begun to look at her
grew in spite of him into the feeling that he was looking at a
stranger. After all, what did he know about her? Who
was she? What had happened to her, during all the years
that he had not known her, in that strange free European
life which he had tried to imitate, and which at heart he
secretly distrusted? What had she ever really told him,
and what had he ever really divined of her? For perhaps
the first time in his life he realized how little one person
may know of another, particularly a man of a woman.
And he remembered Shaban again, and that phrase about
his wife being safer than Hélène. Had Shaban really
meant anything? Was Hélène 'safe'? He acknowledged
to himself at last that the question was there in his mind,
waiting to be answered.

Hélène did not help him. She had been standing for some
time at an odd angle to the pool, looking into it. He could
see her face there, with the eyes turned away from him.

'How mysterious a reflection is!' she said. 'It is so real
that you can't believe it disappears for good. How often
Madame Pomegranate must have looked into this pool,
and yet I can't find her in it. But I feel she is really there,
all the same — and who knows who else.'

'They say mirrors do not flatter,' the Pasha did not keep
himself from rejoining, 'but they are very discreet. They
tell no tales?'

Hélène raised her eyes. In the little room the servants
had cleared the improvised table and had packed up everything again except the candles.

'I have been up here a long time,' she said, 'and I am rather tired. It is a little cold, too. If you do not mind, I think I will go down to the house now, with the servants. You will hardly care to go so soon, for Zümbül Agha has not finished what he has to say to you.'

'Zümbül Agha!' exclaimed the Pasha. 'I sent him away.'

'Ah, but you must know him well enough to be sure he would not go. Let us see.' She clapped her hands. The servant of the lantern immediately came out to her. 'Will you ask Zümbül Agha to come here?' she said. 'He is on the porch.'

The man went to the door, looked out, and said a word. Then he stood aside with a respectful salaam, and the eunuch entered. He negligently returned the salute and walked forward until his air of importance changed to one of humility at sight of the Pasha. Salaaming in turn, he stood with his hands folded in front of him.

'I will go down with you,' said the Pasha to his wife, rising. 'It is too late for you to go through the woods in the dark.'

'Nonsense!' She gave him a look that had more in it than the tone in which she added, 'Please do not. I shall be perfectly safe with four servants. You can tell them not to let me run away.' Coming nearer, she put her hand into the bosom of her dress, then stretched out the hand toward him. 'Here is the key — the key of Pandora's box. Will you keep it for me please? Au revoir.'

And making a sign to the servants she walked out of the kiosque.

IV

The Pasha was too surprised, at first, to move — and too conscious of the eyes of servants, too uncertain of what he should do, too fearful of doing the wrong, the un-European, thing. And afterwards it was too late. He stood watching until the flicker of the lantern disappeared among the dark trees. Then his eyes met the eunuch's.

'Why don't you go down too?' suggested Zümbül Agha. The variable climate of a great house had made him too perfect an opportunist not to take the line of being in favor again. 'It might be better. Give me the key and I will do what there is to do. But you might send up Shaban.'

Why not? the Pasha secretly asked himself. Might it not be the best way out? At the same time he experienced a certain revulsion of feeling, now that Hélène was gone, in the way she had gone. She really was prodigious! And with the vanishing of the lantern which had brought him a measure of reassurance he felt the weight of an uncleared situation, fantastic but crucial, heavy upon him. And the Negro annoyed him intensely.

'Thank you, Zümbül Agha,' he replied, 'but I am not the nurse of madama, and I will not give you the key.'

If he only might, though, he thought to himself again!

'You believe her, this Frank woman whom you had never seen five years ago, and you do not believe me who have lived in your house longer than you can remember!'

The eunuch said it so bitterly that the Pasha was touched in spite of himself. He had never been one to think very much about minor personal relations, but even at such a moment he could see — was it partly because he wanted more time to make up his mind? — that he had never liked Zümbül Agha as he liked Shaban, for instance. Yet more honor had been due, in the old family tradition, to the former. And he had been associated even longer with the history of the house.

'My poor Zümbül,' he uttered musingly, 'you have never forgiven me for marrying her.'

'My Pasha, you are not the first to marry an unbeliever, nor the last. But such a marriage should be to the glory of Islam, and not to its discredit. Who can trust her? She is still a Christian. And she is too young. She has turned the world upside down. What would your father have said to a daughter-in-law who goes shamelessly into the street without a veil, alone, and who receives in your house men who are no relation to you or her? It is not right. Women only understand one thing, to make fools of men. And they are never content to fool one.'

The Pasha, still waiting to make up his mind, let his fancy linger about Zümbül Agha. It was really rather absurd, after all, what a part women played in the world, and how little it all came to in the end! Did the black man, he wondered, walk in a clearer, cooler world, free of the clouds, the iridescences, the languors, the perfumes, the strange obsessions, that made others walk so often like madmen? Or might some tatter of preposterous humanity still work obscurely in him? Or a bitterness of not being like other men? That perhaps was why the Pasha felt friendlier toward Shaban. They were more alike.

'You are right, Zümbül Agha,' he said, 'the world is upside down. But neither the madama nor any of us made it so. All we can do is try and keep our heads as it turns. Now, will you please tell me how you happened to be up here? The madama never told you to come. You know perfectly well that the customs of Europe are different from ours, and that she does not like to have you follow her about.'

'What woman likes to be followed about?' retorted the eunuch with a sly smile. 'I know you have told me to leave her alone. But why was I brought into this house? Am I to stand by and watch dishonor brought upon it simply because you have eaten the poison of a woman?'

'Zümbül Agha,' replied the Pasha sharply, 'I am not discussing old and new or this and that, but I am asking you to tell me what all this speech is about.'

'Give me that key and I will show you what it is about,' said the eunuch, stepping forward.

But the Pasha found that he was not ready to go so directly to the point.

'Can't you answer a simple question?' he demanded irritably, retreating to the farther side of the fountain.

The reflection of the painted ceiling in the pool made him think of Hélène — and Madame Pomegranate. He stared into the still water as if to find Hélène's face there. Was any other face hidden beside it, mocking him?

But Zümbül Agha had begun again, doggedly: —

'I came here because it is my business to be here. I went to town this morning. When I got back they told me that you were away and that the madama was up here, alone. So I came. Is this a place for a woman to be alone in — a young woman, with men working all about, and I don't know who, and a thousand ways of getting in and out from the hills, and ten thousand hiding-places in the woods?'

The Pasha made a gesture of impatience, and turned away. But after all, what could one do with old Zümbül? He had been brought up in his tradition. The Pasha lighted another cigarette to help himself think.

'Well, I came up here,' continued the eunuch, 'and as I came I heard madama singing. You know how she sings the songs of the Franks.'

The Pasha knew. But he did not say anything. As he walked up and down, smoking and thinking, his eye caught in the pool a reflection from the other side of the room, where the door of the latticed room was, and where the cypress-wood chest stood as the servants had left it in the middle of the floor. Was that what Hélène had stood looking at so long? he asked himself. He wondered that he could have sat beside it so quietly. It seemed now like something dark and dangerous crouching there in the shadow of the little room.

'I sat down, under the terrace,' he heard the eunuch go on, 'where no one could see me, and I listened. And after she had stopped I heard —'

'Never mind what you heard,' broke in the Pasha. 'I have heard enough.'

He was ashamed — ashamed and resolved. He felt as if he had been playing the spy with Zümbül Agha. And after all, there was a simple way to answer his question for himself. He threw away his cigarette, went into the little room, bent over the chest, and fitted the key into the lock.

Just then a nightingale burst out singing, but so near and so loud that he started and looked over his shoulder. In an instant he collected himself, feeling the black man's eyes upon his. Yet he could not suppress the train of association started by the impassioned trilling of the bird, even as he began to turn the key of the chest where his mother used to keep her quaint old furs and embroideries. The irony of the contrast paralyzed his hand for a strange moment, and of the difference between this spring night and other spring nights when nightingales had sung. And what if, after all, only calamity were to come out of the chest, and he were to lose his last gift of hope? Ah! He knew at last what he would do! He quickly withdrew the key from the lock, stood up straight again, and looked at Zümbül Agha.

'Go down and get Shaban,' he ordered, 'and don't come back.'

The eunuch stared. But if he had anything to say, he concluded not to say it. He saluted silently and went away.

V

The Pasha sat down on the divan and lighted a cigarette. Almost immediately the nightingale stopped singing. For a few moments Zümbül Agha's steps could be heard outside. Then it became very still. The Pasha did not like it. Look which way he would, he could not help seeing the chest — or listening. He got up and went into the big room, where he turned on the water of the fountain. The falling drops made company for him, and kept him from looking for lost reflections. But they presently made him think of what Hélène had said about them. He went out to the porch and sat down on the steps. In front of him the pines lifted their great dark canopies against the stars. Other stars twinkled between the trunks, far below, where the shore lights of the Bosphorus were.

It was so still that water sounds came faintly up to him, and every now and then he could even hear nightingales on the European side. Another nightingale began singing in his own woods—the same one that had told him what to do, he said to himself. What other things the nightingales had sung to him, years ago! And how long the pines had listened there, still strong and green and rugged and alive, while he, and how many before him, sat under them for a little while and then went away!

Presently he heard steps on the drive and Shaban came, carrying something dark in his hand.

'What is that?' asked the Pasha, as Shaban held it out.

'A revolver, my Pasha. Zümbül Agha told me you wanted it.'

The Pasha laughed curtly.

'Zümbül made a mistake. What I want is a shovel, or a couple of them. Can you find such a thing without asking any one?'

'Yes, my Pasha,' replied the Albanian promptly, laying the revolver on the steps and disappearing again. And it was not long before he was back with the desired imple- ments.

'We must dig a hole, somewhere, Shaban,' said his master in a low voice. 'It must be in a place where people are not likely to go, but not too far from the kiosque.'

Shaban immediately started toward the trees at the back of the house. The Pasha followed him silently into a path that wound through the wood. A nightingale began to sing again, very near them — *the* nightingale, thought the Pasha.

'He is telling us where to go,' he said.

Shaban permitted himself a low laugh.

'I think he is telling his mistress where to go. However, we will go too.'

And they did, bearing away to one side of the path till they came to the foot of the tall cypress.

'This will do,' said the Pasha, 'if the roots are not in the way.'

Without a word Shaban began to dig. The Pasha took the other spade. To the simple Albanian it was nothing out of the ordinary. What was extraordinary was that his master was able to keep it up, soft as the loam was under the trees. The most difficult thing about it was that they could not see what they were doing, except by the light of an occasional match. But at last the Pasha judged the ragged excavation of sufficient depth. Then he led the way back to the kiosque.

They found Zümbül Agha in the little room, sitting on the sofa with a revolver in either hand.

'I thought I told you not to come back!' exclaimed the Pasha sternly.

'Yes,' faltered the old eunuch, 'but I was afraid something might happen to you. So I waited below the pines.
And when you went away into the woods with Shaban, I
came here to watch.' He lifted a revolver significantly.
'I found the other one on the steps.'

'Very well,' said the Pasha at length, more kindly. He
even found it in him at that moment to be amused at the
picture the black man made, in his sedate frock coat, with
his two weapons. And Zümbül Agha found no less to look
at, in the appearance of his master's clothes. 'But now
there is no need for you to watch any longer,' added the
latter. 'If you want to watch, do it at the bottom of the
hill. Don't let any one come up here.'

'On my head,' said the eunuch.

He saw that Shaban, as usual, was trusted more than
he. But it was not for him to protest against the ingratitude of masters. He salaamed and backed out of the room.

When he was gone the Pasha turned to Shaban.

'This box, Shaban — you see this box? It has become
a trouble to us, and I am going to take it out there.'

The Albanian nodded gravely. He took hold of one of
the handles, to judge the weight of the chest. He lifted his
eyebrows.

'Can you help me put it on my back?' he asked.

'Don't try to do that, Shaban. We will carry it together.'

The Pasha took hold of the other handle. When they got
as far as the outer door he let down his end. It was not
light.

'Wait a minute, Shaban. Let us shut up the kiosque,
so that no one will notice anything.'

He went back to blow out the candles. Then he thought
of the fountain. He caught a last play of broken images
in the pool as he turned off the water. When he had put

out the lights and groped his way to the door, he found that Shaban was already gone with the chest. A drop of water made a strange echo behind him in the kiosque. He locked the door and hurried after Shaban, who had succeeded in getting the chest on his back. Nor would Shaban let the Pasha help him till they came to the edge of the wood. There, carrying the chest between them, they stumbled through the trees to the place that was ready.

'Now we must be careful,' said the Pasha. 'It might slip or get stuck.'

'But are you going to bury the box too?' demanded Shaban, for the first time showing surprise.

'Yes,' answered the Pasha. And he added, 'It is the box I want to get rid of.'

'It is a pity,' remarked Shaban regretfully. 'It is a very good box. However, you know. Now then!'

There was a scraping and a muffled thud, followed by a fall of earth and small stones on wood. The Pasha wondered if he would hear anything else. But first one and then another nightingale began to fill the night with their April madness.

'Ah, there are two of them,' remarked Shaban. 'She will take the one that says the sweetest things to her.'

The Pasha's reply was to throw a spadeful of earth on the chest. Shaban joined him with such vigor that the hole was soon very full.

'We are old, my Pasha, but we are good for something yet,' said Shaban. 'I will hide the shovels here in the bushes,' he added, 'and early in the morning I will come again, before any of those lazy gardeners are up, and fix it so that no one will ever know.'

There at least was a person of whom one could be sure! The Pasha realized that gratefully, as they walked back through the park. He did not feel like talking, but at least he felt the satisfaction of having done what he had decided to do. He remembered Zümbül Agha as they neared the bottom of the hill. The eunuch had taken his commission more seriously than it had been given, however, or he preferred not to be seen. Perhaps he wanted to reconnoitre again on top of the hill.

'I don't think I will go in just yet,' said the Pasha as they crossed the bridge into the lower garden. 'I am rather dirty. And I would like to rest a little under the chestnut trees. Would you get me an overcoat please, Shaban, and a brush of some kind? And you might bring me a coffee, too.'

How tired he was! And what a short time it was, yet what an eternity, since he last dropped into one of the wicker chairs! He felt for his cigarettes. As he did so he discovered something else in his pocket, something small and hard that at first he did not recognize. Then he remembered the key — the key. — He suddenly tossed it into the pool beside him. It made a sharp little splash, which was reëchoed by the dripping basins. He got up and felt in the ivy for the handle that shut off the water. At the end of the garden the Bosphorus lapped softly in the dark. Far away, up in the wood, the nightingales were singing.

LITTLE SELVES

BY MARY LERNER

MARGARET O'BRIEN, a great-aunt and seventy-five, knew she was near the end. She did not repine, for she had had a long, hard life and she was tired. The young priest who brought her communion had administered the last rites—holy oils on her eyelids (Lord, forgive her the sins of seeing!); holy oils on her lips (Lord, forgive her the sins of speaking!), on her ears, on her knotted hands, on her weary feet. Now she was ready, though she knew the approach of the dread presence would mean greater suffering. So she folded quiet hands beneath her heart, there where no child had ever lain, yet where now something grew and fattened on her strength. And she seemed given over to pleasant revery.

Neighbors came in to see her, and she roused herself and received them graciously, with a personal touch for each. — 'And has your Julia gone to New York, Mrs. Carty? Nothing would do her but she must be going, I suppose. 'T was the selfsame way with me, when I was coming out here from the old country. Full of money the streets were, I used to be thinking. Well, well; the hills far away are green.'

Or to Mrs. Devlin: 'Terence is at it again, I see by the look of you. Poor man! There's no holding him? Eh, woman dear! Thirst is the end of drinking and sorrow is the end of love.'

If her visitors stayed longer than a few minutes, however, her attention wandered; her replies became cryptic. She would murmur something about 'all the seven parishes,'

or the Wicklow hills, or 'the fair cove of Cork tippy-toe into
the ocean'; then fall into silence, smiling, eyes closed, yet
with a singular look of attention.   At such times, her callers
would whisper: 'Glory b' t' God! she's so near it there's no
fun in it,' and slip out soberly into the kitchen.

Her niece, Anna Lennan, mother of a fine brood of children, would stop work for the space of a breath and enjoy
a bit of conversation.

'Ain't she failing, though, the poor afflicted creature!'
Mrs. Hanley cried one day.   'Her mind is going back on
her already.'

'Are you of that opinion?   I'm thinking she's mind
enough yet, when she wants to attend; but mostly she's
just drawn into herself, as busy as a bee about something,
whatever it is that she's turning over in her head day in,
day out.   She sleeps scarce a wink for all she lies there so
quiet, and, in the night, my man and I hear her talking to
herself.   "No, no," she'll say.   "I've gone past.   I must
be getting back to the start."   Or, another time, "This is
it, now.   If I could be stopping!"'

'And what do you think she is colloguing about?'

'There's no telling.   Himself does be saying it's in an
elevator she is, but that's because he puts in the day churning up and down in one of the same.   What else can you
expect?   'T is nothing but "Going up! going down!" with
him all night as it is.   Betune the two of them they have
me fair destroyed with their traveling.   "Are you lacking
anything, Aunt Margaret?"   I call out to her.   "I am
not," she answers, impatient-like.   "Don't be ever fussing
and too-ing, will you?"'

'Tch! tch!'

'And do you suppose the children are a comfort to her?
Sorra bit.   Just a look at them and she wants to be alone.

"Take them away, let you," says she, shutting her eyes. "The others is realer." '

'And you think she's in her right mind all the same?'

'I do. 'T is just something she likes to be thinking over — something she's fair dotty about. Why, it's the same when Father Flint is here. Polite and riverintial at the first, then impatient, and, if the poor man doesn't be taking the hint, she just closes up shop and off again into her whimsies. You'd swear she was in fear of missing something?'

The visitor, being a young wife, had an explanation to hazard. 'If she was a widow woman, now, or married — perhaps she had a liking for somebody once. Perhaps she might be trying to imagine them young days over again. Do you think could it be that?'

Anna shook her head. 'My mother used to say she was a born old maid. All *she* wanted was work and saving her bit of money, and to church every minute she could be sparing.'

'Still, you can't be telling. 'T is often that kind weeps sorest when 't is too late. My own old aunt used to cry, "If I could be twenty-five again, would n't I do different!" '

'Maybe, maybe, though I doubt could it be so.'

Nor was it so. The old woman, lying back so quietly among her pillows, with closed eyes, yet with that look of singular intentness and concentration, was seeking no lover of her youth; though, indeed, she had had one once, and from time to time he did enter her revery, try as she would to prevent him. At that point, she always made the singular comment, 'Gone past! I must be getting back to the beginning,' and, pressing back into her earliest consciousness, she would remount the flooding current of the years. Each time, she hoped to get further, — though remoter shapes were illusive, and, if approached too closely, vanished, — for, once embarked on her river of memories, the descent was relentlessly swift. How tantalizing that swiftness! However she yearned to linger, she was rushed along till, all too soon, she sailed into the common light of day. At that point, she always put about, and laboriously recommenced the ascent.

To-day, something her niece had said about Donnybrook Fair — for Anna, too, was a child of the old sod — seemed to swell out with a fair wind the sails of her visionary bark. She closed her mind to all familiar shapes and strained back — way, way back, concentrating all her powers in an effort of will. For a bit she seemed to hover in populous space. This did not disturb her; she had experienced the same thing before. It simply meant that she had mounted pretty well up to the fountain-head. The figures, when they did come, would be the ones she most desired.

At last, they began to take shape, tenuously at first, then of fuller body, each bringing its own setting, its own atmospheric suggestion — whether of dove-feathered Irish cloud and fresh greensward, sudden downpour, or equally sudden clearing, with continual leafy drip, drip, drip, in the midst of brilliant sunshine.

For Margaret O'Brien, ardent summer sunlight seemed suddenly to pervade the cool, orderly little bed-chamber. Then, 'Here she is!' and a wee girl of four danced into view, wearing a dress of pink print, very tight at the top and very full at the bottom. She led the way to a tiny new house whence issued the cheery voice of hammers. Lumber and tools were lying round; from within came men's voices. The small girl stamped up the steps and looked in. Then she made for the narrow stair.

'Where's Margaret gone to?' said one of the men. 'The upper floor's not finished. It's falling through the young one will be.'

'Peggy!' called the older man. 'Come down here with you.'

There was a delighted squeal. The pink dress appeared at the head of the stairs. 'Oh, the funny little man, daddy! Such a funny little old man with a high hat! Come quick, let you, and see him.'

The two men ran to the stairs.

'Where is he?'

She turned back and pointed. Then her face fell. 'Gone! the little man is gone!'

Her father laughed and picked her up in his arms. 'How big was he, Peg? As big as yourself, I wonder?'

'No, no! Small.'

'As big as the baby?'

She considered a moment. 'Yes, just as big as that. But a man, da.'

'Well, why are n't you after catching him and holding him for ransom? 'T is pots and pots o' gold they've hidden away, the little people, and will be paying a body what he asks to let them go.'

She pouted, on the verge of tears. 'I want him to come back.'

'I mistrust he won't be doing that, the leprechaun. Once you take your eye away, it's off with him for good and all.'

Margaret O'Brien hugged herself with delight. *That* was a new one; she had never got back that far before. Yet how well she remembered it all! She seemed to smell the woody pungency of the lumber, the limey odor of white-wash from the field-stone cellar.

The old woman's dream went on. Out of the inexhausti-ble storehouse of the past, she summoned, one by one, her much-loved memories. There was a pig-tailed Margaret in bonnet and shawl, trudging to school one wintry day.

She had seen many wintry school-days, but this one stood out by reason of the tears she had shed by the way. She saw the long benches, the slates, the charts, the tall teacher at his desk. With a swelling of the throat, she saw the little girl sob out her declaration: 'I'm not for coming no more, Mr. Wilde.'

'What's that, Margaret? And why not? Have n't I been good to you?'

Tears choked the child. 'Oh, Mr. Wilde, it's just because you're so terrible good to me. They say you are trying to make a Protestant out of me. So I'll not be coming no more.'

The tall man drew the little girl to his knee and reassured her. Margaret O'Brien could review that scene with tender delight now. She had not been forced to give up her beloved school. Mr. Wilde had explained to her that her brothers were merely teasing her because she was so quick and such a favorite.

A little Margaret knelt on the cold stone floor at church and stared at the pictured saints or heard the budding branches rustle in the orchard outside. Another Margaret, a little taller, begged for a new sheet of ballads every time her father went to the fair. — There were the long flimsy sheets, with closely printed verses. These you must adapt to familiar tunes. This Margaret, then, swept the hearth and stacked the turf and sang from her bench in the chimney-corner. Sometimes it was something about 'the little old red coat me father wore,' which was 'All buttons, buttons, buttons, buttons; all buttons down before'; or another beginning, —

> 'O, dear, what can the matter be?
>   Johnnie's so long at the fair!
> He promised to buy me a knot of blue ribbon
>   To tie up my bonny brown hair.'

Then there was a picture of the time the fairies actually bewitched the churn, and, labor as you might, no butter would form, not the least tiny speck. Margaret and her mother took the churn apart and examined every part of it. Nothing out of the way. ' 'T is the fairies is in it,' her mother said. 'All Souls' Day a-Friday. Put out a saucer of cream the night for the little people, let you.' A well-grown girl in a blue cotton frock, the long braids of her black hair whipping about her in the windy evening, set out the cream on the stone flags before the low doorway, wasting no time in getting in again. The next day, how the butter 'came'! Hardly started they were, when they could feel it forming. When Margaret washed the dasher, she 'kept an eye out' for the dark corners of the room, for the air seemed thronged and murmurous.

After this picture, came always the same tall girl still in the same blue frock, this time with a shawl on her head. She brought in potatoes from the sheltered heaps that wintered out in the open. From one pailful she picked out a little flat stone, rectangular and smoother and more evenly proportioned than any stone she had ever seen.

'What a funny stone!' she said to her mother.

Her mother left carding her wool to look. 'You may well say so. 'T is one of the fairies' tables. Look close and you'll be turning up their little chairs as well.'

It was as her mother said. Margaret found four smaller stones of like appearance, which one might well imagine to be stools for tiny dolls.

'Shall I be giving them to little Bee for playthings?'

'You will not. You'll be putting them outside. In the morning, though you may be searching the countryside, no trace of them will you find, for the fairies will be taking them again.'

So Margaret stacked the fairy table and chairs outside.

Next morning, she ran out half reluctantly, for she was afraid she would find them and that would spoil the story. But, no! they were gone. She never saw them again, though she searched in all imaginable places. Nor was that the last potato heap to yield these mysterious stones.

Margaret, growing from scene to scene, appeared again in a group of laughing boys and girls.

'What'll we play now?'

'Let's write the ivy test.'

'Here's leaves.'

Each wrote a name on a leaf and dropped it into a jar of water. Next morning, Margaret, who had misgivings, stole down early and searched for her leaf. Yes, the die was cast! At the sight of its bruised surface, ready tears flooded her eyes. She had written the name of her little grandmother, and the condition of the leaf foretold death within the year. The other leaves were unmarred. She quickly destroyed the ill-omened bit of ivy and said nothing about it, though the children clamored. 'There's one leaf short. Whose is gone?' 'Mine is there!' 'Is it yours, John?' 'Is it yours, Esther?' But Margaret kept her counsel, and, within the year, the little grandmother was dead. Of course, she was old, though vigorous; yet Margaret would never play that game again. It was like gambling with fate.

And still the girls kept swinging past. Steadily, all too swiftly, Margaret shot up to a woman's stature; her skirts crept down, her braids ought to have been bobbed up behind. She let them hang, however, and still ran with the boys, questing the bogs, climbing the apple trees, storming the wind-swept hills. Her mother would point to her sister Mary, who, though younger, sat now by the fire with her 'spriggin'' [embroidery] for 'the quality.' Mary could crochet, too, and had a fine range of 'shamrogue' patterns.   So the mother would chide Margaret.

'What kind of a girl are you, at all, to be ever lepping and tearing like a redshanks [deer]?   'T is high time for you to be getting sensible and learning something.   Whistles and scouting-guns is all you're good for, and there's no silver in them things as far as I can see.'

What fine whistles she contrived out of the pithy willow shoots in the spring!   And the scouting-guns hollowed out of elder-stalks, which they charged with water from the brook by means of wadded sticks, working piston-wise! They would hide behind a hedge and bespatter enemies and friends alike.   Many's the time they got their ears warmed in consequence or went supperless to bed, pretending not to see the table spread with baked potatoes, — 'laughing potatoes,' they called them, because they were ever splitting their sides,—besides delicious buttermilk, freshly-laid eggs, oat-cakes and fresh butter.   'A child without supper is two to breakfast,' their mother would say, smiling, when she saw them 'tackle' their stirabout the next day.

How full of verve and life were all these figures!   That glancing creature grow old?   How could such things be! The sober pace of maturity even seemed out of her star. Yet here she was, growing up, for all her reluctance.   An awkward gossoon leaned over the gate in the moonlight, though she was indoors, ready to hide.   But nobody noticed her alarm.

'There's that long-legged McMurray lad again; scouting after Mary, I'll be bound,' said her mother, all unawares.

But it was not Mary that he came for, though she married him just the same, and came out to America with their children some years after her sister's lone pilgrimage.

The intrusion of Jerry McMurray signaled the grounding of her dream-bark on the shoals of reality.   Who cared

about the cut-and-dried life of a grown woman? Enchant-
ment now lay behind her, and, if the intervals between
periods of pain permitted, she again turned an expectant
face toward the old childish visions. Sometimes she could
make the trip twice over without being overtaken by suffering. But her intervals of comfort grew steadily shorter;
frequently she was interrupted before she could get rightly
launched on her delight. And always there seemed to be
one vision more illusive than the rest which she particularly
longed to recapture. At last, chance words of Anna's put
her on its trail in this wise.

When she was not, as her niece said, 'in her trance, wool-
gathering,' Anna did her best to distract her, sending the
children in to ask 'would she have a sup of tea now,' or a
taste of wine jelly. One day, after the invalid had spent a
bad night, she brought in her new long silk coat for her
aunt's inspection, for the old woman had always been
'tasty' and 'dressy,' and had made many a fine gown in
her day. The sharp old eyes lingered on the rich and truly
striking braid ornament that secured the loose front of the
garment.

'What's that plaster?' she demanded, disparagingly.

Anna, inclined to be wroth, retorted: 'I suppose you'd be
preferring one o' them tight ganzy [sweater] things that fit
the figger like a jersey, all buttoned down before.'

A sudden light flamed in the old face. 'I have it!' she
cried. ' 'T is what I've been seeking this good while. 'T
will come now — the red coat! I must be getting back to
the beginning.'

With that, she was off, relaxing and composing herself, as
if surrendering to the spell of a hypnotist.

To reach any desired picture in her gallery, she must
start at the outset. Then they followed on, in due order —
all that procession of little girls: pink clad, blue-print clad,

bare-legged or brogan-shod; flirting their short skirts, plait-
ing their heavy braids. About half way along, a new figure
asserted itself — a girl of nine or ten, who twisted this way
and that before a blurred bit of mirror and frowned at the
red coat that flapped about her heels, — bought oversize,
you may be sure, so that she should n't grow out of it too
soon. The sleeves swallowed her little brown hands, the
shoulders and back were grotesquely sack-like, the front
had a puss [pout] on it.

' 'T is the very fetch of Paddy the gander I am in it.
I'll not be wearing it so.' She frowned with sudden intentness. 'Could I be fitting it a bit, I wonder, the way mother
does cut down John's coats for Martin?'

With needle, scissors and thread, she crept up to her little
chamber under the eaves. It was early in the forenoon
when she set to work ripping. The morning passed, and
the dinner hour.

'Peggy! Where's the girl gone to, I wonder?'

'To Aunt Theresa's, I'm thinking.'

'Well, it's glad I am she's out o' my sight, for my hands
itched to be shaking her. Stand and twist herself inside
out she did, fussing over the fit of the good coat I'm after
buying her. The little fustherer!'

For the small tailoress under the roof, the afternoon sped
on winged feet: pinning, basting, and stitching; trying on,
ripping out again, and re-fitting. 'I'll be taking it in a
wee bit more.' She had to crowd up to the window to
catch the last of the daylight. At dusk, she swept her dark
hair from her flushed cheeks and forced her sturdy body into
the red coat. It was a 'fit,' believe you me! Modeled on
the lines of the riding-habit of a full-figured lady she had
seen hunting about the country-side, it buttoned up tight
over her flat, boyish chest and bottled up her squarish little
waist. About her narrow hips, it rippled out in a short

'frisk.' Beneath, her calico skirt, and bramble-scratched brown legs.

Warmed with triumph, she flew downstairs. Her mother and a neighbor were sitting in the glow of the peat fire. She tried to meet them with assurance, but at sight of their amazed faces, misgiving clutched her. She pivoted before the mirror.

'Holy hour!' cried her mother. 'What sausage-skin is that you've got into?' Then, as comprehension grew: 'Glory b' t' God, Ellen! 't is the remains of the fine new coat, I'm after buying her, large enough to last her the next five years!'

' 'T was too large!' the child whimpered. 'A gander I looked in it!' Then, cajolingly, 'I'm but after taking it in a bit, ma. 'T will do grand now, and maybe I'll not be getting much fatter. Look at the fit of it, just!'

'Fit! God save the mark!' cried her mother.

'Is the child after making that jacket herself?' asked the neighbor.

'I am,' Margaret spoke up, defiantly. 'I cut it and shaped it and put it together. It has even a frisk to the tail.'

'Maggie,' said the neighbor to Margaret's mother. ' 'T is as good a piece o' work for a child of her years as ever I see. You ought not to be faulting her, she's done that well. And,' bursting into irrepressible laughter, 'it's herself will have to be wearing it, woman dear! All she needs now is a horse and a side-saddle to be an equeestrieen!'

So the wanton destruction of the good red coat — in that house where good coats were sadly infrequent — ended with a laugh after all. How long she wore that tight jacket, and how grand she felt in it, let the other children laugh as they would!

What joy the old woman took in this incident! With its

fullness of detail, it achieved a delicious suggestion of per-
manence, in contrast to the illusiveness of other isolated
moments. Margaret O'Brien *saw* all these other figures,
but she really *was* the child with the red coat. In the long
years between, she had fashioned many fine dresses —
gowned gay girls for their conquests and robed fair brides
for the altar. Of all these, nothing now remained; but she
could feel the good stuff of the red kersey under her little
needle-scratched fingers, and see the glow of its rich color
against her wind-kissed brown cheek.

'To the life!' she exclaimed aloud, exultantly. 'To the
very life!'

'What life, Aunt Margaret?' asked Anna, with gentle
solicitude. 'Is it afraid of the end you are, darling?'

'No, no, asthore. I've resigned myself long since, though
't was bitter knowledge at the outset. Well, well, God is
good and we can't live forever.'

Her eyes, opening to the two flaring patent gas-burners,
winked as if she had dwelt long in a milder light. 'What's
all this glare about?' she asked, playfully. 'I guess the
chandler's wife is dead. Snuff out the whole of them staring candles, let you. 'T is daylight yet; just the time o'
day I always did like the best.'

Anna obeyed and sat down beside the bed in the soft
spring dusk. A little wind crept in under the floating white
curtains, bringing with it the sweetness of new grass and
pear-blossoms from the trim yard. It seemed an interval
set apart from the hurrying hours of the busy day for rest
and thought and confidences — an open moment. The old
woman must have felt its invitation, for she turned her head
and held out a shy hand to her niece.

'Anna, my girl, you imagine 't is the full o' the moon
with me, I'm thinking. But, no, never woman was more in
her right mind than I. Do you want I should be telling

you what I've been hatching these many long days and nights? 'T will be a good laugh for you, I'll go bail.'

And, as best she could, she gave the trend of her imaginings.

Anna did not laugh, however. Instead — with the ever-ready sympathy and comprehension of the Celt — she showed brimming eyes. ' 'T is a thought I've often myself, let me tell you,' she admitted. 'Of all the little girls that were me, and now can be living no longer.'

'You've said it!' cried the old woman, delighted at her unexpected responsiveness. 'Only with me, 't is fair pit-'yus. There's all those poor dear lasses there's nobody but me left to remember, and soon there'll not be even that. Sometimes they seem to be pleading just not to be forgotten, so I have to be keeping them alive in my head. I'm succeeding, too, and, if you'll believe me, 't is them little whips seem to be the real ones, and the live children here the shadders.' Her voice choked with sudden tears. 'They're all the children ever I had. My grief! that I'll have to be leaving them! They'll die now, for no man lives who can remember them any more.'

Anna's beauty, already fading with the cares of house and children, seemed to put on all its former fresh charm. She leaned forward with girlish eagerness. 'Auntie Margaret,' she breathed, with new tenderness, 'there's many a day left you yet. I'll be sitting here aside of you every evening at twilight just, and you can be showing me the lasses you have in mind. Many's the time my mother told me of the old place, and I can remember it well enough myself, though I was the youngest of the lot. So you can be filling it with all of our people — Mary and Margaret, John, Martin and Esther, Uncle Sheamus and the rest. I'll see them just as clear as yourself, for I've a place in my head where pictures come as thick and sharp as stars on a frosty night, when I get thinking. Then, with me ever calling them up, they'll be dancing and stravaging about till doomsday.'

So the old woman had her heart's desire. She recreated her earlier selves and passed them on, happy in the thought that she was saving them from oblivion. 'Do you mind that bold lass clouting her pet bull, now?' she would ask, with delight, speaking more and more as if of a third person. 'And that other hussy that's after making a ganzy out of her good coat? I'd admire to have the leathering of that one.'

Still the old woman lingered, a good month beyond her allotted time. As spring ripened, the days grew long. In the slow-fading twilights, the two women set their stage, gave cues for entrances and exits. Over the white counterpane danced the joyous figures, so radiant, so incredibly young, the whole cycle of a woman's girlhood. Grown familiar now, they came of their own accord, soothing her hours of pain with their laughing beauty, or, suddenly contemplative, assisting with seemly decorum at her devotional ecstasies.

'A saintly woman,' the young priest told Anna on one of the last days. 'She will make a holy end. Her meditations must be beautiful, for she has the true light of Heaven on her face. She looks as if she heard already the choiring of the angels.'

And Anna, respectfully agreeing, kept her counsel. He was a good and sympathetic man and a priest of God, but, American-born, he was, like her stolid, kindly husband, outside the magic circle of comprehension. 'He sees nothing, poor man,' she thought, indulgently. 'But he does mean well.' So she set her husband to 'mind' the young ones, and, easily doffing the sordid preoccupations of every day, slipped back into the enchanted ring.

THE FAILURE

BY CHARLES CALDWELL DOBIE

I

AT an unearthly hour in the morning John Scidmore sat
up suddenly in his bed and remembered Julia Norris's telephone message. He rose at once, switched on the shaded
light on the bureau, and looked at his watch: the minute
hand had just swung past three o'clock.

Undisturbed by her husband's nocturnal prowling, Kitty
Scidmore slept with almost childish naturalness. He
plunged the room into darkness again and felt his way out
into the hall and down the short flight of stairs to the
dining-room.

The night was unusually warm. As he opened the garden window, pungent odors of dry stubble wet with a late
October dew floated toward him. He leaned out and drew
in a deep breath, but his attempts at calmness failed
utterly.

He knew that it was absurd to fret; he might just as
well go back to bed and sleep peacefully. One could not
place a line of insurance at three o'clock in the morning.
Upon what day had Julia Norris telephoned? Was it last
Friday? Yes, he remembered now, perfectly. He had
been busy with a peevish customer who haggled about a
twenty-five-cent overcharge. In the midst of the con-
troversy, in her characteristically impulsive way, Julia
Norris had rung up:—

'O John! is that you, John? Place ten thousand dollars
with the Falcon Insurance Company on my flats in the
Richmond District.'

He had recognized her voice even before she gave her name. And he had been *so sure* he would not forget. Why, he had been so *very* sure that he had not troubled to make a memorandum. And to think that the excitement of arguing a twenty-five-cent overcharge should have so completely put to rout Julia Norris's order!

A sudden rage at his carelessness seized him. How he loathed his life, his work, and the soul-killing routine and cramped vision of the figurative counting-house! He switched on the light and peered into the mirror over the mantel, smiling satirically at the reflection greeting him, — the reflection of plain Johnny Scidmore, insurance broker's clerk, a commonplace, rather undersized, law-abiding citizen just turning forty, whose face showed the lack of that forceful ability necessary to convert opportunity into success.

As he drew back from the glass with a shrug of disgust, the futility of his life flashed over him. He still could remember the time when he went blithely to the day's work, buoyed by youth's intangible hope of better things. But the years soon took their toll of enthusiasm, and there were days when John Scidmore went through his paces like a trick horse urged by the whip of necessity. Lately he had been worried to find how easily he was forgetting things — telephone messages, instructions from his chief, orders to place insurance. So far nothing very important had slipped by him, but now he felt quite sure that he could never trust himself again. There were many reasons why he should have remembered Julia Norris's orders. First, because she was his wife's friend; second, because a ten-thousand-dollar order to his credit was not an everyday occurrence; and third, because the circumstance that had overshadowed it was relatively of so little importance.

For over a week, then, Julia Norris's property had gone

without insurance protection. What if it had burned up?
What if it were burning up at this very moment? He sat
down suddenly.

He got up again, fumbled about, and found cigarettes
and a box of matches. Two cigarettes quieted him. He
began to think that he was a silly fool, mooning about
when he should have been sleeping. In the morning he
would take an early train to San Francisco and place the
line without further ado. Yes, after all, he was as silly
and notional as a young schoolgirl. He put down the
window, turned off the lights, and crawled upstairs to bed.

II

True to his resolve, John Scidmore took an early train
to San Francisco next morning, although he could not have
said why. It was as impossible to place insurance at eight-
thirty as it was at three A.M., since no self-respecting insurance office opened until nine. Still there is a certain
comfort in even futile activity when one has the fidgets.

It was a beautiful October morning such as often veils
the Berkeley hills in faint purple and draws a soft glamour
over the city of San Francisco; and as Scidmore walked
briskly down the elm-shaded streets of Berkeley toward
the train, he felt elusively happy, notwithstanding the rip-
ples below the surface of his content.

The office-boy was taking books out of the safe when he
arrived at the office. In a corner by the wash-basin one
of the stenographers stood, fluffing up her hair. A janitor
dusted the desks with casual attention.

As Scidmore entered he noticed a woman sitting near
the counter. She rose instantly, lifting her veil, smiling a
welcome at him. He crossed over to her — it was Julia
Norris. His heart began to beat violently, but the next

moment he had recovered himself and was able to smile back at her in perfect self-control.

'You are early,' he said, offering her his hand.

'Yes, and I'm in trouble. You know those flats I insured last week — they burned down early this morning. They tell me there is n't a stick left standing.'

His hand fell as if a blow had wilted it. 'The flats you insured last week — ' he echoed, sparring for time. 'I don't believe I — understand.'

'Why, did n't you get my telephone message? I 'phoned last Tuesday. I thought I talked to *you*. I was sure it was your voice. Could I have rung up the wrong office?'

Her uncertainty steadied him. Unconsciously she opened a door of escape. Scidmore laid his hat on the counter. Julia Norris fluttered back to her seat and he sat down beside her.

'I suppose I've bungled things again,' she went on. 'Usually I leave everything to Mr. Rice, but this insurance matter I took into my own hands. I wanted you to have the business, so I left positive instructions with Mr. Rice to let me know when the next insurance policy expired. That was last Friday. I 'phoned you at once. I can't imagine — '

As she rattled on, pointing an accusing finger at herself, John Scidmore grew surer and surer of his next step. There was not the faintest note of calculation in his attitude; confused and dazed he merely followed her lead.

'And you never received any policy?' he questioned. 'Not after a week? You must have thought we were rather inattentive — or slow.'

She shook her head. 'I forgot the whole transaction — until this morning. Rice 'phoned me at eight o'clock.'

'But there may still be a chance,' Scidmore suggested, shamed by the very ease with which he was escaping.

'Perhaps another clerk got the message. I'll question them all. Or — maybe you rang up the Falcon's office direct.'

She laid a gloved hand on his arm as she shrugged.

He shook his head. 'You can't imagine how this bothers me,' he went on. He began to feel a certain boldness, such as thieves feel when they put over a sharp trick. He wanted to prolong the discussion, to dally with danger. 'To think that in trying to be of service to me you should have gone astray. I would n't have had it happen for — Let me see, what was the amount of your order?'

'Ten thousand dollars.'

'*Ten thousand dollars!* That's a lot of money.'

'Yes,' she admitted slowly, as she moved toward the door. 'I'm pretty comfortable, but nobody likes to throw money into the street.'

He thrust his hands into his pockets in an effort at nonchalance. He could feel his temples throbbing. But his confusion cleared before Julia Norris's unruffled smile, deepening a growing sense of irritation. She was not greatly concerned, first, because she did not have to be, and second, because her faith in his integrity was unshaken. Her complacency and trustfulness enraged him. What was ten thousand dollars to her?

In the midst of his musings, her voice, curiously remote, roused him.

'I'm going to have lunch with Kitty,' she said, almost gayly.

'Lunch with Kitty?' he echoed. Then, floundering with mingled consternation and embarrassment, he finished, 'Oh, yes, — won't that be fine! Yes, by all means do!'

And yet, unnerved as he was, he went through the conventional motions of courtesy, bowing her to the door, pressing her hand cordially, sweeping her a good-bye with

exaggerated warmth. Even when she was gone her unper-
turbed smile mocked him. She did not have the slightest
suspicion of his unworthiness, and therein lay the essence
of the sudden and unqualified hate he began to feel for her.

John Scidmore questioned all the clerks as they entered
the office. Had any one received a telephone message
about a week ago from Mrs. Julia Norris? He was playing
his game so earnestly that he would not have been surprised to find somebody acknowledging the transaction.
The manager came in at ten o'clock; Scidmore even presented the case to *him:* Mrs. Julia Norris, a client of his,
had telephoned an order for insurance over a week ago.
Nobody remembered it. The property to be insured had
burned up. Of course, Mrs. Norris might have been mis-
taken (she admitted as much), but there was just a
chance —

The manager, instantly interested, adjusted his glasses.
A ten-thousand-dollar line neglected! Incredible! He
began to investigate personally, calling up one clerk after
another, while Scidmore listened like a highwayman,
tempting chance from a spirit of sheer bravado. Nobody
remembered, even under the most searching cross-exam-
ination. The private exchange operator, who was usually
very keen about such matters, could not place the call.

Then came a discussion as to how to prevent such a lapse
should one occur. Scidmore sat at the manager's desk,
quite the hero of the hour — a very important personage,
whose ten-thousand-dollar client had come to grief. It
was years since he had figured in a question of office policy.
Gradually the uniqueness of his position pushed Julia
Norris and her loss into a hazy background.

He returned to his routine work with a gay spirit.
Several times during the morning the manager called him
for further conference and inquiry. Finally a letter was

drafted to Mrs. Julia Norris, to the effect that the California Insurance Brokers' Company regretted exceedingly to inform her that upon closer examination no trace could be found of her telephone message. They could only conclude that she inadvertently had rung up the wrong office. Inquiry at the Falcon Company's office, however, developed that no such insurance had been placed, even by a rival firm. They hoped that this unfortunate occurrence would not stand in the way of other favors at her hands, and so forth.

John Scidmore signed the letter with a flourish.

All morning the fiction of Julia Norris's mistake still persisted. Why had she not taken greater precautions? The idea of telephoning in a line of insurance and not inquiring the name of the person who took the message! Common sense would dictate such a course. He began to feel abused, as if Julia Norris had betrayed him in some way.

III

It was not until John Scidmore had scrambled aboard the ferryboat on his way home and had seated himself in his usual place, under the pilot-house, that his inflated spirits began to collapse. The afternoon had been spent in a mad rush of business, — an avalanche of petty orders and details such as periodically afflicts an insurance broker's office.

The sense of security which had enveloped him all day fell away before a vague uneasiness. Before an audience, he had played his part spiritedly; without the spur of interested auditors his performance lagged. There was an element of excitement in serving moral fiction to unsuspecting listeners, but hoodwinking himself proved a boresome task. The boldest highwayman had a cleaner record:

at least such an outlaw made bold plays and took great chances. He had not risked so much as his little finger on his enterprise, and his victim's cheek was still warm with the kiss of betrayal. Lies, thievery, murder — one by one these suggestions of outlawry mentally passed in review and sank into insignificance before this sinister word — *betrayal*. In all the calendar of human weaknesses, John Scidmore could recall none that served so contemptible an end as betrayal. And he, John Scidmore, had been guilty of this crowning meanness.

If the memory of Julia Norris's confidence stabbed him, what of the attitude of his superiors at the office? *They* had never even thought of questioning him. As he looked back on the events of the morning he was appalled. It seemed that all these years he had built up barriers of moral responsibility only to see them swept away before a freshet of fears.

A tramping of feet warned him that the boat was swinging into the slip. He rose mechanically. The exertion of following the scrambling crowd and finding himself a seat on the train interrupted his self-accusation. By the time he was comfortably settled again, he mentally had begun his defense.

Why should he make such an absurd fuss over confessing his fault to Julia Norris? She was rich; her husband had left her a cool million. Ten thousand dollars did n't matter, and besides, she was Kitty's friend. Had he the right to purchase a quiet conscience at the expense of Kitty's pride?

What had he given Kitty in the fifteen years of their wedded life? Had he played the game boldly and well? Did she hold her head high at the mention of his name? No, he had fallen short of his own standards. How much more must he have fallen short of her hopes for him! And now he was lacking the courage to swallow his medicine. He was ready to whimper and whine at the load which his own inefficiency had forced upon his conscience. He argued that strong men made bold plays and damned the consequence; in other words, they took a chance. But his soul was tricking itself out in a dramatic subterfuge. What he really had discovered was something to excuse his weakness, and this something loomed up conveniently in the person of Kitty Scidmore, his wife.

When Scidmore arrived home, he went directly to his room and closed the door. The thought of meeting Kitty troubled him. But after he had slipped on an old coat and freshened up, he felt better.

At the dinner table he noticed a tired, pinched look about his wife's mouth. Julia Norris was every day as old as his wife, but time had dealt kindly with her. Her face was still fresh and rosy; there was not even a glint of gray in her hair. Resentment began to move him, resentment at Julia Norris, at her fortune, at her friendship for his wife, at every detail connected with his memory of her.

Kitty began to talk. Scidmore sat silent, crumbling his bread. Finally the dread subject came to life. Kitty looked up and said, —

'Julia was late to-day, as usual. Poor dear Julia, what a generous soul she is!'

Scidmore began to fidget. 'Late? How did that happen? She left our office long before ten o'clock.'

'Oh, but you don't know Julia! She did a thousand and one things before she arrived here. And such a disheveled creature as she was! And so full of apologies and troubles! Nothing to speak of — she laughed them all away in five minutes.'

'Then she did n't tell —'

'About the insurance? I should say she did. She was

so worried for fear you'd be distressed about it all. She admitted that *she* was to blame. But she knows how conscientious you are, and she was afraid — '

Scidmore impatiently interrupted his wife. 'Julia Norris ought to have some business sense, Kitty; upon my word she should. And it *has* worried me. A woman like that — one never can be sure of just what she does think. It's an even chance that deep down she believes that she delivered the message to me, and that *I* neglected it.'

He could feel his face flushing with mingled indignation and disapproval as he voiced his displeasure.

Kitty got up to pour a glass of water.

'Why, John,' she half chided, 'I'm sure Julia would n't be guilty of such a thought. You don't know her — generous — impulsive. Why, she'd forgive you for neglecting, if you really had neglected anything. As a matter of fact she said very decidedly, "If I'd been dealing with anybody but John Scidmore, I do believe I'd be inconsistent enough to try to blame the other fellow, but of course I know — " '

'Yes,' he broke in excitedly, 'that's just it. That's the way she puts it, to you. But such a remark as that just bears out what I say — she's not altogether satisfied. I know what she thinks; I saw it in her face this morning — *this is what comes of trying to help one's poor friends.*'

His wife stopped pouring water and laid down the pitcher.

'Nonsense. Julia Norris has perfect faith in you.'

'Why should she have?' he persisted hotly. 'Is n't it just as possible for me to forget, to overlook a telephone message, as the other fellow? I'm not infallible any more than she is.'

'No,' Kitty returned very quietly. 'I don't think she imagines that you are infallible. But she knows that if you took her message and forgot it, you'd admit it.'

He rallied from this blow with a feeling of fierce antagonism.

'Well,' he sneered sarcastically, 'if she's silly enough to have any such notions, she *does* need a guardian! As a matter of fact, I'd conceal my mistakes as quickly as any one else would.'

Kitty began to laugh, a full-throated, indulgent laugh, that made him bite his lips.

'What a lot of foolish brag you're indulging in, Johnny Scidmore. Well, after all, let's forget about it; Julia herself laughed it off.'

He crumpled the napkin in his hand. 'Yes, that's just it. *She* can laugh over it, while we — why, if we lost ten thousand it would be a tragedy. I could n't help thinking to-day after she'd left the office, suppose, just suppose, I *had* received Julia Norris's 'phone message — and forgotten it. The very thought made me sick all over.'

He paused, frightened at the lengths to which his uneasiness had forced him. His wife's smile gave way to a puzzled look as she returned very quietly, —

'Do you really think it worth while to face these imaginary situations?'

His resentment flared again at the comfortable evenness of her tone. 'Yes, I do,' he snapped back. 'It helps one to exercise one's morals. I wanted to know just how I would act in such an emergency. And I've found out. The very thought frightens me too much. I know that I should feel morally bound to confess, but I'd never have the courage of my convictions. Now, what do you suppose you would advise me to do in a situation like that? What would you tell me to do?'

Kitty Scidmore looked straight at her husband. He dropped his eyes.

'I would not advise you, John,' she said, distinctly.

He glanced up at her. 'You 'd not say a word?'

She shook her head. 'No, it would n't be necessary.'

He began to stir his tea. His hand was shaking, and his spoon rattled noisily against the teacup.

IV

After he had helped Kitty with the dishes, John Scidmore left the house for a walk. It was a calm, beautiful night, lit by a slender moon hung high in the heavens and stars twinkling cheerily. As he went along the elm-shaded streets, he drew in deep breaths, striving to steady the tumult within him.

Kitty's words hummed themselves into his inner consciousness. 'No, John, it would n't be necessary.' What did she really mean? Did she think he had the courage to settle such a question decisively — righteously? Did — He stopped, turning the phrase over in his mind. He knew that materially he had been a failure. People called him a *nice* fellow and let it go at that. Was it possible for his wife, the wife who had lived so close to all his weaknesses, to glorify him with so large a hope? The thought began to thrill him.

He heard the Old Library clock on the University campus chime nine. He began to walk slowly in the direction of the chiming clock. He was still undecided, still battling with his cowardice. The shrill whistle of an incoming train arrested him. This same train would swing back to San Francisco in ten minutes. He retraced his steps. In ten minutes — His legs seemed weighted. He wondered whether he would really catch it.

Standing before the massive façade of the Hotel Fairmont, John Scidmore had a fleeting hope that Julia Norris

would not be at home. But almost as instantly he felt a
desperate need to clear himself at once. If he waited even
an hour he could not vouch for the outcome. He walked
rapidly into the lobby, gave his name to the hotel clerk,
and awaited the reply with beating heart. Mrs. Norris
was in. A bell-boy, answering the clerk's summons,
showed him to her apartments.

A maid ushered him into a reception room. He sank
into one of the luxurious chairs, drumming upon its arms
with nervous fingers.

A lamp on the centre table threw a rich, golden light
over the surroundings. Thrown over a chair a lace scarf
fell with the undulating softness of a cascade. Near a
vase of blood-red roses a long white glove had been dropped
carelessly.

He did not wait long. Julia Norris came toward him
with her usual warm smile, and a hand outstretched in
welcome. He stood up. She was very simply dressed, in
white, and a band of velvet at her throat set off a fine
cameo ringed with pearls, but her air of quiet elegance
caught and held his resentful eyes.

A fierce, unreasoning hate began to sway him; for a
moment his vision blurred.

As she stepped back to pick up her lace scarf from the
chair, John Scidmore recovered his poise.

'I was afraid you would be out,' he began inadequately.

She threw the scarf about her shoulders. 'I was preparing to drift downstairs to watch the dancing,' she
answered. 'You caught me just in time.'

He stood irresolutely, almost awkwardly, watching her
dainty manipulations of the filmy lace. Then quite suddenly, so suddenly as to surprise even himself, he blurted
out, —

'I lied to you this morning. I took your order for insurance. I forgot to place it.'

She stood for a moment in silence.

'What made you —'

John Scidmore shrugged. His vision was clearing. He felt quite calm.

'You suggested the idea yourself. You were so ready to take the blame. I suppose it was self-preservation. I began to strike blindly — as any desperate man would. I'm not what they call a success — I never have been. You know how it is, some people — Oh, well! Some of us don't get by, that's all.'

He turned away. Julia Norris touched him on the shoulder.

'John, can't you see that the ten thousand dollars does n't matter to me? But you and Kitty — you and Kitty *do* matter.'

He began to crush his hat between his clasped hands.

She threw the scarf from her shoulders. 'Look here, John —'

He stopped her with an abrupt gesture. 'I've won this victory for Kitty's sake,' he said. 'This is the first time in my life I've lived up to her hope of me. If you were a failure you'd realize how much that means.'

She was standing by the vase of roses, scattering petals with ruthless fingers. She crossed over to him and put both her hands in his.

'You're not a failure, John Scidmore,' she said simply.

The rose-petals were dropping in a steady shower on the table. He saw them lying lightly on the white glove. He felt a great relief as he put his clenched hand to his eyes.

V

As John Scidmore rode home he felt desperately tired.
He could not remember a day which had seemed longer.

He dragged up the elm-shaded street, down which he
had whistled his confident way twelve hours before, a
shuffling, ineffectual figure. As he opened the front door
his hand shook.

He lingered in the hall, hanging his hat with unnecessary
care, twisting his necktie into shape, smoothing the thin
wisps of hair about his temples.

He found Kitty in the living-room. A tiny fire crackled
in the grate. Standing in the doorway he watched the
needle which Kitty deftly plied slipping about its task
with fascinating gleams. Her face was happily flushed
and she was humming softly to herself. The elegant
memory of Julia Norris rose before him. He saw again
the golden shower of light from the huge table-lamp, the
vase of American Beauty roses, the lace scarf thrown carelessly across a brocade chair. He pressed his lips together
and entered the room.

Kitty looked up.

He stopped short. 'Something new?' he ventured.

She gave a little laugh. 'New? I should say not. Just
freshening up a bit for to-morrow.'

'To-morrow?' he echoed dully. 'What's on for to-
morrow?'

'Guest day at the club. Mrs. Wiley has asked me to
pour tea. What kept you out so late, Johnny?'

He crossed over to the fire, pulling his easy chair into
place.

'I went over to the city — to see Julia Norris.'

He stood a moment, undecided, his back turned toward
Kitty, his hand upon the chair. He was waiting for Kitty

to question him. Finding that she did not answer, he turned and looked at her. She was intent on her sewing, but he fancied that the flush of happiness suddenly had fled her cheeks.

'I went over to see Julia Norris,' he repeated desperately. 'You said your advice would n't be necessary.'

He sank into a chair. Across the room he heard the monotonous ticking of a clock.

He was wondering what Kitty would say. Of course she understood; the whiteness of her face told him that her feminine intuition had bridged the gaps in his explanation. He began to have a terror lest she would come up to him, or speak — perhaps even weep. The fire in the grate flared up suddenly, turned faintly blue, and died. Still Kitty said nothing; still the clock ticked rhythmically.

He leaned back, closed his eyes, and drew a long breath. Kitty was stirring. She came over and dropped gently before the fire, leaning her head against him.

'I forgot to tell you,' she said slowly. 'I asked Julia Norris over for Sunday dinner. She's so awfully stuffed up in that horrible hotel.'

Her bravery smote him more than tears could have. He did not answer, but he just put out his hand and touched her hair caressingly, as she finished, —

'It's very grand, I know, and all that. But, after all, it is n't home, Johnny, is it?'

BUSINESS IS BUSINESS

BY HENRY SEIDEL CANBY

I

Six hours on the train had nearly exhausted Joseph Cargan. He had read all the available magazines, looked up his connections twice in the railway guide, and even gazed for an hour out of the window. But there were only woods and farms to be seen, scarcely a bill-board, and no automobiles. He dropped his cigar wearily into the spittoon by his chair in the club car and relapsed into lethargy. With dull iteration he ran over the plans for the deal in prairie land that he hoped to put through to-morrow, and guessed lazily at whether $6000 would purchase the tract of which they had written him. He thought of his wife, and hoped that his telegram would be telephoned over to the Runkles' so that she might meet him at the station with the clean shirt he had asked for. Afterwards he cut his nails, yawned loudly, and was just going to sleep when they stopped at Joline and a boy came in with papers.

Cargan turned first, as usual, to the stock-market reports. There were only two items of interest since he had left the tape. Montana Pacific had gone off a little more. But 200 shares of Benningham Common had sold at 17, a drop of ten points! His eye caught an explanatory note: the dividend on the preferred had been cut; the surplus was heavily reduced. His mind, searching rapidly over their business, fixed upon two marginal accounts — Jim Smith's and Waldron's. In each case the collateral deposited had already been insufficient. Drawing out his note-book he swiftly figured. 'That old gambler Smith's always on the edge,' he reflected. 'We can hold him a little longer. Gotta sell Waldron out. Must have made a thousand dollars out of that account first and last. Too bad.' A momentary sense of Waldron's calamity swept over him, but quickly evaporated. 'Business is business,' he thought, and remembered, with a little angry satisfaction, Anita Waldron's coming-out dance and how the Runkles, who were invited, kept talking about it all winter. 'Old Waldron won't be so darn particular next year.'

As the train pulled into his home town he hurried out upon the station platform, and saw with pride and pleasure that his wife was just stepping out of the Runkles' motor. Looking about to see who might be there to note the company she was keeping, his eye fell on a tall and stooping gentleman with a trimmed beard and eyeglasses, who was searching with weary eyes the train windows; but even while he frowned at the recognition, his wife had seized him by the shoulder, caroling, 'Hello, Jimmy. Give me a kiss, dear, and take your old shirt.' She was a graceful woman, stiffened by an obvious corset, and faintly powdered. A long yellow feather dangled from her orange hat, big pearls were set in her ears, and her shoe-buckles glittered as she walked.

He kissed her admiringly. 'Say, Martha, you look great,' he chuckled. 'I hate to have to go right on. You tell the kids I'll bring 'em something when I get back.'

The train was starting; indeed he had just time to dash up the steps of his car. 'Good-bye, dear,' she caroled. 'Good-bye, dee-ar,' hummed the brakeman, and slammed down the swinging floor of the vestibule. Cargan was already balancing himself along the corridor of the club car. A lurch of the train swung him heavily out among the chairs; to save himself he caught a shoulder and dropped into a seat. His neighbor had but just sat down. It was Waldron.

They shook hands as if nothing were in the air, and then compared watches to see if the train were on time. This done, Waldron took off his glasses, swung them on their black cord, and began to polish them nervously, blinking with short-sighted eyes into the space that hurried past the car windows. Cargan offered him a cigar, but he put it aside quickly.

'No, thank you; no, thank you — Well — they cut the dividend.' He looked at Cargan with a wan smile. 'What'll I do, Cargan? They told me I'd find you on the train, and I thought I'd ask your advice.'

Cargan was relieved. 'Sell, Mr. Waldron,' he answered earnestly, 'sell right off. That Brogan crowd's runnin' the company now, and they're no good. sell quick.'

Waldron looked at him in doubt. 'How much do I lose?' he asked feebly.

''Bout six thousand'— against his will Cargan made the tone apologetic. 'Say, put up only five thousand more collateral and we'll carry you till better luck.'

The old man blinked rapidly, then conquered his pride. With punctilious care he unbuttoned his gray cutaway, took out a wallet from under the button of the Society of Colonial Wars, drew forth a sheet of note paper, and with a pencil inscribed a broad O. 'There's my collateral, Mr. Cargan,' he said whimsically.

He was so helpless, and so elegant in his helplessness, that the bully awoke in Cargan. With an effort he broke through the nervous deference with which Waldron always inspired him and spoke roughly: —

'We don't do business without either collateral or cash, Waldron.'

The gentleman put his wallet back hurriedly as if some

one had laughed at it, and cast a quick, hurt look at his broker.

'You have n't been thinking of selling me out — after all the business I've given you?'

Cargan nodded.

Incredulity, horror, resolve, passed over Waldron's face. 'You cannot! It's impossible!' he said firmly.

The assertion in his tone was irritating. 'What's goin' to stop us?' Cargan asked coolly; shoved his hands into his pockets, and puffed clouds from his cigar.

Different worlds of imagination revolved in the two men's minds. Theophilus Waldron thought of the children, and of his father the governor, and of the family pride. Sudden poverty was as bad as disgrace. 'I did n't mean it that way,' he answered hurriedly. 'I'm in temporary difficulties. My house is mortgaged. I've borrowed money from my wife — and other places.' — He was too proud to add, 'This is confidential.' — 'My boy's just entered college, my girl's just come out. It is n't just the money —' a gush of emotion reddened his face — 'You've got to pull me through, Cargan. It's impossible; it's out of the question for me to break now!'

But Cargan was remembering how he lost his job in the department store and could n't pay the rent. When *he* was kicked out, nobody said it was impossible! Nobody said it was impossible when they went into the top of a tenement! The contrast made him bitter; but it was the thought that he had never felt it to be impossible, the inescapable inferiority always forced upon him in the presence of Waldron, which roused his temper.

'Business is business, Mr. Waldron,' he said curtly. 'Ab-so-lute-ly, we won't take the risk.'

They were rattling through coal-sheds and grain-elevators

at the edge of a town. Waldron got up stiffly and carefully brushed the cinders from his coat.

'This is Bloomfield, I think,' he said coldly. 'I'm meeting my family here. Mr. Cargan, there are considerations above business.' His voice failed a little. 'This is a matter of life and death.'

Cargan had heard that bluff before. 'What d' you mean?' he grunted.

Mr. Waldron was staring fixedly out of the window. 'I mean,' he faltered, 'that I may not be able to stand up under it.' And then his voice resumed its desperate certainty. 'I mean, sir, that what you propose is impossible. I mean that ab-so-lute-ly you cannot sell me out.'

He bowed and felt his way down the corridor.

'I can't, can't I!' Cargan flung after him; then jerked a sheet from the telegraph pad in the rack beside him and wrote: 'Sell out Waldron at noon to-morrow unless 5000 collateral.' 'Something'll drop for you, old boy,' he growled, addressed the telegram to his partner, and gave it to the porter.

Outside, Cargan heard a burst of merry voices and saw Waldron hurried away by two laughing girls to an automobile waiting with a trunk strapped behind it. Mrs. Waldron followed. She was a stiff woman, a little faded, quietly dressed. Her face was troubled, and when they reached the motor, she caught her husband's elbow gently as if to ask him something, but he merely nodded and turned her glance toward Cargan's window. She bowed and smiled very sweetly in his direction, and Cargan smiled sourly in return. Then the children hustled the old folks into the tonneau and they were off, just as the train started.

Cargan felt hardly used. 'A man's got to look out for himself,' he thought angrily. 'Business is business —

that's the thing for him to remember. "It's impossible"!'
Nevertheless, in self-defense he began to calculate what it
might have cost to carry the account, until the appalling
magnitude of the risk shut off the discussion. 'The darned
old self-confident aristocrat!' he murmured, working himself up into a fury. 'Thinks he can bluff me, but he'll find
out what's impossible, believe *me!*' Then he dispelled his
irritation by a cocktail and hurried into the diner.

He snored in his berth while the train ran out farther
and farther upon the great Kansas plain; slept while signs
of culture disappeared one by one, and arose in the midst
of an endless, unfamiliar world of grass. When he sat
down in the diner for his morning meal, the great wheel of
the horizon rimmed round his little train without a notch
on the perfect circle; over night the outer world had
changed, but he was absorbed in fitting his choices into a
sixty-cent breakfast.

The train stopped quickly and firmly, and lay dead upon
the prairie.

'Eccentrics or hot-box,' said the man who jumped off
the step beside him. 'Nothing much else goes wrong with
an engine nowadays. What is it, Bill?'

And the conductor, looking about him to see that no
more passengers were within earshot, answered, 'Eccentrics — two hours anyway.'

Cargan flung his cigarette on the ground. 'I'll miss my
connection at Hay Junction!' he protested. 'I've gotta be
in Hamden this afternoon.'

'Walk then,' said the conductor stolidly. 'It's only ten
miles from here straight across.'

There was no house in sight, no road, nothing but the
dead train, the new land of endless shimmering prairies,
and, beyond the ditch, a single horseman looking curiously

at the long cars and the faces strained against the glass of the windows.

'Say, you!' Cargan called, 'can you get an auto anywhere here?'

The figure looked at him impassively, then shook its dusty head.

'Or a team?'

It shook its head again.

'Or a — horse?' Cargan hesitated. He had never ridden a horse.

A sudden gleaming idea shot across the man's solemn features. He slid off his pony and led him nearer the ditch.

'Say' — he suddenly became voluble, — 'you said you wanted to get to Hamden. Well, if you'll make it five plunks, and give me your ticket, you can take this horse, an' I'll go round by train. Say — do you want to?'

Cargan was tempted. All you had to do was to stick on.

'What'll I do with my suit-case?'

'Gimme it to take for you. I guess it ain't worth more'n my horse.'

II

They helped him on, and pointed out the dim line of telephone poles which marked a road a mile beyond. He walked his horse onward, not daring to trot, struck the dusty highway, rode on over an imperceptible roll of the plains, and was alone on a vast bare earth, naked as when born from the womb of time.

Plover swung up before him with melancholy cries. A soft haze rose from the plains. They grew more vast, more endless. In the north, a white cloud-mass piled itself up and up until it seemed as if it might topple over upon the flat world beneath. He had never before looked at the country except as real estate, never seen the plains, and a curious new sense of the bigness of the earth oppressed him. He felt very small and very mean. The humiliation of his spirits was a novel feeling and an unpleasant one; he tried to hum it away: —

> 'Just wait till I strike Broadway
> And watch me with the girls,
> For I'm the man that invented it —
> The hair that always curls.'

His harsh voice in the stillness was ridiculous, — even to him, — but when he stopped singing, the silence flowed over him as a stream that had been held back. The sky was enormous; he was only a speck on the vast floor. As he plodded on and on and on through the dust, he began to grow dizzy from the glare and the heat. He could not collect his thoughts for business. A curious sense of weakened identity perplexed him, and his head was full of drifting pictures — Waldron's face among them. That face lingered. He saw him looking vaguely out of the car window — saying that he could n't stand up under it — that it was 'impossible.' He wondered if it was a bluff, after all. The face faded away leaving a dull pity behind it, a struggling remorse. Cargan shifted uneasily in his saddle, and tried to think of business. But instead of business queer childish ideas began floating in and out of his mind, accompanied by words remembered from Sundays in his boyhood. He was alone with God. God saw into his heart. A little nervous shiver ran over him, and when he checked it with a laugh there followed a wave of superstitious emotion.

A low wave of the prairies had hidden from him a little house and barn standing crudely new against the sky in the distance. Tiny figures were moving behind the buildings, and a dust-cloud rose from the highway in front.

Cargan suddenly became conscious of his appearance — his serge suit, his straw hat, his awkward seat in the saddle. The loneliness of the plains had shaken his usual self-assurance.

'Maybe they'll think I stole this horse. Guess I'll go round,' he said aloud. He jerked his steed from the road into the grass, and urged him into a trot. Instantly he found himself beaten and jolted like a ship in a tempest. He lost a stirrup, he slipped sidewise on the saddle; then in a panicky fright he began to shout and saw at the bit. Frightened by the voice and the thunder of hoofs, a chaparral cock darted from beneath the horse's nose. It was enough to make the beast swerve, then toss his head, and in a panic madder than his rider's, break into a run and dash unrestrainably onward. Cargan, numb with fright, leaned over his neck and wound his hands in the mane. The speed sickened him. The flat earth swung beneath, the sky swam dizzily. He dared not pull on the reins; he could only hold on grimly and shut his eyes. Once he slipped, and, screaming, saw for an instant a blur of grass before he could pull himself back to safety. And then the speed increased, the sweaty shoulders labored beneath him, and his senses whirled.

He did not note how far they ran; but at last came a slower motion, a gallop, and then a trot. Weak from exhaustion, he was bumped from the saddle, and found himself clutching and kicking with both arms around his horse's neck. Flinging himself outward, he rolled over on the soft ground, and lay groaning on the prairie. The well-trained horse stopped and began to graze; he too was quivering with fatigue, but his fright was over. The sun was burning near the zenith. The world again was empty, and this time there was no road.

Cargan was lost.

When he recovered a little, he caught the horse, and, too shaken to mount him, limped on, leading him by the bridle, in what direction he did not know. Pangs of hunger and faintness assailed him. The awful loneliness chilled him through in spite of the blaze of heat and light. He remembered stories of men who had wandered on the prairie, round and round in an endless circle, until they had gone crazy and blown out their brains. A profound pity for himself stirred him. Never had he so felt the need of humanity, of human aid. He would have given a hundred dollars to be walking up Main Street, with the boys calling to him from Rooney's cigar store, and the world where it was yesterday.

Just in front a little calf stumbled to its feet and ran toward them, mooing piteously. It, too, was lost. Cargan stroked its nostrils, and a sympathy for all suffering things flowed through his heart. He thought with a shudder of Waldron, pacing somewhere like himself, alone, lost, helpless, his pride gone. In his awakened imagination, he saw him wandering nearer and nearer the fatal act. 'He'll shoot himself. I ought to done something,' he whispered, with a sudden rush of unfamiliar emotion; and all the sentiment in his nature heaved and struggled to the light.

A cow lowed somewhere beyond them; his horse pricked up his ears, and the calf ambled off in the direction of the sound. Cargan limped after hurriedly, leading his horse. A hundred yards brought them to the edge of a slight bowl in the plains, with a little moisture around which pewees were flying, and his heart leaped to see beside it a tiny house of unpainted boards. Wires stretched from one window, along the depression which led westward, until they disappeared in the endless horizon; and, as he paused to survey, a sharp bell rang.

'Hello, is that Annie?' came faintly across the silence.

He looked at his watch, and saw that it was only eleven. 'I'll talk to Casey about Waldron,' he said guiltily. Relief for his escape, and still more the hush of that enormous plain, the solemnity of the great and shining sky, filled him with high and noble thoughts.

'Say, is Hamden near here?' he asked of a slim woman in a gingham dress who appeared at the door.

She nodded.

'And say, can I use your telephone?'

She hesitated, looking him over, then motioned him incuriously to the stool behind the pine table. Solitude seemed to have made her unready of speech. He called Cargan & Casey, then waited, fidgeting. Silence invaded the little kitchen. The clock ticked in a hush; the chickens droned in whispers; the woman herself worked over the stove with slow fingers, moving the kettles gently. Cargan & Casey were 'busy.' He fumed for an instant, then gave his own home number.

'It's Jim,' he said, and heard his wife's carol of surprise. He could see her tiptoeing at their telephone. 'I'm all right,' he shouted in response to her eager words; and the thought of their little sitting-room, and the kids playing behind her, warmed his blood. 'I got run away with on the plains, but I'm all right —' Her frightened ejaculation thrilled him with loving pride — 'honest I am.' And then suddenly a wave of generous emotion mounted to his head. 'Martha,' he called quickly, — 'tell Casey not to sell out Waldron — tell him right away. I'll explain to-morrow.'

The connection roared and failed. He hung up the instrument. The quiet room, the gently moving woman, the immensity without, rushed back on his sight. Exhilarated, clear-hearted, looking heaven in the face, he asked the necessary questions, mounted his horse, and pushed onward.

Hamden was already a blotch upon the horizon. 'Say, it's great to get into a *big* country,' he murmured, lifted his bare head to the free air, and in a curious exaltation of mind rode on dreamily. He noticed the flowers in the coarse grass, watched the wild doves flying with their quick, strong wing-beats, and swung his eye joyfully around the blue horizons that receded until one felt the curve and pitch of the world.

The mood lasted until Cargan reached the first straggling houses of the village street, so that he entered upon the rutty highway between dirt sidewalks with regret, as one whose holiday was ending. He scarcely noticed the loiterers who stared at him, or thought of his streaked face, his trousers split at the knee, his hat lost on the wild ride.

But as he plodded onward the atmosphere of town had its effect. His eye began to take note of the size of the shops glittering under their false fronts, the new houses behind rows of stiff young trees, the number and make of automobiles. His subconsciousness grasped the financial level of Hamden, although his thoughts were still in the wide spaces of the plains. A boy ran out from the sidewalk to sell him a paper. He stuck it in his side pocket, and suddenly began to feel like a man of this world again.

'Say, sonny,' he called; 'who sells land in this burg? — Dubell — John Dubell? — Thanks.'

He went more and more slowly.

A drug-store, blazing with marble and onyx in the afternoon sun, made Cargan's dry throat wrinkle with thirst. He pulled his horse toward that side of the street. There was a row of customers along the soda-water counter, and through the open windows came scraps of conversation: two boys were teasing each other about a girl; a group of men were talking auctions, options, prices, real estate. He drank their talk in greedily, with a pang of homesickness and a rush of returning common sense. Dismounting stiffly, he tied his horse, and stood for an instant on the cement pavement, feeling his dirt and tatters, wondering if they would throw him out for a bum. Then he slid inside the door, and ordered a chocolate soda.

The clerk was reading the paper while he juggled the milk-shakes. Cargan, carefully concealing his torn trousers, climbed a stool, and began to look back upon the vagaries of the day with sullen wonder. He brushed furtively at the caked dust on his legs, remembering, irritably, the elegance of Waldron, whom he had saved. In the mirror of the soda fountain he saw himself, torn, dirty, shrinking, and the sight filled him with disgust and anger. He felt as ridiculous as when he had come out with a glass too much from the Stoneham bar, and tripped over the steps of the main entrance. 'Gimme a cigar,' he called to the boy at the magazine counter; bit off the end, lit it, and began to think business.

The clerk, swirling a cataract of milk from glass to glass, revealed the inner sheet of the paper propped before him. Cargan read beneath his arm the full-page advertisement of a land sale — the land sale he had come through all this tomfoolery to reach. His eyes bulged as he saw that they were going to throw a thousand acres on the market. 'Good gosh,' he gulped inwardly, 'what a chance!' It was a sure thing for the man with the money.

The last of his fine sentiments evaporated. Except for Waldron he could have scooped it all in; but now four hundred was all he dared touch, — and perhaps not that. Raging against his softness back there on the plains, which seemed a hardly recognizable world, he ground his teeth,

and coughed and choked over his soda. Soft-headed donkey! The reaction was complete.

Suddenly a little thought no bigger than a minute rose
in one corner of his brain, and spread, and spread. He
looked furtively at the clock over the clerk's head, and saw
that it was only half-past two. With guilty deliberation
he rose and walked slowly toward the door of the telephone booth, keeping back from full consciousness just
what he was about to do. Then he slammed himself
within, and shouted Casey's address to the operator. As
he waited, his wrath mounted. 'What in heck was the
matter with me anyway!' He smoked furiously in the
stifling box.

'Go ahead,' said the operator, — and, at the word, 'Hey
there, Casey,' he yelled at the dim voice on the wires,
'I've gotta have five thousand quick! Sell that Benningham Common — yes, Waldron's.' At the name his
anger broke loose. 'The old high-brow tried to bluff me.
What!! —' The connection failed and left him gasping.

'What! Sold it! He told you to! — No, I dunno anything about a court decision. Up 15 points on a merger!
Well what do you think —' He gulped down the sudden
reversal and felt for words. 'Say, tell him, —' he licked
his lips, — 'tell him I'm sure glad I saved him. I'm sure
glad.'

The wires roared again, — and Cargan, putting down
the receiver grinned shamefacedly into the dirty mirror.
But gradually a sense of conscious virtue began to trickle
pleasantly through his veins. 'I'm sure glad,' he repeated
more vigorously; 'carryin' him to-day was what did it.'
A vision of Mrs. Waldron's happy face rose to bless him;
the exhilaration of the morning coursed back into his
heart, with a comfortable feeling of good business about
it. He felt better and better. From somewhere a saying

floated into his head: 'Doing good unto others is the only happiness.' 'By heck, that's true,' he commented aloud, and sat smoking peacefully, his mind aglow with pleasant thoughts.

The bell whirred raucously. He saw that he had forgotten to replace the receiver, and putting it to his ear caught Casey's voice again: —

'Say, Carg, Jim Smith's in the office, and won't leave till he's heard from you. Montana Pacific's off two points more. Say, do you want to carry *him?* He says he's done for if you sell him out.'

A fire of indignation rushed through Cargan. 'What d' you think I am — a damned philanthropist?' he yelled. 'Sell out the old gambler! Sell him out!' And he hung up.

NOTHING

BY ZEPHINE HUMPHREY

THIS is not going to be an easy story to write. Its theme is precisely that which I have chosen for my title; and naturally its positive significance is not obvious. But I must somehow get the thing into words. The spiritual value which I found in the experience may come home to some reader. At any rate, it is good for us all to stop now and then and challenge the conventional standards of our lives.

To begin with, I presume that there are few sympathetic students of humanity who will not agree with me that the strain of mysticism which sometimes appears in the New England character is one of the most interesting and touching of all the manifestations of our human nature. It is so unexpected! The delicate pearl in the rough oyster is not more apparently incongruous, rarer, or more priceless. Nay, it is more than that. The development is so impossible as to be always a miracle, freshly wrought by the finger of God.

There are all sorts of elements in it which do not appear in other kinds of mysticism: humor (that unfailing New England salt!), reserve, and a paradoxical mixture of independence and deference. It knows how inexplicable it must seem to its environment, how it must fret its oyster; so it effaces itself as much as possible. But it yields not one jot of its integrity. It holds a hidden, solitary place apart — like a rare orchid in the woods, like a hermit thrush. Even to those who love it, it will not lightly or often reveal itself. But when it does — well, I would take

a weary, barefoot pilgrimage for the sake of the experience
which I had last summer. And here I may as well begin
my narrative.

I

I sat behind her in the little country church; and when
I had studied her profile for a few moments, I was glad
of a chance to rise and sing the Doxology. She was a
woman of fifty-odd, a typical Vermonter, with the angular
frame and features peculiar to her class. Her mouth was
large, her cheek-bones high; her thin, dark hair, streaked
with gray, was drawn smoothly down behind her ears.
But her expression! — that gave her away. Not flagrantly,
of course. To discover her one had to be temperamentally
on the watch for her. Apparently, like all the rest of us,
she was looking at the flowers before the pulpit; but I was
sure that her wide blue eyes were really intent on something behind and beyond. Her mouth brooded, her forehead dreamed, her whole face pondered grave and delect-
able matters. I am afraid that I did not hear much of the
sermon that morning.

When church was over, I followed her out, and waited
to see in what direction she turned her homeward steps.
Then I made up my mind to devote the next week to taking
walks in that same direction. The minister's wife saw me
looking after her, and approached me with a smile which
I understood. She was about to say, 'That is one of our
native oddities, a real character. I see that she interests
you. Shall I take you to see her? You will find her a
curious and amusing study.' But I headed her off by letting the wind blow my handkerchief away. Nobody should
tell me anything about my mystic — not even what her
name was, or where she lived!

I was fully prepared not to find her for several days.

I went forth in quest of her in the spirit in which I always start out to find a hermit thrush — ready to be disappointed, to wait, humbly aware that the best rewards demand and deserve patience. But she was not so securely hidden as the thrush. Her little house gave her away to my seeking, as her expression, the day before, had given her away to my sympathy.

It was just the house for her: low and white, under a big tree, on the side of a brook-threaded hill, a little apart from the village. I recognized it the instant I saw it; and when I had read the name — 'Hesper Sherwood' — on the mailbox by the side of the road, I confidently turned in at the gate.

She was working in her garden, clad in a blue-checked gingham apron and a blue sunbonnet. When she heard my footsteps, she looked up slowly, turning in my direction, and, for the first time, I saw her full face.

It was even better than her profile. Oh! when human features can be moulded to such quietness and confidence, what an inexplicable pity it is that they ever learn the trick of fretfulness! In Hesper Sherwood, humanity for once looked like a child of God.

I was not sure at first that she saw me distinctly. Perhaps the sun dazzled her shaded eyes. Her expectant expression held itself poised a little uncertainly, as if she were doubtful of the exact requirements of the situation. But when I said something — commonplace enough and yet heartful — about the beauty of the view from her gate, her face lighted and she came forward.

'It's better from the house,' she said, shyly, yet eagerly. 'Won't you come up and see?'

It was indeed as fair a prospect as threshold ever opened out upon. Close at hand was the green hillside, dropping down to the smiling summer valley; and beyond were the

mountains, big and blue, with their heads in the brilliant
sky and with cloud-shadows trailing slowly over them.
Directly across the way, they were massive; in the distance,
where the valley opened out to the south, they were hazy
and tender. One of them loomed above the little house,
and held it in its hand. Everywhere, they were com-
manding presences; and it was clear that the house had
taken up its position wholly on their account.

Plain enough in itself it was, that house. Its three small
rooms were meagrely furnished; and its windows were
curtainless, inviting the eyes beyond themselves. It was
utterly restful. It made me want to go home and burn up
half the things I possess. Later, as I came to know it and
its owner better, I understood what perfect counterparts
they were. She, too, invited the gaze beyond herself.

It is, of course, not my intention to trace the development of our friendship. Though we trusted each other
from the beginning, we took the whole summer to feel our
way into each other's lives. It was a beautiful experience.
I would not have hurried it. But now I want to proceed at
once to the conversation in which she finally told me ex-
plicitly what had not happened to her. It was but the
definite statement of what I had known all along: that
here was a life which God had permitted Himself the luxury
of keeping apart for his own delectation.

We were sitting out on the front steps, in the face of the
mountains and valley; and we had said nothing for a long
time. Our silence had brought us so close that when she
began to speak, my ear ignored the uttered words and I
felt as if my thoughts were reading hers.

'It's queer about folks' lives is n't it?' she said thoughtfully — though I am not sure that she was any more aware
of her lips than I was of my ears. 'How they follow one
line; how the same things keep happening to them, over

and over. I suppose it's what people call Fate. There's no getting away from it.

'Take my brother Silas. As a boy, he was always making the luckiest trades; couldn't seem to help it. Then when he married and moved to his new farm, be began to get rich; and now he couldn't stop his money if he wanted to. He must be worth fifteen thousand dollars.

'Take my sister Persis. She's had eleven children.

'Take my uncle Rufus. He's been around the world three times, and is just starting again.

'Take —'

She paused and hesitated.

'You,' I supplied softly.

'Well, yes, take me.' She turned and flashed a sudden smile at me. 'I've always wanted everything, and I've had — nothing.'

She spoke the word as if it were the pot of gold at the foot of the rainbow.

'It took me a long time to understand,' she went on quietly, as I made no comment. 'I suppose that was natural. I was young; and I had never happened to hear of a case like mine. At first, I thought that, just because I wanted a thing, I was bound to have it. There was my mother.'

Again she paused, and a tender, glowing light appeared in her face, like the quickening of a latent fire. It was eloquent of all sorts of passionate, youthful, eager things.

'I guess I worshiped my mother,' she submitted simply. 'Maybe you think that, anyway, I had her. But, no, I hadn't. She liked me well enough. Mothers do. But we had a big family, and we lived in a big house, and she was very busy. It bothered her to have me get in her way with my huggings and kissings. Why in the world couldn't I wait until bedtime? Poor mother! She never did seem to know what to make of my devotion. People don't like to be loved too well; it embarrasses them.

'She died when I was fourteen. And I thought I'd die too.'

There was no shadow on Hesper's face as she remembered her young, far-away anguish; rather, there was a strange deepening of peace. But she was silent for two or three minutes; and I noticed that she put out her hand and caressed an old-fashioned, crocheted tidy that lay on the arm of a chair which she had brought out on the porch. When she resumed her story, she spoke somewhat more rapidly.

'I was sick a long time. If I had n't been, I think I might have gone crazy. But pain took my attention, and weakness made me sleep a good deal; and when I came to get up again, I was quieter. I spent lots of time in the fields and woods. I had always loved them, and now they seemed to help me more than anything else. There was something about them so big that it was willing to let me love it as much as I wanted to. That was comforting. When I was in the woods, I felt as if I had hold of an endless thread. You know how it is?'

She appealed to me.

'Indeed, yes!' I answered her. And I quoted William Blake, —

> 'Only wind it into a ball, —
> It will lead you in at heaven's gate,
> Built in Jerusalem's wall.'

She nodded soberly, yet glowingly, and pondered the words for a moment. Then, 'That's very good,' she said. 'Please say it again.

'Well, by and by,' she continued, touching her finger as if she were half unconsciously enumerating the points of a discourse, — there was something indescribably simple and downright in her manner of unfolding her experience, — 'by and by, somebody gave me a card to the village library, and I began to read. Of course I had always gone to school, but the pieces in the readers didn't interest me particularly, and I hadn't followed them up. A reader isn't a book, anyway; it's a crazy quilt. I guess I shan't ever forget that summer. I couldn't do anything but read. I read stories and poems and books about travel and history and peoples' lives. I had a hiding-place up in the woods, where I used to go and stay for hours, sometimes whole days. My older sister couldn't get anything out of me in the way of housework. It was wonderful.' Her voice rose a little, and something of the old exultation came flooding back into her face. 'Isn't it silly to talk of books as if they were just print and paper, when they are really stars and seas and cities and pictures and people and everything! There was nothing my books didn't give me that summer; and yet, on the other hand, there was nothing they didn't make me want. I wanted to travel, to go everywhere, to see and hear everything; above all, by way of a beginning, I wanted to go to school.

'I was always an impatient child; and it did seem as if I couldn't wait till autumn, when the schools opened. There's a good school at Fieldsborough, over the mountain. I coaxed my father to let me go there; and, after a while, he consented. On the day he wrote to enter my name, I ran up in the woods and lay in a bed of ferns and cried for joy. I hugged every tree that came in my way. I tried to hug the brook. Dear me!' Again she broke off, and the light which had begun to burn in her eyes softened into a smile. 'That's the way I was then. I was so hot-hearted. I didn't understand.'

'But you went?' I inquired, my sympathetic eagerness suddenly breaking bounds. It seemed to me that I could not stand it if she had been disappointed. 'Oh! why not?' My voice faltered, for she shook her head.

'My eyes,' she said briefly. 'They had always bothered me; and, before he let me go to school, father had them examined by a city doctor who was boarding in the village. He said I'd surely be blind some day; and that, of course, the more books I read, the sooner the end would come.'

She spoke as if she referred to the wearing out of an umbrella or a pair of shoes; and, fortunately for us both, my distress kept me dumb.

'It was pretty hard at first — a real blow. But I was sixteen years old, and I had suffered once. Then, too, I thought I had to make a choice, and I needed all my wits about me. So I held on to myself, and went off to the woods to think. Should I go to school, or should I keep my eyes as long as I could? As soon as I had put my mind to it, however, I found that there was n't any real question there. Of course I'd got to keep my eyes, and the school must go. There were all sorts of reasons. I wanted to see the woods and mountains as long as possible. I didn't want to become dependent on any one. My memory wasn't very good; and I knew, most likely, if I went to school and stuffed my mind full that year, I'd soon forget everything, and there I'd be — worse off than ever. So I gave over thinking about it, and just lay in the ferns all the afternoon.

'Maybe you'll hardly believe me when I tell you that I was happy that day. I don't know what it was. Something moved in the treetops and in the shadows. I watched it closely; and, by and by, when I was just on the point of seeing it, I realized that both my eyes were closed. If I had n't been so surprised by that discovery and so taken up with wondering how I had happened to shut my eyes without knowing it, I believe I'd have seen —'

Her voice trailed off into silence; and I presently found myself wondering if she had left that sentence unfinished also without knowing it.

II

'My father died the next year,' she continued, after a few thoughtful minutes, 'and my sister married, and I came to live in this little house. I had it fixed over to suit me, so that it was as simple and convenient as possible; and I set myself to learn it by heart. I did a lot of my housework after dark. Inside a year, I was so independent that I knew I need never worry about having to get anybody to help me. By taking plenty of time, I managed to learn some books by heart too; and I found it was much more interesting to sit and think about one paragraph for an hour than to read twenty pages. Even a few words are enough. Take, "Be still, and know that I am God"; or, "Acquaint now thyself with Him, and be at peace." There's no end to those sentences.

'Well,' — She touched her third finger, and then, for the first time, she came to a full pause, as if she were not sure about going on. Her face grew shy and reserved and reluctant.

I looked away—not for anything would I have urged her further confidence. But she went on presently. She had committed herself to the stream of this confession, and she would not refuse to be carried by it wherever it might wind.

'After a while I had a lover. He was a man from the city, and I met him in the woods. We were never introduced; and, for a long time, I did n't know anything about him — except that I loved him and he loved me. We could n't help it, for we felt the same way about the woods. I had never known any one like him before, and never expected to, because I'm so different from most folks. He made me understand how lonely it is to be different. I — we —'

But, after all, she could not dwell on this experience, and I did not want her to. The poignant beauty of the relation was already sufficiently apparent to my imagination.

'One day he told me that he had a wife at home,' she concluded; 'and I never saw him again. I think it was then that I really knew and understood.'

Knew what? Understood what? She had an air of having said all that was necessary, of having come to the end of her story; and I shrank from putting any crude questions to her. But it seemed to me that, if she did not tell me something more of her secret, I should just miss the most significant revelation I had ever caught a glimpse of.

Perhaps she read my suspense. At any rate, she said presently,—

'It was very simple. If it had n't been, I could n't have understood it; for I was never a good hand at trying to reason things out. It was just that I was n't ever to have anything I wanted. When I once knew and accepted that, I felt as if I'd slipped out into a great, wide, quiet sea.'

This was, to her own mind, so definitely the end of her narrative, that, after sitting a moment in silence, she half rose as if to go into the house and attend to some domestic task. But I put out my hand and held her apron's hem.

'You mean —' I stammered.

Really, she must tell me a little more!

A look of perplexity, almost of distress, came into her tranquil face, and she shook her head.

'I told you I was no hand at working things out,' she said. 'It's better just to know.'

'Please!' I insisted.

It was crass in me; but I felt that something as precious as life itself depended on my grasping the full significance of this story.

Gently, but very resolutely, she stooped and released her apron from my clutch.

'I've some bread in the oven,' she said, and disappeared.

III

She was gone so long that I had time to do what I would with the fragments of the story which she had so non-committally delivered to me. Since analysis was my way, I should have full scope for it. I sat with my head in my hands, my elbows on my knees. The sunset deepened and glowed around me, but I paid no attention to it. The cloudy abstraction which hovered before my inner vision, and let me grasp here a fringe, there a fold, was all-absorbing to me.

Souls that want greatly, like Hesper, are doomed to failure or disappointment. No earthly having can possibly satisfy them. For what they really want is simply God, and earth represents Him very imperfectly. Hesper had not been happy with the thing she had come nearest having — her mother. Would she have been happy with her lover? Would he have let her love him 'too well'? Books and education and travel are all finite and fragmentary means to an end which never arrives. Only adventurous spirits can escape the torment in them. And, with all her eagerness, Hesper was not adventurous. She was too earnest and humble, she was too direct. Fate had been good to her; and, in giving her nothing, had really given her everything. Everything: that was God. Well, her story had not once referred to Him, but it had been as instinct with Him as a star with light. It was He who had beckoned and lured her by lurking in her three definite interests, and then had shattered them before her in order that she might find Him. She had Him fast at last, and He had her. There was no mistaking the heavenly surrender of her face. I was awed with the apprehension of the passionate seeking and finding between a human soul and its Maker. Did she recognize and acknowledge the situation? Or, here again, did she prefer a blind certainty?

Blind! The word had dogged me for several weeks, but I had evaded it. Now, when it suddenly confronted me, I was all but staggered by it. I think I groaned slightly; I know I pressed my hand closely over my eyes. Then my own action admonished me. Here was I, deliberately shutting myself away from the sight of the outer world in order that I might hold and marshal my thoughts in the presence of reality. The hills and sky are distracting; the whole flying glory of creation is a perpetual challenge and disturbance to the meditative spirit. How supremely excellent it would be if one could only look long and hard and adoringly enough at it to see through it once; and then never see it again, for the rapt contemplation of That which lies behind!

I had come to this point in my revery when Hesper softly returned and stood in the doorway behind me. I looked up at her. She returned my smile, but I thought that her eyes did not quite fix me. Neither did she glance at the sky when I commented on the beauty of the sunset — although she assented to the comment convincingly. As she sat down beside me, her hands and feet made a deft groping. I said nothing; and I have never known whether she or any one else knew that she was blind.

The minister's wife waylaid me, as I passed her house that evening on my way back to my room.

'You've been to see Hesper Sherwood again?' she remarked, with a righteous, tolerant air of ignoring a slight. 'I'm so glad! Her life is so empty that any little attention means riches to her.'

'Empty!'

The expostulation was a mistake, but I really could not help it.

'I have never known such a brimming life,' I added, still more foolishly.

The minister's wife stared at me.

'Why, she has nothing at all,' she said.

'Precisely!' I commented, and went on my way.

A MOTH OF PEACE

BY KATHARINE FULLERTON GEROULD

ANNE MARMONT, of old the pupil of the nuns, had told her about Andecy: an ancient place, half-manor, half-farm, in the Marne valley, whence you could walk over a wind-swept plain to the battlefields of the Hundred Days.

'The nuns, being exiled, of course can't keep it up any longer, and no one wants to buy. I remember it as a place of heavenly peace — though in my day they used to make the oldest and crossest nun in the order superior at Andecy. However, Madame Françoise de Paule is dead now, and there aren't any nuns anyhow. Do take it, dear. If you want quiet' — Anne Marmont swept her arms out as if to embrace illimitable horizons. 'Nothing but a church-spire or a clump of trees to be seen from edge to edge of the plain. The unstable ocean is nothing to it. And if you want variety, you can walk over to Champaubert and look at the house where Napoleon stayed, the night before the battle. Riddled with bullet-holes it is. There used to be a foolish ancient there who remembered the Hundred Days. He's dead now, I suppose — but then, so is Madame Françoise de Paule, thank Heaven, and her cane, too. I hope they buried the cane. Do take it, darling. It's dirt cheap, and my dear nuns would be so pleased. They'd probably send the money to the new Nicaragua convent.'

And Miss Stanley had gone to Andecy, had been conquered by the insuperable peace of the plain, and had set up her little household. No place that she had ever seen seemed so good to wait in. When Edmund Laye came

back from the Argentine to marry her, she would submit
to London; but already she had hopes of enticing him to
Andecy for the honeymoon.   The chill of the slow spring
warmed her northern blood; she liked the reluctance of
the season's green, the roaring fire that met her in the
salon, the sharp cold click of her boots on the brick-paved
corridor.

She was well cared for: a Protestant and a foreigner, who
was, none the less, a mysterious well-wisher of 'ces dames,'
she found a shy allegiance springing up about her steps as
she traversed the plain.   There was always a hot *galette* for
her at 'la vieille Andecy,' an obsequious curtsy at Congy
château from the housekeeper, who showed with mumbling
pride the bed where Henri Quatre had slept; and a welcoming smile from St. Eloi, that holy humorist, in the
Champaubert chapel.   She sat until twilight, often, on the
sinister shore of l'Etang des Loups.   Even the legended
'Croix Jeanne,' leaning against its pine thicket, seemed
glad of her awkward Protestant dip.   It was a good place
— and all for the price of a second-rate hotel splotched
with Baedekers.

Loneliness, in the sense of removal from the social scene,
did not afflict her.   She who shrank almost morbidly from
human encounters, had no fear of the peasants.   Slim,
shy, timorous, she felt safe here.   Her terrors were all of
people and what people could do to her.   The plain ignored
her self-distrust.   Letters came from Edmund, regularly,
if you granted the delay of driving to Sézanne to fetch
them.   The months rounded slowly, punctually, to winter
and her marriage.   So might a châtelaine have waited,
powerless but trusting.

Then, in full summer-time, the lightning struck, choosing
again the Montmirail plain, after a hundred years' respite.
The first rumors were vague and vivid — all detail and no

substance, like news in the Middle Ages.   There was war,
and she scarcely knew more.   Jacques or Étienne turned
over night into a reservis`, and departed; but had it not
been for that, she would . ardly have known.   The two
maid-servants whom she ha brought with her clamored
for Paris; she gave them money a=d had them driven to
Sézanne.   After the mobilization they must have got
through, for she never heard again.   It did not occur to her
to strike out, herself, for the capital; for her common sense
told her she was better off where she was until Paris had
cleared the decks for action.   Besides, Paris frightened
her.   She hated being jostled in streets; she resented even
a curious stare.

Old Marie and her husband, with their grandchild, came
up from their cottage to the manor to sleep; and with the
son and nephew gone, there was nothing for them to do but
potter about rheumatically in her behalf.   For many days,
the click of the rosary was never stilled among the corridors
of Andecy.

And still the rumors grew, terror capping terror, until
it seemed that even at Andecy blood might rain down at
any moment from the arched heaven.   At first Miss
Stanley forced herself to drive the fat donkey into Sézanne
for news — a half-day's trip with only more terror at the
end.   The feeble crowds beset the bulletins posted outside
the *mairie*, and scattered, murmuring their own comments
on the laconic messages.   Sometimes crones and half-
grown children on the edge of the crowd got her to report
to them, as she emerged from the denser group in front of
the mairie wall.   She did so as gently as she could, for they
were all involved: fathers, husbands, sweethearts, brothers,
sons, were facing the enemy at some point or other that
only the War Office knew.   If some creatures had had

nothing to give, it was only because the Prussians had taken all they had, in '70.

There was no insane terror; the people were strangely calm; yet they and theirs had been, of all time, the peculiar food of the enemy, and there was pessimism afloat. The plain was as defenseless as they: its mild crops as fore-ordained to mutilation by feet and hoofs and wheels as they to splintering shells.

Miss Stanley, who was so shy of unfamiliar action, felt Sézanne too much for her. She stopped going, after a week, and resigned herself to not knowing. She chafed under the censorship, though she knew that Edmund Laye would tell her that it was well done of the 'Powers that Were' to stanch the leakage of news as you would stanch blood from an artery. The General Staff was better off not drained of its vital facts. To be sure, Miss Stanley never read newspapers. Even less, did she sub-scribe to them. But she longed now for a neutral America, where the extras came hot and hot, where experts of every kind fought out the battles on the front page, and good journalese stimulated the lax imagination.

Her determination to go no more to Sézanne led her for exercise to other quarters of the plain. She would walk quickly, tensely, for an hour, her eyes fixed on a clump of trees or a church-spire far ahead of her at the end of the unswerving road, until the clump and the spire rose up to match her height and she came to the first whitewashed cottage. Champaubert church was never empty, these days, of worshipers who gazed up at gaudy St. Eloi as if he could help. The crops that waved on the old Montmirail battlefield were thinly harvested by women and an im-peding fry of children. The steep little streets of Congy were dirtier than ever, and the ducks and the infants plashed about more indiscriminately in the common mud-puddles. No more galettes at 'la vieille Andecy': the old woman was prostrated by the loss of her reservist grandson.

Finally she gave up the plain too, and withdrew into Andecy itself, waiting, always waiting, for word of Edmund Laye. There had been a touch of loyalty to him in her staying on without plan of escape. News of him would reach her here sooner than elsewhere. If she left, she would be lost in a maelstrom, and might lose some precious word. Until she heard from Edmund of his sailing, or of a change of plan, she would stay where he thought of her as being. When she heard, she would go.

Some atavistic sense in Miss Stanley caused her to look, all through early August, to the provisioning of the manor — some dim instinct to hoard food, that might have sprung from the heart of a colonial ancestress behind a stockade of logs: premonition against death and savages. She sent old Marie to buy thriftily, making it clear that her fortress was not for herself alone, but for all who might be in need. Together, she and Marie and the granddaughter piled provisions in the empty rooms and the dark cellars; and they lived frugally on milk and eggs and *soupe aux choux.*

Sometimes she wondered whether the danger was not a mere fixed idea of the foolish peasants who had all been touched in the wits by '70. True, the able-bodied men were gone, but the reports these people brought her made no sense. Their quality verged on folk-lore. Something gigantic was going on, somewhere, but it had nothing to do with Edmund Laye in the Argentine, or with her at Andecy. Paris in danger? Perhaps: but how to take it on their word? Belgium flowing with blood? Just what did it mean? An aeroplane over Sézanne at dawn? It must often have happened, *allez!* The air was never free, now-adays. The Germans in France? They had been seeing Germans behind every bush for forty years. So she talked with old Marie, scarcely sure whether she or old Marie were the fool.

Since the household no longer drove the fat donkey to Sézanne, none of them knew even what the War Office said — unless what old Séraphine from the next farm reported that her granddaughter had heard in Champaubert from a woman whose married daughter had been to Sézanne two days before, could be called a War Office report. And never, from the first, on the plain of Andecy, had anyone understood *why*. According to the plain, all things were to be believed of the German Emperor, who was usually drunk; but, on the other hand, who could trust an atheist government? The soil of the Hundred Days had never recovered from Bonapartist tendencies, Miss Stanley had often noted; and even old Marie would sometimes mix up '15 and '70. The White Paper — which Miss Stanley had never heard of — would have been wasted on Champau-bert and Montmirail.

Wonder stirred at last even in old Marie's fatalistic mind at the lack of panic in this shy young foreigner — who could not chaffer, who could not bully, who could not endure even the mimic urbanity of Sézanne. Strange that she should be willing to stay quietly pacing up and down the cobbled courtyard of Andecy for sole exercise! Past mid-August, Marie put a vague question.

'When I hear from him, I shall go, Marie,' Miss Stanley answered. 'But I leave everything here to you and Thé-ophile. The British fleet holds the sea, they say, and I shall be better off in England. I shall surely come back when the war is over, and perhaps I shall bring my husband with me.'

Some dim muscular effort deepened the wrinkles in the old woman's face. It was as if a knife had cut them in the living flesh.

'I hope so — if Théophile and I are here. To be sure, you must go where it is your duty. We will keep such of the provisions as can be kept —'

'Keep nothing. It is all for you who have been so kind to me — you and yours. Not a child, not a creature, for a dozen miles about that I would not wish to share with, as you know. But — listen, Marie.' Miss Stanley blushed faintly as she bent her head nearer Marie's good ear.

'It *is* my duty. My first duty, that is, must be to my future husband. When he returns from America' (she had long ago learned the futility of distinguishing, for Marie, between 'l'Amérique du nord' and 'l'Amérique du sud'; and was patient with her belief that New York was a suburb of Cayenne) 'he will wish me there. He was to have sailed last month. A letter — a telegram — must have gone astray in the confusion. When I hear, he will doubtless be in England. And when he reached England, I was to go to my friends and be married to him. My heart bleeds for France; but I am not French, and my duty is not here. I am American, you see, dear Marie, and my *fiancé* is English.'

'Ah!' Marie shook her head. 'My old head is turned with all they tell me, and the buzzing in my bad ear is like cannon. But I had thought that the English, for some reason I do not understand, were fighting with us. They have been telling us for ten years that we do not hate the English — that we love them. And Théophile thought that an English army was against the Germans. But perhaps I am wrong. *Monsieur votre fiancé* will not have to fight, then? I congratulate you, mademoiselle.'

'The English are fighting with the French, Marie. But

all Englishmen are not soldiers.   Monsieur Laye is not a
soldier.   He is an engineer.'

'He is perhaps past the age.'

'There is no conscription in England, Marie.   No man
is a soldier unless he chooses.'

'No service to make?'

'None.'

'*C'est beau, ça!*   All Frenchmen must fight.   So England
may go to war, and still have men to till the fields.   But
where do their armies come from?'

'Any man who wishes may go.   But none are compelled
— except the soldiers by profession.   There will be enough,
never fear.   England will not desert France.'

The old woman nodded.   'I am not afraid of that.
And you are not afraid that *monsieur le fiancé* will fight?
I do not understand these things.   As Théophile says,
what I comprehend I do not hear, and what I hear I do not
comprehend.   I go to fetch mademoiselle's soup.   They
are lucky, all the same, to get the crops in, in time of war.'
She clattered from the room.

Miss Stanley felt her heart grow heavy, she did not know
precisely why.   If only word would come!   Perhaps she
was a fool to stay.   There must be trains through to Paris
now.   Anything to get nearer Edmund, away from this
historic, war-bound plain!   She crouched by the window
to eat her *soupe aux choux* and stale bread.   If only some
boy would come riding into the courtyard with a letter for
her!   She had bribed half the urchins who loitered by the
mairie in Sézanne to rush to her hot-foot with anything
that came.

The lightning that had struck once at Champaubert and
Montmirail was to strike again before she heard from
Edmund Laye.   Suddenly, with no warning, the heavens
opened with that reiterant flash.   Frightened stragglers

over the plain, refugees from the north pushing on from
beyond Sézanne in a blind stumbling dash to the southward; rumors that sprang up out of the ground so that she
had but to stand still to hear the world move; indescrib-
able distant noises, commotions less seen than sensed, on
the far horizon; a casual smudge of aeroplanes on the great
blue round of heaven; an earth, for no visible reason,
tumultuously vibrating beneath her, — and then, at last,
one hot noon, a frightened boy falling exhausted at her
feet. She gave him the piece of gold which for many days
had been waiting for him in her pocket, and bade him rest
where he lay until he was ready for food. Marie and
Théophile crouched beside him, listening to his winded
babbling.

Armies, armies, fighting, men riding on horses, guns and
wounded — like '15, like '70, like Hell. People like themselves leaving their cottages and farms, making, with such
portable treasures as they had (food, relics, poultry, babes
in arms), for the shelter of a town. No town could avail
them, for in the towns sat the officers, and the market-
place offered only a bigger, a more organized destruction.
But the hope of shelter would take them far afield. Anything was better than to see sabres splintering your walls,
and a greasy flame replacing all that had been ancestral
and intimate. Better to die in the open with friends—not
smoked out of your own cellar to fall on a bayonet. They
knew the secular ways of war: the dwellers on the plain
were the foredoomed type of the refugee, the world over.
Once in so often men fought, and poor people were home-
less. And now none of the 'vieux de la vieille' were there to
guard.

These were the visions that assembled in Miss Stanley's
brain while Marie, her lean fists clenched, reported the
boy's wild talk. The lumps of fat hardened on her con-

gealing soup; and still her mind went painfully, shuttle-wise, back and forth from her telegram — infinitely delayed, but clearly authentic — to the apocalyptic events surrounding her. Like most Americans perpetually defended by two oceans, Miss Stanley had no conception of invasion as a reality. The insult of an enemy on your own ground was one which she had never steeled herself to meet. There was no weapon in her little arsenal for a literal foe. Her knees trembled under her as she rose to look out of the window, after Marie, spent with eloquence, had left her.

Edmund Laye, by this, was with his regiment — even she might not know where. No point in trying to break through to London: his telegram, dated the day of his arrival in England, was already too old. The letter he promised her would go the way of all the letters he must have written, that she had never had. And she herself was caught: she had waited too long on that predestined plain. The noises she heard seemed rumblings of the earth and cracklings of the inflamed sky. Andecy manor had not yet seen one soldier, unless you reckoned the pilots of those soaring monoplanes. But their hours were numbered: soon — any moment, now — all that hidden rumor would break forth into visible fruit of fighting men — men with rifles, men with lances, men with mitrailleuses or howitzers. She was trapped. To try, even with no luggage, to make the miles to Sézanne, would be not so much to take her life in her hands as to kick it from her. Caught; and her nervous nostrils feigned for her a subtle odor of smoke. She turned from the window and went to the quiet room that had once been the chapel. Out of those windows she could not look, thank Heaven! The life of the Virgin, in villainous stained glass, barred her vision.

She was absolutely alone. Old Marie and Théophile were not people: they were strangers, creatures, animals — what not. She scarcely knew. 'Allies' meant nothing to her at the moment but marching men. Even Edmund — who would be killed, because all beautiful things were killed unless they hid in caves and let their beauty rot in the dark. Fool that she had been not to go to England while there was time! Fool that she had been to forget that Edmund Laye, landing in England, would be first of all a Territorial — one of the thousands of slim reeds on which Kitchener was so heavily leaning. She had been obsessed with peace: sure that war could not touch her or what was privately, supremely, hers. She was a creature of peace; a little doctrinaire who supposed that, in the inverted moral world in which she walked, right made might. There was a deal of most logical self-pity in her tears. How did any of it concern her, that she should be cooped in a country manor to await horrors from unknown people? Why should Edmund Laye, who had chosen an antipodal career, be dragged back to present himself as a mark for some Prussian shell? The senselessness of it angered her. Nations meant little to her; the cosmos nothing. Alone in the chapel, she treated herself to a vivid personal rage. And still the strange tumult, that was more than half made of vibrations too slow for sound-waves, beat upon her nerves like an injury to the internal ear.

By twilight, the physical need of action came to her. She felt, in the subtler fibres of her mind, that if she stayed longer there half prone in her worm-eaten arm-chair, groveling mentally in this welter of concrete alarms, she should sink into a pit whence reason could not rescue her. She had been so calm in her folly, so lulled by the sense of her sacred detachment from this bloody business, so sure that neutrality protected you from fire and steel even in the thickest *mêlée* — she could not have been more ridiculous if she had worn a dress cut out of the Stars and Stripes. Now, some obscure inhibition told her, she must act. She must move her hands and feet, limber her cramped muscles, set the blood flowing properly in her veins, make herself physically normal, or her worthless mind would let her go mad. She must not think of death or outrage or torture.

She must forget the things she had heard those first days at Sézanne. She must forget the gossip of Marie and Théophile and Séraphine, inventing, inventing, with a mediæval prolixity and a racial gift for the *macabre*, on chill evenings by the fire. They had no need of news. They dug up out of the bloody deeps of the past things the like of which she had never expected to hear. She must forget — shut her staring mouth and forget. Whatever visited itself on Andecy must not find a gibbering mistress there. Perhaps, if she pretended that Edmund knew, moment by moment, what she was doing, she could master her faltering flesh and her undisciplined mind. She had lost him forever, but she would try to be some of the things he thought her. Edmund Laye had called her flower-like. Well: flowers were broken, but they did not go mad. She must be — decent.

Her brisk pacing of the chapel did not allay her fears, but it brought back to her a sense of decorum. Her body had never lent itself to an immodest gesture; what — she caught at the notion — could be more immodest than visible fear? So gradually, by artificial means, she brought herself back into some dignity; scolding and shaking herself into a trooper's demeanor. She could not trust her mind, but perhaps she could get her instincts into fighting form. Cautiously she tried them — as you try a crazy foothold to see if it will bear your weight. Her muscles seemed to respond: suppleness, strength, coördination, were reported satisfactory. She thought she could promise not to fall a-shivering again. The noise in her ears faded; the vibrations ceased to rock her nerves. Miss Stanley flung open the chapel door, and walked firmly, ignoring echoes, down the brick-paved corridor to the kitchen.

Marie, Théophile, and little Jeanne watched, in a kind of apathy, the pot on the fire. In the dim corners of the big kitchen, Miss Stanley thought she saw strange figures. Inspection revealed a few frightened women and children from farms that had once been dependencies of Andecy. Here was something to do — more blessed exercise for hands and feet.

'You, Françoise? and the little ones? And you, Mathilde? and the girl? Good! It is time the children had food and went to bed. We must economize candles, so we will all eat here. The dining-room, in half an hour, will be a dormitory. Jeanne shall sleep in my room. Milk and gruel for the little ones, Marie, and *soupe aux choux* for the rest of us. Milk we will use while we have it. Eggs also. We cannot expect to keep the livestock forever. Bread we have not — until I bake it in my own fashion. It may come to that. Jeanne, you will eat with us older ones. Come and help me make beds for the children. Luckily, there are cots for a whole community. In half an hour' — she took out her watch — 'the babies sup and say their prayers. To-morrow, I prepare the chapel and the pupils' old dormitory for wounded. Wounded there will be, if what we hear from Sézanne — though they are all fools in Sézanne, from the fat mayor down — be true. My fiancé is at the front. We wait here for our men, hein?' And she beckoned to Jeanne.

She had made her speech blindly, recklessly planning as

she spoke, thinking that if she could convince her hearers
she could perhaps convince herself. She looked for the
effect on them when she had done. The speech had
worked. If it worked for them, it must work for her, too.
It could not be madness, if it had lighted up those sodden
faces. And as she looked from one to another, she saw a
flicker of pride, of patriotism, reflected in their eyes. Reflected from what? From her, without doubt. There
must have been pride in her voice and glance when she
spoke of Edmund Laye. Good! That was the line to
take. There should be a brave show: she would work her
muscles to death to keep it going. Every due emotion
should be cultivated in each limb and feature; every surface inch of skin should play its part. The drum and fife
should play all the more bravely because her heart was
hollow. Perhaps, if she got a fair start, a fine physical
impetus toward courage, she could keep it up to the end.

'Come, Jeanne.' She beckoned the child.

The women stirred, and the children huddled against
their skirts crept out upon the floor.

'Théophile, is the great gate locked?'

The old man shook his head vaguely. He had gone near
to losing his few wits with the rumors from Sézanne which
his ears had drunk up so greedily. His shaken mind was
wandering windily about in reminiscences of '70 and leg-
ends of '15.

'It had best be locked at once. The lantern, Jeanne.
Come.'

The child looked at her piteously.

'Oh, very well!' Miss Stanley pushed her gently aside.
'I shall not need it. There is still light enough. Fetch
the bowls for the babies, Jeanne. We must all get to bed,
and be up with the dawn.'

Alone, she left the house and crossed the innumerable

cobblestones of the huge courtyard to the outer gate. She knew the way of the heavy bolts and bars, for she had often escorted Théophile on his rounds before the official *coucher* of the household; but her shaking fingers tapped the rusty iron ineffectually. She loathed her fingers: insubordinate little beasts! She struck her right hand smartly with her left, her left with her right, to punish them with real pain. The fingers steadied; she drove the foolish, antiquated bolts home.

Something white fluttered about her feet in the twilight: the hens had not been shut up. Miss Stanley was very angry, for a moment, with Théophile; then angry with herself for her anger. Théophile was frightened because he *knew:* '70 had been the moment of his prime. She did not know; she had no right to be frightened. Tales of the Civil War, she remembered now, had always bored her; she had never listened to them. Her duty now was to secure the poultry. They must have eggs while they could, and chicken broth for the children. Mathilde's little girl was a weakling. So she ran hither and yon, trying to drive the silly handful toward the little grange where they were kept. With traditional idiocy, they resisted; and the last stragglers she lifted and imprisoned ruthlessly in her skirt. She hated the creatures; to touch them made her flesh crawl; but at last she got them all in, squawking, and fastened the door upon them. How like the stupid things, to make extra trouble because there was a war! Her anger against them was quite serious, and sank into proper insignificance only when her task was done.

A stone wall, continuing the house wall all the way round, bounded the courtyard; but through the grille she could see rocket-like sputters of flame far off on the horizon, and here and there a patch of light in the sky which meant fires burning steadily beneath. The pounding vibrations had ceased. There was trouble, a mighty trouble, upon them all; and with the dawn, perhaps, all the things those chattering fools by the fire had spent their phrases on.

Strangest of all to her was the sudden thought that Edmund, separated from her now by the innumerable leagues of destiny, might be, as the crow flies, not so far away. A few fatal miles might be replacing, even now, the friendly, familiar ocean whose division of the lovers had been a mere coquetry of Time. On that thought she must not dwell; besides — irony returned to her at last — did she not gather from those idiots within that all soldiers one ever saw were Germans? One's own armies were routed somewhere; but one encountered, one's self, only the victors, ever. Then the jealous captain to whom she had given the command reminded her that such reflections meant mutiny.

Slim, straight, hollowed out with fear, but walking delicately ahead, she went back to the house and superintended the babies' supper. Then the grown-ups ate — standing about the table as at the Passover, faces half-averted toward the door — and she marshaled them all to their appointed sleeping-places. Marie and Théophile abdicated their dominion with an uncouth relief. If mademoiselle, so shy, so small, could be so sure of what they ought to do — doubtless hers was a great brain in a frail form. After prayers, in which Miss Stanley herself joined, borrowing a *chapelet*, they went off to snore peacefully in the guardianship of that great brain so opportunely discovered.

'You have not an American flag?' old Marie asked, as she shuffled off.

Théophile, past any coherent reflections, was mumbling over the dying fire.

'No, nothing of the sort. I am sorry. I should use it if I had.'

'You could not make one?'

'Impossible, to-night. To-morrow I will see.'

Marie apologetically offered a last suggestion to the great brain. 'A white flag? It would do no harm to have it ready. Françoise swears they are in Sézanne to-night.'

'I will see. *Allez vous coucher.*'

And Miss Stanley turned on her heel and sought the little room where Jeanne was already restlessly dreaming.

Save the babies, Andecy found no deep sleep that night. The old people napped and woke and napped again, according to their habit. The mothers rose and walked beside their children's cots, then fell limply back and dozed. Miss Stanley slept from sheer exhaustion until an hour before dawn. Then she rose and dressed herself, and, when dressed, sent Jeanne to wake her grandparents. Whatever the day might bring, it should not find them either asleep or fasting. They would eat, if it was to be their last meal.

Alone in her room, by candle-light, Miss Stanley made a white flag out of a linen skirt. She sewed hastily but firmly, that it might be no flimsier than she could help. By the first streaks of daylight, she groped for and found, in a lumber-room, a long stick to fasten it to — probably, it flashed across her, Madam Françoise de Paule's cane, never buried, as Anne Marmont had hoped. When the flag was finished, she loathed it: loathed its symbolism, loathed its uselessness. No: whatever happened, she would have nothing to do with that. What could be more humiliating than to hold up a white flag in vain? Another idea came to her; and while breakfast was preparing and the children were being dressed, she carried it swiftly into execution. Slashing a great cross out of a scarlet cape, she sewed it firmly to the white ground. *That* she might hang to the dove-cot, after breakfasting.

She carried it martially with her into the great kitchen, and placed it in a corner. The sun itself was hardly up, but the children brought the flag out into the firelight and old Marie was jubilant. The wonderful idea! The great brain of mademoiselle! She fussed almost happily over the simmering skillet of milk. But the great brain was pondering apart in the lessening shadows. Better the American flag, if she could manage it. She would beg an old blue smock of Théophile's, for she had nothing herself. Those wretched stars! It would take her a long morning; and she felt convinced that this day's sun would not rise peacefully to the zenith. This thing she had made was a lie. Incalculable harm could be done by assuming a badge you had no right to — incalculable harm to those who had the right. She was mortally afraid; but she would not do anything in pure panic. That would make it worse for every one in the end.

An American flag: it must be made. How many states were there? She had no notion, but she fancied they were as the sands of the sea. It would take a woman all day to cut out those stars and sew them to a blue field hacked out of Théophile's smock. And what a makeshift banner, in the end! Even if the enemy politely waited for her to finish it, would they not detect it at once? Was not that the kind of thing every German knew better than she — how many little silly stars there were, safe and far away, sending senators to Washington? A sullen tide of mirth was let loose in her far below the surface. Here she was, quivering with terror, with a lot of foolish livestock on her hands — livestock that she could not give up to slaughter as if they had been the sheep that they really were.

Miss Stanley caught up one of the children to her lap

and fed it great spoonfuls of warm milk — choking it hope-
lessly.   Luckily the mother was too apathetic to reproach
her.   She could not even feed a child without wetting it all
over!   Disgusted, she put the child down again.   It
whimpered, and the mother, roused, moved over to it.
Miss Stanley looked at her cup.   Chocolate — no coffee,
for the coffee was gone.   Coffee might have cleared her
brain, but this mess would do nothing for her.   Still, she
drank it.   And gradually, as their hunger was appeased,
they crept about her.   Even those who did not move their
chairs turned and faced her.   She could not meet so many
eyes.   She had nothing to do with them — these tellers of
old wives' tales, who expected her to deliver them from
the horrors their own lips had fabricated.   Why did they
stare at her as if she might have an idol's power over
events?   Whispering, almost inaudibly, their strung and
beaded prayers, yet blasphemously looking to her!

The shadows still lessened in the great kitchen.   The
sun lay in level streaks on the centre of the stone floor, and
even the twilight in the corners was big with noon.   The
women sat in a helpless huddle, not knowing how to go
about the abnormal tasks of the abnormal day.   The
far-off thunders of the plain began again: vibrations as of
earthquake first, then explicit sounds, unmistakable and
portentous.   To-day, you could distinguish among those
clamors.   Miss Stanley, with the first sounds, expected to
have a tiny mob to quell; but their apathy did not leave
them.   Even the children turned that steady, hypnotized
stare on her.   And then Jeanne — how could she not have
missed Jeanne from the assembly? — ran down the corridor with a sharp clatter.

'They are there!   Soldiers — on horseback — at the
gate!'

And indeed now, in the sudden tragic hush, Miss Stan-

ley could hear the faint metallic thrill and tinkle of iron
bars, at a distance, struck sharply. Old Théophile roused
himself as if by unconscious antediluvian habit, but Marie
plucked him back and ran for the flag with the scarlet
cloth cross. This she thrust into the American girl's hand.
No one else moved, except that Mathilde flung her heavy
skirt over her little girl's head.

For one moment, Miss Stanley stood irresolute. She
had never dreamed of such a tyranny of irrelevant fact.
She must, for life or death, — for honor, at all events, —
respond to a situation for which nothing, since her birth,
had prepared her. Peace had been to her as air and sunlight — the natural condition of life. This was like being
flung into a vacuum; it was death to her whole organism.
Yet, somehow, she was still alive.

Irony took her by the throat; and then the thought of
Edmund Laye — linked, himself, with events like these,
riding or marching beneath just such skies, on just such a
planet, under just such a law. Never had there been,
really, immunity like that which she had fancied to be the
very condition of human existence. It was all human, with
a wild inclusiveness that took her breath. And, whatever
happened, paralysis like that which even now crept slowly
up her limbs, was of the devil. Against that last ignominy
she braced herself.

Her muscles responded miraculously to her call for help,
and she felt her feet moving across the floor. If feet
could move, hands could. She rolled up the little banner
and threw it in the very centre of the fire. It occurred to
her as a last insult that she did not know enough German
even to proclaim her nationality; but she did not falter
again. Some residuum of human courage out of the past
kept her body loyal — some archaic fashion of the flesh
that dominated the newness of the mind. Past genera-

tions squared her shoulders for her, and gave her lips a phrase to practice.

As she passed down the corridor, she flung each door wide open. She paused, a mere fraction of an instant, in the big front door of the house; but from there she could see only a confusion of helmets, and horses nosing at the grille. Almost immediately she passed through the door and walked, hatless, her arms hanging stiffly at her sides, across the innumerable cobblestones, to the gate.

IN NO STRANGE LAND

HE was in the heart of the crowd, in it, and of it — the crowd of late afternoon whose simultaneous movement is the expression of a common wish to cease to be a crowd. His was one of the thousand faces that are almost tragical with weariness, tragical without thought. At five o'clock the sparkle of the morning is forgotten. There is no seeking of hidden treasure in the face opposite, for the face opposite, whosesoever it may be, has become too hatefully intrusive with its own burden to yield any light of recognition.

He was running down the Elevated stairs at the appointed minute, when his foot slipped and he fell. It seemed hardly a second before he was up again, angered by the sudden congestion about him. One white-cheeked woman put her hand to her mouth and gave a cry.

'Let me by!' he exclaimed, straining to break through the fast-pressing barrier. The very throng of which he had been an undistinguishable member had suddenly closed round him, focusing its Argus glance upon him, nearer and nearer, and it was only by extreme struggle that he was able to push away and be free.

He sat down in the train, breathless from his final sprint. He felt as if the incident had roused him from some deep lethargy of which he had hitherto been unaware. With his quickened pulse, his thoughts ran more quickly, more crystally onward. He felt as if a wonderful but unknown piece of luck had befallen him. An ecstatic sense of fortune made him wonder at himself.

'What am I so damned happy about, all of a sudden?'
he thought.

He made an indifferent survey of his fellow passengers,
and as he noted the familiar heads and shoulders, he had a
most curious sensation of utter bliss, and thanked heaven
that his lot was not theirs.

'Am I dreaming?' he asked himself. 'Am I about to discover a gold-mine, or what?'

As the train moved out he sank comfortably back into
his seat, and with his chin on his hand he took up his accustomed nightly gaze on the outer landscape. His thoughts
ran back to the morning. He saw the room where he had
gone to wake his children. It was a large, square room,
with colored nursery pictures on the walls and a collection
of battered toys in the corner. The place was fresh and
cool with the sparkling air of early day, and through the
open windows he had seen the lawn thick spread with cob-
webs. And in each of the three small beds a pretty child of
his lay stretched in a childish attitude of sleep. Very tender they looked, very lovable, in their naïve curlings-up,
a young, shapely arm flung out in the restlessness of approaching day, lips and nostrils just stirred by the tiny
motion of their breathing, and an unbelievable, blossomy
hand spread in fairy gesture across a pillow. As he walked
through the room, he heard the boy John murmur in his
waking dreams. Alicia sat up suddenly, as thin and
straight as a new reed in her prim nightgown. Her eye-
lashes were black and her eyes were heather-purple.

'Father!' she had cried, 'I know what day it is!' And
in a moment three small whirlwinds stood up on the floor,
dropped their nightgowns, and began to fling their arms
and legs into their morning apparel, and there was a great
deal of loud conversation full of the presage of festivity.
Their father had forgotten that he had a birthday until his

wife and children had recovered it from obscurity and made it a day of days.

As he left the house he had looked at Maggie, his fragile, high-hearted wife, and urged her not to get tired with the nonsense. She had looked back at him with mock haughtiness and warned him not to be late to supper, or make light of feast days. He did not notice her words; he was curiously unable to grow accustomed to her face. The more he saw it, the more unbelievably beautiful, the more eloquent in delicate and gentle meanings, it became to him. She looked into his eyes quickly, with a question for his sudden absent-mindedness.

'Because your face is so heavenly,' he answered reverently.

As the train moved on, he saw that a fresh, green haze had begun to veil and adorn the landscape which through the cold months had been so gaunt and ugly to his daily observation. The hint of fever was in the air — the slight madness that accompanies the pangs of seasonal change.

Love glowed in his heart and touched all the veins of his body with its winelike warmth, its inimitable winelike bouquet. 'Life is sweet! Life is sweet!' his body said, echoing and reëchoing through all the channels of his being. And as the train carried him on through the fields and woods outside the city, something almost like the fervor of genius took hold of him, plucking at his heart for words, crying to him out of the silent fields and woods for words, words!

A slight rain was in the air, darkening the twilight, when he stepped down from the train. He was grateful for the darkness, for the soft air on his face, grateful indeed for the silence. Evening had brought him back to his obscure town, a small station marked by one lantern swung in the stiff grasp of an ancient man. The usual handful of three or four passengers alighted, and exchanging remarks up and down the village street, quickly disappeared within the generous portals of their hereditary houses. The sound of a door opening and shutting, the pleasant light of lamps, the brief glimpse of a shining supper-table, the departing whistle of the train as it shot away through field and thicket, and the remote town was undisturbed again.

He was grateful indeed for the nightly renascence of his spirit in the clear air and gracious heaven of the place. On this May night of mist and darkness he took up again the thread of his real existence. Only to-night it seemed more golden, more palpitating with hope and mystery — a still moment wherein one could only half distinguish between the future and the past. He was thirty years old to-day, he told himself, and he had a wife and three children. A short swift time it had been! Had he them then, or was it a dream? Where were his footsteps taking him down the empty street? To Babylon, or some lost coast of gods and visions? He turned a familiar corner. A fresh breeze struck his face with a sudden shower of drops, and he saw in the dim light the heads of crocuses shaking in the grass beside the walk. He flung open the door and heard Maggie's voice in the dining-room and the laughter of Alicia.

'Hallo!' he called; and getting no answer, he walked into the dining-room. There was a circle of candles on the table, unlighted as yet, and a bowl of flowers.

Maggie was sitting by the fire, cracking nuts, and telling a story to the children who sat about her in white frocks, the firelight on their faces. The boy John was staring into the flame with the look that made his mother believe that she had given habitation to a poet's soul, and that inspired her to tell the most extravagant tales of wonder that her brain could conjure. Vibrant mystery rang in the low monotony of her voice.

Their father checked himself at the doorway, thinking that he had done violence to the etiquette of birthdays by allowing himself to view the preparation. He laughed and stepped out again.

'Oh, I see you don't want me. I really did n't look at a thing!' And he called back from the stair, 'How soon *may* I come?'

He heard nothing but the cracking of nuts, Maggie's enchanting tone, and the short laughter of Alicia.

'O Maggie, dear!' he called again.

No reply, — only the soft continuance of the magic tale in the inner room.

'By the way,' — He stepped down a stair. 'By the way, Maggie, may I see you a second?'

The story had ceased, but Maggie neither answered nor came. He stepped to the dining-room door with a curious sense of apprehension. There was a touch of surprise in his tone.

'Maggie!'

She looked round and on her face was the quick and strange reflection of his bewilderment. Yet she looked beyond him, through him, as if he had not been there. The boy John was still staring into the fire, folded deep in the robe of enthrallment his mother had made. As if from the hushed heart of it, he said, --

'What did you hear, mother?'

She gave him a startled glance, and then she smiled upon him, tenderly, warmly.

'Only the wind outside, dear child. It is a rainy and windy night.'

She looked again toward the door of the room.

'Maggie!'

Such was the sudden torture and fear in his breast, he could scarcely lift his voice. He put one hand to his head and stepped nearer his wife.

As if to find tranquillity in a moment of nervousness, she rested her soft glance on Alicia, the child of delicate hands and delicate thoughts.

Robbie, the importunate youngest, leaned against his mother with heavy and troubled eyes.

'I thought I heard something, mother,' he said.

She bent over him, visibly trembling.

'What did you think it was, darling?' she asked.

'I thought it was the rain hitting the window and trying to get in.'

She laughed and rose uneasily from her chair, and taking the child in her arms, she walked up and down before the friendly fire. For a long time there was no sound in the room except the vague sound of wind, of flame, and of Maggie's footsteps.

Suddenly Robbie gave a little cry from her shoulder.

'Why does n't father come?'

The man rushed toward his wife to clasp her and the child in his arms, crying, —

'O Maggie!'

She sank to her chair, trembling and stroking the head of her child with fearful compassion.

'O heavy mystery! Is this life,' he cried, 'or death?' He stretched out his arms in vain. The impassable gulf lay between them. Then, as he turned away from her, the walls of the house grew heavy upon him, the fire sent forth a smothering heat, and incomprehensible, unendurable became the spectacle of human grief.

He went toward the door. Hesitating he looked back again. Robbie's face was buried in her breast; her eyes were deep and dark with the half-guessed truth.

There came a sound at the door, that caused Maggie to start piteously. He forgot his desire to be free in his desire to clasp her again and console her.

She left the children and went unhesitating and pale to answer the summons, he hovering beside her. What a flower she looked and how fragilely shaken, like the rain-beaten crocuses in the grass!

As the door opened he saw two men standing in the dark and wet. For a moment neither spoke. One looked at the other, and broke out, —

'You tell her, for God's sake!'

This came to him dimly as if he were a thousand miles away. He heard no more. He had gone out into the wind and rain. It struck his breast again with its incomparable sweetness. He saw dark hills lying before him. Gateways long barred within him rushed open with a sound of singing and triumph. He felt no more sorrow, no more pity, — only incredible freedom and joy. The stone had been rolled away.

'Death is sweet! Death is sweet!' echoed and reëchoed through all the passages of his being. He smelt the icy breath of mountains, and he knew the vast solitude of the plains of the sea. The veins of his body were the great rivers of the earth, sparkling in even splendor. His head was among the stars, he saw the sun and the moon to-gether, and the four seasons were marshaled about him. The clouds of the sky parted and fell away, and across the blue sward of heaven he saw the procession of glowing, gracious figures whose broken shadow is cast with such vague majesty across the face of the earth.

LITTLE BROTHER

BY MADELEINE Z. DOTY

IT was a warm summer's day in late August. No men were visible in the Belgian hamlet. The women reaped in the fields; the insects hummed in the dry warm air; the house doors stood open. On a bed in a room in one of the cottages lay a woman. Beside her sat a small boy. He was still, but alert. His eyes followed the buzzing flies. With a bit of paper he drove the intruders from the bed. His mother slept. It was evident from the pale, drawn face that she was ill.

Suddenly the dreaming, silent summer day was broken by the sound of clattering hoofs. Some one was riding hurriedly through the town.

The woman moved uneasily. Her eyes opened. She smiled at the little boy.

'What is it, dear?'

The boy went to the window. Women were gathering in the street. He told his mother and hurried from the room. Her eyes grew troubled. In a few minutes the child was back, breathless and excited.

'O, mother, mother, the Germans are coming!'

The woman braced herself against the shock. At first she hardly grasped the news. Then her face whitened, her body quivered and became convulsed. Pain sprang to her eyes, driving out fear; beads of perspiration stood on her forehead; a little animal cry of pain broke from her lips. The boy gazed at her paralyzed, horrified; then he flung himself down beside the bed and seized his mother's hand.

'What is it, mother, what is it?'

The paroxysm of pain passed; the woman's body relaxed, her hand reached for the boy's head and stroked it. 'It's all right, my son.' Then as the pain began again, 'Quick, sonny, bring auntie.'

The boy darted from the room. Auntie was the woman doctor of B. He found her in the Square. The townspeople were wildly excited. The Germans were coming. But the boy thought only of his mother. He tugged at auntie's sleeve. His frenzied efforts at last caught her attention. She saw he was in need and went with him.

Agonizing little moans issued from the house as they entered. In an instant the midwife understood. She wanted to send the boy away, but she must have help. Who was there to fetch and carry? The neighbors, terrified at their danger, were making plans for departure. She let the boy stay.

Through the succeeding hour a white-faced little boy worked manfully. His mother's cries wrung his childish heart. Why did babies come this way? He could not understand. Would she die? Had his birth given such pain? If only she would speak! And once, as if realizing his necessity, his mother did speak.

'It's all right, my son; it will soon be over.'

That message brought comfort; but his heart failed when the end came. He rushed to the window and put his little hands tight over his ears. It was only for a moment. He was needed. His mother's moans had ceased and a baby's cry broke the stillness.

The drama of birth passed, the midwife grew restless. She became conscious of the outer world. There were high excited voices; wagons clattered over stones; moving day had descended on the town. She turned to the window. Neighbors with wheelbarrows and carts piled high with household possessions hurried by. They beckoned to her.

For a moment the woman hesitated. She looked at the mother on the bed, nestling her babe to her breast; then the panic of the outside world seized her. Quickly she left the room.

The small boy knelt at his mother's bedside, his little face against hers. Softly he kissed the pale cheek. The boy's heart had become a man's. He tried by touch and look to speak his love, his sympathy, his admiration. His mother smiled at him as she soothed the baby, glad to be free from pain. But presently the shouted order of the departing townspeople reached her ears. She stirred uneasily. Fear crept into her eyes. Passionately she strained her little one to her.

'How soon, little son, how soon?'

The lad, absorbed in his mother, had forgotten the Germans. With a start, he realized the danger. His new-born manhood took command. His father was at the front. He must protect his mother and tiny sister. His mother was too ill to move, but they ought to get away. Who had a wagon? He hurried to the window, but already even the stragglers were far down the road. All but three of the horses had been sent to the front. Those three were now out of sight with their overloaded wagons. The boy stood stupefied and helpless. The woman on the bed stirred.

'My son,' she called. 'My son.'

He went to her.

'You must leave me and go on.'

'I can't, mother.'

The woman drew the boy down beside her. She knew the struggle to come. How could she make him understand that his life and the baby's meant more to her than her own.   Lovingly she stroked the soft cheek.   It was a grave, determined little face with very steady eyes.

'Son, dear, think of little sister.   The Germans won't bother with babies.   There is n't any milk.   Mother has n't any for her.   You must take baby in your strong little arms and run — run with her right out of this land into Holland.'

But he could not be persuaded.   The mother understood that love and a sense of duty held him.   She gathered the baby in her arms and tried to rise, but the overtaxed heart failed and she fell back half-fainting.   The boy brought water and bathed her head until the tired eyes opened.

'Little son, it will kill mother if you don't go.'

The boy's shoulders shook.   He knelt by the bed.   A sob broke from him.   Then there came the faint far-distant call of the bugle.   Frantically the mother gathered up her baby and held it out to the boy.

'For mother's sake, son, for mother.'

In a flash, the boy understood.   His mother had risked her life for the tiny sister.   She wanted the baby saved more than anything in the world.   He dashed the tears from his eyes.   He wound his arms about his mother in a long passionate embrace.

'I ll take her, mother; I'll get her there safely.'

The bugle grew louder.   Through the open window on the far-distant road could be seen a cloud of dust.   There was not a moment to lose.   Stooping, the boy caught up the red squirming baby.   Very tenderly he placed the little body against his breast and buttoned his coat over his burden.

The sound of marching feet could now be heard.   Swiftly he ran to the door.   As he reached the threshold he turned. His mother, her eyes shining with love and hope, was wav-

ing a last good-bye. Down the stairs, out the back door,
and across the fields sped the child. Over grass and across
streams flew the sure little feet. His heart tugged fiercely
to go back, but that look in his mother's face sustained
him.

He knew the road to Holland: it was straight to the
north. But he kept to the fields. He did n't want the
baby discovered. Mile after mile, through hour after
hour he pushed on, until twilight came. He found a little
spring and drank thirstily. Then he moistened the baby's
mouth. The little creature was very good. Occasionally
she uttered a feeble cry, but most of the time she slept.
The boy was intensely weary. His feet ached. He sat
down under a great tree and leaned against it. Was it
right to keep a baby out all night? Ought he to go to
some farmhouse? If he did, would the people take baby
away? His mother had said, 'Run straight to Holland.'
But Holland was twenty miles away. He opened his coat
and looked at the tiny creature. She slept peacefully.

The night was very warm. He decided to remain where
he was. It had grown dark. The trees and bushes loomed
big. His heart beat quickly. He was glad of the warm,
soft, live little creature in his arms. He had come on this
journey for his mother, but suddenly his boy's heart
opened to the tiny clinging thing at his breast. His little
hand stroked the baby tenderly. Then he stooped, and
softly his lips touched the red wrinkled face. Presently
his little body relaxed and he slept. He had walked eight
miles. Through the long night the deep sleep of exhaustion held him. He lay quite motionless, head and shoulders resting against the tree-trunk, and the new-born babe
enveloped in the warmth of his body and arms slept also.
The feeble cry of the child woke him. The sun was coming

over the horizon and the air was alive with the twitter of birds.

At first he thought he was at home and had awakened to a long happy summer's day. Then the fretful little cries brought back memory with a rush. His new-born love flooded him. Tenderly he laid the little sister down. Stretching his stiff and aching body, he hurried for water. Very carefully he put a few drops in the little mouth and wet the baby's lips with his little brown finger. This proved soothing and the cries ceased. The tug of the baby's lips on his finger clutched his heart. The helpless little thing was hungry, and he too was desperately hungry. What should he do? His mother had spoken of milk. He must get milk. Again he gathered up his burden and buttoned his coat. From the rising ground on which he stood he could see a farmhouse with smoke issuing from its chimney. He hurried down to the friendly open door. A kindly woman gave him food. She recognized him as a little refugee bound for Holland. He had some difficulty in concealing the baby, but fortunately she did not cry. The woman saw that he carried something, but when he asked for milk, she concluded he had a pet kitten. He accepted this explanation. Eagerly he took the coveted milk and started on.

But day-old babies do not know how to drink. When he dropped milk into the baby's mouth she choked and sputtered. He had to be content with moistening her mouth and giving her a milk-soaked finger.

Refreshed by sleep and food, the boy set off briskly. Holland did not now seem so far off. If only his mother were safe! Had the Germans been good to her? These thoughts pursued and tormented him. As before, he kept off the beaten track, making his way through open meadows, and patches of trees. But as the day advanced, the heat grew intense. His feet ached, his arms ached, and, worst of all, the baby cried fretfully.

At noon he came to a little brook sheltered by trees. He sat down on the bank and dangled his swollen feet in the cool, fresh stream. But his tiny sister still cried. Suddenly a thought came to him. Placing the baby on his knees he undid the towel that enveloped her. There had been no time for clothes. Then he dipped a dirty pocket handkerchief in the brook and gently sponged the hot, restless little body. Very tenderly he washed the little arms and legs. That successfully accomplished, he turned the tiny creature and bathed the small back. Evidently this was the proper treatment, for the baby grew quiet. His heart swelled with pride. Reverently he wrapped the towel around the naked little one, and administering a few drops of milk, again went on.

All through that long hot afternoon he toiled. His footsteps grew slower and slower; he covered diminishing distances. Frequently he stopped to rest, and now the baby had begun again to cry fitfully. At one time his strength failed. Then he placed the baby under a tree and rising on his knees uttered a prayer: —

'O God, she's such a little thing, help me to get her there.'

Like a benediction came the cool breeze of the sunset hour, bringing renewed strength.

In the afternoon of the following day, a wagon stopped before a Belgian Refugee camp in Holland. Slowly and stiffly a small boy slid to the ground. He had been picked up just over the border by a friendly farmer and driven to camp. He was dirty, dedraggled, and footsore. Very kindly the ladies' committee received him. He was placed at a table and a bowl of hot soup was set before him. He

ate awkwardly with his left hand. His right hand held
something beneath his coat, which he never for a moment
forgot. The women tried to get his story, but he remained
strangely silent. His eyes wandered over the room and
back to their faces. He seemed to be testing them. Not
for an hour, not until there was a faint stirring in his coat,
did he disclose his burden. Then, going to her whom he
had chosen as most to be trusted, he opened his jacket.
In a dirty towel lay a naked, miserably thin, three-days-
old baby.

Mutely holding out the forlorn object, the boy begged
help. Bit by bit they got his story. Hurriedly a Belgian
Refugee mother was sent for. She was told what had happened, and she took the baby to her breast. Jealously the
boy stood guard while his tiny sister had her first real meal.
But the spark of life was very low.

For two days the camp concentrated its attention on
the tiny creature. The boy never left his sister's side.
But her ordeal had been too great. It was only a feeble
flicker of life at best, and during the third night the little
flame went out. The boy was utterly crushed. He had
now but one thought — to reach his mother. It was impossible to keep the news from him longer. He would have
gone in search. Gently he was told of the skirmish that
had destroyed the Belgian hamlet. There were no houses
or people in the town that had once been his home.

'That is his story,' ended the friendly little Dutch
woman.

'And his father?' I inquired.

'Killed at the front,' was the reply.

I rose to go, but I could not get the boy out of my mind.
What a world! What intolerable suffering! Was there
no way out? Then the ever-recurring phrase of the French

and Belgian soldiers came to me. When I had shuddered at ghastly wounds, at death, at innumerable white crosses on a bloody battlefield, invariably, in dry, cynical, hopeless tones, the soldier would make one comment, —

'C'est la guerre; que voulez-vous?'

WHAT ROAD GOETH HE?

BY F. J. JOURIET

A SMOKY lantern, suspended from the roof by a piece of spun-yarn, described intricate curves in the obscurity of the forecastle. Black chasms gaped on every side. Oilskins and sodden clothing slapped against the walls. The air was impure, saturated with moisture, and vibrant with the muffled roar of the storm outside. A thin sheet of water washed over the floor as the ship rolled.

A sea-chest broke from its lashings, and carried away to leeward. The deck rose, and the chest slipped aft, amid a raffle of wet boots and sou'westers; it sank, and the heavy chest shot forward across the slippery floor, to fetch up sharply against one of the bunks. Again the ship rolled, and the chest glided to leeward. Mutterings came from the chasms, and pale faces, distorted with yawns, appeared above the bunk boards. The owner of the chest awoke and crept stiffly from his bunk; the ship rolled, the water splashed about his feet, and the chest swooped toward him. He made it fast and climbed into his bunk again without drying his feet. The faces had disappeared. The ship rose and fell, the lantern swung, the hanging clothes bulged and flattened and bulged again; gloomy shadows wavered and seemed ever threatening to advance from the walls. The sound of the storm outside was dull and persistent.

Boom! A solemn stroke of the bell on the forecastlehead woke one of the sleepers. He sat up, expectant, for a moment, and then sank back. As he did so the door slid open, the storm bellowed as a man stepped through, and was deadened again as he forced the door to behind him. He vanished into the starboard forecastle, and reappeared with a short pipe that gurgled as he smoked. He seated himself on a chest, and the man who had awakened looked down on him.

'What time is it?' he asked.

The smoker looked up. 'That you, Bill? It's gone six bells.'

The other grumbled. 'I heard one bell from the fo'c's'le-head.'

'She rolled bad just now. Tolled the bell herself.'

'Humph!' said the man in the bunk thoughtfully.

'Shut up!' called a voice. 'I want to sleep.'

Bill lowered his voice. 'How's the weather?' he inquired, looking down anxiously at the smoker's glistening oilskins.

'Heavy. The Old Man hain't left the deck for a minute.'

After that the man in the bunk could not sleep again. He heard the other leave the forecastle, and swear as the flying spray struck his face; he heard a great body of water come over the bows and wash aft; he heard the heavy breathing about him. He lay in his clothing (it was wet and his blankets were wet — 'Warm wet, anyhow,' he thought), and shivered at the sound of the water washing about in the darkness below him, and at the thought of the weather outside. He counted the minutes grudgingly, and lay dreading the sound of the opening door. Wide-eyed, he watched the lantern swinging in the gloom, the pendulous clothing on the wall, the starting shadows, until some one beat frantically on the door, and, staggering into the forecastle, turned up the light and called the watch.

'A-a-all hands! Eight bells there! D' ye hear the news, you port watch? Eight bells there!'

Men stirred and yawned. Tired men kicked off blankets

and sat up, swearing. Cramped men eased themselves from their bunks, and pulled on sodden boots. They stumbled about the heaving deck, cursing their cold oilskins, cursing the ship, cursing the sea.

'Come, shake a leg, bullies!' continued the inexorable voice. 'Weather bad an' goin' to be worse! Get a move on you, or the mate 'll be for'ard with a belayin'-pin!'

'Anything up?' inquired one.

'Heard the Old Man tell the mate to take in the fore-lower tops'l.'

Thereupon they fell anew to cursing the captain, his seamanship, and, above all, his want of knowledge of the weather.

The watch went out into the tumult of the night, out into a chaos of smashing seas and howling wind, out into a furious abyss of darkness and uproar.

They collided blindly with other men; they called out angrily. Great seas crashed over the bulwarks and smothered them; invisible torrents poured off the forecastle-head and washed aft, beating them down, stunning them. From somewhere out of the darkness came the voice of the mate, bawling orders. They felt for the clewlines, making the most of the intervals between the boarding seas. High above them they knew a man was making his way aloft in the darkness to ease up the chain sheets. They hauled and swore, arching their backs against the seas that tore at their gripping fingers and washed their feet from under them. And always the mate's voice sounded, cheerful, threatening, dauntless. Then up into the black night, ratline by ratline, panting, clutching, and climbing; out upon the invisible yard, along invisible foot-ropes, grasping invisible jack-stays; swaying in the darkness, spat upon by the storm, beating the stiff canvas with bleeding hands; unheeding the tumult of the sea, the pounding wind, the lurching yard; with no thought save for the mate's voice below, and the lashing canvas under their hands. From the foretop, as they descended, they looked far down on the narrow hull, rolling, pitching, and shivering, beneath them. Out from the darkness pale seas rushed, roaring, toward the ship; and, roaring, passed to leeward. Seething masses of water rose over the bows, smashed down on the deck, and surged aft, forward, and over the side. Hissing foam creamed about the lee chains; vicious rain-squalls drove across the flooded decks; the cold was penetrating.

In the empty forecastle the lantern swung, the shadows rose and crouched, the voice of the storm sounded deep and steady. Ends of blankets dangled from the deserted bunks and flicked at the murmuring water on the floor. The deck soared and swooped, soared and swooped, minute after minute, hour after hour, and still the lantern swung, and the shadows moved and waited.

The door slid back, the storm bellowed, and three men staggered into the forecastle, bearing another. They laid him awkwardly in one of the lower bunks, and stood for a moment looking down at him. The ship rolled, and the shadows on the wall started as if they, too, would gather around that gloomy berth. Again the deck dropped, the shadows retreated, and the three men turned and left the forecastle.

The man in the bunk lay inert, as they had left him. His body sagged lumpishly to the roll of the ship. A dark stain appeared and spread slowly on the thin pillow.

A little later another man entered. He came to the edge of the bunk and gazed for a few minutes, then deliberately removed his dripping oilskin coat and sou'wester. The man in the bunk began to moan, and the other leaned over him. The moans continued, and the watcher sat down on a chest beside the bunk. Soon the sufferer's eyes opened and he spoke.

'What time is it?' he asked.

'Lie quiet, Bill,' the other cautioned. 'It's gone six bells.'

'My head hurts,' complained Bill. He tried to raise it, and moaned a little.

The elder man placed a hand gently on his shoulder. 'Don't you worry,' he said. 'You got hurted a little when the spar carried away. That's all.'

'Spar!' repeated Bill, and pondered. 'What watch is it?'

'Middle watch.'

'I thought I been on deck,' said Bill. 'It was blowin'.' His hands were groping about. 'Who bandaged my head?'

'The steward. They carried ye down into the cabin, first. Want a drink, Bill?'

Bill assented, and the other, bracing himself against the chest, lifted the injured man's head slightly and he drank.

'I may as well go to sleep,' he said, and closed his eyes. Instantly he reopened them. 'Why ain't you on deck, Jansen?' he asked.

'The Old Man sent me in to sit by you.' Jansen fingered his long gray beard, and the bright eyes under the shaggy brows blinked uneasily. 'You see, it's this way, Bill. You was hurt, an' the Old Man thought mebbe you'd want something.' He looked at the swinging lantern as if seeking inspiration. 'Anything I can do for ye, Bill?' he asked at last.

The other stirred. 'I can't move me legs,' he complained.

'Mebbe the spar hurt your back a little,' suggested Jansen timidly. 'You remember, don't ye, Bill?'

Again the injured man pondered. 'Me back's broke?' he said finally, and Jansen nodded.

'Me back's broke, an' me head's broke,' Bill went on, 'an' there's a pain in me side like Dago knives.'

'D' ye want another drink?' asked Jansen.

'It's eight bells, an' my watch below for me,' said Bill; and again Jansen nodded.

Silence fell. The muffled roar of the storm, the plunging forecastle, the waiting man on the chest, the dim light, the swinging lantern, the pendulous clothing, and the shadows, all seemed accessory to the great event about to take place.

'The pain in me side is awful!' groaned Bill; and Jansen shivered.

'The Old Man said he'd come for'ard as soon as he could leave the poop,' he said, as if hoping there might be comfort in the thought.

'I don't need him,' gasped the sufferer. 'I'm goin', I think.'

Old Jansen folded his hands, and repeated the Lord's Prayer. Then he leaned forward. 'Is — is there anybody ashore you'd want me to write to?' he asked.

'No,' answered Bill between his moans. 'Me mother's dead, an' there's nobody else that matters. I never was no good to any of 'em.'

After a time the moans ceased. A great sea boomed on the deck outside, and washed aft. The lantern swung violently, and the ship's bell tolled. Jansen looked into the bunk; Bill's eyes were fixed on him.

'I want to ask you, Jansen,' he said in a low voice. 'D' ye think there is any chance for me?'

The other hesitated. 'I — I'm afraid not,' he stammered.

'I don't mean a chance to live,' explained Bill. 'I mean, d' ye think I've got to go to hell?'

Jansen's tone grew positive. 'No,' he said, 'I don't.'

'I wisht there was a parson here,' muttered the man in the bunk. 'There used to be a old chap that come regular to the Sailors' Home — gray whiskers, he had, an' a long coat — I wisht he was here. He'd tell me.'

The man on the chest listened, his elbows on his knees, his head on his hands.

'I shook hands with him many a time,' continued Bill. 'He'd tell me —'

Jansen started, and looked up. His bright, deep-set eyes had taken on a look intent, glowing.

'Shall I read to ye a bit?' he asked. 'I've got a book — it might strike ye — now.'

'All right,' said Bill indifferently.

The old man crossed the forecastle, opened his chest, and, delving deep into its contents, brought forth a small, thin book.

It had seen much usage; the binding was broken, the leaves were stained and torn. The old man handled it tenderly. He held it high before him that the light from the swinging lantern might fall upon the text, and read stumblingly, pausing when the light swung too far from him, and making grotesque blunders over some of the long words.

'What is that book?' asked Bill after a time. 'It ain't the Bible?'

'No,' said Jansen. 'It ain't the Bible.'

'Then who is it says them things?' demanded Bill. 'He talks like he was Everything.'

Jansen lowered the book. 'I don't exactly understand what they call him,' he answered, 'they give him so many names. But I reckon nobody but God talks like that, whatever they call him.'

'Where did you get it? the book, I mean,' persisted Bill.

'I was cleanin' out a passenger's cabin, two voyages back,

an' I found it under the bunk. I've been readin' it ever since. It's all full o' strange, forrin names, worse 'n the ones in the Bible.'

'Well, neither of 'em stands to help me much,' commented Bill. 'I ain't never been good. I've been a sailor-man. That book' — he broke off to groan as the ship rolled heavily, but resumed — 'that book says same as the Bible, that a man's got to be pious an' do good an' have faith, an' all that, else he don't have no show at all.'

'Listen!' said Jansen. He turned the pages, and read a few lines as impressively as he could.

'That sounds easy,' said Bill. 'But I ought to ha' knowed about that before. It's no good desirin' anything now. It's too late. He'd know I was doin' it just to save my own skin — my soul, I mean.'

'Bill,' said Jansen. 'I'm goin' to ask you something.' He closed the little book over one finger, and leaned toward the bunk. 'Do you remember how you come to be hurted this way?'

'The spare spar that was lashed to starboard fetched loose, an' I tried to stop it,' answered Bill readily. 'I see it comin'.'

'Why did you try to stop it?'

'Well, a big sea had just washed the Old Man down in the lee scuppers, an' if the spar had struck him it would ha' killed him.'

'It's killed you, Bill,' said Jansen. 'Did n't you think o' that?'

'Me!' exclaimed Bill scornfully. 'Who's me?'

'But why did you want to save his life?' insisted Jansen.

'The ship 'ud stand a likely chance in a blow like this without a skipper, would n't she?'

'Then you thought —'

'Thought nothin'! There was no time to think. I see

the spar comin' an' I says, "Blazes! That'll kill the skipper!" an' I tried to stop it.'

'You ain't sorry you did it?'

'Sorry nothin. What's done's done.'

'See here, Bill,' said old Jansen earnestly. 'I'll tell you what you did. You did your duty! An' you laid down your life for another. You saved the captain's life, an' mebbe the ship, an' all our lives through him. An' you did it without thought o' reward. Don't you s'pose you'll get a little credit for that?'

'I'm thinkin',' said Bill. He lay silent for a minute. 'Read that again,' he requested.

Old Jansen did so, and after a pause he added, 'Now, if I was you I would n't worry no more about hell. Just make your mind as easy as you can. That's a better way to go.'

'I've got that,' said Bill. 'It's all right. Go on; read to me some more.'

Jansen lifted the book and resumed his reading. He turned the pages frequently, choosing passages with which he was familiar. The other moaned at intervals. With every roll of the ship, water plashed faintly underneath the bunks. The lantern swung unwearied, and sodden clothing slapped against the walls. Dark shadows rose and stooped and rose again as if longing and afraid to peer into the narrow berth. The sound of the storm outside was grave and insistent.

The reader came to the end of a passage, and laid the book on his knee. Suddenly he realized that the moans had ceased. He leaned over and looked at the man in the bunk. He was dead.

Old Jansen sat motionless, deep in thought. At length he reopened the little book, and read once more the lines

which he had already repeated at the dying man's request:—

> He is not lost, thou son of Prithâ! No!
> Nor earth, nor heaven is forfeit, even for him,
> Because no heart that holds one right desire
> Treadeth the road of loss!

He closed the book and again meditated. Later, he rose,
replaced the book in his chest, drew the dead man's blanket
over his face, and went out on deck.

THE CLEARER SIGHT

BY ERNEST STARR

NOAKES leaned over a stand in one of the Maxineff laboratories and looked intently into a crucible, while he advanced the lever of a control-switch regulating the furnace
beneath it. He held a steady hand on the lever, so that he
might push it back instantly if he saw in the crucible too
sudden a transformation. As he watched, the dull saffron
powder took on a deeper hue about the edge, the body of
it remaining unchanged. For several minutes he peered
with keen intentness at the evil, inert little mass. No
further change appeared. He leaned closer over it, re-
gardless of the thin choking haze that spread about his face.
In his attitude there was a rigidity of controlled excitement
out of keeping with the seeming harmlessness of the experiment. He was as a man attuned to a tremendous hazard,
anticipation and mental endurance taut, all his force fo-
cused on one throbbing desire. He bent closer, and the
hand on the lever trembled in nervous premonition. The
deepened hue touched only the edge, following regularly the
contour of the vessel; it made no advance toward the centre
of the substance.

'It shall!' Noakes breathed; and as if conning an oft-
repeated formula, he said, 'The entire mass should deepen
in color, regularly and evenly. Heat! Heat!'

His glance shifted to the control-switch under his hand.
Its metal knobs, marking the degrees of intensity of the
current it controlled, caught the light and blinked like so
many small, baleful eyes. Particularly one, that which
would be capped next in the orbit of the lever, held him

fascinated; the winking potentiality of it thralled him, as the troubled crystal devours the gaze of the Hindu magi.

He jerked back his head decisively; he would increase the current.   The thought burned before him like a live thing; and in the light of it he saw many pictures — heliographs of happenings in and about the laboratories: flame, smoke dense and turgid, splintered wood, metal hurtling through air, bleeding hands, lacerated breasts, sightless eyes.

'That's the trouble with high explosives,' he half groaned.

He turned away from the stand and went to the single window that lit the room.   Through it he saw shops, store-houses, and small buildings similar to his own, all a part of the plant of Maxineff.   He thought of each small labora-tory as a potential inferno, each experimenter a bondman to ecstasy, the whole frenzied, gasping scheme a further-ance of the fame and power of Henry Maxineff, already world-known, inventor of the deadliest high explosives. One of the buildings had been turned into a temporary hos-pital.   He thought of the pitiful occupant — his face scarred, one socket eyeless — and shivered.

'It is n't that I want to hedge,' he said.   'I shall take the chance; but having risked everything, I will go to her able and whole, offering it all without an apology.'

His gaze was drawn back to the crucible.   In the thin haze above it a face seemed to shine.   Avidly he gave him-self to the spell his tight-strung imagination had conjured — a face oval and delicately tinted; lips joyously curved; gray eyes not large, but brimming with enthusiasm, fearless-ness, and truth; a white brow beneath simply arranged light hair.

'Let me bring with an avowal all that you have now, more! — for in your life there can't be anything bigger than my love.   And it's that which makes the deal right.   Don't

judge me yet!   Wait until I've finished, and grant me that
it's worth while.'

He whispered to the face, and his breath made little
swirls and eddies in the haze about it.   The filmy curves
wafted toward him, bringing it close to his lips.   The lids
fluttered.   Then an acrid odor filled his throat and nostrils.
The face vanished.   He started back, distraught.

A rushing recollection of Maxineff's tragedies came to
him, more vivid even than the face.   Halsey, who jarred
the nitro, had been annihilated.   Ewell was mad from the
violent termination of an experiment similar to that now in
development.

'A year ago!'   Noakes said, 'and still Ewell lives and
raves!'

How alike the cases were!   The difference lay in the
crucible.   If the mixture there were properly prepared,
added heat would metamorphose it calmly from its present
harmlessness into something new, wonderful, deadly.   It
would become imbued with marvelous possibility, a thing
for which royal military bureaus, imperial navies, would
pay a great price.

A twist of the lever would do it.   Yet how alike — And
Ewell was mad, injured gruesomely, living dead.

Again the blinking switch caught him, but he shrugged
away its evil suggestiveness.   He sought to flee the strain
of the moment, to make it seem natural and like the smaller
risks of his daily occupation.   He assumed a tottering
bravado, and as he put his hand to the lever, he smiled
crookedly.

A light, quick tread sounded on the walk outside, on the
double step; as the knob turned, a voice said, 'May I come,
Mr. Alchemist?'

His hand left the lever as if it pricked him.

'You!'

'Am I a wraith?'

Noakes looked at her silently. In the moment's abstraction her presence seemed a manifestation of some psychic conduction which he tried lamely to understand — here, now, in a moment of danger of which she unknowingly was the moving force.

'Then exorcise me quickly, but don't sprinkle me with acid; it would be fatal to my clothes.'

Noakes warmed to the aura of light and cheer about her.

'There is n't an alkali in the shop; I won't endanger you,' he replied easily.

She moved into the room and paused a moment near the stand.

'Mrs. Max says you are confining yourself too closely. I've been with her all morning.'

While she spoke she took off her hat and smoothed her hair.

'I'm blown to pieces.   I drove Cornish this morning; he got by everything on the way.   He acted like a *première danseuse* when I passed the cooper's shop.'

His joy at seeing her was discountenanced by his fear for her; and he was afraid of her.   Her insinuated trust in him threw into murky relief the affair which occupied him. When she turned to him a flushed, joyful face, and gray eyes clear and unsullied, it flashed into his soul, as formedly as a *Mene Tekel*, that she would unhesitatingly brush out of her life-path the dust of doubt; that equivocation and willingness to balance motives were no part of her.   He knew that in her were no dim angles of cross-grained purpose, no shadowy intersections of the lines of good and evil.

'I say I'm blown to wisps; could n't you find me a mirror, please?'

'What would I do with a mirror here?   But see —'

He lifted the window sash, pulled in one shutter, and with a gesture of presentation, said, 'As others see us!'

She turned her back while she arranged her hair before the makeshift mirror. Relieved from her direct gaze, he stepped quickly to the stand, and look d into the crucible. There was no change. He had expected none, but he could not be sure. Maxineff himself could not be sure of this new mixture. A run of the same temperature might bring about the change he looked for as readily as an increase. The suspense was unbearable.

'Well, Cagliostro!' she called. 'You alchemists are capable of the utterest abstraction, are n't you?'

'Why have you come?' he said quickly, frowning at her.

'To take you driving,' with an enticing smile.

'Will you not go? Please, at once?'

Her manner lost something of its verve.

'It is n't safe, you know, really,' he added.

'And won't you come?'

'I cannot; not this morning.'

'Well,' she said, with a little sigh, as she thrust in her hatpins, 'Mrs. Max will be disappointed. On her command I came to break up this seclusion of yours. None of us have seen you for — '

'A week, seven days!'

'What are you doing?'

'Oh — I've been working out some ideas.'

'But you are so quiet about it! What are the ideas?'

Noakes hesitated, and she laughed merrily as she went toward the door.

'We laity are hopeless, are n't we? You are thinking that I could n't possibly understand?'

'No, I was n't, because I scarcely understand myself.'

'Of course, some secret formula Mr. Max has you on.'

'Indeed, no,' he said. 'Mr. Max knows nothing about it — that is,' he continued hurriedly, 'it's the sort of thing— At any rate, I'll soon be through.'

She stood in the doorway, outlined against the bright incoming mid-daylight, her face turned back to him.

'And then you will come out into the world again? Mrs. Max and Cornish and I shall be honored.'

'Then I shall be free.'

He spoke the words with singular feeling.

'Truly, though, Mr. Noakes,' she said in a straightforward manner, 'you are too busy. Mrs. Max says you are to break out, break out with the measles if nothing else will interrupt you, and you are to have tea with her this afternoon.'

Noakes looked doubtful. She went down the steps and turned again.

'Oh, I almost forgot — here's a letter for you.'

'Where —'

'It came in the Maxineffs' mail this morning. Mrs. Max suggested my bringing it to you.'

Noakes took the long, foreign-stamped envelope. The typed superscription was noncommittal, but at the Berlin postmark his eyes narrowed and the knuckles of the hand by his side whitened. He drew a quick breath and looked keenly at the girl.

'Was Mr. Maxineff at home this morning?' he asked quietly.

'No; I believe he is in the city.'

'Oh!' he breathed. 'Thank you very much.'

He slipped the letter into his pocket.

'Well, I can't stay any longer.'

Noakes pressed her hand.

'And, Cagliostro, when the puzzle's solved, come to see me. I'll sing away the worries. Good-bye.'

'Good-bye, Miss Becky. Excuse my untractableness, won't you?'

With a pat to her hat and a smile to Noakes, she was gone.

He watched her a moment, then strode rapidly to the stand. Looking through the faint haze, he saw her pass down the straight path which led to the great gate of the Maxineff work-yard. When she was close to it he grasped the switch-lever with cramped fingers. His face was colorless. He moved the lever forward with a jerk, and lifting his eyes, saw her pass out of the gate.

Beyond reach of time he waited. Evenly, insistently, a dull brown suffused the mass. Still he waited, fearfully wondering at the stability of this new thing. It kept its even coloring. He pushed back the lever, watched again, and waited.

He was afire with joy. He had succeeded; he had created a thing new to the world, an explosive which would be more powerful than the deadliest in existence; he had perfected the work of a week's exquisite danger; he had won.

'I am glad, glad!' he said faintly.

As he straightened up he found himself suddenly weak. The strain had been galling, and the madness of gratification consumed his strength. He moved toward the door, stepping very gently, for he knew not how slight a vibration might shatter the delicate affinity in his discovery.

He remembered the foreign letter, and taking it from his pocket, tore open the envelope.

He looked through the open door, conscious for the first time of the perfectness of the day. It was good to be alive, he thought, free, something accomplished, with leave to tell a girl —

A tall man entered the gate and took the walk toward the laboratory. Noakes looked at him in a moment of amazement, almost of stupefaction. The necessity of instant action startled him to movement. As quickly as he thought, he pushed the door three-quarters shut, replaced the jars from which he had taken his materials, filled a second crucible with a harmless haphazard mixture, and placed it over a dead furnace in a stand in the corner behind the door. He lifted the window-sash. With all his strength he hurled his priceless crucible. By a marvel of speed he had the sash lowered, and was behind the door, when the building was shaken by an explosion.

'What is that, Mr. Noakes?' came in deep, calm tones from the door.

'Good morning, Mr. Maxineff,' said Noakes, turning slowly. 'The racket? Some half-baked fulminate I put in the ditch out there an hour ago.'

'So long since?' said the older man, advancing toward the window.

'Yes, sir. I think the jarring of the wagon you see leaving the chemical house caused it.'

A hole several feet in diameter marked the spot where the crucible fell. The stuff had delayed not an instant in working its havoc. Noakes was glad there was too little of it to cause a suspicious deal of damage.

Maxineff looked reflectively about the yard, while Noakes nervously eyed his chief's expressive profile. His eyes wandered to the fine gray head of this tall, straight man. He could not fail to be impressed afresh by the forceful exterior, significant of the inner attitude which had won for Henry Maxineff a name honored among nations.

'What of your work?' he said.

Noakes was glad those seeing eyes were not on him.

'I'm beat,' he said. 'I've gone at it every way I know, and I have been consistently and finally unsuccessful.'

In the ensuing pause Noakes realized that this was the

first admission of failure he had ever made to his chief. The surprise it called forth was grateful to him.

'What's the trouble? But I think the trouble with you is that you have overreached yourself, Noakes.'

'Oh, no; the idea is a fine, tremendous one. Sheer stupidity is my trouble, I think.'

His humility seemed real, and perhaps the unusualness of it brought a curious expression to Maxineff's face, and into his eyes a contemplative light that Noakes did not care to meet.

'I met Miss Hallam as I entered,' Maxineff said carelessly.

The remark may have meant much, or it may have had merely an intentional indication of the intimacy accorded Noakes above the other assistants in the laboratories.

'Yes? She came to tell me that Mrs. Max will permit me to have tea with her this afternoon.'

'You are coming, I hope?'

'Indeed, yes. I confess I am tired out. I gave up the experiment early this morning. I understood the fulminate was running low, and spent my morning blundering over making some. I could n't do that even, familiar as I am with the process.'

'Well, leave it all and come with me over the yard. I am inspecting this morning. Be my secretary for a while.'

Five o'clock had passed when they emerged upon the New England town's stolid main street. They walked beneath the venerable flanking trees toward the Maxineff villa, which surmounted a wooded continuation of the street.

In a high gray-and-white room they found Mrs. Maxineff. She touched a bell as she said in an odd manner of inflecting, 'But you are late!'

Moving to one end of the spindle-legged sofa, she made

place at her side for Maxineff, and motioned Noakes to a
chair near them.

'Ah, I see it: you will be a second Max — all science, all
absence, and a woman waiting at home!   Immolation, you
call it?' she continued, her hands moving quickly among
the appurtenances of the tea-table.   'That is what you
prefer, my young Mr. Noakes.'

'I am under orders, you know, Mrs. Max,' said Noakes,
with a deferential inclination of the head toward Maxineff.

A servant brought in buttered rusks, and served the men
with tea.

'Orders!   For orders do you permit circles about your
eyes as dark as they themselves are?   Then you are easily
immolate!'

Over his cup Maxineff smiled encouragement to his wife.

'You are practical, my friend.   Confess now, there is a
reason for your — your application?'

Noakes's attitude was uncompromising.   He placed his
cup on the table before he spoke.

'The reason you are thinking of, Mrs. Max, is not for
a poor man.'

Mrs. Maxineff lifted her shoulders and displayed her
palms in a manner that marked her nationality.

'So!   Science has made your dark skin white; love for
this business of killing men has kept you hid a week.'

'Of saving men,' Maxineff corrected, while his wife
smiled as at the recurrence of a customary witticism.

'And you gave the orders, Max!   You are to be blamed
for this display of energy.'

'Don't scold, dear.   It will be a wonderful thing!'

'A new explosive?' she interrupted.

'Do you remember the day we motored from Stoneham?
I first thought of it then.   I have been too busy to work on
it, so I turned the idea over to Noakes.'

'And I have made application to a home for the feeble-minded, Mrs. Max,' Noakes said. 'Mr. Max will never commission me again.'

'I'll be with you to-morrow, and we shall see wherein is the difficulty.'

'But, Max, another? Now I see your scheme of universal peace quite puffed away!'

'This will bring it nearer!' Maxineff said enthusiastically.

Mrs. Maxineff shrugged her shoulders as she walked toward the long windows.

'Stay to dinner, will you?' she said to Noakes.

'Thanks, but I could n't with propriety. I forgot to have luncheon to-day, and your tea has given me a keen anticipation for dinner; my zest would be embarrasssing to you, and past my control. Besides, I shall take a half-mile walk to-night.'

'Lucky Becky! Then come again soon. Max, dear,' she said, turning to her husband, 'I cannot hear that again. I shall be on the porch.'

When she passed through the window, Noakes seated himself to listen to a new exposition of the subject which chiefly aroused Maxineff's interest and loosed his speech. Frequently he bent his head in acquiescence, and occasionally interjected a pertinent question under the guidance of his secondary mind; but his thoughts moved in a circle of smaller radius.

What to him was a policy of world-peace? He cared not a jot what scheme of universal pacification men dreamed over. Maxineff's argument was not new to him; when he gave it serious attention he doubted its practicability.

The older man's voice seemed far away, as it said, 'Each new explosive deals a blow at war, — war!'

Noakes had heard the same thing when his chief concluded with the government an agreement which secured to it the exclusive use of his latest product.

'This new thing will make war too dreadful a course for the least humanitarian nation to pursue. That the variance of nations tends toward equilibrium is incontrovertible. Granted then —'

Noakes was practical. He placed before himself a definite goal. He exerted every power to attain it, and used the means at his disposal. If he encompassed it, he put it to the use for which it was intended. He gave no thought to the extraneous influence it exerted on other phases upon which his life touched. He had made a great discovery — not a fortunate accident like that of the man who discovered nitro. With great danger to himself, he had followed a line of reasoning to its proximate end; the resulting discovery he would use to his individual advantage. He did not accord to himself the godlike privilege of casting discord among the nations, and he did not care what peaceful zoo the lion, the bear, and the various species of eagle found as common refuge.

'On the other hand, if to each is given coextensive power —' The voice slipped away, as Noakes humorously wondered why Maxineff had never been a delegate to a Peace conference.

The great man's argument was advanced step by step. The light faded. Secure in the dusk, Noakes no longer maintained a semblance of attention. He weighed the chances of the present and actualized his long-time dreams.

A servant clicked soft light from the wall, and removed the tea-table.

Noakes rose, uttered a commonplace, and bade his chief good-night.

Soon he was descending the village street, keeping pace with his rapid thoughts.

From the exchange he dispatched a messenger to the house a half-mile away.

He dressed quickly, the while reading repeatedly his foreign letter. When dressed, he sat on the bed, chin in his palms, and looked at the blank bedroom wall. A frown hung between his brows. Later he sat before the shelves in his study, absently scanning the backs of the books.

'When? When?' he said aloud.

In the morning Maxineff would come to search for that which he had found. He might be there for weeks, from morning till night. In that case the work must be delayed and misguided. The proportions were finely calculated; the method could not be bettered. He could duplicate it in an hour. If only he could repeat the experiment before —

'To-night!' he said, and left the room with a firm step.

He dined well, though with few words for the kindly lady in whose home he lived.

He took the path by the side of the road which led in the opposite direction from the Maxineff place. He lit his first pipe since morning. How good life was! The town, the plant, Maxineff, were all behind him. Ahead was a goal toward which he bore with increasing lightness of heart. Clearly defined decisions, unregretted, faded into the brightness of anticipation. His pack of problems dropped from him. One day more and he could speak — one evening of companionable friendship.

Her yard was a gnomish alternation of unsullied light and alluring shade. The moon utilized impartially natural and artificial features of landscape as detail for the picture of gray, black, and silver. Noakes traversed less rapidly the curved driveway, pausing where it was cut by a paved way to the door.

Through a window he saw her seated on the piano-bench, her head bent forward, her mellow-tinted hair coiled low. She was singing softly.

She came to the door to meet him.

'Will duty call you back before you have been with me just a little while?' she asked as they entered the room.

'No, duty has lost her voice at present.'

She dropped into a big arm-chair. He turned his back to the light, and sat facing her.

'What have you been doing this week?'

'Singing mostly.'

'Sing now, please.'

'No, let's talk first.'

'Well, how did Cornish behave on your way back?'

'Quite as well as if you had been with us, Noakes.'

He leaned forward quickly.

'Do you know, that's the first time you've called me "Noakes"?'

'It slipped. Mrs. Max says it, you know; I am weak about taking on colloquialisms.'

'And you are sorry you have been so easily influenced?' Noakes asked in ponderous aggrievement.

'You do not seem to be overjoyed.'

'I am,' he said gently.

'Don't be hilarious over it.'

'I will; I wish —'

'Well, certainly; "Noakes" it shall be.'

'Thanks, Miss Beck.'

'Have n't you done anything but work these days?'

'I have thought more or less.'

'Strange; what about?'

'You, of course.'

'Steady! Spring has passed.'

'And to-night I heard a queer thing about you.'

'What?' she asked in an engaging manner of invitation to confidence.

'That you are to be married. I have it on the word of my landlady.'

'I?'

'So it is rumored in the village.'

'I am glad my family is not so anxious to thrust me off as my friends are.'

'And you are unwilling to be thrust off, as you put it?'

'Married? No, not unwilling; unprepared. It is so very final, you know. A woman gives up everything.'

'Not necessarily.'

'Oh, yes she does: freedom, family, associations.'

'And in return?'

'From the right man she gets — a sort of compensation.'

'Not a high valuation.'

'A true one; she knows she cares more than he does.'

'No, no!' Noakes spoke from a full heart.

'She does; and knowing it, she need not expect equal return — only part compensation. But how good he ought to be!'

'Good?' he asked doubtfully.

'Yes, everything she thinks he is.'

'No man loved of woman is that.'

'Noakes, you are disillusioning, and incorrect, and moreover traitorous to your kind.'

'Not a bit of it; you overpraise my kind.'

'But — let's be definite — you know he may be all — '

'And may not always have been; in which connection he may not be expected to enlighten the dreaming lady, may he?'

'I think he may.'

'But he may possess a certain masculine trait, a kind of secretiveness.'

'Secretive,' she mused. 'Then he is a bit of a coward, I think.'

'He would be a cad,' Noakes said quickly, 'to tell her things that would pain her.'

'Understanding will come sooner or later,' she said oracularly. 'It is better to become accustomed to a thing than have it come as a revelation.'

'I see,' Noakes said; 'like taking a tonic in midwinter to fend off spring fever. You forget,' he continued in a different tone, looking at her speculatively, 'that understanding may never come.'

'Then he has put her on a lower intellectual plane; he has withheld from her, as he might from a child.'

'No, he has loved her too well to hurt her.'

'Loved her so ill that he has deceived her from the beginning.'

'To my mind there is something active in deception; this would be rather an omission.'

'An omission that is an insult to her.'

'Not at all!' Noakes spoke somewhat vehemently.

'Don't think I mean,' she said, 'that there should be a detailed interchange of trivial confidence. That would be tiresome. If, however, there were one big thing in his life that might influence her feeling toward him, he should tell it, and let her judge.'

'Not smooth over a disagreeable occurrence?'

'Never! It would be cruel.'

Noakes sat very still.

'If I were the girl, — ' she began, and checked the speech with a faint laugh. 'But we will not be dramatic, nor personal.'

Noakes told himself he had always known that this was her thought; she was too clear-hearted to feel anything else. The understanding of which she had half-seriously spoken must never come, and the only means of avoiding it was to-night's silence, the silence of all the days to follow. He foresaw the revelation which might come, and realized that any abnegation was worthless except the sacrifice of his love. Alive, aware of its possible fulfillment, he could not condemn himself to the sacrifice. She had not asked it of him, and he would not face that which she might ask if he obeyed the weak voice which counseled a surrender to her judgment. To the last intoxicating drop he would drink, in reverent loving-thankfulness for the draught vouchsafed him. He would care, not in fearful accumulation of credit against a day of reckoning, but in surrender to the brimming abundance of their store. He would secure to her freedom from that possible pain by following the inevitable trend.

His regard was a compelling force with which he had lived and grown since he had known Becky. He had not spoken of it to her, silenced by the piteous bane of insufficient income; but now almost he was free. When he spoke, the breadth and depth of the thing it was would induce her assent. Of this he was so sure that he did not consider the possibility of refusal. His failure to anticipate such a chance was by no means due to an under-estimation of her powers of will, determination, or selection; rather to the feeling which, with the beat of his heart, knocked for freedom to go out, out, about the world, and with its sweeping lines converged again, to enter and permeate a heart attuned to reception and response.

He sat beside her on the piano-bench, and placed before her the songs he liked best.

Her voice was a pure soprano, of an expressive sweetness which affected Noakes as nothing else he had known. It seemed to him that her clarity of soul found expression in her exquisitely pure singing tones.

With hands tight-clasped between his knees, fearing to look at her, Noakes listened while she sang him into a half-visualized dream, as obsessing as it was immanent, which he clung to and enjoyed to the full in order that he might ignore the longing then to speak his thought. His dream keyed him to a responsiveness which made his throat throb in sympathy with the vibration of her tones.

Presently he went away.

Alone in the silver-splotched yard, the spell yet held him; but when the white road pointed a way back to what he had left behind, a fog of uncertainty encircled him, dissipating the glow of his dream, checking his anticipation, crushing his problem close to him in the narrow circle of his vision, so close that, although a thing solved and set aside, it loomed ominous and insistent.

He followed the road back to what he had left behind.

In the laboratory Noakes bent over a crucible. The room was still. Not even the night-sounds penetrated the shut door and closed window. The light from a single bulb played upon the set lines of his jaw, and upon the still hand which lay on the switch-lever. He drew a deep breath that quivered through the room with startling distinctness. He bent closer to the tiny quantity of powder in the bottom of the vessel.

Suddenly he stood erect and looked about him. His glance slowly circled the room, and fell to the hand on the switch-lever. Then he advanced the lever.

It came as a burst of light taken up and radiated by clouds of fume and gas with which the air was instantly impregnated. Around Noakes was a white-hot brilliance which he could not face, and could not escape. His eyes pained horribly. He heard a crescendo roaring as of a billow breaking on the shore; as suddenly as it had come, the light went out. He was in darkness. He trained his gaze into the void and succeeded only in augmenting the pain back of his eyes. The darkness was impenetrable. He began to realize what had happened. With a low moan he crumpled and sank to the floor.

Late in the afternoon of the next day, behind a livery horse, two men were covering the roadway between town and the Hallam place. To one the way seemed long. He leaned back wearily and pulled a soft hat down over his bandaged eyes.

'Where are we?' he asked.

'At the gate,' the driver replied.

Noakes stiffened. The gate closed behind them, and the wheels rumbled on the driveway.

'Is — is any one in front?'

'Miss Hallam is on the porch, sir.'

The vehicle came to a stop.

'Afternoon, Miss Beck,' Noakes called.

He tried to make it sound pleasant and commonplace, and knew that he failed.

Grasping the side of the vehicle, he descended clumsily.

Becky took his hand and pressed it warmly. She turned and took a step toward the house, still holding his hand. He withdrew it.

'I — don't, please; I know the way.'

With the shuffling tread of the blind he ascended the walk, stopping uncertainly at the foot of the steps. He heard Becky, at his side, draw a quick breath, as if about to speak. He half-turned to her, and hearing nothing more, mounted the steps heavily.

'Do you know,' he said, as he paused at the top, 'I've never counted these steps before. I did n't know there were so many. Let's sit inside, if you don't mind.'

He went a little way, and Becky put her hand on his arm.

'It's this way, Noakes,' she said gently, as she guided him into the room in which they were the night before.

'Thank you. It's a bit hard to be led,' Noakes said huskily.

They sat on a deep couch.

'Noakes, was it wise to come? I am glad you are here, but won't it hurt you, retard your recovery?' Becky asked anxiously.

'I had to come.'

'Mr. Max told me — both he and the doctor telephoned me early this morning — that in spite of all they said to you, you insisted on coming.'

'I am fit, sound except for my eyes; that's the shame of it,' he said bitterly. 'They could n't persuade me that I should rest now, rest to recover from a shock that will last a lifetime.'

'I thought — I was afraid you might add fresh danger by coming out so soon.'

'I tell you I had to come!' he said with level forcefulness. 'As for my eyes, the harm is done.'

'Is it irremediable?'

'I am blind.'

'But soon — some day, surely — '

'No. The doctor gives me banalities for answers. I suppose he thinks I would go to pieces if he told me the truth.'

'Yes, perhaps he thinks you could not bear the truth,' Becky assented very gently.

Her low, feeling tones brought a lump to Noakes's throat. He felt the sympathy which quivered in her voice, and it nearly unmanned him; but he misunderstood her meaning. He thought that she felt with him the sting of being deprived of full knowledge of his condition, the hurt of their doubting his strength. That Becky mear something far different, he might have known from her humble acquiescence, and the sudden touch of her hand on his arm.

'I've been trying to think it out,' Noakes said, his voice low at first, roughening and increasing in volume as he spoke, 'but here I am, unweakened in mind and body, and put aside — Not to see, never to see for myself the beautiful things about me; shut out from everything; with power to do, and ability to appreciate, yet put out in darkness; never to — O Becky, you, I can't ever see you again!'

'Don't! You must n't, please!'

'I did n't intend to speak so to you. I have n't the right. You must pardon me.' He was silent a moment. 'I came to say something else.'

He turned his head about impatiently, calling upon his bandaged eyes to perform their function.

'Is it dark yet?' he asked.

'We are in the gloaming,' Becky answered softly.

Noakes shut his lips, taking counsel of his powers of control before he spoke.

'Becky,' he began, and gave a tired little sigh. 'Let me call you "Becky" to-day.'

'Yes,' she acquiesced quietly.

'Becky,' he continued, lingering over the word, thinking of the privilege of its use as an accolade conferred by her, 'you need not speak when I have finished; I'll go away then.'

'What is it?' Becky asked. 'Tell me.'

Noakes leaned forward, pressing his temples; then sat erect and turned his face toward her.

'I love you,' he said. 'I think it has been through more lifetimes than this; I know I shall always love you. I could no more grow away from it than I could add a cubit to my stature by taking thought. I kept silent because I was poor. Don't think of this as a bit of sordidness creeping in. My love would not ask of you any sacrifice. I could not give you the things you are accustomed to, so I said nothing. I planned and worked for a time when I would be privileged to speak.'

He heard an inarticulate sound at his side, and quickly continued: —

'Last night I thought the time was close at hand. I thought in a few days I could come to you, and ask you for your love. Success of a certain kind was about to crown an effort of a despicable kind. Of that I must tell you. To-night I am confessing a wrong I have done you. That's what it is. O, Becky, the explosion last night took away my sight, made me a useless blind man, but it opened my eyes too! It is as if a scroll were outspread before me, on which is a record of all my tendencies and crucial acts. I can see my failures at the crises of my life, and I can trace them back to causes, can see wherein a lightly taken determination has later borne bitter fruit. Last night I thought I had reached the pinnacle of attainment; in reality I had fallen lower than ever before. The success which was to be the beginning of all good things was stolen. I robbed Maxineff of it. He gave me an idea to work out. I followed his instructions to a point where I knew a different treatment might bring about a fine result. I saw great possibilities in the experiment and determined to keep for myself the benefits of it. From that point I followed my own ideas, and called the thing mine. I opened correspondence with the representatives of a foreign government. They agreed to buy the secret in case of a successful test. It was an excellent bargain I made — I put a high price on the betrayal of my benefactor! The experiment was successful. I was forced to destroy the result, why it is needless to say. Last night, when I left you, I went back to repeat the experiment, intending to make a small quantity to be used in the test which would have taken place to-morrow. Something went wrong with the unstable stuff, — and you know the rest.'

In relief from the tension of his confession, his voice dropped lower as he said, 'Now you know me!'

He shifted his position, stretching out his hands toward her. He touched her face, started, and drew back.

'And Becky, do you realize that it was after I left you last night that I went back? After what you told me? O Becky, I am glad I cannot see you now!'

His voice quivered off to a whisper.

'It is poor consolation that I know myself for what you judge me. I know bitterly well; I see much now. I could not come to the weakest agreement with the self I want to be, until I had told you of the wrong I have done you. And let me think my love is not distasteful to you. I know I am past your caring for, and I'll never ask it of you, but let me keep on loving you. Won't you, Becky?'

He paused and listened. He heard Becky's uneven breathing.

'I don't offer any excuse; there is none to offer. I want only the comparative peace of the assurance that those I have wronged understand now. I have talked with Mr. Maxineff. He was with me afterwards, when the pain — He hushed me far too gently, but he will not forget. You will not forget either, Becky, and you will not excuse. If, though, you should ask me why, I would say again, I love you. It is the only reason. I was thinking of you while I was making myself unfit for you to think of me.'

'Do you care so much?' Becky asked softly.

'Yes. May I keep on caring?'

'To what good?'

'For the sake of the little good in me, which love of you
will keep alive and growing.'

'You ask nothing of me.   What will you find in caring
for me?'

'There will be a constant joy in knowing that you permit
me to care.'

Becky was silent.

'If you won't let me, I am afraid it will make no difference, because I cannot help it, you know.   I don't want to
help it; you don't mind my saying so?'

For a moment neither of them spoke.   Noakes rose.

'I — Becky, I thank you for hearing me out.'

He went a step away from her.

'I'm going.'

She did not rise.

'I am glad you have not spoken of my — my mistake;
and somehow I am sorry.   I know what you —'

'How do you know what I think?'

'I know; that's all.'

'Don't go, please,' Becky said.

'Had n't I better?   I'm tired, and the doctor — A last
acknowledgment: I am afraid to hear you.'

'But I don't want you to go,' she said softly.

Something in her tone made Noakes turn sharply.

'Becky!'

'Yes, Noakes?'

'You don't —'

'Yes!'

'You love me, and blind?'

'You are brave!'

Her hands were in his when he sat by her side.

'I talked with the doctor this morning,' she said.

'As I did.'

'No.   He gave me a message for you.'

'A message from the doctor?'

'It was Mr. Max's notion that I should tell you.'

'What is it?' Noakes asked quickly.

'Your eyes — they will be well in time, if you are very careful.'

As Noakes breathed deep in relief and gratitude, one of his hands engaged two of Becky's, and he found a different use for the other.

'Noakes,' Becky said, 'I'll take care of the eyes.'

THE GARDEN OF MEMORIES

BY C. A. MERCER

THE garden looked dreary and desolate in spite of the afternoon sunshine. The lilac and lavender bushes were past their prime; their wealth of sweetness had been squandered by riotous offshoots. The wind played among the branches, and cast changing sun-flecked shadows on the grass-grown paths, narrowed by the encroachment of the box borders that had once lined the way with the stiff precision of troops before a royal progress.

The flowers had the air of being overburdened with the monotony of their existence. They could never have had that aspect if they had been only wild flowers and had never experienced human care and companionship. That made the difference.

The gate hung on rusty hinges; it answered with a long-drawn-out creaking, as it was pushed open by a man who had been a stranger to the place for nearly twenty years.

Yes, the garden was certainly smaller than it had been pictured by his memory. There had been a time when it had appeared as a domain of extensive proportions, and the wood beyond of marvelous depth and density.

He was conscious of a sense of disappointment. The property would scarcely realize as high a price in the market as he had hoped; and it was incumbent upon him to part with it, if he would be released from the narrow circumstances that hemmed him in.

He had arranged to meet the lawyer there that afternoon. One of the latter's clients had already made a bid for the estate. The timber, at all events, would add to the value.

The house faced southward upon the garden. It was here the man had been brought up by an old great-aunt. He guessed later that she had grudged him any of the endearments that death had denied her bestowing upon her own children. Her affections had all been buried before he was born. Besides, he took after the wrong branch of the family.

She must have possessed a strong personality. It was difficult to bring to mind that it was no longer an existent force. Every one, from the parson to the servants, had stood a little in awe of her. He remembered the unmoved manner in which she had received the news of the death of a near relative. It had overwhelmed him with a sudden chill, that so she would have received tidings of his own. It had taken all the sunshine in the garden to make him warm again.

In the mood that was growing upon him, it would not have much surprised him to find her sitting bolt upright in her carved high-back chair, as she had sat in the time of his earliest recollections, — the thin, yellow hands, on which the rings stood out, folded in her lap. On one occasion she had washed his small hands between hers. The hard lustre of the stones acquired a painful association with the ordeal. The blinds would be partially drawn in the musk-scented parlor, to save the carpet from further fading, for there had been a tradition of thrift in the family from the time of its settlement, — a tradition that had not been maintained by its latest representative.

Like the atmosphere of a dream, the years grew dim and misty between now and the time when summer days were longer and sunnier, and it had been counted to him for righteousness if he had amused himself quietly and not given trouble.

A stream that he had once dignified with the name of

river formed a boundary between the garden and the wood.
Although it had shrunk into shallow insignificance, — with
much beside, — a faint halo of the romance with which he
had endued this early scene of his adventures still clung to
the spot.

As he came to the stream, he saw the reflection of a face
in the water — not his own, but that of one much younger.

It was so he met the boy.   The child had been placing
stepping-stones to bridge the stream, and now came across,
balancing himself on the slippery surfaces to test his work.
It was odd that he had remained unobserved until this moment, but that was due to the fact of the water-rushes
on the brink being as tall as he.

The boy's eyes met those of the man with a frank, un-
clouded gaze.   He did not appear astonished.   That is the
way when one is young enough to be continually viewing
fresh wonders; one takes everything for granted.   He saw at
a glance that this other was not alien to him; his instinct
remained almost as true as those of the wild nature around.

For his own part, he had an unmistakable air of possession about him.   He appeared to belong to the place as
much as the hollyhocks and honeysuckle; and yet, how
could that be?

'Probably a child of the caretaker,' the man told himself.

He had authorized the agent to do what was best about
keeping the house in order.   He had not noticed what signs
it had to show of habitation.   Now he saw from the distance that it had not the unoccupied appearance he had
expected of it; nor the windows, the dark vacant stare of
those that no life behind illumines.

'Do you live here? ' he asked of the boy.

'Yes.'   The boy turned proudly toward the modest gray
pile in the manner of introducing it, forgetting himself in
his subject.   'It's a very old house.   There's a picture over

the bureau in the parlor of the man who built it, and planted the trees in the wood.   Hannah says —

'Hannah!'

It was a foolish repetition of the name.   Of course there were other Hannahs in the world.   The old servant of that name, who had told the man stories in his boyhood, had been dead more years than the child could number.

'Yes, — don't you know Hannah?   She'll come and call me in presently, and then you'll see her.   Hannah says they — the trees — have grown up with the family' (he assumed a queer importance, evidently in unconscious mimicry of the one who had repeated the tradition to him), 'and that with them the house will stand or fall.   Do you think the roots really reach so far?'

There was an underlying uneasiness in the tone, which it was impossible altogether to disguise.

As the other expressed his inability to volunteer an opinion on this point, the boy went on, seeing that his confidences were treated with due respect:

'I dug up one myself once — I wished I had n't afterwards — to make myself a Christmas tree like I'd read about.   I just had to hang some old things I had on it. It was only a tiny fir, small enough to go in a flower-pot; but that night the house shook, and the windows rattled as if all the trees in the forest were trying to get in.   I heard them tapping their boughs ever so angrily against the pane. As soon as it was light, I went out and planted the Christmas tree again.   I had n't meant to keep it out of the ground long: they might have known that.'

'Have you no playfellows here?'

The boy gave a comprehensive glance around.   'There are the trees; they are good fellows.   I would n't part with one of them.   It's fine to hear them all clap their hands when we are all jolly together. There are nests in them, too, and squirrels. We see a lot of one another.'

This statement was not difficult to believe: the Holland overalls bore evident traces of fellowship with mossy trunks.

The boy did most of the talking. He had more to tell of the founder of the family whose portrait hung in the parlor, and of how, when he — the child — grew up, he rather thought of writing books, as that same ancestor had done, and making the name great and famous again. He had not decided what kind of books he should write yet. Was it very hard to find words to rhyme, if one tried poetry? He was at no pains to hide such fancies and ambitions, of which his kind are generally too sensitive or too ashamed to speak to their elders, and which are as a rule forgotten as soon as outgrown.

'Shall we go in the wood now?' said the boy. 'It's easy enough to cross over the stepping-stones.'

'Yes, let us go.' The man was beginning to see everything through the boy's eyes. The garden was again much as he had remembered it, inclosed in a world of beautiful mystery. Nothing was really altered. What alteration he had imagined had been merely a transitory one in himself. The child had put a warm, eager hand into his; together they went into the wood, as happy as a pair of truant school boys; they might have been friends of long standing.

'So this is your enchanted forest?' said the man.

'Not really enchanted,' replied the boy seriously. 'I once read of one, but of course it was only in a fairy tale. That one vanished as soon as one spoke the right word. It would be a very wrong word that could make this vanish.' He had a way of speaking of the wood as if it were some sacred grove.

His companion suddenly felt guilty, not quite knowing why.

'Of course some one might cut them down.' The boy lowered his voice; it seemed shameful to mention the perpetration of such a deed aloud. 'It would be terrible to hear them groan when the axe struck them. The young ones might n't mind so much; but it would be bad for the grandfather trees who 've been here from the beginning. Hannah says one would still hear them wailing on stormy nights.'

'Even if they had been felled and carted away?'

'Yes, even then; though, to be sure, there would be no one to hear the wailing if it's true that the house must fall, too, at the same time. But we need n't trouble about that; none of it is likely to happen. You see, if it did, where should I be?'

He laughed merrily. This last argument appeared to him to be quite conclusive. Such an important consideration placed the awful contingency quite out of the question, and transformed it into nothing more than a joke.

The child's laughter died away as they both stood still to listen. Each thought he had heard his own name called.

'It's Hannah,' said the boy; and off he raced toward the house, barely saving himself from running into the arms of another person who had turned in at the gate.

'Who was the boy who ran round by the espaliers a minute ago? One would scarcely have judged him to be a child of the caretaker.'

The man's heart sank with a dull thud: something had told him the answer before it came.

'Child!' The lawyer looked puzzled. 'I did not see one. No children have any business in this garden; neither is there any caretaker here. The house has been shut up altogether since the old servant you called Hannah died, eleven years ago.'

They had reached the veranda. The westering sun had faded off the windows. It was easy to see that the house was empty. The shutters were up within, and the panes dark and weather-stained. Birds had built their nests undisturbed about the chimney stacks. The hearthstones had long been cold.

'My client is willing to purchase the property on the terms originally proposed,' the lawyer was saying. 'He contemplates investing in it as a building site. Of course the timber would have to be felled —'

A breeze passed through the treetops like a shudder. The younger man interposed:—

'I am sorry you should have had the trouble of coming here, but I have decided to keep the old place after all — stick and stone. It is not right it should go out of the family. I must pull my affairs together as well as I can without that.'

The little phantom of his dead boyhood was to suffer no eviction.

THE CLEAREST VOICE

BY MARGARET SHERWOOD

THE little business frown which John Wareham usually wore only at his office, and put off as he put on his hat in starting for home, lingered that evening, persisting through the long street-car ride, the walk past rows of suburban houses, and even to the brook at the foot of the hill below his home. Here it vanished, for the brook marked the spot where the world stopped, and Alice began. He watched with a meditative happy smile the rough stone fence which bordered this bit of meadow land, with the trailing woodbine and clematis that made it a thing of beauty; and, as he climbed the hill, the deepening color in the sunset clouds, and the notes of a wood thrush from the forest edge not far away, became part of a deep sense of harmony, breaking a mood of anxiety and fear.

Then came the comforting glimpse of the red brick house through the encompassing green, with its white daintiness of porch, fan-window, and window-facings. It all looked like her; in its serene and simple distinction it seemed to embody her; her creative touch was everywhere. The bay window, about which they had disagreed when the house was planned, had, surprisingly, turned out to the liking of both. As he fumbled at the latch of the gate, and pinched his finger as he always did, a vexed sense of triumph came to him, for it surely would have worked better if he had insisted on having his own way! Everywhere were traces of little worries and little triumphs, the latter predominating. It was the very soul of home, from the threshold to the branches of the tall elm which touched the roof protectingly; it was wholly desirable,— and it might have to go.

As he followed the brick walk, in bitterness he closed his eyes that he might not see, and so ran into a porch pillar, the one on which Alice's red roses were blossoming; the queer little groan that he gave in some strange way took on the sound of 'Railroads!' and again 'Railroads!' as he beat his head against the pillar once or twice purposely; and his voice had a note of contempt. He had not felt that way about railroads when he had invested his savings, partly in the stock of a new railroad in the West, partly in the stock of an old railroad in the East that was doing wild things in the way of improvements. Then there had been nothing too good for him to say about the earning power of railroads, the wise management of railroads, the net profits of railroads. Now, both railroads were in trouble; dividends were cut, and the stock which he had hoped to sell at a profit had dropped almost to zero; the mortgage loan on his house was due in a month; and he, a man earning only a moderate salary in a real-estate office, had nothing in the world wherewith to meet the emergency. Even the savings-bank deposit had gone into railroad stock, in order that the mortgage might be paid off more quickly.

But his face lighted up with a smile both sad and bright which made quite a different face of it as he crossed the threshold, that threshold on which Alice had stopped to kiss him the day he had married her and brought her home. There was something here that shut out all the trouble in the universe: about the doorway his wife's laughter seemed to be always floating,— that laughter, merry, touched with tenderness, made up of mirth and sorrow, as all wise laughter is. Just then came little Jack to meet him, speeding madly down the baluster; and John, as he picked up his boy, kissed him, and reproved him for coming downstairs that way, had nothing to answer, when his son averred that it was lots better than a railroad, save 'That might well be.'

'There's ice-cream for dinner,' the boy exploded; and the father, roughly smoothing Jack's tousled hair, started as he caught a sound of chatter from the living-room, and stood still in dismay. That to-day of all days should be the time of the family gathering which brought two uncles, two aunts, and three cousins to the house! How completely he had forgotten! He hung up his hat and grasped little Jack's hand; he would tell them nothing about his troubles, nothing; he would be the ideal host, concealing his personal vexations under a cordial smile.

But hardly had he opened the door, with his office bag still held absentmindedly in his hand, when they were upon him. The cordial smile did not deceive them for a minute. Aunt Janet, who was sitting by the fireplace, looked the most troubled of all, though she said nothing. It was 'Why, John, what's the matter?' from Aunt Mary, and 'Well, John, how goes it?' from Uncle Philip, who looked as if he knew that it went very badly indeed; and 'What makes you look so worried? With a home like this, no man ought to look worried,' from his Cousin Austin, who had recently become engaged and was thinking about homes. He nodded approvingly at the room, which was simply furnished, soft in coloring, with English chintzes, a few pictures of trees and of water, — all out-of-door things, — and a fireplace that showed signs of constant use.

John's face brightened as he caught this look of admiration; not all the confusion of greeting and inquiries in regard to health, not all the business worries in the world could check the sense of peace that always came to him in entering this room, which, more perfectly than any other spot, expressed the personality of Alice. He managed to make his way through the little crowd of sympathetic wrinkled faces, and wondering smooth faces. There were, it was discovered, comfortable chairs enough for all, and John found himself, as host, the centre of a little group bent on probing his affairs, in friendly fashion, to the bottom.

It was his sister Emily who finally started the flood of questioning that led to the betrayal of the secret he had meant to keep for the present. She came bustling in through the door leading to the dining-room, looking anxious as soon as she glanced at her brother; and from the brass bowl of yellow roses held unsteadily in her hand, a few drops spattered to the floor.

'Are you ill, John,' she asked, 'or have you lost—'

Among all the many voices of inquiry, comment, question whereby she was interrupted, the voice of Alice was the clearest, making the others, no matter how near the speakers stood, seem to come from far away. Little Jack came and climbed upon his father's knee, a curious reproduction of the family look of worry appearing on his chubby face. John the elder leaned his head back in the chintz-covered chair, shutting his eyes for a minute with a sense of warmth and satisfaction, and the nearness of the cuddling body of his son.

'Everything's the matter,' he said wearily, 'everything'; and he had a momentary twinge of conscience, realizing that he was not being the ideal host.

They all watched him anxiously, sympathetically, in silence; and Aunt Mary, near the window, went on drawing her needle in and out with exquisite precision, her gray head bent over a centrepiece which she intended to present to the house.

'Oh no, I'm not ill,' said John Wareham, suddenly sitting upright; 'but the Long Gorge Railroad has gone into a receiver's hands, and three days ago the New York and Nineveh cut its dividend. I'm done for.'

Emily gave a little gasp, and said nothing. 'You will pull through all right,' asserted Uncle Philip, stirring up the fire in order to hide his face. And Cousin Austin slapped John's shoulder, saying facetiously, 'Take courage, Jeremiah. The worst is yet to come.'

John laughed in spite of himself, and struck his fist upon the knee not occupied by Jack.

'Every dollar I had in the world I had drawn out and put into those two cursed things. Now I've nothing, no capital, no credit. The place has got to go.'

'No, no!' cried the women-folk.

'The place has got to go,' repeated John Wareham, his face in little Jack's hair. 'And I feel as if I could rob a bank or a jewelry store to prevent that.'

Jack burst into a delighted giggle, through which John heard, 'You wouldn't do any such thing, and you mustn't talk that way before Jack.' It was Alice who spoke, with a little catch in her voice that sometimes came, half way between a laugh and a sob; and it was echoed by the two aunts.

'Railroads!' growled John, with supreme contempt. 'It would have been a great deal better if railroads had never been invented. Jack, we shall have to get a prairie schooner, and trek to the West.'

Jack's eyes shone like stars, but he got no chance to say anything, for, with that outburst, the springs of speech were loosened. There was the clamor, the chorus clamor, of relatives, indignant, inquisitive, sympathetic relatives, all eager to help, and all uneasily conscious that their own small measure of prosperity would hardly stand the strain. He shook his head sadly in answer to the inquiry as to whether he could not borrow: he had no security. Aunt

Mary did not fail to remind him that she had warned him at the time; Aunt Janet, in a thin but affectionate voice, admitted that she had suffered in the same way heavily. And then the clock ticked through a brief silence.

'Why don't you read your letters?' asked Emily suddenly. She stood, absent-mindedly arranging the flowers with one finger, busy already with plans for the future.

There was a small pile of letters on the centre table, quite within John's reach; he began tearing open the envelopes in mechanical fashion, throwing them untidily upon the floor. As each one fell, Jack slid down and picked it up, climbing back to his father's knee. One was a wedding announcement; one was a plumber's bill; at the third, John paused, read, looked up bewildered, and read again.

'Why, Emily!' he exploded, boyishly. 'This can't be. Read that, will you, and tell me if I have lost my mind.'

Emily put down the roses, and read the letter slowly, wonderingly, smiling even as her brother had smiled.

'Not Uncle John! And we were always so afraid of him!'

'Twenty thousand dollars!' murmured John.

Open-mouthed silence waited upon them, until Cousin Austin broke the spell with,—

'I say, would you mind if I looked over your shoulder?'

And John flung him the letter with a little whoop of joy.

'Is this plain living, or is this a fairy story?' he demanded quizzically. 'I never thought of myself as a dark-eyed hero with a fortune dropping into my hands just in the nick of time! A title ought to go with it.'

The vibrant energy of the man was back again; the dry humor which, in sunny seasons, quivered about his mouth, was once more there; the mocking incredulity of his words belied the growing look of peace and security in his face. The years seemed slipping from him, bringing him a mellow boyhood.

'Twenty thousand dollars is n't exactly a fortune, John.'

'It will buy the place twice over,' exulted the man, 'and we shan't have to start for the West in a prairie schooner right away!'

'Shan't we, papa?' asked little Jack, in hungry disappointment.

But the child's shrill voice had little chance where everybody was speaking at once. Aunt Mary's 'Well, I hope you hang on to this, and not be foolish again,' and Cousin Austin's 'You deserve it, John,' and Uncle Howard's 'Well, I *am* glad. Shake!' and several other congratulatory remarks all came at once.

'The poor old fellow; the poor old fellow,' said John to himself softly, rubbing his hands. 'I suppose he died out in Oklahoma all alone. How he happened to will this to me, I give up; he did n't like me very well.'

The very atmosphere of the room had changed; once more a feeling of quiet pleasure pervaded it. The full sense of home, peace, security came back, with a suggestion of a kettle singing on the hearth, though there was no kettle nearer than the kitchen.

'But there's Frank — ' It must have been Alice who suggested this, and a something disturbing, questioning, crept into the air.

'Frank!' said John Wareham suddenly. 'Why, I'd forgotten all about Frank! We have n't heard of him for more than fifteen years or so, have we?'

'More than that,' answered Emily. 'He was in Mexico, the last we knew.'

'He may be living,' suggested John. 'Mexico is always in such a state — I suppose the mails can't be trusted.'

'We ought to find out,' said Alice.

'Uncle John had cast him off,' suggested Emily tentatively, anxiously.

'But he was Uncle John's own son,' said Alice, earnestly, compellingly; 'and wasn't Uncle John in the wrong?'

'Uncle John was a queer customer,' said John hastily. 'He was cranky, no doubt about it, but he was n't crazy; and if this lawyer's statement is correct, I've got a good legal right to the twenty thousand, haven't I?'

'Of course you have!' said Aunt Mary.

'But the moral right?' whispered Alice.

'What was the quarrel about, anyway?' asked Austin. 'Frank's marriage, was n't it? I never heard much about it.'

'That was part of it,' said Aunt Janet. 'Frank, you know, fell in love with a little country girl whom his father did not want him to marry, but he insisted on having his way, and married her.'

'Good for him,' nodded Austin approvingly.

Little Jack, glancing from one to another with wide blue eyes, was silently weaving his philosophy of life, and his interpretation of humanity.

'Religion was mixed up in it in some way,' contributed John. 'Uncle grew to be something of a fanatic, and he wanted them both to believe what he believed, and they would n't, or did n't, or could n't. It was incompatibility of temper all round, I dare say.'

'Frank was a good son,' reminded Alice. 'He was patient with his father, and he all but gave up his life for Uncle John, nursing him through diphtheria.'

More and more the sweet, persistent voice brought trouble and question into the atmosphere from which trouble and question had so suddenly cleared. The new security began to seem unstable; the new-found joy a stolen thing. Even in the pauses, the personality of the woman spoke from curtain and cushion and fireplace of this room of her devising. She dominated the whole, seeming the only presence there; brother and sister and guests shrank in the radiance of her.

'Do you really think I ought to hunt Frank up?' asked the man.

Emily shook her head, but doubtfully.

'You probably couldn't find him, after all these years.'

'I could try,' admitted John.

'Nonsense!' cried Aunt Mary, over her embroidery. 'You stay right where you are, and pay off your mortgage. A man who has worked as hard as you have, and has had as much trouble, ought to take a bit of good luck when it comes.'

'Think how much good you could do with it,' murmured Aunt Janet.

'As the pickpocket said when he put the stolen dime in the collection plate,' said Austin; but fortunately Aunt Janet did not understand.

'Uncle had a right to do what he pleased with his own,' said John defiantly. 'If he chose to cast off his son, for reasons which he considered sufficient, he had the right.'

'But you cannot cast off your son,' persisted Alice. 'John, we have a boy of our own. You know that the obligation is one of all eternity; you cannot get rid of fatherhood.'

'O papa, papa, you hurt me,' squealed little John, suddenly interrupted in his philosophy-weaving.

'Confound it all!' cried John with sudden irritation. 'Is n't this just like life! To hold out the rope, just to grab it away again with a grin — I won't, I say. What is mine is mine.'

'But it is n't yours.'

'Did Frank have any children?' he asked.

'Several, I believe,' admitted Emily reluctantly.

'And he never got on?'

'He never got on.'

'And the twenty thousand might save their pesky little Mexican souls.'

The child's laughter rippled out across the shocked silence of the elders.

'Maybe Uncle John left them something,' suggested Emily. 'For a man who tried such big things this does n't seem much money.'

Her brother shook his head.

'"The entire sum of which he stands possessed,"' he read from the lawyer's letter.

'You might make a few inquiries through the post. I rather imagine the Mexican mail service is n't very trustworthy,' suggested Aunt Mary, hopefully.

He looked at her, but in abstracted fashion, as if it were not to Aunt Mary that he was listening.

'I'll write to this Oklahoma lawyer, and then I must go to Mexico.'

'Is n't it a little quixotic?'

'It's most likely all kinds of foolishness, like everything else I do,' groaned the man. 'But it's what I'd want done for my little chap if I were dead and he alive, and I had quarreled with him. I suppose I could keep this money and save my skin, but —'

'You couldn't keep it without finding out,' murmured Alice, 'because you are you, and the real you is incapable of doing a mean thing.'

'You must do as you think best,' said Emily at last. 'Maybe, if you find Frank, he won't want it all, but will divide, knowing that his father willed it to you.'

'That may be as it may be,' said the man, leaning back in his chair with the face of one listening. 'But I go to

Mexico. It's a queer game we play here, and I'll be dashed if I can understand it, but I'm going to play it as fairly as I know how.'

So the voice of Alice won, of Alice, who had been dead for five long years.

THE MARBLE CHILD

BY E. NESBIT

ALL over the pavement of the church spread the exaggerated cross-hatching of the old pews' oak, a Smithfield market of intersecting lines such as children made with cards in the old days when kings and knaves had fat legs bulging above their serviceable feet, and queens had skirts to their gowns and were not cut across their royal middles by mirrors reflecting only the bedizened torso of them and the charge — heart, trefoil, or the like — in the right-hand top corner of the oblong that framed them.

The pew had qualities: tall fat hassocks, red cushions, a comparative seclusion, and, in the case of the affluent, red curtains drawn at sermon-time.

The child wearied by the spectacle of a plump divine, in black gown and Geneva bands, thumping the pulpit-cushions in the madness of incomprehensible oratory, surrendered his ears to the noise of intonations which, in his own treble, would have earned the reprimand, 'Naughty temper.' His eyes, however, were, through some oversight of the gods of his universe, still his own. They found their own pasture: not, to be sure, the argent and sable of gown and bands, still less the gules of flushed denunciatory gills.

There is fair pasture in an old church which, when Norman work was broken down, men loved and built again as from the heart, with pillars and arches, which, to their rude time, symbolized all that the heart desires to materialize, in symbolic stone. The fretted tombs where the effigies of warrior and priest lay life-like in dead marble, the fretted canopies that brooded above their rest. Tall pillars like the trunks of the pine woods that smelt so sweet, the marvel of the timbered roof — turned upside down it would be like a ship. And what could be easier than to turn it upside down? Imagination shrank bashfully from the pulpit already tightly tenanted, but the triforium was plainly and beautifully empty; there one could walk, squeezing happily through the deep thin arches and treading carefully by the unguarded narrow ledge. Only if one played too long in the roof aunts nudged, and urgent whispers insisted that one must not look about like that in church. When this moment came it came always as a crisis foreseen, half dreaded, half longed-for. After that the child kept his eyes lowered, and looked only at the faded red hassocks from which the straw bulged, and in brief, guarded, intimate moments, at the other child.

The other child was kneeling, always, whether the congregation knelt or stood or sat. Its hands were clasped. Its face was raised, but its back bowed under a weight — the weight of the font, for the other child was of marble and knelt always in the church, Sundays and week-days. There had been once three marble figures holding up the shallow basin, but two had crumbled or been broken away, and now it seemed that the whole weight of the superimposed marble rested on those slender shoulders.

The child who was not marble was sorry for the other. He must be very tired.

The child who was not marble, — his name was Ernest, — that child of weary eyes and bored brain, pitied the marble boy while he envied him.

'I suppose he does n't really feel, if he's stone,' he said. 'That's what they mean by the stony-hearted tyrant. But if he does feel — How jolly it would be if he could come out and sit in my pew, or if I could creep under the font beside him. If he would move a little there would be just room for me.'

The first time that Ernest ever saw the marble child move was on the hottest Sunday in the year. The walk across the fields had been a breathless penance, the ground burned the soles of Ernest's feet as red-hot ploughshares the feet of the saints. The corn was cut, and stood in stiff yellow stooks, and the shadows were very black. The sky was light, except in the west beyond the pine trees, where blue-black clouds were piled.

'Like witches' feather-beds,' said Aunt Harriet, shaking out the folds of her lace shawl.

'Not before the child, dear,' whispered Aunt Emmeline.

Ernest heard her, of course. It was always like that: as soon as any one spoke about anything interesting, Aunt Emmeline intervened. Ernest walked along very melancholy in his starched frill. The dust had whitened his strapped shoes, and there was a wrinkle in one of his white socks.

'Pull it up, child, pull it up,' said Aunt Jessie; and shielded from the world by the vast silk-veiled crinolines of three full-sized aunts, he pulled it up.

On the way to church, and indeed, in all walks abroad, you held the hand of an aunt; the circumferent crinolines made the holding an arm's-length business, very tiring. Ernest was always glad when, in the porch, the hand was dropped. It was just as the porch was reached that the first lonely roll of thunder broke over the hills.

'I knew it,' said Aunt Jessie, in triumph; 'but you would wear your blue silk.'

There was no more thunder till after the second lesson, which was hardly ever as interesting as the first, Ernest thought. The marble child looked more tired than usual, and Ernest lost himself in a dream-game where both of them got out from prison and played hide-and-seek among the tombstones. Then the thunder cracked deafeningly right over the church. Ernest forgot to stand up, and even the clergyman waited till it died away.

It was a most exciting service, well worth coming to church for, and afterwards people crowded in the wide porch and wondered whether it would clear, and wished they had brought their umbrellas. Some went back and sat in their pews till the servants should have had time to go home and return with umbrellas and cloaks. The more impetuous made clumsy rushes between the showers, bonnets bent, skirts held well up. Many a Sunday dress was ruined that day, many a bonnet fell from best to second-best.

And it was when Aunt Jessie whispered to him to sit still and be a good boy and learn a hymn, that he looked to the marble child with, 'Isn't it a shame?' in his heart and his eyes, and the marble child looked back, 'Never mind, it will soon be over,' and held out its marble hands. Ernest saw them come toward him, reaching well beyond the rim of the basin under which they had always, till now, stayed.

'Oh!' said Ernest, quite out loud; and, dropping the hymn-book, held out his hands, or began to hold them out. For before he had done more than sketch the gesture, he remembered that marble does not move and that one must not be silly. All the same, marble *had* moved. Also Ernest had 'spoken out loud' in church. Unspeakable disgrace!

He was taken home in conscious ignominy, treading in all the puddles to distract his mind from his condition.

He was put to bed early, as a punishment, instead of sitting up and learning his catechism under the charge of one of the maids while the aunts went to evening church. This, while it was terrible to Ernest, was in the nature of a reprieve to the housemaid, who found means to modify her own consequent loneliness. Far-away whispers and laughs from the back or kitchen windows assured Ernest that the front or polite side of the house was unguarded. He got up, simulated the appearance of the completely dressed, and went down the carpeted stairs, through the rosewood-furnished drawing-room, rose-scented and still as a deathbed, and so out through the French windows to the lawn, where already the beginnings of dew lay softly.

His going out had no definite aim. It was simply an act of rebellion such as, secure from observation, the timid may achieve; a demonstration akin to putting the tongue out behind people's backs.

Having got himself out on the lawn, he made haste to hide in the shrubbery, disheartened by a baffling consciousness of the futility of safe revenges. What is the tongue put out behind the back of the enemy without the applause of some admirer?

The red rays of the setting sun made splendor in the dripping shrubbery.

'I wish I had n't,' said Ernest.

But it seemed silly to go back now, just to go out and to go back. So he went farther into the shrubbery and got out at the other side where the shrubbery slopes down into the wood, and it was nearly dark there — so nearly that the child felt more alone than ever.

And then quite suddenly he was not alone. Hands parted the hazels and a face he knew looked out from between them.

He knew the face, and yet the child he saw was not any of the children he knew.

'Well,' said the child with the face he knew; 'I've been watching you. What did you come out for?'

'I was put to bed.'

'Do you not like it?'

'Not when it's for punishment.'

'If you'll go back now,' said the strange child, 'I'll come and play with you after you're asleep.'

'You dare n't. Suppose the aunts catch you?'

'They won't,' said the child, shaking its head and laughing. 'I'll race you to the house!'

Ernest ran. He won the race. For the other child was not there at all when he reached the house.

'How odd!' he said. But he was tired and there was thunder again and it was beginning to rain, large spots as big as pennies on the step of the French window. So he went back to bed, too sleepy to worry about the question of where he had seen the child before, and only a little disappointed because his revenge had been so brief and inadequate.

Then he fell asleep and dreamed that the marble child had crept out from under the font, and that he and it were playing hide-and-seek among the pews in the gallery at church. It was a delightful dream and lasted all night, and when he woke he knew that the child he had seen in the wood in yesterday's last light was the marble child from the church.

This did not surprise him as much as it would surprise you: the world where children live is so full of amazing and incredible-looking things that turn out to be quite real. And if Lot's wife could be turned into a pillar of salt, why should not a marble child turn into a real one? It was all quite plain to Ernest, but he did not tell any one: because he had a feeling that it might not be easy to make it plain to them.

'That child does n't look quite the thing,' said Aunt Emmeline at breakfast. 'A dose of Gregory's, I think, at eleven.'

Ernest's morning was blighted. Did you ever take Gregory's powder? It is worse than quinine, worse than senna, worse than anything except castor oil.

But Ernest had to take it — in raspberry jam.

'And don't make such faces,' said Aunt Emmeline, rinsing the spoon at the pantry sink. 'You know it's all for your own good.'

As if the thought that it is for one's own good ever kept any one from making faces!

The aunts were kind in their grown-up crinolined way. But Ernest wanted some one to play with. Every night in his dreams he played with the marble child. And at church on Sunday the marble child still held out its hands, farther than before.

'Come along then,' Ernest said to it, in that voice with which heart speaks to heart; 'come and sit with me behind the red curtains. Come!'

The marble child did not look at him. Its head seemed to be bent farther forward than ever before.

When it came to the second hymn Ernest had an inspiration. All the rest of the churchful, sleepy and suitable, were singing, —

> 'The roseate hues of early dawn,
>   The brightness of the day,
> The crimson of the sunset sky,
>   How fast they fade away.'

Ernest turned his head towards the marble child and softly mouthed, — you could hardly call it singing, —

> 'The rosy tews of early dawn,
>   The brightness of the day;
> Come out, come out, come out, come out,
>   Come out with me and play.'

And he pictured the rapture of that moment when the marble child should respond to this appeal, creep out from under the font, and come and sit beside him on the red cushions beyond the red curtains. The aunts would not see, of course. They never saw the things that mattered. No one would see except Ernest. He looked hard at the marble child.

'You must come out,' he said; and again, 'You must come, you must.'

And the marble child did come. It crept out and came to sit by him, holding his hand. It was a cold hand certainly, but it did not feel like marble.

And the next thing he knew, an aunt was shaking him and whispering with fierceness tempered by reverence for the sacred edifice, —

'Wake up, Ernest. How can you be so naughty?'

And the marble child was back in its place under the font.

When Ernest looks back on that summer it seems to have thundered every time he went to church. But of course this cannot really have been the case.

But it was certainly a very lowering purple-skied day which saw him stealthily start on the adventure of his little life. He was weary of aunts — they were kind yet just; they told him so and he believed them. But their justice was exactly like other people's nagging, and their kindness he did not want at all. He wanted some one to play with.

'May we walk up to the churchyard?' was a request at first received graciously as showing a serious spirit. But its reiteration was considered morbid, and his walks took the more dusty direction of the County Asylum.

His longing for the only child he knew, the marble child, exacerbated by denial, drove him to rebellion. He would run away. He would live with the marble child in the big churc.. porch; they would eat berries from the wood near by, just as children did in books, and hide there when people came to church.

So he watched his opportunity and went quietly out through the French window, skirted the side of the house where all the windows were blank because of the old window-tax, took the narrow strip of lawn at a breathless run, and found safe cover among the rhododendrons.

The church-door was locked, of course, but he knew where there was a broken pane in the vestry window, and his eye had marked the lop-sided tombstone underneath it. By climbing upon that and getting a knee in the carved water-spout — He did it, got his hand through, turned the catch of the window, and fell through upon the dusty table of the vestry.

The door was ajar and he passed into the empty church. It seemed very large and gray now that he had it to himself. His feet made a loud echoing noise that was disconcerting. He had meant to call out, 'Here I am!' But in the face of these echoes he could not.

He found the marble child, its head bent more than ever, its hands reaching out quite beyond the edge of the font; and when he was quite close he whispered, —

'Here I am. — Come and play!'

But his voice trembled a little. The marble child was so plainly marble. And yet it had not always been marble. He was not sure. Yet —

'I *am* sure,' he said. 'You did talk to me in the shrubbery, did n't you?'

But the marble child did not move or speak.

'You did come and hold my hand last Sunday,' he said, a little louder.

And only the empty echoes answered him.

'Come out,' he said then, almost afraid now of the

church's insistent silence. 'I've come to live wiu. vou altogether. Come out of your marble, do come out!'

He reached up to stroke the marble cheek. A sound thrilled him, a loud everyday sound. The big key turning in the lock of the south door. The aunts!

'Now they'll take me back,' said Ernest; 'you might have come.'

But it was not the aunts. It was the old pew-opener, come to scrub the chancel. She came slowly in with pail and brush; the pail slopped a little water on to the floor close to Ernest as she passed him, not seeing.

Then the marble child moved, turned toward Ernest with speaking lips and eyes that saw.

'You can stay with me forever if you like,' it said, 'but you'll have to see things happen. I have seen things happen.'

'What sort of things?' Ernest asked.

'Terrible things.'

'What things shall I have to see?'

'*Her*,'— the marble child moved a free arm to point to the old woman on the chancel steps, — 'and your aunt who will be here presently, looking for you. Do you hear the thunder? Presently the lightning will strike the church. It won't hurt us, but it will fall on them.'

Ernest remembered in a flash how kind Aunt Emmeline had been when he was ill, how Aunt Jessie had given him his chessmen, and Aunt Harriet had taught him how to make paper rosettes for picture-frames.

'I must go and tell them,' he said.

'If you go, you'll never see me again,' said the marble child, and put its arms round his neck.

'Can't I come back to you when I've told them?' Ernest asked, returning the embrace.

'There will be no coming back,' said the marble child.

'But I want you. I love you best of everybody in the world,' Ernest said.

'I know.'

'I'll stay with you,' said Ernest.

The marble child said nothing.

'But if I don't tell them I shall be the same as a murderer,' Ernest whispered. 'Oh! let me go, and come back to you.'

'I shall not be here.'

'But I must go. I must,' said Ernest, torn between love and duty.

'Yes.'

'And I shan't have you any more?' the living child urged.

'You'll have me in your heart,' said the marble child — 'that's where I want to be. That's my real home.'

They kissed each other again.

'It was certainly a direct Providence,' Aunt Emmeline used to say in later years to really sympathetic friends, 'that I thought of going up to the church when I did. Otherwise nothing could have saved dear Ernest. He was terrified, quite crazy with fright, poor child, and he rushed out at me from behind our pew shouting, "Come away, come away, auntie, come away!" and dragged me out. Mrs. Meadows providentially followed, to see what it was all about, and the next thing was the catastrophe.'

'The church was struck by a thunder-bolt was it not?' the sympathetic friend asks.

'It was indeed — a deafening crash, my dear — and then the church slowly crumbled before our eyes. The south wall broke like a slice of cake when you break it across — and the noise and the dust! Mrs. Meadows never had her hearing again, poor thing, and her mind was

a little affected too. I became unconscious, and Ernest —
well, it was altogether too much for the child. He lay
between life and death for weeks. Shock to the system,
the physician said. He had been rather run down before. We had to get a little cousin to come and live with
us afterwards. The physicians said that he required young
society.'

'It must indeed have been a shock,' says the sympathetic friend, who knows there is more to come.

'His intellect was quite changed, my dear,' Aunt
Emmeline resumes; 'on regaining consciousness he demanded the marble child! Cried and raved, my dear,
always about the marble child. It appeared he had had
fancies about one of the little angels that supported the
old font, not the present font, my dear. We presented
that as a token of gratitude to Providence for our escape.
Of course we checked his fancifulness as well as we could,
but it lasted quite a long time.'

'What became of the little marble angel?' the friend in-
quires as in friendship bound.

'Crushed to powder, dear, in the awful wreck of the
church. Not a trace of it could be found. And poor Mrs.
Meadows! So dreadful those delusions.'

'What form did her delusions take?' the friend, anxious
to be done with the old story, hastily asks.

'Well, she always declared that *two* children ran out to
warn me and that one of them was very unusual looking.
"It was n't no flesh and blood, ma'am," she used to say in
her ungrammatical way; "it was a little angel a-taking care
of Master Ernest. It 'ad 'old of 'is 'and. And I say it was
'is garden angel, and its face was as bright as a lily in the
sun." '

The friend glances at the India cabinet, and Aunt Emmeline rises and unlocks it.

'Ernest must have been behaving in a very naughty and destructive way in the church — but the physician said he was not quite himself probably, for when they got him home and undressed him they found this in his hand.'

Then the sympathizing friend polishes her glasses and looks, not for the first time, at the relic from the drawer of the India cabinet.   It is a white marble finger.

Thus flow the reminiscences of Aunt Emmeline.   The memories of Ernest run as this tale runs.

THE ONE LEFT

BY E. V. LUCAS

I

HE had become very ill — could hardly move from
where he lay; and she, who loved him, and was to have
married him, and spent all her waking hours in thinking
what she could do for him, persuaded him to have a telephone installed and brought to his bedside so that he and
she could talk, and he could talk with others, too.   Every
night he rang her up and they had a long conversation;
many times in the day also.   Nothing, as it happened,
could have saved his life, but this modern device lightened
his last weeks.

His death, although it blasted her hopes, made no difference to her devotion.   She merely installed his memory in
the place of his rich personality and loved that.   He, almost more than ever, was her standard.   What he would
have liked, she did; what he would have disliked, she left
undone.   Although dead, he swayed her utterly, and under
his dominion she was equable and gentle, although broken
at heart.   She took all things as they came, since how could
anything matter now that everything that mattered was
over?

One perplexity only had power to trouble her, and that
was the wonder, the amazement, the horror, not only that
so much knowledge and kindliness and sympathy and all
that made for the world's good and happiness should be so
wantonly extinguished; but that no touch of the vanished
hand should be permitted to the one soul (now left behind)
with whom his soul had been fused.   This she could neither

understand nor forgive. Religious she had never been in the ordinary sense, although such religion as must sway a true idealistic lover was hers; but now she broke even from such slender ties as had held her to orthodoxy. She threw off the creed of her parents as naturally and simply as if it were a borrowed garment, and sank into her sorrow, which was also her joy, without another thought of here or hereafter.

So it went on for a year or so, during which time his house had remained empty, save for a caretaker, — for she (who was rich) could not bear that any one else should live there, — and his room exactly as he had died in it.

II

One evening she dined out. Her next neighbor on one side was a young American engineer, and in their conversation they came in time to the topic of invention and the curious aptitude for inventiveness shown by the American race. It was a case, said the engineer, of supply following demand; all Americans required time- and labor-saving appliances, and they obtained them. Where servants abounded and there was no servant problem, as in England and on the Continent, the need for such contrivances was not acute. And so on. The conversation thus begun reached at last specific inventions, and the engineer told of a remarkable one which had come under his notice just before he left New York.

'You will probably not believe me,' he said; 'the thing sounds incredible; but then who would have believed once that there could be a telegraph, and still less a telephone? Who would have believed that the camera would ever be anything but a dream? I will tell you what this is. It is a machine in which you insert a portion, no matter how small, of a telephone wire, and by turning a handle you compel this piece of wire to give back every message that has ever passed over it.'

She held her heart. 'This really exists?' she forced herself to ask.

'Actually,' said the engineer. 'But when I left home the inventor was in a difficulty. All the messages were coming out all right, but backwards. Naturally the reproduction would be from the most recent to the less recent. By writing down the words and then reversing them the investigator could of course get at what he was wanting, — I may say that the invention is for the New York police — but my friend is convinced that he can devise some mechanical system of reversing at the time which will make the messages read forward as they should. Just think of the excitement of the detective, listening through all the voices and ordinary conversations on the wire for the one voice and the one sentence that will give him his long desired clue! — But are you ill?'

'No, no,' she said, although her face was a ghastly white, 'no, it is nothing. The room is a little hot. Tell me some more about your inventive friend. Is he wealthy?'

'Indeed, no,' said the engineer. 'That is his trouble. If he had more money, or if he had some rich backers who believed in him, he might do wonders.'

'I should like to help him,' she said. 'This kind of work interests me. Could you not cable him to come over and bring the thing with him? I would gladly finance him. I want some sporting outlet like that for my money.'

'Cable?'

'Yes, cable. There are things that one does by impulse or not at all. The butler here will get you a form.'

III

She had been to the empty house that day with an em-
ployee of the telephone company, and they had extracted
a foot of the precious wire. A few minutes ago she had
held it in her trembling fingers and placed it in the machine.
Now she carefully locked the door and drew the heavy
curtain over it and carried the machine to the farthest corner of the room. There, with a sigh of relief and tense and
almost terrible anticipation, she sat down and placed her
ear to the receiver and began to turn the handle.

His voice sounded at once: 'Are you there?' It was
quite clear, so clear and unmistakable and actual that her
hand paused on the handle and she bowed her throbbing
head. She turned on; 'Are you there?' the familiar tones
repeated. And then the reply, 'Yes, who is it?' in a
woman's voice. Then he spoke again: 'Ernest,' he said.
'Is it Helen?' Again her hand paused. Helen — that
rubbishy little woman he had known all his life and was on
such good terms with. She remembered now, that she had
been away when the telephone was installed and others had
talked on it before her. It could not be helped: she had
meant to be the first, but circumstances prevented. There
must be many conversations before she came to her own;
she would have to listen to them all. She turned on,
and the laughing, chaffing conversation with this foolish
little Helen person repeated itself out of the past now so
tragic.

To other talks with other friends, and now and then with
a tradesman, she had to listen; but at last came her hour.

'Is that you?' she heard her own voice saying, knowing
it was her own rather by instinct than by hearing. 'Is
that you? But I know it is. How distinctly you speak!'

'Yes, it's me' — and his soft vibrant laugh.

'How are you, dear?'

'Better, I hope.'

'Have you missed me?'

'Missed you!'

And then the endearments, the confidences, the hopes and fears, the plans for the morrow, the plans for all life. As she listened, the tears ran down her face, but still she turned on and on. Sometimes he was so hopeful and bright, and again so despairing.

She remembered the occasion of every word. Once she had dined out and had gone to the theatre. It was an engagement she could not well refuse. It was an amusing play and she was in good spirits. She rang him up between the acts and found him depressed. Hurrying home she had settled down to talk to him at her ease. How it all came back to her now!

'Are you there, my dearest?'

'Yes, but oh, so tired, so old!'

'It is a bad day. Every one has been complaining of tiredness to-day.'

'You say that because you are kind. Just to comfort me. It's no use. I can see so clearly, sometimes, I shall never get well — to-night I know it.'

'My darling, no.'

And then silence, — complete, terrifying.

She had rung up without effect. He had fainted, she thought, and had dropped the receiver. She was in a fever of agony. She leaped into a cab and drove to his house. The nurse reassured her; he had begun to sob and did not want her to know it, and now he was asleep.

But there was no sleep for her that night. What if he were right — if he really knew? In her heart she feared that he did; with the rest of her she fought that fear.

As she listened, the tears ran down her face, but still she

turned on and on. She sat there for hours before the last words came, the last he was ever to speak over the wire.

It was to make an engagement. He had rallied wonderfully at the end and was confident of recovery. She was to bring her modiste to his room at eleven o'clock the next morning with her patterns, that he might help in choosing her new dress. He had insisted on it — the dress she was to wear on his first outing.

'At eleven,' he had said. 'Mind you don't forget. But then you never forget anything. Good-night once more, my sweet.'

'Good-night.'

She had never seen him again alive. He died before the morning.

She put the machine away and looked out of the window. The sun had risen. The sky was on fire with the promise of a beautiful day. Worn out, she fell asleep; to wake — to what? To such awakening as there is for those who never forget anything.

IV

Every night found her bending over the machine. She had learned now when not to listen. She had timed the reproduction absolutely, and watch in hand she waited until the other messages were done, and her own voice began. There was no condensing possible; one must either each time have every conversation or stop it. But how could she stop it before the end?

Locking the door and drawing the heavy curtain, she would sit down in the far corner and begin to turn. She knew just how fast to turn for others; so slowly for herself. When the watch gave her the signal she would begin to listen.

'Is that you? Is that you? But I know it is. How distinctly you speak!'

'Yes, it's me,'— and the soft vibrant laugh.

'How are you, dear?'

'Better, I hope.'

'Have you missed me?'

'Missed you!'

THE LEGACY OF RICHARD HUGHES

BY MARGARET LYNN

I

RACHEL MARQUIS paused a moment with her hand on the library-door. She had had John placed in here because it was the room she herself loved best, and she knew that it was here she would prefer to sit beside him in these last hours of waiting. Yet she had hesitated to come down, and even now, with her hand on the door-knob, she lingered again to re-strengthen herself before entering. The very unusualness of an unfamiliar sight in the familiar room would add, she knew, to the sharp strangeness of the whole event. She almost hoped, as she waited this moment, for another practical duty of some sort, which would postpone again her entrance to the room.

But no sound came from any part of the silenced house, and she opened the door and entered. The long casket stood awkwardly across the blank fireplace, for she had chosen to give no direction to the undertaker and he had followed his own professional judgment. Everything was arranged, however, with a sort of intention which indicated the intrusion of the professional into the private. In spite of the stronger feeling of the moment, Rachel Marquis noticed this, with sharp disapproval. But she went directly to the chair which had been placed beside the casket and seated herself, bowing her head long on her folded arms before she looked on the familiar face beside her.

It was now only twenty-four hours since the strange accident had happened, and she had not yet adjusted herself, even so far as to determine her fundamental emotion.

It was grief, of course, but the kind or degree of that grief was still undefined. The hours since they had brought him home had been so full of the unfamiliar practical things which arise at such a time, of the sudden necessities and small perplexities which muddle and chafe sorrow, that there had been scarcely a moment for her to look consciously at the great fact. Even now, as she covered her eyes, to be the more alone with herself, she felt rather a welcoming of momentary inactivity, than the relaxation of grief. She realized, with a sort of pang of disapproval, that she did not need to relax from any tension of anguish. She did not know what she wished to say to herself in this communion. She was sorry, bitterly sorry; but what elements went into the making of that grief? — She could not yet tell.

So she leaned with covered eyes, almost as if she were waiting for something outside of herself to give her a cue. As the minutes passed, however, the great simple fact that John was dead and that his place beside her would now be empty, engrossed all supplementary feelings, and her genuine regret had its way. She wept long, and ever more bitterly, absorbed, as one may be, in a mere physical expression of grief. The activity of sorrow overcame thought for the time, and left her no energy for analysis of feeling. Death alone seemed enough to weep over, and her tears still fell.

At last, as if having reached a natural period, she rose and moved away to the window and sat down there, in a quiet reverie of sadness. She was sorry for the life cut off, shocked at the abruptness and completeness of the tragedy, — John himself, she was sure, the assertive, energizing John, would have hated this sudden subduing of himself, and she sympathized with such revolt, — sorry, sorry for it all.

As she thought, she looked gravely out across the garden, the gay stretch to which John had given so much time. She had never understood his devotion to that garden. He had not been ready to spend money on things to give æsthetic pleasure in the house, although in practical matters he had been willing enough to make outlays, ever since his business had been secure. She thought of their new car, of the signs of prosperity in their living. 'Poor John!' she said at last with a deep sigh, when, aware of the nodding line of rare dahlias on which her eyes were resting, she thought of all the pains he had taken in the propagation and selection of them. She had come to recognize this lavishness of care and money as a sort of blind expression of the one æsthetic element in his nature, and had felt a quiet approval of it. 'Poor John!' she sighed again, and turned from the window to go.

But even as she did so, the simplicity of her mood passed, and the old complexity of feeling returned with a keenness which was for the moment bewildering. As she left the window, the long black shape across the fireplace confronted her again, and she paused, startled anew; it was so strange and so tremendous a thing in her room.

For the library was, above everything else in the world, hers. It was such a room as shows it has been taking on character through succeeding decades, cumulative of its type, slowly drawing to itself an atmosphere of fineness and greatness. The credit of it belonged only remotely to Rachel Marquis. She was the possessor, but not the maker of it. She had kept it and loved it, but her own contribution to it had been slight. A few shelves of new books not yet mellowed down to the tone of the others, standing as if waiting to be proved, and a bit of renewing of texture here and there, whose freshness showed need of the softening of time, were the only marks of her hand or taste. But it was such a room as any lover of the long effects of books would cherish.

In the midst of its harmonies, the heavy black box undoubtedly looked harsh and intrusive. Rachel recognized, as a sort of confidence with herself, that bringing it here was an invasion. Because she loved the room herself she had placed John here, without thought of the inappropriateness of the act. But now the incongruity of the choice struck her. Why should he be brought here, she thought pitifully, to the room he never frequented, where she scarcely welcomed him, she acknowledged? Why should she sit beside him here, when she had so seldom done so before? She remembered very well the manner with which he occasionally sought her here, tentative, unfamiliar, and yet assertive. She had resented every element of that manner. Anywhere else in the house he was more nearly himself; here everything she did not desire in him was accentuated.

It had been, she thought, with an instinctive desire to do the best for him in every way, that she had directed that he should be placed here; just as she had ordered everything of the choicest and had given her most careful attention and taste to every detail. But this thought had been a failure.

'Poor John!' she said gently once more, with a pity in her thought all the greater for this very incongruity, as she came over and stood beside him. But as her eyes rested on his face, she felt almost compelled to withdraw the phrase. The dead man seemed to allow no such pity. The unfamiliar in the familiar, which is stranger than a new thing, held her startled attention as she looked. She had thought that she knew John Marquis to the last shred of his character, but death seemed to have laid a fineness she had never known over the stubbornness and taciturnity of the face. The dignity of the last great experience of his life seemed to mark him. He seemed to be gathering himself away from her pitying kindness. Very soon she went out again and closed the door.

II

When Richard Hughes, the last of his family, left his mother's old home to John and Rachel Marquis, no one had wondered. Rachel was a sort of cousin and John, too, a distant connection by somebody's marriage. And they lived in the town and nothing was more natural than that he should give them a home there, and whatever else he had to leave.

What no one knew but Rachel was that Richard Hughes had wished to marry her, and that she had refused him and chosen John Marquis instead. Richard Hughes, fifteen years her senior, quiet and inexpressive, shut in with books and remote from life, was far less to her mind than John Marquis, who was of her own generation, with whom she went to parties and talked the light talk of youth, and had a thousand things in common, as she thought. John was bright and jolly, and played tennis and danced with her and took her out in a canoe, and was sweet-tempered and loved to laugh, and between times talked seriously about the business he was starting and the money he expected to make. John belonged to the whole format of her life at that time, and it was perfectly natural to choose to marry him, with the expectation that life would go on as she and John had both known it and liked it in other homes, comfortable, sensible, ambitious of practical things, real, as their kind would call it. It seemed an impossible thing for her not to marry John.

In the first years of their marriage she was proud of coming quickly to understand John's business. She was proud of her management and her well-timed economies, proud that John could talk affairs over with her with satisfaction, that she was beginning to take the place her mother and other successful women had taken in practical life. But after two or three years had passed, the space taken by practical things in her life began to shrink; her familiarity with them detracted from their interest and allowed her to dispose of them more readily. She began to feel a restlessness which called for new interests.

At the same time John's affairs were not prospering. Difficulties he could not manage hampered him. All Rachel's advice and economies were of little help among the inevitable conditions of the time. She was becoming tired of the continual effort to acquire, and impatient of the atmosphere of practical things. But she made a show of readiness when he suggested that they give up the cheerful modern home they had fitted about themselves, with the conventions of comfort and the furnishings and decorations to which they had been adapted.

It was just at this time that Richard Hughes left them his home and the little money he owned. Nothing could have been more opportune for them. Whatever other feelings John may have had were absorbed in sheer relief at the assistance the bequest brought him. The money, with that from the sale of their own house, tided him over his difficulties and even helped to develop his business further. Rachel concealed her reluctance at moving into the out-of-date old house with its antiquated furnishings, and made a show of welcoming their fortune as a good partner should.

She could hardly tell when her consciousness of the house began to have its influence upon her. From the first, John, absorbed in business, left all practical things to her, feeling that the house was more hers than his anyway. She, in a mood of vague compunction and desire to compensate for she hardly knew what, made it a point of honor to dispose of all their own furniture, chosen with such satisfaction and complacency, and settled among the dull tones and quiet spaces of the old house.

'Gay old place, is n't it?' said John, walking through the house after they were established.

Rachel assented with a cheerful smile.

'Oh, well,' he went on, settling down with his trade-journals, which looked sadly out of place in the dim library, 'we can stand it for a while. Some time we can have what we want again.'

It was months before he recurred to the subject directly. Then, one Sunday, he looked about him as he sat stretched in an old easy-chair, and said abruptly, 'We are getting pretty well settled down here. I did n't think the old place would be so comfortable.'

'It is more than comfortable,' said Rachel quietly.

'I wonder why Richard ever left it to us. Have you ever figured it out?'

'Oh, he had no nearer relatives that he knew.' Rachel tried to speak in a matter-of-fact way, but instead she hesitated and flushed a little.

John looked at her closely. 'Do you know any other reason?' he asked curiously.

Rachel hesitated again. Mere reticence on past affairs was one thing; positively keeping a secret from her husband was another. 'Richard wanted to marry me once,' she said. 'But I don't think that had anything to do with it,' she added hastily.

'When was that?'

'Oh — before I was engaged to you,' said Rachel, and smiled at him.

John said nothing more, but sat tapping his knee with

his folded newspaper, as was his habit when in thought. Presently he rose and strolled away.

Rachel could not help resenting his silence, which left her in discomfort. When so much had been said he should have said more, if only to put her at her ease. For days afterwards she expected him to return to the subject, and when he did not do so, she continued to resent the implication he seemed to be making.

At this time the house itself had already begun to have its effect upon her. Rachel could hardly tell when she stopped looking wistfully at the sectional bookcases and mission furniture of her acquaintances. But soon after she moved into it, the house had ceased to be to her merely a house. With her conventionally modern notions of beauty in furnishings, she had first been surprised to find how at rest and how satisfied she was in this house, which had met in a generous way the needs and tastes of another generation, but met few of those to which she had been trained. She had not known that it was in her to find a charm in such a house. But from the time when she first became aware of a positive quality in the place, she became more and more awake to its existence; she wondered at it, but it held her attention constantly more firmly.

At last she found that behind the entity of the house lay that which had made it — the personality of the generations gone and especially of its last owner. The quality of the whole place, with its solidity of walls and generosity of room, along with its plain sincerity in every detail, seemed to indicate praiseworthiness, not only in the first builder, but in all later possessors. It became a meritorious thing to have and to keep a house like this. She remembered something of the sacrifices that Richard Hughes had made to retain it, and warmed with pride of him at the recollection.

The whole place reflected him and the people who had made him. Gradually Rachel grew in pride of the house and of her heritage. As she lived there month by month she found herself enveloped in its atmosphere and growing toward its proportions. At first she entered the library with timidity and an uncomfortable strangeness. Even one who had only very superficial intellectual tastes must have felt a sort of awe before its accumulation of books and their accompaniments. When Rachel and John had first begun to make a home, they had placed the making of a library among their ambitions for it, and had taken pleasure in adding a few gayly bound novels each year to the small united collection with which they had begun. They had enjoyed seeing their few shelves grow, and knowing that they had so many of the popular books of which their friends talked. When they came to the Hughes home, Rachel had crowded their parti-colored collection into the shelves of the library there, weeding out others to make room for their own.

But on a later day, as she reëntered the room, she felt a shock at the incongruity presented and, to John's puzzlement, gathered their own books into a corner by themselves where a curtain safely hid them. Their garish triviality had no place among these mellowed, long-tried volumes. John, however, had looked the old volumes over and pronounced them a dry lot — give him something fresher.

But Rachel perceived that there had been something in the choosing of these books which she had never really known. To her, books had been an accessory, an incidental thing, hypothetically an enrichment of life, but not an essential. She had thought of intellectual exercise as an intermittent thing, to be taken up or laid down as suited the mood of the time. But here was a people who chose books not merely as a desirable possession, an ornamental furnishing, but as an unquestioned necessity.

Gradually, as she continued to handle and to know their books, she evoked for herself the earlier presences of the house, most of all Richard Hughes. In the long hours which she now spent alone about the house, she found herself living more constantly in a companionship with those minds. They were not only an atmosphere, but sometimes almost a positive presence. It entertained her to go over the books one by one, sometimes, deciding who had chosen this one and that one, and for what reason, and picturing the occasion of its coming to his hand. As her knowledge of the library grew, she took more and more pleasure in this, tracing the taste of one owner or another in the recurrence of a subject or in successive accretions. She, as she learned, glowed over her collection of first editions of modern works, since they had been chosen, not as first editions, but, in their own time, as works for which an appreciative hand was eagerly waiting.

And since Richard Hughes was the only one of her predecessors in the library whom she had known, she found herself embodying all the others in him. She knew him now better than she had ever known him. She could detect his additions to the treasures of the house, and, as her own knowledge increased, could trace his using of the resources which had been handed down to him. She began to take pleasure in following what she thought had been his path in taste and knowledge, gradually matching her mind to his own.

Her pride in the room went through successive stages. In her first days of satisfaction in mere proprietorship of so respectable and worthy a possession, she took pleasure in unostentatious exhibition of it. She liked to take guests there, in a natural sort of way, and to be found sitting

there, by unexpected callers. She liked the eminently admirable background of the rows of books, for social epi-
sodes. But as her knowledge of the library grew, that
stage passed. As she went from familiarity to intimacy,
she began to desire that it should be an exclusive intimacy.
She no longer took callers to the room, and when familiar
acquaintances found their way there, she was uneasy at
their handling of the books and impatient of their discussion of them. She now seldom spontaneously took strangers there. In time she had come to group John with all the
others. The only companionship that she desired in the
library was an imagined one.

John's attitude had more and more set her apart in this
companionship. His dislike for the house had grown
steadily more obvious as the months and years passed.
It showed itself in a lack of home-pride, in open contempt
for the old-fashioned elements of the place, in reluctance to
make even necessary expenditure upon it.

But Rachel herself had hardly guessed the strength of
his feeling until one day when she discovered among Richard Hughes's papers what seemed to be a memorandum
for a codicil to his will, which would make a gift of a
thousand dollars to the little public library of the town.

She took the note directly to John. 'I think we ought
to do this,' she said.

John looked at the paper and laid it down. 'I don't see
that we are obliged to,' he answered shortly.

'It is what he intended to do — and we got the money,'
she said, with too patient a manner, as if explaining the
moral point to him. 'We should give it in his name.'

'It is enough to have to live in Richard Hughes's house.
I don't care to set up a memorial for him besides.'

'But John,' she urged herself to argue, 'is it honest?'

'There is more than one kind of honesty,' said John

shortly, in a tone which checked further answer. 'I can't afford it,' he added after a moment, as the final word.

She left him in an anger which it seemed to her she would feel all her life. But gradually it became less an active feeling than a part of all her unformulated opinion of him. He had not followed her a single step in the development which had resulted from her awakening to the spirit of the house. In time he came to ignore the library altogether as part of the house, and by degrees fitted up an incongruous little lounging-place upstairs. Rachel came to regard his whole attitude toward the place and the man who had owned it as belonging to his mental and æsthetic plane; his jealous ingratitude seemed not a separate feeling, but only an element in his character.

Richard Hughes, she now understood very well, had known her very little, and had loved only her prettiness and light girlishness, charms which were different from anything in his own life. The recollection of that episode did not flatter her now, or even afford her any special gratification. But she loved to live side by side with the embodiment she had re-created for herself, and was proud to feel her spirit matching its spirit. She sometimes felt, with her growing imagination, that she was living in the house, not with John, but with these presences of the past — most of all with Richard Hughes.

But in the mean time the matter of the bequest assumed for her constantly greater proportions. After some time had passed she ventured to mention it again. He answered as before, 'I can't afford it!' She knew that he could afford it. About the same time he bought a strip of ground lying beside them and began his garden. Rachel suggested that he take a piece of their own grounds, but he bluntly rejected the proposal. A growing taciturnity marked his manner, and often a willful crudeness of phrase and speech, which annoyed her almost to the point of reproof. So far as was possible, however, she kept the recognition of all this far in the background of her thought and forebore any conscious criticism of him, even to herself. But her warmest feeling for him was tinged with pity.

Yesterday he had been taken. This accident, sudden as a lightning-flash and more unforeseen, had ended the relation between them — though not the puzzle. Rachel had never been one to revise her opinion of a man because he was dead. Her tears had fallen now, but she had no compunctious self-deception, and her long-framed feelings were only complicated, not really altered. She saw as clearly as ever the incongruity of her husband's presence in this room where Richard Hughes had had his life, and where she now had her own.

III

All waited for the coming of John's brother, David Marquis. David was an elder brother, retired from business on some pretext or other, now loitering his way profitably and pleasantly through the later half of his life. It had been his custom to visit them frequently, spending weeks at a time idling about the house, quiet, keen of look, ready to talk with interest on any general topic, but incommunicative of opinion on any personal matter. Rachel had always felt, as she saw his observant eye first upon John and then upon her, that he saw the difference between them and sympathized with her. For this reason, although she had never critized John to him, she had sometimes spoken freely of herself and of her own tastes and wishes; and he had listened, quietly as ever, but responsively.

She had a sort of feeling now that she would find her poise through him when he came. A sympathetic eye would help her to adjust the degree of her grief to the limits of her previous feeling.

It was eight o'clock when he arrived. The pretext of dinner in the house was over, and even the neighborly and professional attentions of the day were withdrawn. Rachel descended from her room in the quiet house at the sound of his entrance, and met gratefully the brotherly kindliness of his manner. They sat a few minutes in the hall, in question and answer of his journey and of the accident and all the circumstantial things which cluster about death itself. Rachel answered freely and fully, discovering a relief in breaking the instinctive repression of the day, and finding the sort of rest she had hoped for from his presence. David listened to her quietly, as he had always done, with his ready eye upon her.

At last he rose, turning away from her with a comprehensive look about him.

'Where is he?' he asked abruptly.

'In the library,' said Rachel, with a movement to lead the way for him.

'In there?' exclaimed David, with the emphasis of surprise. Then he closed his lips again and followed her, without meeting her questioning look.

But inside the door he paused again. Rachel had, constrained by long habit, looked first at the room, as she entered, and then at the casket, as a separate thing. The room had so long served to give her poise that she felt a sort of appeal to it even now. David's eyes rested first on the casket and then swept the room in a disapproving look.

'Why is he here?' he asked, with a curtness in his easy voice which Rachel had never heard from him before.

'Why —' she began hesitatingly, and then added vaguely, 'It seemed best.'

'Best for him?' responded David with the same curtness.

Then he turned and dropped his head slowly over the figure in the coffin, and Rachel slipped away. David's manner seemed to put her entirely outside of the occasion.

Later he joined her where she waited in the dim parlor. The still chilliness of the room was stiffening and depressing, but she had not made a fire because its open cheerfulness would not have seemed appropriate. David walked up and down the long room a few minutes in a silence which Rachel, not knowing his mood, did not break.

Then he said, as abruptly as before, 'Can you have him moved in the morning?'

'Moved? — Where?'

Rachel had not supposed that her brother-in-law would have the same feeling of incongruity that she had.

'Anywhere but there. Here — I don't know — there is no place in the house that seems to belong to him. The hall might do — at least he went through there every day,' he finished with an irony none too subtle.

He began to walk up and down the length of the room, alternately facing her with a challenging air, and turning abruptly away again when he had neared her seat. But Rachel, absorbed still in her mood, was unappreciative of his manner.

'John never fitted into the house very well, anywhere,' she said, with reserved regret.

'Fitted into it!' exclaimed David, as he turned toward her at the end of the room. 'My — Did the house ever fit into him? It is the business of a house to suit the people that live in it,' he flung over his shoulder as he wheeled away again.

Rachel was silent, puzzled at this surprising change of manner in David, and not knowing how much of his emotion was merely the impatience of grief.

'Is there a corner of the house where it is appropriate

for him to lie now, except that little cubby-hole of his upstairs?' demanded David, continuing, but as one who knows that an answer is impossible.

He suddenly abandoned his walk and came over and sat down opposite her, in front of the empty fireplace. He sat silent a moment, his gray figure drooping in a big chair. Rachel, looking carefully at him for the first time, noted with a kind of surprise the mark of brokenness and relaxation upon him, of submission to tremendous grief. It had not occurred to her that John could be mourned in that way. After a moment he said quietly, 'This house has never been a home for John.'

'I was always hoping,' said Rachel, as if this subject were one which they had discussed before and agreed upon, 'that he would feel more at home here in time.'

'What would have been necessary to bring that about?' asked David quietly.

'Well,' said Rachel, with reluctance in criticism even greater than usual, 'he would have had to change in many ways.'

'In what ways?' persisted David.

Rachel hesitated again. The thing, when baldly said, seemed so much harsher than when it was merely held in thought.

'John's taste was different from that of the people who made the house,' she said.

'Yes, I know. These pictures, and the old books in the library, and so on. Is that what you mean?'

'Well, the insides of the books, and other pictures which we don't have — and so on,' she finished indefinitely.

'Yes. You thought John was crude and rather coarse in feeling.'

'Oh, no — not that indeed!'

'You wouldn't call it just that, of course. But the difference between you was the same, whether it put you up high or him down low. Is n't that so? You were sorry for yourself because John was not on your level?'

'Yes,' admitted Rachel, reluctantly voicing the word.

'Were you ever sorry enough for John because you were not on his level? — There are different kinds of lonesomeness,' he added after a pause. 'I never saw a worse case than John's.'

Rachel sat upright, looking at him in a sort of amazement, as much at himself as at the idea. She had never dreamed that behind his apparently sympathetic observation of her lay any condemnation of her attitude.

He met her look with one as direct, and asked, in a way which made the question a sort of arraignment, 'Did it ever occur to you what a tragedy John's life was?'

Rachel merely shook her head slowly as she tried to connect, in an impersonal sort of way, the notion of tragedy with John — John the successful, the obstinate, the simple in desire, the objective. There had been no real disappointment in all his life. She looked back half-indignantly at David, rejecting the suggestion.

David rose and took a turn up and down the parlor again, pausing in the shadows at the farther end of the room. Then he came back to his seat and faced her determinedly.

'What *I* had always hoped was that you would come to understand John without any outside interference. I came back over and over to see, but I always kept from butting in.' He paused again. 'I would n't say anything now, only your tone, your "Poor John" way, shows you are just the same as ever. I won't have him buried without your knowing something more about him — if I can show you,' he added more gently.

'Please tell me,' said Rachel quietly. Her mind was still half as much on David as on what he was going to say.

'There is nothing to tell that you should not have seen for yourself. You were his wife and you lived with him. From the time you came to this house one side of John's life ended. In a way he had no home and no — wife. A man wants a companion.'

Rachel almost spoke, in startled contradiction. It was she who had been uncompanioned.

'You were proud, I know, of never finding fault with John. Don't you know that he would have been glad if you had openly found fault with him? As it was, it seemed as if you thought him hopeless. When he said things about the house or anything in it, he really wanted you to contradict him and argue with him, and give him a way to come to the same place where you were—don't you see?'

'Did he tell you?'

'No. But of course I used to sit round with him a good deal. And I had always been used to understanding him,' he added, with a drop in his voice. 'John had a lot of imagination,' he went on.

Rachel looked up in real surprise.

'I could see every year how the house was getting more on his nerves. Sometimes when he was feeling it more than usual he would say little things that I understood. For him it was like living with some one who did n't want him round. But he might have liked it.'

'You don't understand,' said Rachel, as if pricked into coming to her own defense. 'John did n't like the way the house came to us in the first place. You did n't know —'

'Yes, I did,' he responded as she hesitated, 'I found out.'

'And yet,' she went on, 'we used the house and the money —'

'You have n't known much about the business for several years, have you? Of course you do know that the house has been in your name from the beginning, almost.

But you don't know that the few thousands Richard Hughes left have been invested for you ever since two years after he died. It crippled John for a while after he took it out of the business. But he always took good care of that money — it amounts to quite a little now.'

'John did n't like it because Richard —' Rachel hesitated again.

'You thought he was jealous. He did that after one day when you weeded out a lot of his books and put them away in some corner. And it was after he had those New York electric men here that evening and you seemed not to want to have them in the library, that he bought that corner of ground over there and made his garden. Don't you understand?'

Rachel dropped her face upon her hands, partly for relief from David's serious face, which forebore to rebuke her and yet of necessity did so, partly to close herself in with her own bewilderment. To reconstruct John's life meant to take a new view of her own also.

David leaned suddenly toward her. 'If John had been jealous, would n't he have had reason, Rachel? I know you were n't — untrue to him. But still —' He felt the formulation of the thought with her.

'I have n't judged you harshly, Rachel,' he went on in a moment, 'but it is not right that a man's brother should know him better than his wife does. I had to make you know, even at the last.'

Then, as if he were compelled to say the final hard thing, he added, 'Was n't there something you had already thought you should do when everything was in your hands?'

Rachel, startled and flushing, faced him again, in involuntary confession. 'I had always thought it would be right to carry out a plan of Richard Hughes's.'

'Yes, I know. I am sure that was only a momentary notion of his. He had a great habit of making notes of things. His will was made only a few days before he died, and that idea was probably earlier. I was an executor, you remember. But anyway, several years ago John made a large gift to the library of Richard's college, in Richard's name. He took no chances on being unfair. He should have told you,' he added, 'but John had a hard sort of pride to manage, and I suppose he never did.'

'No,' said Rachel, 'he never did.'

She rose, with a sudden dropping of her hands at her sides, as if relinquishing something they had held, and moved vaguely toward the door.

'Don't you think,' pursued David, 'that he might be brought in here — or somewhere?'

Rachel hesitated, her hand faltering on the door-frame. 'No,' she said at last, 'let him stay there now.' And she herself went out through the dim chill hall. She lingered a moment at the closed library door, and then went slowly on up to her own empty room.

OF WATER AND THE SPIRIT[1]

BY MARGARET PRESCOTT MONTAGUE

'I WANT to tell you — I *must* tell you all about it.'

With a kind of grave finality, the little woman in the deck chair next to mine snapped together the collapsible drinking-cup with which she had been playing, and sat up, laying a small eager hand on my arm. It was as if her groping thoughts had suddenly pushed open a door into action. I wondered if she guessed that I had been peeping at her from under dropped lids. She had the colorless make-up of a small middle-aged mouse, but her expression was amazing. It startled and arrested one. All the old lines of the face were set to small ambitions and sordid desires, but the look which should have accompanied these lines was clean gone — wiped into something big and still and simple — and her manner was that of an earnest child.

'I was in Belgium when it commenced,' she began. 'But I guess I better go back and tell it all right from the beginning,' she broke off.

'Please do,' I begged.

I did my best to speak naturally, but my voice seemed to break some spell, for her face blurred suddenly to self-consciousness.

'I — I reckon I ought to apologize for speaking to a stranger,' she stammered primly. And now her words exactly matched all the old small lines of her face. It was as if her little self, aware of something big and overwhelming that threatened to sweep her out of her depth, made a desperate clutch at conventionality.

[1] Published also in book form and here republished through the courtesy of E. P. Dutton & Co.

'But I want to hear,' I protested eagerly. 'Please tell me.'

She must have seen that I was in earnest, for the little conventional self disappeared at that, and she answered simply, 'And I want to tell you — it seems like I've just *got* to tell you.'

It was September, 1914. We homing Americans were churning through an extraordinarily blue ocean toward New York and peace, while back there, just over our shoulders, a mad world was running red.

'It was like bein' torn all to pieces and put together again different,' she said. 'But I'll go back like I said, and start right from the beginning.'

For a moment she was silent, staring thoughtfully down at the cheap little metal cup, screwing the rings softly round and round, and drawing, as it were, inspiration from the sight of it.

'I come from Johnson's Falls,' she began at length. 'You would n't know where that is. It's just a little place down in West Virginia, but it's right close to the Virginia state line, and we have some mighty nice people in town. Why,' she exclaimed, 'I reckon we have some of the very best blood in the South there! But — but that is n't what I set out to tell you,' she caught herself up.

She fell into such a prolonged silence, turning the little cup, and looking at it, that at last I ventured a question to start her again.

'And I suppose,' I said, 'you belong to one of the oldest families there.'

I was sorry as soon as I had said it.

'No, I don't,' she answered simply, looking straight up at me. 'That was how it all commenced. My father kept the livery stable. But of course it would n't matter — keepin' a livery, I mean — if your family was all right.

Jeff Randolph kept the grocery. Being a Randolph, of course he could. But my name's Smithson — Sadie Virginia Smithson — and my grandfather was a carpenter. I'm a dressmaker myself. That's the reason they did n't elect me to the Laurel Literary Society.' She paused a moment. 'I reckon you would n't understand about the Laurel Literary Society?' she questioned a trifle wistfully.

'Perhaps not,' I admitted.

'Well, it's a literary society, of course. The members read papers, and all like that, but it's a heap more'n that. Belonging to it kind of marks a person out in Johnson's Falls and gives 'em the — the — well, I reckon you'd call it the *entray* to all the best homes in town. If you don't belong — well, I reckon it came kinder harder on me, not belonging, than it did on some of the others. Why, I'd have said the girls that started it were my very best friends. We'd played together as children, and I called 'em all by their first names, and they *knew* I was just as smart, an' liked readin' an' all that just as well as any of 'em did. So when I was n't asked to join — well, it just seemed to knock me right out. I was n't but nineteen then, an' when you're young things hurt more, I reckon. Anyhow the slight of it got just fixed in my mind, an' I made a kind of a vow that I'd belong to that society some day if I *died* for it. And then, after a while it came to me, maybe if I could just save money enough to go abroad, they'd ask me to read a paper before the society when I got back, 'cause mighty few people have traveled much from our town. — Well,' she looked thoughtfully away at the blue water, many an' many a night I've put myself to sleep thinking how it would be when I read that paper. You know, when you're young and kind of unhappy and slighted, how you make up things to sort of comfort yourself?'

I nodded.

'Well, I could just see the whole thing, me standing there reading an' all, and when I'd get through I could almost hear the applause. They'd some of 'em have on gloves, you know, so it would sound softer an' more genteel-like than just common bare-hand clapping. Well, it takes time for a country dressmaker to save. It took me twenty years. I did have most enough once, but then my sister was taken sick an' what I'd saved had to go for her. But I just gritted my teeth an' commenced again, and at last this spring I had enough, an' I joined a party and went. Ours was n't a regular party. It was just a professor an' his wife who were goin' anyhow, an' would take a couple of ladies with them, so there were just the four of us. Well, we traveled for a month or more, an' you better b'lieve I stretched my eyes to see all there was to see. An' then, all at once, the world just tipped itself right over an' went crazy.

'We were in Brussels when it came. The professor was sure everything would quiet down in a little bit, an' he said we'd better stay right there. And anyhow, it was n't easy to get away. It was all just awful, with one country after another slipping in. Only things came so quick a person did n't hardly have time to catch their breath an' think "how awful," 'fore something worse was jumping right on top of it. Well, we stayed and stayed, till at last the Germans came. It certainly was a sight to see 'em — but I ain't goin' to tell about that, I'm just goin' to skip right along to what I set out to tell.

'The professor and his wife had left their only child, a mighty sickly little thing, with her grandmother in Paris, and when things got so bad they were pretty near distracted to get to her. Well, one morning the professor came in and told us he'd run across a young American, a Mr. Grenville, who was being sent to Paris on some special diplomatic business. He had a big automobile, and he thought maybe he could get it fixed to take us all, too. It looked like a mighty crazy thing to do, but there wasn't any holdin' the professor an' his wife on account of their child, and me and the other lady, we was afraid to be left behind. Well, after a lot of runnin' around from one official to another, they did finally get it all fixed for us to go, an' the next day we started out with an American flag on the front of our car. Of course we were stopped a lot of times and all our papers gone through and everything, but each time they let us go on account of Mr. Grenville bein' a United States official. We'd started early, an' by noon we'd come a right smart piece, an' about that time we began to hear firing on in front. Did you ever hear them big guns?' she broke off to ask, her childlike eyes questioning me.

I shook my head.

'Well, you needn't never want to hear 'em,' she said. 'When they commenced we all kind of looked at one another, an' I reckon we was all scared. Anyhow, I know I was. Why, at home I'm 'fraid of a thunderstorm. But still we kept on. The sound of the firin' got louder an' louder, but it was never very close, and along late in the afternoon it sort of died off, an' we commenced to draw breath again, and think everything was goin' to be all right. I'm 'most sure now we must have missed the way, for just about that time we ran upon a piece of road that was all tore up. There were big holes in it from the shells, an' those tall poplars alongside were all snapped off, an' their branches stripped down like a child peels a switch. You could smell the fresh sap like you can in lumber camps at home. Well, we had to slow up an' kind of pick our way, and on round the very next turn we ran right up on them.'

'On the fighting!' I gasped.

'No — no; the fightin' was all over then. Just for a flash, comin' on 'em so quick like, I did n't know what they were. They looked like little sprawled brown heaps. But in the second I was wonderin', one of 'em flung up an arm and groaned.'

'How *awful!*' I cried aghast.

'Yes,' she assented simply, 'it certainly *was* awful. My words ain't big enough to tell you how awful. Runnin' up on 'em so unexpected like that, kind of cut my breath right off an' choked me. There they were, layin' all about acrost the road, an' in a wheat-field alongside, with the sun just shining down like it was any kind of a summer day. A good many of 'em were dead, but there were a plenty that were n't. They blocked the road so we had to stop, an' right where we stopped there was a young man layin' flung over on his back. He'd snatched his shirt open at the breast, an' the blood had all dripped down into the dust of the road. He opened his eyes, an' stared right up in my face, an' cried, "Water, for God's sake!" He said it over an' over in the awfullest voice, an' like it was one word — "Water-for-God's-sake, water-for-God's-sake" — like that. I had this little drinkin' cup, an' there was a good-sized creek just a piece across the field, so I grabbed my hand-bag an' jumped out. Well, at that all of 'em in the car commenced to holler an' scream at me to get back, that we could n't stop — it would n't be safe — an' we could n't do anything, an' anyhow the stretcher-bearers would be along d'rectly. But I just said, "He wants water, an' I've got my cup here, an' there's the branch, an' anyhow," I says, "he looks kind of like my sister's oldest boy," an' with that I started on to the creek.

'Well, the professor an' Mr. Grenville jumped out of the car an' came runnin' after me, but I just turned 'round

an' looked at 'em. "You all go on," I says. "He asked me
for water for God's sake, an' if you try to put me back in
that car I'll fight you like a wildcat." I never did anything like that, — fightin', I mean,' — she broke off to
explain earnestly, 'but I would have, an' I reckon they
knew it. The professor tried to argue. "You'll be a rav-
ing maniac if you stay here," he says. "Well," I says,
"look what's here now — what difference does it make
if I am?" Somehow that was the way I felt. Everything was so awful it did n't seem to matter whether anything awful happened to me or not. So I just kept on to
the creek, and Mr. Grenville said, "For Heaven's sake,
let her stay if she can do anything. I wish to God I could
stay too." But he could n't, he was carryin' some mighty
important dispatches that he just *had* to get on with. An'
then he calls out to me, "Good luck and God bless you,
Miss Smithson!" An' when I looked back he was standin'
with his hat off. He was a mighty nice young man. But
all the time the other ladies in the car was screamin' an'
hollerin' for them to come on, so they had to go.'

'They left you all alone!' I cried.

'They had to,' she returned. 'Mr. Grenville had to get
on with his dispatches, an' it was the last chance the professor an' his wife had of gettin' through to their child. An'
the other lady — Well, she could n't do nothin' but scream
anyhow. By the time I was comin' back from the creek
the car was just pullin' out of sight. Somehow, to see it
go like that gave me a kind of funny feelin'. I was scared,
I reckon, but all the same I felt kind of still too. It seemed
like for the last few weeks I'd been hustled along in a wild
kind of a torrent, but now I'd touched bottom an' got my
feet under me. I reckon a woman does touch bottom
when there's anything she can do — anyhow, one raised
to work like I've been does. But, oh, my Lord!' she cried

suddenly, dropping her face to her hands, 'I wish I could keep from seein' it all still — an' hearin' it too! Did you ever hear a *man* scream?' she demanded. 'Not just groan, but shriek, an' scream?'

'In hospitals,' I said, uncertainly, 'I've heard people screaming when they were coming out of ether.'

She shook her head. 'That's different. You knew there were people, nurses and doctors, to do things for 'em; but out there there wasn't anything but the trampled wheat, an' the big empty sky. There was plenty of 'em who wanted water, an' begged an' cried for it; but I just said, "I'll be back to you all presently," an' went on to the first one. He was kind of delirious, but he could drink the water, an' was mighty glad to get it. I brushed the flies all away, an' spread a clean handkerchief over his wound, — he was too far gone to try an' do anything else for him, — an' went on back to the creek. Water, that was the main thing they wanted. The most of 'em that could be were bandaged already. Some of the medical outfit had been around an' got 'em tied up, but after that, I reckon the fightin' must of changed an' cut 'em off from their friends, for the stretcher-bearers didn't come, an' didn't come.

'It was all so strange an' kind of shut away there, like destruction had lit for a spell an' then flown on to the next place. The wheat was all laid over an' tramped, and lumpy with khaki bodies, an' with caps an' guns an' things flung around in it, an' the red sun sailin' down an' down in the West, an' every here an' there awful splatters of blood in the wheat. But I didn't have time to look an' think too much — an' it was mighty lucky I didn't have. They were all English an' had run upon a German battery an' been shot to pieces 'fore they hardly knew what was happenin.' I guess some of 'em must have got away, but there was a plenty that did n't. They'd been layin' there since dawn, an' — an' they were *hungry* — ' her voice broke. 'An' I did n't have anything to give 'em,' she whispered.

'They say after a while you get kind of numb to things,' she went on presently, with her grave simplicity. 'I don't know how that is, but I know the things I saw made me stop every now an' then down by the creek out of sight, an' just wring an' wring my hands together in a kind of rage of pity. Once, goin' through the wheat, I tramped on something soft, an' when I looked, it was — it was just a piece of a man. I thought I'd lay right down then an' die, but I says to myself, "They want water, they want water" — an' that way I kind of drove myself on. But all the time I could see my heart under my waist just jumpin' up an' down, like it was fightin' to jump out an' run away. An' then another time —' But she broke off. 'No,' she said, 'I won't tell about that. It's so peaceful here with that blue water an' sunshine an' all, I reckon I ought n't to tell what it's like underneath when Hell takes the lid off. An' maybe some day the Lord'll let me forget.

'But it's funny,' she went on again presently, 'how your mind grabs ahold of any foolish thing to steady you.' She paused, staring down at the little cup as though she drew remembrance from it. 'I recollect as I went back and forth, back and forth, weaving out paths through the wheat, a silly song that we used to sing to a game at school kept runnin' in my head:—

> I don't want none of your weevily wheat,
> An' I don't want none of your barley;
> An' I don't want none of your weevily wheat
> To bake a cake for Charley.

'I was mighty glad it did. For all it was so silly, it kept me from flyin' right off the handle. An' so I kept on an' on, carryin' 'em water. Some of the men thought it was funny I should be there, an' they wanted to talk an' ask me questions; but the most of 'em were sufferin' too bad to care, an' some of 'em were busy goin' along into the next world, an' were done with bein' surprised over anything in this. Most of 'em called me "Nurse" or "Sister," an' some way I liked to have 'em do it. Some of 'em certainly were brave, too. Why, I saw one young fella jump straight up to his feet an' fling his arms out wide, an' holler right up at the sky, "Are we downhearted? — No!" an' pitch over dead. You know,' she paused to explain simply, her extraordinarily childlike eyes lifted to mine for understanding and sympathy, 'it just seems to snatch the heart right out of you to see a person stand up to death like that — 'specially when they're so young, like that little fella.'

'Of course,' she went on after a moment, 'I did n't just give 'em water. I'd do any other little thing I could besides. An' every time I could do anything, I certainly was glad. Doing things seemed to ease up a little that terrible rage of pity I felt. I took my skirt off an 'rolled it up for a pillow for a little fella who could n't move an' was layin' with his head in a kind of a sink-hole. He tried to thank me but he could n't, — he just sobbed, — but he caught ahold of my hand an' kissed it. That made me cry. It was so sort of young an' pretty of him. After that I went on for a spell with the tears just pourin' down my cheeks. But presently I found the one who could n't drink the water, an' I quit cryin' then. My tears were n't big enough; only God's would have been big enough for that.

'The man's face was all gone, — eyes, mouth, everything, — an' still he was alive. He must have heard me an' known somebody was there, for he commenced to scream an' moan, tryin' to say things down in his throat, an' to reach out his hands an' flop about — O my God! It was like a chicken with its head off! I thought I'd *have* to run. But I did n't. I just sort of fell down beside him, an' caught ahold of his hands, an' patted them an' talked to him like you do to a child in a nightmare. I don't know what I said at first. Just a crazy jumble of pity, I reckon; but after a little bit I found I was prayin'. I know *I* needed it, an' it seemed to help him too, for after a little bit, he stopped that awful tryin' to speak down in his throat, an' lay still just grippin' my hands. I was so crazy I couldn't think of a thing to say but "God bless us an' keep us an' make his face to shine upon us an' be merciful unto us." An' I just said that over an' over.

'I guess it was n't the words that he wanted, it was the feelin' of havin' God there in all that awful dark and blood, an' some human bein' beside him who was sorry. Anyhow, every time I'd stop he'd snatch at my wrists so hard it would hurt; look.' She broke off to push up her gray sleeve, and there on her thin wrist, still vividly black and blue, were the bruised prints of fingers. 'But I was glad to be hurt — I *wanted* to be hurt. I wanted to have a share in all the sufferin'. It just seemed like my heart would break. An',' she added with great simplicity, 'I reckon that's just what it did do, for I know I broke through into something bigger than I ever had been.

'Well, after a while, God did have mercy on that poor soul, for he quit pullin' at my hands, and began to die, an' when I came 'round again to him he was gone. But that got me started, an' I left off sayin' that foolishness about the weevily wheat, an' said the little prayer instead. I said it to myself first, but after a little bit, I found I was sayin' it out loud. I don't know why, but it seemed like I *had* to say it every time I gave one of 'em water. Just "God bless us an' keep us an' make his face to shine upon us and be merciful unto us." It was somehow like a child's

game — like havin' to touch every tree-box goin' along
the street, or steppin' over every crack. Each one of 'em
had to have the water an' the little prayer, an' then on to
the next, or back down to the creek for more. Most of
'em did n't seem to notice, but some of 'em laughed, an'
some stared like I was crazy, — an' maybe I was a little, —
an' again some of 'em were glad of it.

'So I kep' on an' on, an' the sun went down, an' the
dark came, an' it seemed like a kind of a lid had shut us
away from all the world. It was n't right dark, for the
stars were shinin'. It was about that time that I found
the little officer. He was dyin', off in the wheat all to himself, an' he got me to take down some messages for his folks.
I wrote 'em in my diary. I had a pocket flashlight in my
bag, an' it made a round eye of light that stared out at
every word I wrote. They were the simplest kind of words.
Just love, love to mother, and love to father, and Snippy
and Peg, an' good-bye to 'em all, an' how he was glad to
die for England. But they look mighty strange jumpin'
out there in my diary alongside of travel notes about Brussels. It's like something big an' terrible had smashed its
fist right through all the little fancy things.

'But it was funny,' she went on after a minute, 'how
sort of like children so many of the men were, so trusting
an' helpless. There was one little fella always said the
same thing to me every time I came 'round. "They'll
sure be around for us soon now, won't they, sister?" he'd
say. An' I'd always answer, "Oh, yes, just in a little bit
now." An' he'd settle back again, so trusting an' satisfied,
an' like I really knew. That was the way they all seemed
to me — just children. Even the ones that cursed an'
screamed at me. An' another funny thing,' she added
lifting her grave child's eyes to mine: 'I've never been
married — never known what it was to have children

— but that night all those men were my children, even
the biggest an' roughest of 'em. I felt 'em all *here*' — She
held her hands tight against her breast. 'An' I b'lieve
I would have *died* for any one of 'em. I reckon bein' so
crazy with pity had stretched me up out of bein' a scary
old maid into bein' a mother.

'I recollect there was two loose horses gallopin' about.
They were wild with fear, an' they'd gallop as hard as
ever they could in one direction, an' then they'd wheel
'round an' come to a stand with their heads up, an' their
tails cocked, an' nicker, an' snort over what they smelt, an'
then take out again. Well, once they came chargin' right
down on us, an' I thought sure they were goin' right over
the men. I never stopped to think: I ran straight out in
front of 'em wavin' my arms an' hollerin'. They just
missed gallopin' right over me. But I did n't care; I b'lieve
I'd almost have been glad. It was like I said — I *wanted*
to be hurt too. That was because it was all so lonesome
for 'em. Death an' sufferin' *is* a lonesome thing,' she
stated gravely. 'When they'd scream, I felt like I'd tear
my heart out to help 'em. But all I could do was just to
stand on the outside like, an' watch 'em sufferin' an' maybe
dryin' inside there all alone. That's why it seemed like
bein' hurt too would make it easier.

'Well, along late in the night, the guns broke out again
awful loud, an' presently off against the sky I saw red
streaks of flame go up in two places, an' I knew they were
towns on fire. I just stopped still an' looked, an' thought
what it was like with the folks scurryin' 'round like rats, an'
the fire an' the shells rainin' down on 'em. "That's Hell
— right over there," I says out loud to myself, an' then I
went on down to the creek faster than ever. Maybe I
was gettin' kind of lightheaded then, an' God knows it was
enough to make anybody so; anyhow, I felt like I had to

hold Hell back.   It was loose right over there, an' the only
thing that held it off was the cup of water an' the little
prayer.   So I kept on back an' forth, back an' forth from
the creek, faster an' faster.   I thought if I missed one of
'em it would let Hell in on all the rest, so I kept on an' on.
The guns were boomin', an' the flames goin' up into the
sky, an' all Hell was loose, but the little prayer an' the cup
of water was holdin' it back.   An' then at last, when it
commenced to freshen for dawn, I knew I'd won.'

She drew a deep breath, and paused, looking up at me
with clear, far-away eyes.

'That was because I knew He was there,' she said.

'*He?*' I questioned, awestruck by her tone.

She nodded.   'Yes, God,' she answered simply.   'An'
after that, that terrible lonesomeness melted all away.   I
knew that though I had to stand outside an' see 'em suffer,
He was inside there with 'em — closer to 'em even than
they was to themselves.   So I knew it was n't really lonesome for 'em, even if they were sufferin' an' dyin'.   An' I'm
right sure that a good many of 'em got to know that, too —
anyhow, the faces of some of the ones that had died looked
that way when I saw 'em in the mornin'.   Maybe it was
because I cared so much myself that I kind of broke
through into knowin' how much more God cared.   Folks
always talk like He was a father 'way off in the sky, but
I got to know that night that what was really God was
something big an' close right in your own heart, that was a
heap more like a big mother.

'An' it was all bigger an' sort of simpler than I'd ever
thought it would be.   Right over there was Hell an' big
guns, an' men killin' each other, but here where we were,
were just stars overhead, an' folks that you could do things
for, an' God.   I reckon that's the way,' she said with her
grave simplicity, 'when things get too awful you suffer

through to God, an' He turns you back to the simplest things — just the little prayer, an' the cup of water for men that were like sick children. This is the cup,' she added, holding it out for my inspection. 'An' — an' that's all, I reckon,' she concluded. 'When daylight came, the stretcher-bearers did get through to us. There was a sort of doctor officer with them, an' I never in my life saw any one look so tired.

'"Who are you, an' what in thunder are you doing here?" he stormed out at me — only I don't say it as strong as he did.

'I reckon I must have looked like a wild woman. I had lost my hat and my hair was all falling down, an' I only had on my short alpaca underskirt, 'cause I'd taken off my dress skirt to make a pillow like I said; but I just stood right up in the midst of all those poor bodies, an' says, "I'm Miss Smithson — Sadie Virginia Smithson — an' I've been holdin' Hell back all night."

'I knew I was talkin' crazy but I did n't care — like the way you do comin' out of ether.

'He stared at me for a spell, an' then he says, kind of funny, "Well, Miss Sadie Virginia, I'm glad you held some of it back, for everybody else in the world was letting it loose last night."

'He was mighty kind to me, though, an' helped get me to one of the base hospitals, an' from there over to England. But I don't know what happened to the professor an' his party.'

'Well,' I ventured after a long pause, and not knowing quite what to say, 'the Laurel Literary Society will be glad enough to have you belong to it now.'

She flashed bolt upright at that, her eyes staring at me.

'But — but you don't understand,' she cried breathlessly. 'I've been face to face with war an' death an' Hell an' God, — I've been born again, — do you reckon any of them little old things matter now?'

I was stunned by the white look of her face.

'What does matter — *now?*' I whispered at last.

'Nothin',' she answered, 'nothin' but God an' love an' doin' things for folks. That was why I had to tell you.'

MR. SQUEM

BY ARTHUR RUSSELL TAYLOR

'Why do we go on perpetuating an uncomfortable breed?'

The man who was shaving at the mirror-paneled door of the Pullman smoking compartment looked at his questioner on the leather seat opposite.

'Give it up,' he answered. 'Why is a hen?'

The first man rapped his pipe empty on the edge of a cuspidor.

'You answer the question,' he said, 'in the only possible way — by asking another.'

'Right,' answered the shaver; and began to run the hot water.

A closely built man, in a suit so heavily striped as to seem stripes before it was a suit, lurched into the compartment and settled himself to his paper and cigar.

'That monkey-on-a-stick,' he presently broke out, 'is still taking good money away from the asses who go to hear him rant about God and Hell and all the rest, up in Boston. I am so *damn* tired of him, and of that rich rough-neck Freeze. It's the limit.'

'Pretty much,' said the man with the pipe. 'I was reading about the Belgians just before you came in, and when I jumped away from them I lit on some things about Poland. Then I wondered aloud to this gentleman why we go on multiplying — increasing such an uncomfortable breed. Modoc gods and degenerate millionaires make one wonder more.'

'What is your line, may I ask?' inquired the stripe-suited man.

'Religion.'

'The hell — I beg your pardon. If you mean that you're a preacher or something like that, all I've got to say is, you're a funny one. It's your job, is n't it, to be dead sure that everything's all right, or somehow going to be all right — no matter about all the mussed-upness? Yes, that's certainly your job. Yet here you are, asking why we go on stocking the world with kids. *I* might ask that, — I'm in rubber tires, — but not you. Yes, I might — only I do n't.'

The man who had been shaving had resumed his tie, collar, and coat, and now lighted a cigarette.

'I lay my money,' he said, 'on one thing: that, if men let themselves go, they wind up shortly with God — or with what would be God if there were any. You've come to it early — through the *Ledger*. You'd have got to it sooner or later, though, if you'd been talking about hunting-dogs — provided you'd have let yourselves go.'

'Well, now,' asked the closely built man, 'what is *your* line?'

'Education.'

'High-brow company! Seems to me the pair of you ought to be silencers for a plain business man like me. Rubber is my line — not how the world is run. My opinion on that is small change, sure. Yet I think it ought to be run, — the world, I mean, — even if it's mussed-up to the limit, and I think it's up to us to keep it running. The parson here — if he is a parson — asks why we should; that is, if I get him. And then I think there's a manager of it all in the central office — a manager, understand, though he never seems to show up around the works, and certainly does seem to have some of the darnedest ways.

The professor here — if he is a professor — does n't sense any manager; that is, if I get him straight, with his "if there were any." That was what you said, was n't it? I'm a picked chicken on religion and education, but, honest, both those ideas would mean soft tires for me — yes, sir, soft tires.'

'Broad Street, gentlemen,' said the porter at the door.

The Reverend Allan Dare walked away from the train and down the street. He was Episcopally faced and Episcopally trim, and he was having considerable difficulty in holding his universe together. This is not pleasant at forty-two, when you want your universe held together and things settled and calm. He had an uncomfortable sense that this difficulty had jolted into plain sight on the car.

'Ass!' he addressed himself briefly. 'To let your sag and unsettlement loose in that way! To say such a thing as you said, and in such a place! To parade your momentary distrust of life! Ass — oh, ass!'

He said — or thought — a Prayer-Book collect, one which seemed rather suited to asses, and continued, —

'I suppose I'm three-tenths sag — no more; and "He knoweth whereof we are made," and what a devil of a world it is to be in just now. But that rubber man on the car — he is n't sag at all. Heavens, his crudeness! His beastly clothes, and the bare shaved welt around the back of his neck, and that awful seal ring! But he's fastened. Life is worth pushing at and cheering for — and there's a manager, if he *has* "the darnedest ways." I'd give something for an every-minute mood like that — a carrying night-and-day sureness like that. He's not illuminated — lucky dog!'

Professor William Emory Browne had changed cars and was continuing his journey. In his lap lay a volume of essays just put forth by a member of his craft, a college professor. He opened it, — it chanced at page 27, — and his eye was caught by the name of his own specialty. He read: —

'Philosophy is the science which proves that we can know nothing of the soul. Medicine is the science which tells that we know nothing of the body. Political Economy is that which teaches that we know nothing of the laws of wealth; and Theology the critical history of those errors from which we deduce our ignorance of God.'

'Confound it!' ejaculated Professor Browne, and closed the book.

'Room for one more?' inquired a voice, and the rubber-tire man slid into the seat.

'I just pulled off a little thing out here,' he said, 'that ought to put a small star in my crown. A down-and-out — a tough looker — says to me, "*Please*, mister, give me a dime. I'm hungry." And I says to him, "Get out! What you want is a good drink — go get it," and slips him a quarter. Talk about gratitude! To think there are men — you know it and I know it and he was afraid of it — who'd have steered him to a quick-lunch and put him against soft-boiled eggs!'

'"Man's inhumanity to man"' —

'Sure! Nothing but that ever makes me any trouble about things. Tear ninety, George,' — this to the conductor, — 'and burn this panetella some time. You said you were in education,' he went on. 'I've just blown myself to a Universal History — five big volumes, with lots of maps and pictures and flags of all nations and hanging gardens of Babylon and such things. Gave down thirty-five for it, and my name is printed — Peter B. Squem

— on the first page of every book. Now,' — Mr. Squem grew quite earnest, — 'you'd say, would n't you, that if a man could take those books down, — chew them up, you understand, and take them down, — he'd have an education? Not the same, of course, as normal school or college, and yet an education.'

'I think, if you know what's good for you, you will steer clear of what you call an education. I think I should stick to rubber tires, and a few comfortable certainties — and peace.'

Mr. Squem stared. 'How's that?' he inquired. 'Education is your line, you were saying, and yet you queer your stuff. I'd get quick word from the house, if I handled Mercury tires that way.'

'But you would n't,' rejoined Professor Browne, 'you would n't, because tires mean something. Tires are your life-preserver — they are shaped like life-preservers, are n't they?'

'You've got me going,' said Mr. Squem, 'and no mistake. I don't mind telling you I'd hoped to get some hunch from you — on education. You see, my clothes are right, I always have a room with bath, and I get two hundred a month and fifty on the side. I read the papers — and the magazine section on Sunday — and I got through four books last year. And yet there's something not there — by Keefer, not there! I'd give something to *get* it there — to slide it under, somehow, and bring the rest of me up to regular manicuring and ice-cream forks and the way my clothes fit!'

Mr. Squem was interrupted in the expression of this craving. There was a tremendous jar; the car tore and bumped with an immense pounding over the ties, then careened and sprawled down a short bank and settled on its side. People who have been through such an experi-

ence will require no description.   To others none can be
given.   In the bedlam chaos and jumble, and chorus of
shrieks and smashing glass, Professor Browne, struggling
up through the bodies which had been hurled upon him,
was conscious of a pain almost intolerably sharp in his
leg, and then of a sort of striped whirlwind which seemed
to be everywhere at once, extricating, calming, ordering,
comforting — and swearing.   It was like a machine-gun: —

'*Keep* your clothes on, nothing's going to bite you —
just a little shake-up — Yes, chick, we'll find your ma —
No, you *don't* climb over those people; sit down or I'll
help you — To hell with your valise, pick up that child!
— There go the axes; everybody quiet now, just where he
is — You with the side-whiskers get back, *back*, hear me!
— Now, children first, hand 'em along — women next, so
— men last — Why did n't you *say* you was a doctor?
Get out there quick; some of those people have got broke
and need you!'

Professor Browne was one of these last.   Lifted by
Peter Squem and a very scared brakeman, he lay on two
Pullman mattresses at the side of the track, waiting for the
rabbit-faced country doctor to reach him.   He was suffering very much, — it seemed to him that he had never
really known pain before, — but his attention went to a
white-haired lady near by — a slight, slender woman, with
breeding written all over her.   She had made her way
from the drawing-room of the Pullman, and leaned heavily
upon her maid, in a state approaching collapse.   Professor Browne was impressed by her air of distinction even
in the midst of his pain.   Then he saw a striped arm
supportingly encircle her, and a hand dominated by an
enormous seal ring press to her lips an open bottle of
Scotch.

'Let it trickle down, auntie — right down. It's just
what you need,' said Peter B. Squem.

'What did you think of when the car stopped rolling?'

Professor Browne, lying in his bed, asked this question
of Mr. Squem, sitting at its side.   The latter had got the
professor home to his house and his housekeeper after the
accident the day before, had found the best surgeon in
town and stood by while he worked, had in a dozen ways
helped a bad business to go as well as possible, and now,
having remained over night, was awaiting the hour of his
train.

'Think of?   Nothing.   No time.   I was that cross-eyed
boy you've heard about — the one at the three-ringed
circus.   *Did* you see that newly-wed rooster, — I'll bet he
was that, — the one with the celluloid collar?   "Good-
bye, Maude!" he yells, and then tries to butt himself
through the roof.   He would n't have left one sound rib
in the car if I had n't pinned him.   No, I had n't any time
to think.'

He produced and consulted a watch — one that struck
the professor as being almost too loud an ornament for a
Christmas tree.   An infant's face showed within as the
case opened.

'Your baby?' inquired Professor Browne.

'Never.   Not good enough.   This kid I found — where
do you suppose?   On a picture-postal at a news-stand.
The picture was no good — except the kid; and I cut him
out, you see.   Say, do you know the picture was painted
by a man out in Montana?   Yes, sir, Montana.   They
had the cards made over in Europe somewhere, — Dagoes,
likely, — and when they put his name on it, they did n't
do a thing to that word Montana.   Some spelling!'

'Why, what you have there,' said the professor, taking

the watch with interest, 'is the Holy Child of Andrea
Mantegna's Circumcision, — it's in the Uffizi at Florence.
Singularly good it is, too. I'm very much wrapped up in
the question, raised in a late book, of Mantegna's influence
upon Giovanni Bellini. There's a rather fine point made
in connection with another child in this same picture — a
larger one, pressing against his mother's knees.'

Mr. Squem was perfectly uncomprehending. 'Come
again,' he remarked. 'No, you need n't, either, for I don't
know anything about the rest of the picture. I told you
it was no good. There was an old party in a funny bath-
robe and with heavy Belshazzars, I remember — but the
picture was *this*.'

He rose and began to get into his overcoat.

'There's one thing about this kid,' he said, in a casual
tone which somehow let earnestness through. 'I know a
man, — he travels out of Phillie, and he's some booze-
artist and other things that go along, — who's got one of
those little "Josephs." You know, those little dolls that
Catholics tote around? Separate him from it? Not on
your life. Why, he missed it one night on a sleeper, and he
cussed and reared around, and made the coon rout everybody out till he found it. It's luck, you see. Now this
kid' — Mr. Squem was pulling on his gloves — 'is n't luck,
but he works like luck. He talks to me, understand, and'
— here a pause — 'he puts all sorts of cussedness on the
blink. You can't look at him and be an Indian. I was
making the wrong sort of date in Trenton one day, and I
saw him just in time — sent the girl word I'd been called
out of town. I was figuring on the right time to pinch a
man in the door, — he'd done me dirty, — and I saw *him*
again. Good-night! I'm never so punk that he does n't
ginger me — does n't look good to me. The management
is mixed up with him — and I hook up to him. Here's the

taxi. So long, professor. — Rats! I have n't done one
little thing. Good luck to your game leg!'

It was Sunday morning, and service was under way in
the Church of the Holy Faith. For the thousandth time
the Reverend Allan Dare had dearly-beloved his people,
assembled to the number of four hundred before him,
exhorting them in such forthright English as cannot be
written nowadays, not to dissemble nor cloak their sins
before God, and to accompany him unto the throne of the
heavenly grace. He had had a sick feeling, as he read this
exhortation, so full of pound, rhythm, heart-search, and
splendid good sense, to the courteous abstractedness in the
pews.

'Heavens!' he had thought, 'once this burnt in!' He
had wanted to shriek, — or fire a pistol in the air, — and
then crush the meaning into his people; crush God into
them, yes, and into himself.

He was four-tenths sag that morning — the Rev. Allan
Dare. In the *Jubilate*, a small choir-boy — a phenomenon
who was paid a thousand a year, and was responsible for
the presence of not a few of the four hundred — had sung
'Be sure ye that the Lord he is God,' to the ravishment of
the congregation — not of the rector, who stood looking
dead ahead. The First Lesson had been all about Jona-
dab, the son of Rechab, and drinking no wine — frightful
ineptness! What could it mean to any one? how help any
one? Here was Life, with all its cruel tangles, tighter and
more choking every day. Here was Arnold's darkling
plain, and the confused alarms and the ignorant armies
clashing by night.

There came back to Dare the creed he had heard in the
smoking compartment: 'I think it ought to be run, — the
world, — even if it's mussed-up to the limit, and I think

it's up to us to keep it running.   I think there's a manager of it all in the central office — a manager, understand, though he never seems to show up around the works, and certainly does seem to have some of the darnedest ways.'

'O God!' breathed Allan Dare, 'there are so many things — so many things!'

It was the same Sunday.   Professor William Emory Browne was for the first time on crutches, and stood supported by them at his window.

'Back again,' he ruminated.   'I can probably drive to my classes in another week.   Then the same old grind, showing ingenuous youth — who fortunately will not see it — how "the search hath taught me that the search is vain."   Ho, hum!   How very kind, that Mr. Squem, — he did so much for me, — and how very funny!   I should like to produce him at the seminar — with his just-right clothes, his dream of culture *via* his Universal History, his approach to reality through a picture postal-card!'

He turned on himself almost savagely.   Then, —

'What the devil are you patronizing him for?   Don't you see that he is hooked to something and you are not, that he is warm and you are freezing, that he is part of the wave, — the wave, man, — and that you are just a miserable, tossing clot?'

It was the same Sunday.   Mr. Squem sat in his room — extremely dennish, smitingly red as to walls, oppressive with plush upholstery.   A huge deerhead, jutting from over the mantel, divided honors with a highly-colored September Morn, affrontingly framed.   On a shelf stood a small bottle.   It contained a finger of Mr. Squem, amputated years before, in alcohol.

On the knees of the owner of the room was Volume One

of the Universal History — Number 32, so red-ink figures
affirmed, of a limited edition of five hundred sets.   Mr.
Squem's name was displayed, in very large Old English,
on the fly-leaf, and above was an empty oval wherein his
portrait might be placed.

'No use,' soliloquized the owner of this treasure, 'no
use.   If I *could* chew it up and get it down, — or two of it,
— *that* would n't slide under the thing that is n't there.
Nothing will ever put me in the class of Professor Browne
or that preacher on the car, or bring the rest of me up to
my clothes.'

He rose and stretched.

'Maybe,' he said, addressing a huge chocolate-colored
bust of an Indian lady, 'maybe I can catch up to those
fellows some time — but not here.   Noon, I bet,' — looking at his watch, — 'and it is to eat.'

He contemplated the Mantegna baby.

'So long,' he said, 'you're running things,' and snapped
his watch.

BIOGRAPHICAL AND INTERPRETATIVE NOTES

THE PRELIMINARIES

CORNELIA A. P. COMER, accomplished critic, essayist, and writer of short stories, was educated at Vassar, and afterwards engaged in journalistic work in the Middle West and California. She now lives in Seattle.

The plot of *The Preliminaries* might readily be told in a single paragraph. Its significance lies in its lucid and austere psychology. The young Mr. Oliver Pickersgill appears in four distinct situations; and as we watch him in company with the four dominating and diverse personalities in turn, we are engrossed in the swift and poignant play of his feelings — feelings which finally deepen into a sincere and settled consciousness of attained truth and a confident loyalty to an imprisoned convict. The verisimilitude of both situation and conversation is complete; and in the process there is no exhaustion of emotional values. Henry James would not have treated the situations with more clarity.

The author's further treatment of the problems connected with marriage is seen in two other noteworthy Atlantic stories — *The Kinzer Portraits* and *The Long Inheritance*.

BUTTERCUP–NIGHT

JOHN GALSWORTHY, an English 'novelist of much distinction, and a playwright who has proved that the possession of ideas is not incompatible with popular success. Endowed with an exquisite sense of pity, he has put that sentiment to many chivalrous uses, and since the war he has written in the public service on behalf of various patriotic and humanitarian objects.' Thus Mr. Galsworthy was described in the *London Gazette* as a recipient of the honor of knighthood in the list of New Year (1918) Honors, his declination not having been received in time to forestall the publication.

Buttercup-Night is hardly a story at all. In company with Mr. Galsworthy we live out the quiet but impressive experience of a single evening, night, and morning, all the while breathing the atmosphere of a rare June beauty that completely wins us to its æsthetic favor and repose. The incident of the sick horse, so gently cared for by the faithful keeper, secures our sympathy but does not draw us away from the more insistent wooing of the charms of the buttercup-night and the morning radiance of a suddenly awakened glow of blooming yellow. The commonplace writer would use the scene for romantic effect; Galsworthy enhances the beauty of the setting by a homely but sincere realism. The significant merits of the style are its purity, its restraint, and its complete adaptability to the hoveringly quiescent mood.

HEPATICAS

ANNE DOUGLAS SEDGWICK (Madame Basil de Sélincourt) is of American birth, but has lived in England since her childhood. For many years she has found an admiring audience as a writer of novels and short stories. In 1908 she was married to M. de Sélincourt.

The title of the story hints at a reliance upon mere setting. And the hepatica bed, with all that its associations signify, certainly makes its generous atmospheric contribution to the charm of the narrative. But as domestic entanglements begin to ensue, our interest in the flowers is soon shifted to plot and theme. Our sustained sympathy rests with the mother — the mother who has created in her home an atmosphere of the truest and most sensibly refined culture. The promising son, sharing this atmosphere and even enriching it, yields while at Aldershot before the war to the superficial charm of a chorus girl, and marries her. Her loud and garish presence in the home of quiet beauty and repose provides an interesting but tragic study in contrast, and makes us continually more anxious as we watch its influence upon the mother, yearning pityingly for her absent son, yet plaintively relieved when news comes that he has been killed in the war. Death has released him from the grim necessity of living his mismated life and caring for the child born of parents of such divergent types. The supreme merit of the mother's character lies in her willing acceptance of the burdening problem. The strength of the story, as we view it in its entirety, rests in a skillful merging of effects which allows final emphasis upon character portrayal and thematic situation.

POSSESSING PRUDENCE

AMY WENTWORTH STONE is a resident of Boston, who combines a pleasant sense of the ludicrous with a rare understanding of the spirit of childhood.

This miniature sketch of Amy Wentworth Stone's is admirably handled, and sparkles with the best and kindliest humor — a humor that is in no sense spoiled by the sins that rest so lightly upon the imaginative soul of little Prudence Jane. Her sins hark quickly back to the childhood periods of each reader who sympathetically remembers the world of fancy which conflicted so loudly with dull realism. The charm of this humorous tracery will invite a rereading of Miss Stone's similar triumph in *Capital Punishments*, published in the *Atlantic* for November, 1913.

THE GLORY—BOX

ELIZABETH ASHE is the pen name of Georgiana Pentlarge, a young and promising story-writer living in Boston.

The Glory-Box is an unforgettable story. Its accuracy in the matter of minor household details and commonplace neighborliness creates an atmosphere of intimate realism which readily wins our sympathetic credence in situation and event. We grow easily familiar with the three or four characters who are introduced, and then we discover our interest centering in two of these — Eunice, the sweetheart, and Stephen, the lover — as, in their separated lives, each in fancy penetrates the daily routine and comes fondly to rest in thoughts and plans of marriage. The story interest is enhanced by the contrast of their daily routine. Eunice's time is spent in teaching, relieved by friendly village companionship; Stephen's in the arduous work of the Columbia Law School, relieved by glimpses of fashionable life in Washington Square. All this routine and hope and relaxation end in the tragedy that the earlier realism of the story grimly accentuates and intensifies. The art of the story lies in the author's quiet control of situations which might so easily, in the hands of a lesser craftsman, run a riotous course in the field of pseudo-sentiment.

THE SPIRIT OF THE HERD

DALLAS LORE SHARP, well known as a keen observer both of nature and of human nature, is Professor of English at Boston University.

I have asked permission to extract this episode from a longer article. Professor Sharp was as generous in this as he has been helpful in other matters relating to selections which make up this volume of narratives.

The paragraphs which precede the present beginning are expository in nature, and while they bear interestingly upon the incident, they are not a necessary part of the narrative. The selection breathes the very atmosphere of highly hazardous adventure; and even though the writer quickly generates in us a feeling of confidence in the superior powers of Ranchman Wade and Peroxide Jim, we nevertheless restlessly live through the moments of the wild stampede as it makes its mad and frightened way along the perilous edge of the rim-rock.

IN THE PASHA'S GARDEN

H. G. DWIGHT is the son of an American missionary to the Near East, and lived for many years in Constantinople. Being compelled to leave Turkey after her entrance into the war, he returned to the United States and is now in the government service.

Mr. Dwight in this Stamboul romance has invested his scenes with the languorous and mystical spirit of the orientalism in which his characters so naturally move. We are here far away from the O. Henry type of story, with its startling cleverness, crisp humor, and ingenious surprise. We share instead the leisure and luxury of this eastern way of living — felt all the more strongly because of the presence of the French wife whose independent customs and bearing offend the servants of the easy-going Pasha. The interest, however, is not confined to the atmosphere. We are soon breathing the mystery of the kiosque — a mystery which the author never fully solves, but leaves silently merged in the intangible charm of the pervading orientalism.

LITTLE SELVES

MARY LERNER, a story-writer of Cambridge, Massachusetts, first won attention by the publication of 'Little Selves' in the *Atlantic Monthly*.

I have included this selection because it reveals so delicately and so immediately that quality which we may somewhat paradoxically call *romantic realism*. The scenes which Miss Lerner's old Irish woman so intimately recalls are all peopled by the real creatures of a remembered past, principally her little selves as they lived through their childish joys and sorrows and swiftly sequent perplexities. But each of these experiences, so intimately and realistically portrayed, is seen through memories tinged with the charm of a happy Celtic romance.

THE FAILURE

CHARLES CALDWELL DOBIE is a young writer living in San Francisco.

Mr. Dobie has in this story shown himself more than a mere realist. The realistic details of John Scidmore's home, the early-morning routine of the insurance office, the evening splendor of Julia Norris's hotel apartments, — all are graphically re-created. But the central idea is an ethical one — John Scidmore's wavering action in the midst of a business situation where a frank admission of gross neglect was morally imperative. His immediate failure to meet the situation is grimly contrasted with his wife's expressed faith in his honesty. The story presents a graphic instance of a righteous act silently directed by a strongly influencing personality. It closes with this particular problem solved; but we end the reading with many interesting and conflicting surmises concerning the future domestic life in the Scidmore home.

BUSINESS IS BUSINESS

HENRY SEIDEL CANBY, essayist and critic and occasional writer of stories, is a Professor of English at the Sheffield Scientific School at Yale University. His books include several volumes on the short story.

The commercial theme has been freely exploited by the popular magazine writers. When it is written merely for the sake of getting in line with a popular trend, it is likely to be empty and blusterous. In Mr. Canby's story we are, of course, interested in the business atmosphere; but we are more deeply interested in the portrayal of character. Cargan is most fully drawn, and we watch him with increasing keenness as we see him dominated by the various moods which the other personalities and the shifting incidents and the changing environment engender. The skill shown in the rapid but graphic sketching of Mrs. Cargan and Mrs. Waldron is equally engaging. The story is perfect in its mastery of narrative technique.

NOTHING

ZEPHINE HUMPHREY (Mrs. Fahnestock), long a contributor of essays and stories to the *Atlantic*, is the author of a novel entitled *Grail-Fire*.

In this and other contributions to the *Atlantic* Miss Humphrey has shown an acute sensitiveness to atmosphere and personality. We are here charmingly led into an intimate understanding of the surroundings and character of the little blind woman who lives her lonely life in the simple cottage where, in preparation for the imminent affliction, she had long ago learned to do her work in the silent dark. The story has almost no plot interest, for we trace no significant movement of events—except the few which are fragmentarily imparted in confidential retrospect. The quietness of the style is in thorough keeping with the secured tone— one of those happy revelations so difficult to accomplish, yet when once accomplished suggesting, by its inevitable touch, the easy process of mastership.

A MOTH OF PEACE

MRS. KATHARINE FULLERTON GEROULD, distinguished as a writer of essays and stories and novels, is the wife of Gordon Hall Gerould, Professor at Princeton.

Aside from the unusually strong and flowing style here so impressively revealed, we have a story marked by a sympathetic penetration into the atmosphere of Andecy — an atmosphere, when first felt, richly laden with the languor of a lonely and pervading provincial peace. This peace is suddenly broken by the rumors and processes of war, and we feel the dread of the impending German attack and the personal solicitude of Miss Stanley, the American heroine lovingly anxious for the fate of her

English fiancé. Nearer and nearer comes the threatened danger. Finally the heroine goes out to meet the troop of enemy soldiers without the gates — whether to meet a tragic end, the author does not say.

There is little dialogue and little haste in the action. The narrative is continuously guided by the controlling spirit of Miss Stanley, who grimly triumphs over the fear and dread of the perilous situation. Her body may have suffered defeat; her soul is splendidly victorious. The author's skill at the end is finely revealed in the graphic portrayal of the psychology of the situation.

IN NO STRANGE LAND

KATHARINE BUTLER, a young writer of few and distinctive stories, lives at Danvers, Massachusetts.

The significant merit of this story is the mystical creation of a man's experience with death. The things of earth and heaven become perplexingly intermingled. Realism becomes strongly blended with the thoughts that move in weird circles on the tenuous wings of wanton fancy, and we live a puzzled moment as we try to visualize the man's experiences in his new realm of consciousness with its 'incredible freedom and joy.' The whole narrative is wrought in the delicate tracery of one whose temperament is obviously the temperament of a poet.

LITTLE BROTHER

MADELEINE Z. DOTY, of New York, learned the true story of 'Little Brother' when at The Hague, in the summer of 1915, as a delegate to the Woman's International Congress. Miss Doty is a lawyer by profession; by practice, a writer, investigator, and traveler.

With terrible concreteness *Little Brother* weights our soul-sense with the horror and tragedy of war. The story is told with a bared realism which the poignancy of the occasion freely extenuates. In short crisp sentences the opening scene is exposed. There follow in dizzy succession and in the same quick-breathing style the little tragic ordeals that fill the story with a terrible passion. It penetrates the very essence of our being and starkly confronts us with the bleak mystery of the existing condition of world-carnage — a carnage that wantonly wreaks its unselected vengeance on little sufferers unskilled and unschooled in squaring their strength to ill-proportioned trials.

WHAT ROAD GOETH HE ?

'F. J. LOURIET' is a pseudonym representing the dual authorship of Captain and Mrs. F. J. Green, long of Australia and now of Honolulu.

By the free but not too lavish use of sea terms and common sailor talk, we are brought into immediate and intimate knowledge of the affairs of a ship floundering in a storm. Through graphic sensory images, with their vivid and varied appeals, the whole perilous situation is wonderfully intensified. Seldom indeed are details better massed to secure an intended effect. But the interest later comes to centre in the great theme of sacrifice — a sacrifice all the more significant because it is performed with such absolute spontaneity. The story is a noteworthy example of strong effect secured with great economy of time and material.

THE CLEARER SIGHT

ERNEST STARR, a writer of occasional stories, lives in North Carolina.

The most interesting element in Mr. Ernest Starr's narrative is the dramatic conflict of emotions. Placed first in the gnomish atmosphere of a chemical laboratory, the tone soon changes from scientific to ethical — each interest being intensified and directed by the deep emotion of romantic love. A serious accident in the laboratory creates the crisis; it reveals to Noakes, the young scientist, the inexcusable baseness in his character — a baseness which allowed him to act with direct disloyalty to his employer and with somewhat obvious disloyalty to the ideals cherished by the girl whom he loved. The situation is finally relieved by his confessions and by the physician's hope that the young scientist's physical blindness is not necessarily permanent.

The author shows unusual skill in dialogue, in analysis, and in the handling of both conventional and dramatic situations.

THE GARDEN OF MEMORIES

C. A. MERCER is an American author who has, unfortunately, been altogether silent of late years.

In this story the traditions and influence of Hawthorne are picturesquely revived. The experience is one which is a bit fragile and tenuous, but to readers who reproduce in their fancy the more delicate picturings of their childhood, who delight in the re-creation of mood, who frequently re-live their childhood sentiments — to all such will come a sense of pleasure in the contemplation of the tracery here so artistically etched.

THE CLEAREST VOICE

MARGARET SHERWOOD, a singularly sincere and graceful writer, is Professor of English Literature at Wellesley College.

The clear voice which here speaks under Miss Sherwood's guidance is the voice of the absent. And, individually, as we read the story, we listen sympathetically to the separate messages of those voices which have entered sympathetically into our past experiences and wisely guided or wisely thwarted our separate deeds.

A Harvard graduate who had taken Professor Charles Eliot Norton's course in fine arts was years afterward selecting a cravat pin in a jeweler's shop in Paris. As he finally decided upon one of plain, simple, and silently impressive design, he said, 'I think Professor Norton would have chosen this.' In decisions minor and in decisions major, we are almost invariably influenced by the unconscious thought of those whose counsel we value. This significant truth Miss Sherwood has impressively revealed in *The Clearest Voice*.

THE MARBLE CHILD

E. NESBIT (Mrs. Hubert Bland) is an English writer who for many years has enjoyed widespread and deserved popularity as a writer of children's books.

'The world where children live is so full of amazing and incredible-looking things that turn out to be quite real.' This sentence from the story supplies us with the theme the wording of the bald analyst requires. For him who simply reads for the mere

narrative, no such analyzing is really necessary—provided there
still linger with him the manifold fancies that peopled his childhood. Of course Ernest was an extraordinary child — like
Shelley or William Blake, it may be. Just such a child as Hawthorne would adore. To appreciate the story in all its fineness,
we must ourselves have something of that abnormality. Else
we shall be as impervious as the crinolined aunts, and as unsym-
pathetic toward Ernest's experience as are some readers to Hawthorne's fanciful *Snow Image*.

THE ONE LEFT

E. V. LUCAS is an English essayist, a lover and biographer of
Lamb, known for many delicate and appreciative essays, and
for books of travel in familiar places. It is semi-occasionally
only that Mr. Lucas addresses himself to fiction.

This admirably written story — so brief as to be little more
than a sketch — is rich in emotional values which are safely held
within the bonds of restraint. Scientifically, I am told there is
nothing wrong in the description of the ingenious device which
provides the means for the expression of the emotion, though
readers unfamiliar with such devices may question the verisimilitude of the action. It is but one instance among thousands
which provide modern literature with a broadened range within
the field of realism.

THE LEGACY OF RICHARD HUGHES

MARGARET LYNN, member of the English Department of the
State University of Kansas, at Lawrence, is best known for her
sympathetic appreciation of prairie life.

This story is a tragedy — the tragedy of a wife's failure to
understand the finer side of her husband's nature. She learns her
misjudgment all too late — when the husband lies dead. The
emotional values are the greater because the reader inevitably
contemplates the long years they lived together in their isolation.
The psychology of the situation is portrayed with remarkable
clarity. The method is very different from the method of such
writers as de Maupassant. De Maupassant's analysis and dis-
secting is usually done with cold and relentless indifference; Miss
Lynn's processes are here carried out determinedly, but with full
and lingering sympathy.

OF WATER AND THE SPIRIT

MARGARET P. MONTAGUE, living among the West Virginia mountains, has written many successful stories of the Hill people whom she knows so well.

The chain of incidents narrated by the simple-hearted Virginia dressmaker is of absorbing interest, and seems to be the real experiences of one who had actually endured the tragedy of having lived in the horror of the aftermath of battle. But even more interesting than these scenes of pitiful suffering is the effect produced upon the woman who endures it all. Her whole attitude toward life was changed. What matters it now that her father was not an aristocratic Virginian? What if she were a poor dressmaker at the little village of Johnson's Falls? What though she was not elected a member of the Laurel Literary Society? She had been face to face with war and death and Hell and God. The little things of life had unconsciously sunk away and the great enduring themes had boldly emerged to re-create her spiritual self.

MR. SQUEM

REVEREND ARTHUR RUSSELL TAYLOR, Rector of the Episcopal Church at York, Pennsylvania, whose career as a writer of fiction opened so auspiciously with 'Mr. Squem' and a few companion stories, died very suddenly early in January, 1918.

Here the central interest is in character. In creating such a personage as Mr. Squem, the writer of this story has boldly penetrated the veneer of culture and shown us that the character elements which are of enduring worth may be far aloof from any knowledge of art or religion or philosophy, or any form of polite learning.

It is interesting to note the part which the railroad wreck plays in this story. While there is enough in the situation to have made the wreck a point of central objective interest, it is utilized here simply as the background for the display of Mr. Squem — genial, direct, efficient, ingenuous, dominating, interestingly crude.

In the February, 1918, *Atlantic* Mr. Squem is equally interesting in a different environment.

Soon after the death of Reverend Arthur Russell Taylor, Bishop James Henry Darlington sent to the Atlantic office an interesting appreciation of Dr. Taylor's work and character.   From Bishop Darlington we learn that Dr. Taylor 'had for years been suffering from a tumor on the brain which had totally destroyed the sight of one eye and which by its pressure caused him constant pain, sleepless nights, and the gradual failing of the other eye.   Like Robert Louis Stevenson, he was cheerful and brightened the lives of others until the very last, and almost his final writings were sent to *The Atlantic*.'

St. Mary's Seminary-Junior College